Books in the Abby Wize series
by Lisa Bradley Godward

Abby Wize – AWAY
(e-book, paperback, and hardcover)

Activity and Discussion Guide for Abby Wize – AWAY
(e-book and paperback)

The author plans nine books in the Abby Wize series.
AWAY is the first.

WIZE.MEDIA

Loved Awake
Growing Aware

Abby Wize-Away

by

Lisa B. Godward

Revised Edition

Abby Wize Media

www.wize.media   grow@wize.media

Facebook: Abby Wize and Abby Wize Media

Instagram and Twitter: Abby Wize

First published by AuthorHouse 8/9/2010

ISBN: 978-1-4520-2490-5 (sc)

ISBN: 978-1-4520-2491-2 (hc)

Second edition published by Godwarding LLC 9/19 and 8/21

ISBN: 978-1-7333276-2-6 (hc)

ISBN: 978-1-7333276-0-2 (sc)

ISBN: 978-1-7333276-1-9 (e-book)

Printed in the United States of America

Acknowledgements & Requests

In addition to those crucial Original Edition helpers, whose contributions I continue to build on, Andréana E. Lefton's editorial suggestions elevated the Revised Edition to new heights and Dorothy Hamrang's skillful listening and input were crucial and enjoyable. Rachel R. Hoff helped before graduating to the next world.

Abby opens vistas of world peace, provides peace-savvy folks with interesting particulars, and fuels imaginations. One of Abby's purposes is to inspire us to start building actual, lasting, world peace, wherever we are at the moment. I would love to hear how you've decided to work on the Long Plan for Peace!

Reader feedback is the main fuel that keeps the writing engine going, so **if you like this Revised Edition, please post a positive review on Goodreads, Amazon and Facebook, e-mail me at grow@wize.media , and tell others!**

Like talking about books in groups? Check out the *Abby Wize Activity and Discussion Guide* on Amazon; it coordinates with and extends themes from the novel. Get a group together in person or online, message me and I'll try to visit you!

Also, discuss the Abbyverse with other fans in the Facebook group "Abby Wize Fans." Find ongoing Abby Wize morsels on the two Facebook pages, "Abby Wize" and "Abby Wize Media" and register for email updates on Abby's website, www.wize.media . You can also email me about upcoming audiobooks, foreign translations, and partnerships and funding for our future films.

Lisa Bradley Godward
Revised Edition 2.1, Aug. 2021

⚠ Trigger Notice: Chapter 5, "Packing", portrays an altercation between Abby and her mother.

Feedback on
the original edition:
Abby Wize: AWA ("away")

I loved this book! It was one of those great impulse buys that turned out well. I just love horses, of course, and spirituality. I can't wait for the next one to come out!

—Janet Smith, Competitive Trail Rider, California

Competently written.
-Ronald Tomanio, Author, Radio Talk Show Host, Maine

I bought 2 hardback copies of this book, one for our Bahá'í Library & one for the public library. I just finished reading it. WOW! It is more than a teen book; I am 62 & I loved it. It reveals a world as it could be & I am sure we all wish it to be. I encourage you all to get a couple of copies, read it & share with others. It made my heart sing & uplifted my Spirit.

-Sali in Astoria, Oregon

[Abby] wants to know all about horse-handling – maybe because her mother can't be handled – although the traditional methods of horse-wrangling seem crude and ineffectual. As Abby begins to learn about "horse-whispering," she's thrown from the saddle and wakes up in the future…[in which] everything is unbearably wonderful, thanks to the teachings of Bahá'u'lláh…Bradley is clearly a true believer and wants to share both her religious beliefs and love of horses. She has a talent for communicating both.
– Burl Burlingame, *Honolulu Star-Advertiser*, Nov. 7, 2010

We received our book from Amazon today. Kassie started reading it and said, "This is really good!"
God Bless,
Kay Kelly

Hi Lisa,
I admit giving your book to my granddaughter without having read it … she is IN LOVE with Abby's world … can't put the book down. MAJOR KUDOS to you!

-Gayle Hanke
Grandmother of four from Des Moines, IA

I thought it was wonderful. It really brought back a lot of memories with the prayers and songs. I would like to know when the next one comes out and are you going to make it available as an ebook?
-Kandra Carman, Nevada
Mom, grandma, explorer, world traveler.
Author's reply: Yes, Kandra, it's available as ebook everywhere those are sold.

Warm, wise, well-paced sci-fi. Recommended!
-Will Peterson, owner, Walrus & Carpenter Books, Pocatello, ID

Every Bahá'í should read this book to carry a vision of what we're working so hard to build, then use it with their junior youth, and to help seekers find teachers.
-Mrs. Kathy Rutan-Sprague, equine therapist, retired nurse, grandmother, author.

I really enjoyed the book, especially once Abby "goes into" the future; it was a page turner that I just couldn't put down. When Abby "returned" home, like her, I too was disappointed in having "returned." I look forward to the next installment of the series.
    I really liked many of the thought-provoking things you pose in the book....
-Mrs. Susan Ricci
Manager, Bahá'í, world traveler.

I gave the book to my 12-year-old granddaughter. She's mixed (African American) and bi-lingual (Japanese and English). I was pleasantly surprised when she spontaneously said that she loved the book and wanted to read it again. Although she's an avid, read-everything-in-sight reader, she's not been lavish with commentary, let alone praise. When is the sequel coming out?
—Nancy Barnes, American in Japan with her husband; grandmother, teacher, and rooftop gardener.

Table of Contents

Chapter 1 Moony

Abby Wize's eyes resisted, fluttering, reluctant to leave delicious, precious, horse-infused dreams of happy laughter, enthralled creativity and joyful freedom.

A blurry white object gradually came into focus: her cheap white straw cowgirl hat on the low bureau near her bed. As if swimming out of a deep pond, she eventually remembered that today, she had another chance to make her dream come true: Saturdays in August meant horseback riding lessons. That thought propelled her out of bed as nothing else could.

After her usual milky breakfast of Leprechaun Coins, she packed her old metal lunch box and dressed, turning the tall socks and the underwear inside out so the seams didn't press uncomfortably. She was sensitive that way. She dressed in her longest jeans, a belt, and the lightweight, long-sleeved, tan Western shirt that her sister, Jenn, suggested: a compromise between protecting her pale skin and keeping cool in the blistering Tennessee summer sun. She studied her boots. She had put off telling Mother they were too small, dreading the confrontation. Finally, she braided two pigtails behind her ears and rubbed in sunscreen.

Mother had told Abby to take a check to Tyler this lesson. He'd phoned to say that the money Abby had handed to one of the ranch workers last weekend had never reached him, hinting that cash tended to disappear. Mother had strongly implied that it was Abby's fault for giving the money to just anyone, and accused "those no-good barn rats" of getting drunk or high on that lesson money. Abby privately admitted that Mother might be right, but was offended anyway. She also suspected some of them had spread rumors that she was stuck up. Why else would one of the newest riders have exclaimed, after Abby helped her with her horse, that *she* didn't think Abby was stuck up? No, Abby was just quiet because she was always under fire.

When Ms. Curry and her daughter Chloë arrived to drive Abby to their lessons at The Ride Place, Abby pulled on her tight boots, tucked the envelope holding the check into her back pocket and slid in the Curry's car with a quiet "hi."

Chloë was too busy unwrapping a fancy breakfast bar and popping a straw into a high-priced protein drink to reply.

"Hi, Abby," Ms. Curry replied. "How are you?"

"Okay," Abby said. "Oh, Ms. Curry, I'll be gone to North Carolina to visit Mother's sister for the next two weeks, so you don't have to…"

1

She stopped, afraid she'd get in trouble for telling an adult what to do.

"All right," Ms. Curry said calmly. "I'm sure you'll catch up when you get back. What has Tyler been teaching you?"

"I'm up to catching, bridling and saddling by myself, and next, cantering, and I want to start learning about feeding, because the horses always come whenever there's food ...." Abby trailed off, worried she'd disclosed too much. She glanced at Chloë, who was no help, preoccupied with her breakfast.

"Oh yes, that sounds good," Ms. Curry replied pleasantly. *A nice change from at home,* Abby thought, relieved. After a silent minute, Chloë received permission to turn on the radio, then asked how to switch away from the classical music that played.

"Hit the SEEK button," Ms. Curry instructed, looking over her left shoulder for a merge.

Chloë pushed the SEEK button with her only clean finger, her pinky. The radio spewed a man's voice singing seductively, "You're so hot, you make me want to do it all night, you make me want you ...."

Ms. Curry squawked but was busy switching lanes. Chloë juggled her breakfast for a moment, trying to free up her pinky again. They all endured several more awkward moments of lustful lyrics, while Ms. Curry muttered about the trash on the airwaves these days.

Chloë's second SEEK landed on a family pop station, which offered "Beautiful" by Christina Aguilera, "Unwritten" by Natasha Bedingfield, a Phil Collins song, an Avril Lavigne, a Jack Johnson, and an oldie by Journey. The Currys hummed and sang along until the girls spied the horses in their fields. Abby did not hum or sing; as usual in the morning, her nose was stuffed up. Chloë rolled down her window to see the horses better, letting in the warm, humid air of a typical summer morning in Surely, Tennessee.

Ms. Curry let the girls out at The Ride Place's barn, which was now a tack room and office. The sign said office, but the ranch co-owner's Bulgarian grandfather had called it an *obor* because it still looked like a barn, and the name had stuck and was easier than "barn/office."

"Thank you, Ms. Curry," Abby mumbled unconfidently, trying to be polite, for otherwise, she'd not be able to come out to the horses that fueled her dreams and spirit.

"Bye Mom!" Chloë chirped.

"Bye, girls! Be safe and have fun!" Ms. Curry waved and drove off.

Tyler and his helpers were already gathering the riders in the yard, taking their money, and beginning to name lesson horses. Whoever wanted to ride that horse spoke up. If two kids wanted the same horse, Tyler flipped a coin. Informal, but it worked well and ensured that the kids rode a variety of horses.

Abby won Moony; not her favorite but not the worst. He was fat and slow but didn't actually fight her like some of the other horses. She pushed open the *obor*'s people door next to the wide, sliding barn doors layered in flapping, faded flyers, and walked past the dusty, cobwebby, unused stalls and into the student tack room with several sneezes. She was actually allergic to horse hair, but the doctor had suggested that if she was determined to indulge her passion, she should avoid being in enclosed spaces with horse hair and dander.

A labeled post sticking out from the wall marked Moony's tack. She checked that the short, stiff, fraying lead rope was still attached to the faded nylon halter by a rusty bull clip and carried it and her lunch box into the so-called lounge – former run-in stalls now merged and furnished with a ratty assortment of grungy buckets, boxes and tack trunks set on the dirt floor. It was open to the elements in summer, offering a view of the horses in their yards.

One of the many things Abby loved about The Ride Place was how down-to-earth, literally, it was. She probably ate as much dirt as food in the dusty lounge, but it hadn't killed her yet. Occasionally, a sick horse occupied the one remaining functional stall in the *obor*, at the far end of the lounge, but no creature peered at her from the "horse-pital" now as she parked her battered metal lunch box on a shelf.

The lounge was empty now, but Abby looked forward more than she would dare admit aloud to socializing there after her lesson. Life with Mother had taught her that if she showed she liked something too much, it would probably be taken away from her.

On her way to Moony's pasture Abby noticed two ranch workers uncoiling garden hoses in one of the paddocks.

"Hi, Abby," they said, smirking at each other. Their voices carried a slight "tone" that made Abby wonder if they'd been the ones gossiping about her. Hard to tell.

"Hi, Craig. Hi, Liz," she answered cautiously, distrusting their show of friendship. She walked on, the halter and lead rope swinging from her shoulder, tapping her leg. She had heard that those two were an item and wondered again if they'd kept her money after she'd handed it to Liz last week before lesson.

Tyler passed her in a golf cart, pausing briefly.

"Got the right halter? Remember which horse you have?"

Abby proffered the halter that might once have been green but was now the color of sun, dirt, and rain. Tyler peered at the fading letters on the noseband and confirmed that it was the right one.

"Good job. Is everything okay?" He looked right into her eyes.

Suddenly feeling scrutinized, she ducked her head.

"Yeah."

Even though Tyler was in a hurry, he was still friendly. She felt her chin and her spirits rise along with the sun and the temperature.

Abby turned with an inner smile and headed for Moony's field. Passing Parker the Pony's dirt pen and two paddocks housing private boarders' horses, she slipped through the aged, wooden pasture boards and headed toward Moony. Steadily ripping and chewing withered grass, he eyed her neutrally.

"Hi, Moony, ready for a ride today?" Abby asked.[1] She patted his roan hide heartily, snuck the lead rope around his neck, and hauled up on it. She held the halter open and slid it onto his nose, then flipped the longest strap over his neck behind his ears. She was proud of how quickly she could let go of the crownpiece on his right side and grab it on his left side before it all slid off. A couple of years ago, when she had first tried to halter a horse, she had been totally uncoordinated and incompetent. The horses often got bored and tried to wander off before the job was done.

She was supposed to examine her horse for injuries first. She looked at and felt Moony's mouse-brown nose, his face with black, brown and white hairs, his thick speckled neck and wide, flat back. His legs, black below his knees, seemed fine as well, as did his ample, multicolored rump. His other side was also clear of bites and wounds. She headed toward the gate, pulling on the lead rope.

Moony didn't budge.

Abby clucked and kissed and tugged on the rope but Moony just stretched out his neck and planted his feet. This was the part Abby was not so fond of. Horses were too big for her to force into obedience, but they often resisted. She wasn't sure what to do when they did this.

"Come on, Moony, we'll be late!" she said, frustrated. She pulled the lead rope way to his left, hoping to unbalance him. He took one step and thrust his head down to eat again.

"Moony! Come *on!*" Abby cried out, then scanned the ground, but couldn't find any sticks to hit him with. She did see a rock but decided she'd get in trouble for throwing it at him, especially if she cut him.

She circled around to the horse's right and pulled harder. Miraculously, this worked and he grudgingly relented, although he resisted the pull of the halter with every step.

Abby leaned as if into a strong wind, dragging Moony toward the rusty gate. She remembered to open it wide, but he still nearly knocked her over as he scurried through it. He did not like going through gates. Lots of horses at The Ride Place didn't. It was just how they were.

Still, her cheerfulness returned as she led him to the *obor* (on his left side, as she'd been taught); she'd caught him all by herself and the sweat popping out on her face proved it. The humidity, always high in Tennessee in the summer, seemed especially bad today.

She spied a place to tie Moony at the hitching rails on the side of the *obor*, not too close to a chestnut brown horse that was still upset from stepping on its lead rope. Abby had seen this many times: horses panicked when they felt their heads trapped. They thrashed and fought to get free. If they did this when they were still tied, they could destroy the tie rail and hurt or even kill themselves. They were called "pullers." Abby had heard that one of them had broken its neck, flailing like a trout on a line. They had shot it in the head right there at the hitching rail, then buried it in the far pasture.[2]

Abby led Moony around the wide-eyed horse and poor Chloë, nervously trying to coax Rocket back, ducking low under the rail, careful not to knock off her hat, concentrating on tying the hitching knot correctly. She wasn't sure it was right but thought it would hold well enough if Moony didn't chew on it or wiggle it too much.

Tyler had opened the wide, faded doors of the *obor* to more easily carry the tack out to the horses, but this didn't make the equipment any lighter. Abby staggered from the student tack room under the load of pad, saddle, grooming bucket and bridle, trying not to trip on the dragging stirrups and straps. Just as she reached Moony, it all fell out of her hands and thudded to the ground in a pile.

Wiping her sweaty face on her increasingly dirty sleeves, she fished in the grooming bucket for the rusted metal currycomb and an old body brush. She tried to do what she'd been told – curry in a circle and avoid the bony parts – but it was harder than it sounded and she earned a few glares from Moony as sharp metal teeth scraped the thin skin over his knees and withers. She plopped the saddle pad on his back, followed by the saddle, which was very hard to lift high and plunk on him. Studying her handiwork, she decided the saddle was too far back and pulled the pad and saddle forward. That was better! If only Moony would stop swinging his head around, trying to bite her.

She knocked her hat askew reaching under Moony's belly to get the cinch, which was full of crud from the ground. She plucked off as much junk as she could, tied the cinch knot, unhooked the halter, rebuckled it around his neck and slid the mechanical hackamore up his nose, anchoring it with the crownpiece behind his ears and the throatlatch under his large, round cheeks.

There, Moony was ready for lesson, and she had done it all herself! "Ropes, straps, chaps, and dopes," as Tyler sometimes chanted. Though she hoped she was not a dope. And she didn't own any chaps, nor was she one … she wasn't sure which way it was meant. She liked mottos and pithy sayings, but sometimes the cowboy sayings were confusing.

After she led Moony a few steps, he stopped, stretched his nose to his side, and bit the old, cracked leather fender of the saddle.

"What are you doing? You're going to hurt the saddle. Stop it!" she exclaimed, pushing his head forward. He pinned his ears flat back against his head, and she slapped him for it. Never allow pinned ears or bad manners, that's what she'd been told. He paid her back by snapping at her hand, which she jerked away.

"Let's just get to lesson, huh?" she hissed at him, glancing to see if anyone had noticed her failure. Chloë was closest but focused wholly on learning to clean the underside of Rocket's hoof. Moony chewed hard at the saddle a few more times as Abby stood helplessly, then allowed her to pull him toward the unfenced patch of scruffy land that served as the lesson arena, his ears only half-pinned.

Chapter 2 Riding

The lesson was very basic. Tyler, a high-schooler, and his slightly younger helpers checked the tack on horses as students led them to the dirt patch "arena." Tyler said Abby had done everything right except that the cinch knot was twisted and backward, but he decided it was close enough. Abby and the others mounted from the left side of the horse and reined them onto a primitive dirt track worn into the field behind the *obor*.

"Okay, everyone circle to the right, kick to walk, and a LOUD cluck!" Tyler called from the middle of the lesson arena where he stood with his two helpers, Rana and Cory. The nine students, ranging from very small to very tall, did as they were told and the horses walked in a ragged circle. After a lap or two of walking to the right, Tyler called out, "Ready to stop? Everyone say 'HO!' and pull back!"

"HO!" rang out. Horses in adjoining yards lifted their heads to watch. Some horses stopped and several did not.

"Shout louder and pull back harder on those reins!" Tyler yelled to the students on the moving horses. Eventually they all stopped.

"Everyone turn around and walk the other way! But wait until the horse in front of you is going. Don't ride up on his behind!" Tyler hollered. Some horses turned left, some right, and others not at all. "Make 'em go, show 'em who's boss!" he chided loudly.

After several circles at the walk, he yelled, "Everyone who's not ready to trot, come in!" Three beginners steered their mounts to the middle; the remaining six, including Abby, kept walking. "Ready to trot? Loud clucks, and kick! Kick! Kick!" he urged.

The six students filled the air with kissing and clucking, hunched and drumming their horses' sides. All but one of the horses gave in to their riders' heels and trotted. The lone holdout merely walked faster. He had not trotted in years, but he built confidence in the beginners.

"Try turning while you're still trotting!" Tyler hollered. Abby did her best to keep Moony trotting. He wanted to fall back into a walk at every other step, and she whacked his shoulders with the ends of the reins and kicked him constantly. She tried to turn while still trotting, but Moony wouldn't. Most of the other riders weren't having much better luck, Abby saw, so she didn't feel too bad.

"Make 'em trot; you gotta be boss!" Tyler commanded. Abby tried again in vain, wishing the reins were long enough to hit Moony's rump. After a half-circle of futilely thumping him with her heels, she recalled pictures of cowgirls smacking horses' hind ends with their hats. So, despite Mother's "don't ruin your clothes" warnings in her head, she hit Moony's behind with her hat, making him half-heartedly trot for another quarter-circle. She was pleased at getting such good results and proud of thinking to use her hat. The instructors must have agreed, shouting, "Good job, Abby! Good job, everyone!"

Only one mare and her rider were up to cantering, so the other five trotters gathered in the middle with the three walkers. At one cliffhanging point in her canter, the mare veered off track, heading out of the arena, unseating her young rider. But he clung to the saddle horn and managed to get control of the horse.

"Great start on your rodeo career!" Tyler yelled out. "Calf roping or steer wrestling at the least, I'd say! Maybe bronc riding!" Ten-year-old Kevin grinned, pleased to think he'd done something tough guys do.

Tyler sent the group back onto the track for more walking before calling everyone back to cheerfully argue about which game they'd play. The candidates were Duck Duck Goose, Rescue Race, and Keyhole. In two tosses, Tyler's nickel chose Rescue Race. No matter what they'd argued for, everyone cheered; they loved all the games.

Tyler sent Cory and Rana to help tie the slowest horses and those of the newbies to the hitching rails.

"Put their halters on! Don't tie 'em by the reins! And tie 'em beside a friend! When you get back, stand in the partners line," he hollered after them. The remaining riders lined up their horses at the *obor*-end of the dirt patch, watching Tyler draw a line in the dead grass with his boot heel while the other kids walked to the far end.

"First rider ready? First partner ready?" he hollered, looking at the first kids at both ends of the field, then at his watch.

"*Yes!*" they both yelled back.

"Ready … *Go!*" Tyler cried.

The first rider, a girl of maybe 15, whacked her horse into a trot and headed toward the boy waiting at the far end. Everyone yelled, whistled, and cheered for Patricia. Once at the other end, she pulled hard on the reins to stop the horse and tried to help the small boy up. All the onlookers laughed, cheered, and hollered advice as the kids struggled. In the end, Conall climbed up the rider's leg, holding onto Patricia's arm and the horn. He scrambled over her thigh to sit behind the saddle, holding its cantle. Patricia turned Velvet around and kicked him hard. When this didn't produce a trot, she said something to Conall, who reached back and spanked. They got a few steps of trot and an enthusiastic reception back at the start/finish line.

"Three minutes and eight seconds! Awww-*rrriiiigghhttt*, you two! Wayta go!" Tyler pronounced grandly. He turned to the next team.

"Ready ... Set ... *Go!*" Tyler shouted to Abby.

Abby set her heels into Moony's flanks and used her hat right away. Moony trotted well. She reached her partner, a tallish girl, in good time.

Abby had played this game before, so she told the inexperienced girl, "Here, Sarah, use my stirrup and grab my arm. Get behind me."

On the third try, Sarah swung right up behind her. Abby turned Moony toward the finish line, then kicked him as hard as she could. Unfortunately, so did Sarah, and Moony broke into a canter.

Abby had rarely cantered on any horse, and now she was scared. Moony seemed headed out of the dirt patch and back to the hitching rails, and Abby could only cling to the horn and try not to fall off.

A funny shape hove into view near her right elbow: Sarah's face, leaning over, trying to see around Abby, who noticed a strange, slow, sliding sensation ... yelling ... the saddle slipping ... no, no, it couldn't be ... yes, it *was* ... they hit the dirt.

Abby hit face-first. Her hat flew off when the brim smashed into the ground. She got up slowly, spitting dirt, testing what hurt the most. Time moved strangely, as if everyone waded in syrup.

Sarah was not getting up ... people were running over to her ... Moony ran to the nearest horses ... Sarah moaned ... Abby spit more dirt and tested a tooth that felt funny ... a crowd gathered around Sarah, who lay twisted in the dirt ... someone handed Abby her bent, dirty hat ... Sarah got up slowly, still moaning ... Abby assured people that nothing hurt too bad ... everyone asked Sarah where it hurt ... the girl cried and held her left upper arm ... someone shouted to call an ambulance ... Tyler screamed to start with calling Sarah's mother ... Tyler ordered Rana and Cory to make a human chair and carry Sarah to the *obor* ... Sarah sobbed that as she fell, Moony had kicked her, knocked her around, might have stepped on her ....

Tyler cancelled the game. He called to Abby to wait, however, and when he reached her, he said that her team had crossed the finish line before they fell, with a time of 57 seconds. He held out a small first-place ribbon and walked with her toward Katherine and Kevin, who guided Conall in holding Moony's reins. Tyler quickly loosened the saddle enough for him and Ramey to hoist it back up on Moony. Abby tucked the ribbon in her back jeans pocket and took the reins, discovering more aches as she walked with the supportive group.

"Are you going to be okay?" Tyler asked, holding the loose saddle up on Moony, letting him carry his saddle back to the hitching rails.

"I'm pretty sure it will only be bumps and bruises. And a bent hat."

"Do you want Rana to take a look? She'll be free in a minute."

"Naw, I should be okay. But poor Sarah, she's got a broken arm at the least, huh?"

"Riders break bones. Not if, but when and how bad," Tyler scoffed.

At the hitching rails, they found that two horses had changed their minds about being friends, kicked at each other and pulled back. One had stepped on and broken her reins. That was bad; she wore a bit and might have hurt her mouth. Tyler grumbled about getting in trouble for the broken tack, and blamed the new students for not tying the horses' leads correctly. But Abby knew the lead ropes were hard to tie.

Abby tied Moony the best she could and pulled the loose saddle off him, looking at where Sarah had sat when she kicked Moony "from the back seat." How stupid! She'd kicked him in his tender flanks, breaking a basic safety rule. Was that a mark she'd made? No, just a patch of weird-colored hair. And then leaning over – doubly dumb of her. But it would be terrible if she was disabled from the fall. Didn't anyone tell the new kids how to do things? Someone should've. And what about the cinch knot that wasn't right? Tyler had said it was okay, but the saddle had slipped. What else wasn't taught correctly around here?

Abby walked Moony back to his pasture, lost in wondering if Tyler had missed some other important things with the kids, herself included. She absently brushed off cinch litter from Moony's ample belly, but snapped to attention as his heels whistled past her head when she turned him loose and he spun, kicked out, and bolted back to his buddies. *Two close calls today*, she thought darkly.

Chloë and the kids in the lounge seemed intent on ignoring both Tristan's ruined sack lunch (pillaged by ravenous, wily barn cats) and today's incident. They tried not to watch out the open lounge wall as Sarah's mother picked her up to take her to the hospital. Then they went out of their way to tell ridiculous jokes, throw food scraps to the cats, and spy on Tyler talking to his older brother in the parking lot.

Abby's back hurt now, along with her leg. She figured she should just tough it out, the cowboy – or cowgirl – way. Sitting on a busted saddle on the ground, she ate the bologna-and-cheese sandwich and chips from her lunch box. Loosening her hat's tight hold on her head, she felt the dent in the dirty brim. It didn't bother Abby; after all, many hats were sold pre-distressed. But Mother wanted things to be just-so. No, Abby had better hide the hat when she got home. If Mother saw it, she was sure to attack Abby for it, or claim it was ruined and even throw it away.

Abby's swirling thoughts silently touched on other realizations she didn't feel she could share with the overly rowdy riders: that Sarah had helped cause her own injury, that all of them might likely get hurt and, on a positive note, that she'd won her first-ever riding ribbon!

Chapter 3 Home

The Currys drove Abby home, first sighting the fenced back yard with the maple tree Mother didn't allow anyone to climb and the flower beds she wanted the girls to stay away from. They passed the basement garage's concrete driveway, turned the corner and stopped at the sidewalk leading up to the apricot-colored brick house.

Hot, hairy, and still happy with her ribbon, Abby paused at the bottom of the cement steps, one hand on a black metal handrail. She repeated her usual mental inventory, looking at herself through Mother's critical eyes. Today, she did not pass inspection. Mother didn't mind getting Abby out of the way, especially when someone else drove her, but she never liked the mess her daughter brought back from the ranch.

Abby tapped her hat on a handrail, trying to get more dirt off, but that only seemed to dent it more. Brushing it with her hand only made streaks of dirt; she parked it on her head and wiped her booted feet on the grass and again on the cement steps to get the grass off, but the boots were still dusty and would smudge the carpet. She climbed the steps and sat on the cement stoop outside the door to take them off. Her socks were almost as dirty as her boots because of rolling in the dirt. She took off the socks, shook them over the side of the stoop and stuffed them into her boots. Her only hope was to get inside quickly, hide the bent hat, clean up fast, bury her filthy clothes in her hamper, and hope to be presentable before dinner.

Hat on, boots in hand, she quietly opened the storm door and peered through the slowly opening front door.

Her older sister, Jennifer, watched TV in the large open living room to the left. If Abby was lucky, Daddy would be away working extra hours and Mother would be downstairs sewing, or out in the back yard working. Jenn looked up.

"It's your favorite part, Abs," Jenn said. Abby set down her boots and tip-toed across the Berber carpet.

It was the old movie *Hook*. One of the Lost Boys was telling Robin Williams as Peter Pan that he needed to find a Happy Thought to fly. Abby touched Jenn on the shoulder. Jenn touched her hand in return, a small, silent gesture of welcome affection.

Abby carried her boots down the carpeted hallway that split the house. She passed the doorway into the kitchen on her left, then walked cautiously between the doors leading left to the basement (always open), right to her sister's room (always closed), left to the big bathroom (open unless in use), another left to her door (usually open) and, opposite that, her parents' room (preferably closed). Today her parents' door was open. Abby saw Mother's tall, dark-haired female shape look up sharply and bolt away from a sleeping male form on the bed. Only because Daddy was asleep did Mother hesitate and quietly close their door. Then she sprang to angry life.

"You're filthy!" Mother took in the dirty jeans, the sweat-stained sleeves, and the bent and dusty hat.

Abby was busted. The fastest but most unpleasant way out was straight through.

"I'll just take these off and get—"

"Not on my carpet, you won't!" Mother lashed out. "Go to the bath-room and take them off ... no, it'll get the bathroom floor dirty and I'll have to clean that, as if I don't have enough to do! Stand in the tub to undress. Shake everything out in the back yard." Mother plucked the socks out of the boots Abby held. "What did you do to your socks? They'll never come clean! They're *ruined*, Abigail Clift Wize! You have to throw them away. What else did you ruin today with those beasts?" She jabbed at Abby's chest as she ranted.

They were not *that* kind of beasts, they were the one good thing in her life. And Abby didn't know why Mother complained about cleaning, since she made Jenn and Abby clean almost everything. To be dramatic, probably. Whenever Mother crabbed about Abby being a drama queen with her allergies and sensitivities, Abby privately thought Mother was the one who made such a big deal out of stuff. But she'd get her head chopped off if she ever hinted at having such a thought.

"Nothing, Mother, I'll get started now."

"Don't you lie to me, young lady. Look at your hat! What did you do, beat your horse with it? If you don't straighten out that hat *and your act*," she lectured aloofly with folded arms, sounding proud of her verbiage, "we may have to reconsider this horse-riding business!"

Mother was really on a roll.

"Yes, Mother." Abby dared not look at her lest Mother intuit how close her accusation was, or make good on her threat. Fortunately she marched off down the hall and, in case she threw the final word over her shoulder, Abby sidled away into the bathroom, not willing to actually back away. That seemed too servile.

After trying to straighten out her hat brim, then carefully wiping it with a damp washcloth and setting it on its crown on the sink counter, Abby undressed inside the tub. Mother had given her the ultimatums, but had not said exactly how to do them. Somehow Abby had to keep the dirt off the floor as she took the dirty things outside. *Wrap 'em in a towel?* Then she'd get in trouble for the dirty towel. *Turn 'em inside out?* A hassle with the jeans. *Turn one inside out and put the rest inside it?* Best yet. *Why do I have to figure out such stupid stuff all the time?* She shook some dirt off, turned the T-shirt inside out and folded the jeans inside, socks tucked into the jeans, boots perched on top. She parked the bundle next to the bathroom door and turned on the shower, waiting for the water to warm up.

The house had been built in the 1960s, when earth tones were "in." Vivian had redone the bathroom in a more modern shade of cream. Fetching a towel from the built-in cabinet while avoiding smudging the light doors, Abby caught sight of herself in the vintage frameless mirror over the sink. She examined her face, sprinkled with freckles and streaked with brown mud. She unbraided her shoulder-length, slightly wavy, red-brown hair and surveyed her green eyes with bright yellow flecks and large black pupils. Her ears had collected dirt, threatening to invade the pierced lobes. At least she didn't have any zits, but her neck begged for a good washing.

Mother occasionally said things like: "You are such a pretty girl, Abby, why don't you do something with your hair?" Or: "Be grateful you have such a clear complexion. Take care of it." Somehow it never felt like a compliment, and Abby distrusted that she was pretty. She leaned closer to look, really look, at the eyes that she doubted were as attractive as Mother claimed. Normally she avoided looking directly in peoples' eyes; it seemed to provoke the people she knew. She forced herself to keep looking past the point of comfort, and fell into the large black pools that grabbed and held her.

"The eyes are the window to the soul," she'd heard. Was that what now commanded her attention? Fearfully, she looked and saw … something like the vacuum of black space, with Forces moving, plotting, fighting. She pulled herself back before terror set in. She had to shake her head to get rid of the very disturbing feeling that such awful turmoil lived within her.

Vowing to avoid eyes, she stepped into the back of the out-of-fashion tan tub and washed the horse dirt and happiness down the drain.

Half an hour later, showered, redressed, and the bathroom cleaned, Abby headed toward the back yard with her dirty clothes, holding her boots just above them, but found her mother passing in the hallway.

"Come set the table, Abby," Mother said without preamble.

"Okay," Abby muttered, and followed her mother down the hallway, not too closely, eyes down, trying not to limp.

"We are having cold tuna salad on a bed of lettuce," Mother dictated. "The red and white dishes should set things off."

Abby knew that she was referring to the pleasing colors of the foods against the plate, not to emotional outbursts.

"Which glasses?" Abby ventured.

"The usual … no, the clear ones. There's a slight blue tint to the usual ones that would clash with the red in the dishes. It's past Fourth of July, after all." Mother turned into the kitchen, smiling at her own joke. *As if it were all that funny*, Abby thought. She set her riding clothes just outside the back door, out of sight but not out of her mind.

After rinsing her hands, she fetched four dinner plates. She wondered how many other 13-year-olds in Tennessee knew the difference between dinner, luncheon, and salad plates, and saucers. Not too many, she guessed, although it was actually pretty easy: each was smaller than the last. And the thing about which fork to use when they gave you more than one? Start from the outside and work inward with each new dish. If in doubt, watch the hostess and copy her, Abby recited to herself, but it came out in Mother's voice.

Deep down Abby often felt that, no matter what she did, she was going to get in trouble for breaking some rule. She wondered if there would ever come a time that Mother would not crab at her. Mother seemed to expect her to know tons of rules without being told them, claiming that they came from High French Breeding and that People With Class *Know* These Things.

No one would know they were of Good European Ancestry if they looked at the outdated orange metal cabinets around three sides of the kitchen, Abby snarked as she fetched the dinner things. And since her dad was Scandinavian, Abby was only half French. Ever since the girl at the ranch had accidentally revealed that rumors circulated around the ranch about her being stuck up, she'd worried that Mother's holier-than-thou attitude had rubbed off on her. But if she *was* snobby, maybe she'd be the last to know it. She despaired whenever her thinking took her down that road, so she usually avoided it.

The fourth, far side of the kitchen used to open into the back yard through the back door, but that wall had been removed and a sunroom added. Mother's Crafters Circle work and laptop occupied the low, east-facing counter and spilled onto the breakfast bar. Too bad for Abby, who had looked forward sitting on a high stool to eat, but ate at the small round table placed in the middle of the sunroom. Still, Mother's trees and flowers showed through the sunroom's sliding glass doors. In winter, snow sometimes swirled outside like a snow globe, though ice was more the norm in Tennessean winters.

Abby shut a cabinet door, slowly turning around with her load while pretending it was her horse equipment from today. She carried the dishes carefully through the door opposite, fighting the twinge in her back and the hitch in her leg. She laid the place settings on the dining room table, where the family ate together.

Silverware, napkins, salt and pepper shakers, and the salad dressing cruet on its saucer all had to be brought in trips so nothing fell and broke. *Maybe I should have brought the tack in several trips, too? Had Moony protested the junk stuck on his cinch?* She exchanged occasional glances with Jenn, who had been asked – told – to wash the lettuce leaves, and not to splash Mother's papers.

"Is there anything else?" Abby asked of Mother, who made the tuna salad. Abby averted her eyes and used a voice low enough to avoid being called impertinent but loud enough to avoid being labeled ... not loud enough.

"Yes, Abigail, please go tell your father that it's time to eat. He is in the bedroom resting."

"Okay," Abby replied obediently in the same monotone.

Daddy didn't normally sleep during the day. The bedroom door was still shut, and she wasn't sure what to expect. She tapped softly with the back of her hand. No answer. She tapped a little louder.

"Daddy?" she called.

A grunt answered her.

She didn't know whether to open the door then, as he always did with her door, or not. She decided that as the child she should not open it without permission.

"Mother says it's time to eat." She carefully modulated her voice to reach him through the door without shouting at him.

She heard another grunt and his weight moving on the bed. She still hesitated, not knowing if she was supposed to wait or go, and decided to split the difference by watching from her room.

She wandered over to her windowsill, where several model horses posed on the wide ledge. She cleaned the dustiest, a small flocked gray with its own plastic brush. Daddy had still not come out, she admired her new blue ribbon and placed it precisely between the well-loved, flaking palomino and the high-stepping white gelding.

Daddy finally appeared, wearing jeans and a polo shirt instead of his weekday business suit. He looked like his usual self: wavy brown hair combed to the side, large green eyes accented with bags and lines, and mouth habitually settled into a patient, neutral smile.

His sad eyes met her uncertain gaze and guessed her question, because he said, "I didn't sleep well again last night and was tired today, so I took a nap."

She nodded and followed his medium frame down the hall, through the living room, and into the dining room, where Jenn and Mother waited silently. Abby slid into her chair and waited, escaping already into whatever focal point she could find and noting the pretty golden tone creeping into a few sugar maple leaves in the back yard.

Once seated, Daddy intoned, "Bless us, oh Lord, and these Thy gifts which we are about to receive. Amen." Sometimes he said a different Christian grace, from the Lord's Prayer: "Give us this day our daily bread, and forgive us our trespasses. Amen." But Abby liked a less solemn one better that, ironically, she'd learned at church camp: "Rub-a-dub-dub, thanks for the grub, Good God, let's eat!" She recited it silently now and allowed herself to remember some of the good times there. Hiking, swimming, softball, Capture the Flag, crafts and, every year, an operetta performed for the parents. Better than church camp was Girl Scout camp, because it had horses; she'd earned her Horse Lover and Horse Rider badges there. The most rewarding part was knowing more than the other girls and earning the praise of the instructors, though she hadn't shared that with family or friends for fear it would seem egotistical and earn her scorn.

When she slipped into those memories at the table, though, Mother sometimes caught the vacant look on her face and told her to get her "head out of the clouds." She wondered if her spacey face looked any different when she recalled the stage fright that caused her to completely forget her lines in one operetta, or nearly drowning in the Girl Scout swimming pool. Abby could handle being called a space cadet, but intended to keep up with her fantasies and reminiscences. She worked on keeping her face blank during thoughts she didn't want to be quizzed about.

Mother's dinner conversation usually consisted of, "Elbows off the table, Jennifer; it's bad manners." Or, "Abigail, only vulgar people chew with their mouths open." Abby kept her head down except when spoken to and usually anchored her left hand under her left thigh to keep it off the table until she needed it. Mother had taught the family the "proper French way" to use utensils, using the fork in the right hand to carry bites of food to the mouth and transferring the fork to the left hand when the right hand cut food. Abby knew how to pile the cut food onto the back of her fork in her left hand, too, and bring it to her mouth without spilling anything. She didn't ever tell Mother that at school, she reverted to the "crude" American fashion of holding the fork straight up and down in the left hand while sawing with the knife in the right hand, then delivering food with the right hand.

Near the end of dinner, Mother asked, "Paul, how was your nap?"

"It helped," he said. "It's been harder and harder to sleep right."

Abby regarded him for a moment, wondering what this would mean for the family. She couldn't tell. She removed dishes from Mother and Daddy's right side as they sat chatting and relaxing, thankful that dinner had gone fairly smoothly tonight. Jenn did the dishes; next week they would reverse the chores.

After dinner, Abby made a point of shaking out her clothes where Mother would see her through the sliding doors. She banged her boots together to knock dirt and grass off. Was she supposed to take them back to her room? Or try to leave them outside? "The Dictator" had not said. If she guessed wrong, she'd get more venom. She thought she might escape more trouble if she folded the clothes up and put them in her hamper. The boots could go on newspaper in her closet, preferably keeping them out of Mother's sight. Vivian seemed to forget about things she didn't see; Abby counted on that a lot.

Abby escaped into her reading nook – the little space between her bed and low bureau. This allowed the old family quilt on the bed to remain tidy, as Mother wanted.

She was almost done rereading *Harry Potter and the Order of the Phoenix* – the one she'd understood least – in preparation for the last and seventh book. She had especially enjoyed the part where Harry and his friends rode on the flying thestrals. It must be a lot like galloping on a horse, which she often fantasized about. With today's experience on Moony, going fast would be much easier to imagine, if only she erased the disastrous bits about being scared and falling off. Souvenir bruises and aches were worsening tonight, however, and reminded her about riding realities.

Harry had lost his parents, had just two close friends, and suffered at the hands of the Dursleys. Abby had two biological parents, but often felt her treatment was just as unfair as Harry's. She, too, had only a few friends: her sister Jenn; Chloë Curry at riding; Grace, Kendra, and Maria up the street; and the girls at church … who didn't really count because they only saw each other at church. She, too, never had friends over. It was too hard to make sure Mother wouldn't go off her rocker about some tiny thing.

Harry had adopted Dumbledore as a kind of grandfather figure, but seemed to switch between being angry with him and adoring him. Abby would have been delighted to meet Dumbledore, let alone have him as a grandfather. She knew J.K. Rowling had just imagined him; surely no one could be that funny in real life, that smart, that … *everything*.

Abby had never known either of her grandfathers before they died, which saddened her. Lois, Daddy's stepmother, now lived in Florida, where they had visited her several times. Granny, Mother's mother, lived in New York, where the Wizes used to live. They'd gone back last year for Granny's 70th birthday. Abby liked Lois more because she was much nicer and because she bought one piece of Abby's silver pattern every birthday and Christmas, as did Mother. By the time Abby got married, she might have eight complete place settings, something Mother felt was essential.

At least Abby had her sister Jenn, while Harry only had that awful Dudley. He was a Dud, all right. But Abby and Jenn got along pretty well. They'd played with Barbies and other toys in the basement, back when it was a playroom. They'd gone to neighborhood kids' houses together, and to the closest swimming pool. But now that Jenn was 16 and in high school, the three years between them seemed further than before, creating a strange new gap in their closeness.

Scrunching up in her reading nook, propped against her bed, Abby finished reading. Sliding the thick book into the bottom drawer of her bureau, she saw her diary, pulled it out, and wrote a quick entry about the riding accident before starting her laundry in the basement, putting her dirty jeans and shirt in first. She would finish the laundry after church in the morning, ready for tomorrow night's car-loading so they could leave early Monday morning for North Carolina. She went to bed at 9 p.m., calling "goodnight" down the hall and hearing it echoed back.

That night she dreamt that she called a Pegasus to her by raising a shining halter in the air …

∞   ∞   ∞   ∞   ∞   ∞   ∞   ∞

… it flies down to her, glowing in the sun … bows for her to mount … they rise up and fly over trees … buildings … lakes … she senses the houses where other girls are in trouble … shoots bolts of power to them from her hands, which turn warm … the warmth spreads to her whole body … the winged horse is one with her thoughts, turning as she looks, slowing when she wishes to slow …

∞   ∞   ∞   ∞   ∞   ∞   ∞   ∞

She always loved the dreams where she mastered beauty and control and power, so unlike her real life.

Chapter 4 Church

Sunday morning brought church, heat, humidity, blooming bruises and sore muscles. After her usual breakfast, Abby continued her laundry and took the suitcase Daddy handed her for later. Surveying her clothing choices for church, she pushed aside her favorite peach skort, knowing Mother would say that it was too casual for church. Instead, she took out a short-sleeved flowered yellow summer dress and sandals, along with her biggest gold hoops for her pierced ears. She figured the sunny colors were best for the sunny day.

At least the dress covered the biggest bruises on her legs from yesterday's fall. She planned to avoid mentioning the accident to her family, and would rather not give anyone a reason to find out. She took her prayer book and yellow straw hat into the living room to wait.

Jenn arrived at the same time. They gave each other the once-over.

"Nice dress, where'd you get it?" Jenn asked with a growing grin.

"Best place in town," was Abby's quick, smiling reply. It was a standard joke between them, as many of Abby's nice things were hand-me-downs from Jenn. Neither of them minded it. Mother prided herself on her sewing abilities, and she used to sew matching outfits for them. Abby's favorite was the fancy, identical Easter dresses from a Daisy Kingdom pattern, with coordinating shoes and hats.

Mother often drafted the girls to sew with her. Jenn enjoyed it even though she shared Abby's sentiments about Mother. Jenn's skin must be thicker because Jenn seemed to tolerate the bad parts of sewing with Mother better than Abby. Abby disliked how picky Mother was, and how hard the projects were. Pleats, interfacing, darts, ruffles, buttonholes … weren't there easier sewing projects? Jenn wanted to learn more and use the large stash of interesting fabrics in the former playroom, now the sewing and family room. Jenn had made cloth toys, bedding, dresses, even shirts. She said that this winter she was going to learn how to make down-filled vests.

Jenn wore her latest creation, a simple dress made from a baby blue T-shirt attached to a pieced skirt. It set off her blue eyes well. She had completed her outfit with Huarache sandals, a straw purse, dangly chain earrings, and a simple plastic barrette in the straight brown hair that fell to the middle of her back. She looked comfortable but stylish sitting in the reupholstered armless chair in the living room, leafing through the current issue of the *Keepsake Quilting* catalog.

"Look," she said, pointing.

Abby took the catalog and saw the quilt made of horse pictures.

"Cool," Abby replied, peering at the small photo. Horses of several breeds in various poses adorned the center of the quilt. Border panels depicted horse-related items such as saddles and bridles. The catalog said that directions came with the preprinted fabrics.[3]

She handed the catalog back slowly, imagining owning that quilt, spreading it on her bed or folding it in her reading nook. Her eyes followed the picture as it went into Jenn's waiting hands, so she missed how closely Jenn watched her reaction.

"Thanks," Abby said, coming back to reality. Rather than moving Mother's current knitting project from under the brightest lamp, Abby chose an empty spot on the couch's far end and eyed the neatly displayed magazines on the coffee table. Mother bought them so the girls would be "cultured and knowledgeable," but Abby did like *Muse* (a kids' science magazine), and *Reader's Digest* (for the jokes). The *National Geographic* showed a scary-looking man with slightly bloodshot, scowling brown eyes, looking out over the big gray word "Pakistan." He made Abby uncomfortable.[4]

Abby picked up the magazine to see what the man on the cover was so angry about. She flipped past the current downloadable screensavers and paused briefly at the Culture page in case she could use it to gain points with Mother. This time it showed pictures of foods unique to different regions of the U.S. Nothing was listed for Tennessee, but North Carolina enjoyed "Livermush – pig parts and cornmeal fried in a block." Abby wondered if she'd be expected to eat it during their vacation. She quickly turned to the cover article.

Pakistan was portrayed by poor people and war, but a horse caught Abby's attention. Slightly blurry, framed between a rifle, a dangling strand of bullets, and a soldier's arm, it was harnessed, probably to a cart. Was it an Arabian horse? What breeds did they have there?

Abby liked horse-breed books. She owned two, and checked others out of libraries. What was the name of the bony kind from the Middle East? This dirty-gray horse might be one of those. Its mouth was open; was its driver pulling too hard on the reins? It looked like it was straining to trot; was the load too heavy and the driver forcing it?

Abby had seen a "joke" photo that she didn't find funny at all – a small donkey suspended in midair by its harness, strapped to a cart piled ridiculously high and tipped up on its back edge. Were lots of animals in other countries overworked and under-loved? Abby did not know if she could tolerate a working animal being treated unfairly. She suspected she wouldn't make a very good Peace Corps volunteer.

Mother interrupted her thoughts, swishing into the room and announcing that it was time to go. Abby and Jenn put down their reading, stood up, and straightened their clothes for Mother, who wore a loose, lavender-colored linen skirt with a short-sleeved, silk floral blouse and low brown heels.

"Change those ludicrous earrings, Abigail! Do you want everyone to think you're uncultured?" Mother had a special knack for inserting venom into a mere sentence or two, Abby thought viciously as she trooped down the hall to put on her smaller gold hoops. Her cheerful earrings were ludicrous, she was uncultured, and "everyone" would think she was trash. *Good morning to you too, Mother.*

The two girls followed their parents downstairs, turned right at the bottom, and entered the cluttered basement garage, full of castoffs: boxes of Daddy's old papers, dishes that Mother had tired of, chairs to be refinished. Crowded out, the two cars stayed in the driveway.

Jenn hoisted the garage door and Daddy led the way to their silver four-door sedan, wearing the white, open-throated dress shirt, khaki-colored dress pants, and brown woven dress shoes Mother had bought for him. In her most resentful moments, Abby felt that Mother played Barbies and Ken with the family and house. It made her feel like a thing instead of a person.

Abby headed for her seat behind Mother, who sat with her passenger door open, carefully arranging her skirt so the crisp linen would not wrinkle too badly. Out of habit from when she was younger and weaker, Abby braced herself against the car pillar with her right hand and began to open her door with her left hand. Suddenly, Mother shut her door faster than Abby could jerk her hand away. Her right pinky finger was trapped between the front door and its frame.

"Ow! Ouch! Ooowww!" Abby began to howl in pain. She could not twist around far enough to open Mother's door with her free left hand. But Mother merely stared at her daughter's unseemly outburst.

"The door! Open the door!" Abby cried through her pain, barely getting the words out. Her swelling finger felt like it was being cut off.

"What's the noise about?" Daddy demanded on Mother's behalf.

"My finger, my finger!" Abby would have sunk to the ground from the unlivable pain shooting up her arm and shrieking in her brain, but she was pinned in place.

"Paul, would you see what's the matter?" Mother scowled at Daddy, angry with the delay and the breach of social etiquette.

Jenn said, loudly and calmly enough for the adults to hear, "Mother, her finger is caught in your door; she needs you to open it."

"Oh! Why didn't she say so?" said Mother, irate at the commotion in general and Abby in particular.

Vivian opened her door and released Abby's finger. Blinking and wiping her eyes, Abby could barely see her hand through her tears. Pain shot up her arm with every heartbeat. The pinky was swollen and growing purple, nearly black in a deep crease across the middle bone.

"Well, if it's not bleeding, get in and stop crying!" Mother snapped.

Abby slid into her seat, took the tissue Jenn offered, and quietly sucked on her finger, not knowing what else to do. She resented her mother for not even checking to see if it was broken. But it wasn't bleeding visibly, and no one seemed to consider cancelling church. Abby would have to figure out whether or not any bones were broken during the drive. She did her best to stifle her sobs, watching the purple grow over her ballooning, throbbing finger. It hurt a lot, even worse when she tried to bend it. She knew she'd get an earful, though, if she said anything more about it.

The drive took 20 very long minutes, during which Abby suffered in silence, feeling more and more certain that the whole ordeal wasn't going to be worth it. Church felt like a just fashion show that Mother paraded for.

Jenn didn't dare say anything, but gave her sympathetic glances, once mouthing, "You'll be okay, Abs!" When Abby leaned back, wiped her tears with Jenn's tissue and closed her eyes against the pain, Jenn held her good left hand. Once, when Abby tried resting her hand on her thigh, Jenn tapped Abby's arm, then held up her own right hand in front of herself to model the idea: "Hold it up, not down in your lap." She was right; it throbbed worse when it was down.

Daddy parked the car in one of the slots around the huge building of blond, rough-cut stone. Abby knew Mother required her to appear as normal as possible, so she quickly experimented with different poses to hide her smashed finger. The best answer seemed to be hiding it behind her prayer book at waist height. Jenn glanced stealthily at her as they followed their parents past the carved wooden doors that stood open, inviting them into the T-shaped old church.

St. Zosimo's Episcopal Church was one of the oldest and most respected in Surely, Tennessee. Straight ahead, a huge stained glass window glowed above the elaborate marble altar. Wooden choir stalls faced each other across the chancel, the organ console to the right. Wooden pews filled the nave, holding today's sparse congregation, thinned by summer vacations and heat. Following Daddy up the center aisle to a pew, the females curtseyed after he bowed. They each traced the sign of the cross on their chests before sliding in.

At least the thick stone walls help keep the inside cool, Abby thought, still quietly nursing her finger while covering her bruises with her dress. As usual, her nose was stuffed up. She had to hold her breath to close her mouth around her finger, then open her mouth to take a breath – all while looking down, using her hair as a curtain, sucking noiselessly so her parents wouldn't notice and tell her to stop. She glanced up once to see if the tall old trees outside shaded the stained glass windows high in the walls. The ornate depictions of saints and Biblical events did look darker in patches.

Dr. Laird, the organist, played background music as the congregation sat quietly, scanning the program and the hymn numbers, adjusting their clothes, and scoping each other out. Abby spotted several kids from her Sunday School class.

The music changed, cueing the congregation to stand and began to sing the first hymn. Abby and Jenn shared one hymnal, Mother and Daddy another. A small side door opened to reveal the long-robed processional: lead cross-bearer, minister, two assistant ministers, choir, and final cross-bearer.

The procession sang and walked down the left side aisle, turned the corner in the narthex behind the congregation, and progressed up the center aisle of the nave. As it reached the steps to the chancel, the ministers continued straight to the altar while the choir members filed into their stalls, right and left, still leading the congregation in song. The stately procession was designed to be impressive.

Today's service was a regular one, without Holy Communion. Abby's main challenge was to find something interesting, possibly even useful, to keep her awake.

Abby had taken catechism classes and received her first communion last year. At the small party at their house afterward, Mother and Daddy had given her the prayer book and a necklace she liked and sometimes remembered to wear to church. Its clear Lucite front magnified a tiny mustard seed, and its engraved back showed the Bible quote about having faith like a grain of mustard seed and being able to move mountains with it.[5] Although such allegories sounded nice, they didn't usually make sense, and whenever Abby asked, the answers were so vague that they didn't help. Maybe somewhere, somewhen, she'd get some understandable answers.

Today's sermon covered Jesus returning to Earth.[6]

"The Second Coming is extremely important for Christians," Rev. Davison declared. "One by one, over the centuries, all of the prophesies Jesus made about His return have come true." He quoted Biblical passages predicting the tearing down of the temple in Jerusalem 70 years after Jesus's crucifixion; enemies killing the believers, and love dying; the sun and the moon growing dark; earthquakes, floods, and other terrible natural disasters; and the

Gospel spreading all over the world just before the end, when He would return like a thief in the night to judge who had and who had not obeyed Him. "The righteous will live eternally with the Lord in Paradise, and the cursed will be cast into eternal fire with Satan. Jesus will return on clouds of glory with angels blasting on trumpets. The faithful will be taken up with Him to heaven in the glorious Rapture that all sincere, righteous, pious, deserving Christians yearn for."

Imagining all this, Abby grew alarmed; but when he said he thought these were more like parables than actual mechanics, she relaxed a little.

"We should stay alert, though, continually checking ourselves," the reverend said, "always ready should Jesus return and see us. If we think He wouldn't like something about us, we had better change, because no one knows when He will return."

This worried Abby, who already had to watch her behavior every second around Mother. Now Jesus could arrive any minute, looking at her like that stern Pakistani man, and throw her into Hell with eternal fire. That was too awful to think about.

She sucked quietly on her finger, trying to banish this newest threat from her mind, when the reverend abruptly said, "Let us pray. O Lord God, we thank you for the promise of the return of Jesus Christ when there will be an end to all suffering, sin, and death. May the Holy Ghost grace us so that we gain admittance into His flock when He reappears. In Jesus's name. Amen."

Dr. Laird played again, the choir sang, and the collection plates passed through the congregation. Abby and Jenn put little church-issued envelopes containing their portion of allowance into the collection plates. Daddy put in a larger one for himself and Mother.

Abby imagined how amazing it would be to live in the time of Jesus's return and maybe even fly with Him in Paradise. How she would love being in heaven, happy all the time!

Sadly, the rest of the service was as boring as she expected, broken only by the announcement that today was the church's 130th birthday and, instead of Sunday School, everyone was invited to a celebration on the lawn.

The closing processional filed through the little side door to the final hymn, Rev. Davison at the rear. The organ music stopped as he turned and paused in the doorway, raised his first two fingers and gave the final benediction while slowly sketching the sign of the cross in the air toward the congregation.

"May the Lord bless you and keep you. May the Lord make His face to shine upon you, and be gracious to you. May the Lord lift up

His countenance upon you, and give you peace."[7]

Then he turned and went through the door, which quietly closed.

Abby always liked that little blessing and the way it was done. She needed all the help and goodwill she could get. She rose slowly, trying for smoothness and reverence.

Daddy – relaxed-looking and, for once, holding Mother's hand – led the way out toward the lawn. Abby wished he'd hold her hand as well, but the aisle was too narrow for three abreast. She settled for pretending she was balancing a book on her head to help her walk gracefully, as Mother often urged.

Jenn smirked and copied Abby, linking arms. They glided gracefully down the blond stone steps, stifling goofy giggles, giving Abby a rare light-hearted moment and prompting a wistful, timid prayer for more happiness even before Jesus returned and made everyone happy all the time. Jenn dropped their prayer books in the car, allowing Abby space to wonder if she could purposely dream about Paradise, and if it was sinful to yearn for more happiness, or if she was supposed to just accept whatever came her way with forgiveness. That brought on one of her frequent disagreements with church teachings.

"Jenn, what if heaven on earth means I could ride horses all the time, but it would take Daddy's money away from things *you* want, or even need? Then you and Daddy would be unhappy, right? And that's not your heaven. Or is everyone going to be millionaires then? Or would everything will be free?"

"Yeah, that's why utopias never work," Jenn said, resuming their graceful stroll to the gathering on the lawn. "If we still have bodies and we're still on earth, but everyone can do whatever they want, some people's wants step on others. Then it's not heaven anymore."

The Ladies' Auxiliary bustled around the folding tables on the lawn, laying out the refreshments that featured a sheet cake spelling "St. Zosimo's Church 130 Years" in bright yellow icing. Small, sophisticated, yellow and green sugar roses bloomed brightly in two diagonal corners. Once Asst. Rev. Smythe blessed the cake, the ladies sliced it and poured the punch. It was already getting hot at 10:30 a.m., driving the adults into shady spots under the large trees and in doorways. The youngest children played tag and threw pine cones, the preteens shoved and teased, and the teens dug out their cell phones and stood in two groups, one for boys and one for girls.

Abby and Jenn headed for the group of girls.

"Hey," they said to Kat, Jessica, Laurel, and Deirdre. Another girl, Cissy, left her brother at the cake table and joined the girls.

"Hey, 'sup?" several replied.

"Not much." Abby decided that a slowly clearing nose, a smashed finger and leg bruises didn't rank as news. She didn't want to share her private prayers about going to heaven with Jesus ... or seeing Him return and bring peace to the earth. Wait, first he'd have to return, then the faithful would rapture with Him. But if she was up in heaven, how could she see heaven on earth? Or would she have to be a sinner to stay behind on earth to see it? But that would mean she was in hell. Oh, no!

"Did you hear about Asst. Rev. Gottle?" Kat breathed.

"No, what happened?" the Thomkins sisters rejoined, Laurel leaning forward and Deirdre stopping her compulsive text-messaging.

"They caught him having an affair last week, with Mrs. Talinda! They're deciding what to do with him," Kat imparted secretively.

This was astounding news indeed. Rev. Gottle, an unmarried assistant minister, with Mrs. Talinda? She was, well, *married* ... to Mr. Talinda, with two kids just younger than Abby! Jenn remained more composed than Abby, whose mouth fell open in disbelief and shock.

"What, like send him away?" Deirdre hissed.

"Yeah, like to another church in another state maybe. Or pay a fine. Stuff like that," Kat said, relishing being the one to bring the news.

Abby thought a more fitting punishment would be jail or even stoning like they did in the Bible for sexual crimes. If he followed the Bible, shouldn't he get a Biblical kind of punishment?

"That's all?" she blurted out.

"Well, I don't know, really," Kat backpedaled. "It's just what I heard. It's gonna be decided sometime pretty soon, I guess."

Abby wondered why he had appeared in the processional just like nothing had happened and, come to think of it, even passed right by the Talindas. How could he even be in the same room with her, knowing that others knew? She looked around, but couldn't see him on the lawn, even though both other ministers chatted with church members. Well, maybe at least he had some sense of shame and didn't want to face people who might know about what he did. But maybe he should come out and face his music.

Whatever he should be doing now, Abby felt, he was doing it as a hypocrite. The nerve to even show his face in church wearing that robe and colored shawl, when he'd done something so very wrong. What had *he* thought of Rev. Davison's sermon today? Was that sermon mainly directed at Asst. Rev. Gottle? This news changed how she thought of everyone and everything at church today, it was so ... so ... unminister-like, so un-churchly.

Her aching finger grabbed her attention; she'd forgotten to hold it up, and it throbbed and had turned purple again.

Chapter 5 Packing

To Abby's great relief, her pinky was a bit better through the day. She bandaged the last joint to immobilize it and stop it from hurting every time she bent it. The bruises on her legs matched her purple finger by Sunday afternoon, so she changed into tights after church rather than the shorts the weather suggested.

Finishing laundry and packing for their trip to North Carolina took the remainder of the family's Sunday afternoon. Mother's sister and her three children had invited the Wizes to stay for about two weeks, maybe visiting the ocean a couple of hours away.

"Pack clean pajamas!" Mother dictated, standing in the doorway of Abby's room.

"Yes, I will," Abby replied, hunkered on the floor between a basket of clean clothes and the half-full suitcase.

"Let me see what you have." Mother strode across the tan carpet.

Stifling a groan, Abby stood aside. Mother removed everything Abby had packed.

"The more folds, the more waste," Mother scolded. "Occupy the whole space. Biggest items on the bottom. Like this." She laid the windbreaker out flat at the bottom of the suitcase, folding only the sleeves in. "How many shirts?"

"Six, plus I set aside one to wear on the trip."

Surprisingly, Mother did not find anything to criticize about that, and asked about bottoms.

"Three shorts, two capris, and one jeans. They coordinate with most of my shirts so I can fit the weather." *Though maybe I should leave the shorts home, depending on how long it takes bruises to disappear.*

"Speak properly, Abigail. 'Dress for' the weather," Mother quickly corrected. "Leave the jeans out. It will be too hot for them. Pack one more pair of shorts instead, so you'll only need to do laundry once while we're there. Shoes?"

Abby had not decided on her footwear but tried to sound firm as she said, "One sandals, one tennis shoes, one boots. I'll put them in plastic bags before I pack them."

"Boots?" Mother raised an eyebrow. "There's no riding there, why do you need boots? Leave them here, they take up way too much room. Besides, you want to just stand around and *pet* the horses. Just take your white sneakers, they're nice and clean and look good with everything."

Abby didn't know why she wanted to take boots and jeans. "Just in case" didn't seem a defensible answer, so she said nothing. The petting comment stung, but she knew she would be punished for talking back if she tried to explain the boost, the thrill, of just standing next to a horse. Smelling, seeing, touching, let alone riding it, made Abby's week.

Mother packed the bottoms next, in order of size, then shirts, biggest first, followed by swimwear and panties in the pockets.

"Where are your bras?" Mother asked, looking not at Abby but at the suitcase.

"Um..." Abby stalled.

"You need to take them and wear them, young lady. I have noticed you're not wearing a bra, and you are at the age where you should be."

Abby's heart sank further. She hated the so-called training bras her mother had left on her bed one day. They restricted her arms and cut into her sides. The hooks rested smack on her spine; hard chair-backs made her squirm to get them off her bones.

Mother wasn't finished. "Also, Daddy says you need to shower more often and shave your arms and legs. He says he has noticed a certain odor." She marched out of the room.

Abby hunched over her packing, dwelling on the cruel words.

Mother popped back in and placed a travel-sized deodorant inside the suitcase, giving Abby the "I mean business" look. "Don't forget your toothbrush, either," she added, glowering at Abby.

Abby's humiliation grew. Her toothbrush? She wasn't *stupid*. She opened her toiletry kit to show that it was already packed. Mother seized the pouch and examined the contents.

"Razor?" she demanded.

Abby dropped her head and Mother spun out of the room.

So she stank and was hairy. And Daddy had left it to Mother to deliver his sentiments with the tactfulness of a steamroller. Abby would much rather *he* approached her about something this personal, but ... well, honestly, he didn't really talk to her much at all. But, if Daddy wanted her to shave her pits, but why didn't he shave his?

Mother reappeared and dropped a plastic razor into her toiletry kit.

"You must start shaving your underarms, Abigail. It is very unlady-like to be hairy."

"Men don't. And European ladies don't." Abby voiced her train of thought without vetting it first.

"Do not talk back to your elders!" Mother exploded. She seized her daughter's wrist and dragged her over to the bathroom sink. Abby knew what was coming and stiffened in loathing.

Mother grabbed a handful of Abby's hair, wrenched her head back, jammed the bar of soap into her daughter's mouth twice, then let her go. Abby thought it was over, now that she gagged with the taste of soap. But Mother grabbed Abby's T-shirt and pulled it up. Abby fought to hold it down; whatever Mother planned was bad. Mother won the tussle, tugged off the shirt, and threw it down on the floor, her face a cold mask of fury. Abby grabbed it again to cover herself; but as she straightened back up, Mother slapped her face – hard.

"You're ungrateful and willful! You will not defy me, young lady! You will *do as I say!*" Mother shouted, spit flying.

She grabbed one of Abby's arms, raised it high, and coated Abby's armpit with the spit-moistened soap. Frozen in fear, Abby dared not fight but was unable to cooperate with this assault. Vivian fetched another disposable razor from a drawer and roughly swiped at the few pitiful hairs sprouting from Abby's underarm. The razor cut her, once, twice, before Mother felt that her point had been made and stopped.

"That's how it's done, missy!" Mother announced.

She took a washcloth from the rack by the sink and wet it, wiped Abby's armpit, and tossed the cloth onto the sink countertop in disgust when she saw the blood mingled with the soap lather and bits of hair.

"You bled on my good washcloth!" Mother spat. "Clean it all up! Now!" She stormed out of the bathroom.

Abby allowed herself to sink to the floor in pain and humiliation. This was a new low, even for Mother. Her finger had gotten wrenched again in the tussle, her armpit was cut and bleeding, her mouth was absolutely horrible from the taste of soap – she wondered if she'd soon be a connoisseur of the various brands of soap; Mother would be pleased at her sophisticated palate, no doubt – and even her father had turned against her. Too miserable even to cry, she just wished lightning would strike her now.

But no lightning visited her. And she knew she'd likely get another round of the same treatment if she did not clean up the mess, as unfair and galling as Mother's words were.

Her throat was stuck shut; it was hard to breathe. She listened for Mother to return with more abuse. Tears would not come, but odd vicious thoughts did, filling her with a nightmarish daydream of suddenly being bigger than Vivian and screaming at her, "You hate me? You think I'm your enemy? The Bible says to love your enemy!"

Abby's thoughts grew more and more bitter as she rinsed out her mouth, forcing herself to breathe past the large rock in her throat. (And how *did* one get that horrible taste out?) She lathered the washcloth with the hated soap to get the bloody streaks out, hung it back up – straight, so as not to be hauled into Mother Court for Crooked Washcloths – put away the razor that had been so painfully used against her, and squeegeed the counter clean of water and soap bubbles with the side of her undamaged left hand.

She returned to her bedroom and closed the door quietly lest the sound provoke Mother – wherever she was – and leaned against the cream-colored wall. She'd have to get on with packing, or she'd probably get a beating.

She surveyed the suitcase on the floor, mute testimony to Mother's domination. Would Mother notice if Abby repacked how she preferred, with bottoms and tops already paired? Although she liked pulling out an entire outfit, ready to wear, it probably wasn't worth it. She dug the boxes of bras out of her bureau drawer.

Reluctantly, she set aside the jeans and opted for two more pairs of capris instead of shorts; the bruises would be visible for a while longer.

Last, she slid her shoes into bread bags so that no filth from them could touch her clean clothes.

She was getting hungry, but heard no sounds from the kitchen. The entire house was quiet. Sometimes Mother just drove off when she was upset. It seemed that dinner was do-it-yourself tonight, so she looked cautiously into the refrigerator freezer for a TV dinner, microwaved it, wolfed it down standing over the sink, drank tap water quickly using her left hand, cleaned up fast, and scooted back to her room.

It had been a horrible day from start to finish. So bad it merited an entry in her diary: "M a witch. Shaving, bras." She didn't feel she could handle Harry Potter's woes too, so she got ready for bed at 8:30, hoping tomorrow's drive would be survivable.

Part of her doubted it would be, and she laid down, evaluating the ways she could arrange to be hit by lightning early in what promised to be a miserable trip, praying for a storm, and concocting likely excuses to get out of the car during the storm. (She knew from *Muse* that car designs stopped lightning from harming people inside them.) One possibility was to claim she had to go to the bathroom, but that had to be used sparingly in case of real need. Another option was to point out craft or sewing stores that might tempt Mother to stop. Armed with these desperate plans, she fell asleep wondering who was the more debased tonight: she or Asst. Rev. G.

Chapter 6 Driving

The kitchen hummed with activity the next morning. Abby ate a quick bowl of cereal at the sunroom table with Jenn, who glanced at Abby's pinky finger and raised her eyebrows. Abby silently nodded that her finger was better, but rolled her eyes and scrunched her mouth to let her sister know that another bad thing had happened. Jenn raised her eyebrows again, and Abby jerked her head slightly toward Mother, who made coffee for herself and Daddy. Jenn gave Abby a sympathetic look, but they had no signals for Abby to convey, "Mother attacked me with a razor and soap last night," so they finished breakfast in the customary compatible silence, got up together, rinsed their bowls and spoons, and put them in the dishwasher. Abby noisily shook out her dusty riding clothes and boots once more on the back patio and took them to her room; Jenn followed and quietly shut the door.

"What did she do?" Jenn whispered.

For a moment, Abby's throat closed again and she could not speak. Tears threatened to spill down her face. Jenn's face twisted in shared pain while she waited for Abby to do whatever she needed to do.

In a minute, Abby was able to whisper back, "She made me shave, and washed out my mouth with soap." Abby could not bring herself to say the complete truth out loud; it was too humiliating.

Jenn's eyes opened wide as she filled in the details herself. "Oh no! Abs!" she murmured, squeezing Abby's arm. "Was it bad?"

Jenn's compassion brought it all back again. Abby couldn't stop the tears from running down her face, and her breathing threatened to become a wail squeezing past the lump in her throat.

"Shhhh," Jenn said and brought her into a hug. Abby knew the shush was meant equally to comfort and quiet her lest Mother hear. The door was closed, but still ....

A sob escaped her but fortunately was muffled by Jenn's shoulder.

"Shhhhhh!" Jenn hissed more loudly, and Abby knew she was very worried about what might happen to both of them if they were discovered like this. That fear stifled the crying. Abby got a tissue from her bureau top, blew her predictably stuffy nose, and wiped her eyes. Jenn still studied her, very concerned.

"Are you gonna be okay?" she asked.

Abby gave the only possible answer. "Yeah," she mumbled, not believing it.

Jenn interpreted the answer correctly. She stood there for another long moment, knowing her little sister was not okay but unable to undo

31

Mother's deed. Jenn gently patted Abby's face and quietly left, leaving the door ajar so as not to signal Mother to investigate.

Despite crying, Abby did feel oddly better. Bringing it all up again was no fun, but after the storm cleared, the sun could peek out. It helped when somebody looked straight at her and cared how she was, knew what she went through. Fortunately, she didn't have to explain every last detail. Jenn had plenty of her own run-ins with Mother and was counting down the seasons until she could leave for college, meanwhile extracting the things she wanted from home.

Abby realized that she hadn't put on a bra, and she knew Mother would look. Could you see bras through shirts, or would Mother again rip off Abby's shirt? In front of Daddy in the car? Probably.

Abby crowded next to the closet, out of view from the doorway and anyone peeking into her room through the slit Jenn had left. She peeled off her shirt and took one of the stupid training bras out of the box. Were you supposed to reach behind your back to hook it? Human arms didn't bend like that. She'd have to hook it first, then slide it over her head. And which of the three lines of hooks were you supposed to use? Blindly, she picked the first.

Once she wrestled herself into it, the bra was uncomfortably tight. The hooks sat on her spine again. She wiggled, trying to tweak it into a better position. The hooks did shift a little, and the shoulder straps seemed a tad looser. Probably the best she could hope for.

She reached down for her shirt, only to see her toiletry kit with the deodorant staring accusingly at her. But it was just too much to deal with right now, so she prayed Mother wouldn't detect its absence.

She carried her suitcase through the house, out the front door, and down the cement steps to the street, where Mother directed the car loading. After all the items on both paper and mental checklists were completed and everyone else was in the car, Daddy locked the house door, slid into the driver's seat, and drove away.

Abby positioned her backpack at her feet and checked her saltines, orange drink, and drawing supplies.

Mother handed Abby the treasured *HP #7* and, after carefully looking at its vibrant orange cover for clues about the upcoming story, she held it on her lap while they drove through Surely, past familiar neighborhoods containing friends, her school, and Daddy's medical software office. The silver sedan turned onto I-65 heading north. Once on the interstate, when all was quiet, Abby nudged the bra hooks to one side, settled in, and lost herself in Voldemort's evil, the Malfoys' resentment, and Harry's pain, both physical and emotional.

She looked up when they turned east onto I-40 in Nashville, when

Daddy started fussing about the traffic being so heavy he couldn't use cruise control any more. He drove more jerkily, trying to keep his distance from the many semitrailers.

He seemed to blame the radio. Mother had selected a classical music station, but when the music grew loud, Daddy turned it down, then back up when a softer part started.

After several changes, Mother admonished, "Paul, there are *supposed* to be louder and quieter parts! Please focus on your driving!"

Abby tried to drown out their disagreement by playing a game she'd subversively misemployed from Mother's advice to only remember one thing in museums instead of everything: she looked for a new favorite from the longer, more unusual words in the *HP* book.

Abby and Jenn began a game they always played on long trips: Find Cars From Different States. Abby found the first North Carolina plate, evidence of their destination. "First in Flight," it boasted, featuring a drawing of an early plane.

Past the bustle of Nashville, Jenn pulled out a book of Celebrity Sudoku puzzles. Abby had never done one and asked Jenn to show her how. They worked companionably on several.

Mother knit, occasionally making comments to Daddy about the talk show now coming from the front speakers. He set the car on cruise control, leaned back, and growled replies at the emcee, who debated whether or not President Bush should be impeached because the Iraq war was floundering. The host injected opinions like, "It's time to *dump* the parties, register as Independents, and *protest* the politics in this nation!" It sounded like Mother on a tirade. Abby was glad the sound was low enough that she could ignore the harangue.

As he often did while driving, Daddy took his small clippers from his shirt pocket, moved both hands to the top of the steering wheel, and clipped his thumbnails, eventually stowing the clippers but repeatedly stroking both thumbnails with his thumb pads as he drove.

Climbing out of the cool car to have lunch at a rest stop was like stepping into the hot, steamy school gym showers. Mother handed bags and baskets out of the trunk, then led the way to a shady picnic table, which she covered with a plastic sheet. The girls assembled bologna sandwiches while the adults ate cold roasted chicken and leftovers. Mother grumbled about the "styrofoam hockey pucks" she had to eat – though she daintily held out her pinky as she did – because the doctor had told Vivian that she needed to eliminate several foods she was allergic to, including wheat. Abby had been sensitive ever since she was a newborn (shortly after her emergency Caesarian birth, she'd been covered in a head-to-toe rash, Mother liked to bemoan) and she, too, was allergic to many foods. It made eating together difficult.

Mother handed Abby a plastic tub of green jello with pears. Abby couldn't stand the texture of jello and passed it to Jenn but Mother said, "Take some jello, you're not allergic to it and we need to use it up."

Abby took the smallest scoop possible and put it at the side of her plate. Mother frowned. Abby stirred it and put the spoon in her mouth with only the smallest bits clinging to it. Mother tutted and tsk'd. Abby wanted to distract her and drop some on the ground, but a glob under her seat would invite punishment and she could not throw it far without drawing Mother's attention.

Mother hadn't spanked her with the hairbrush or told Daddy to use the belt on her since fifth grade, but that didn't mean they wouldn't. Perhaps Mother would give her the same choice as with liver years ago: eat it or sit there all night. Abby had resigned herself to sitting in her dinner chair all night rather than eating the vile stuff. Mother had finally seen how it was going to be and let her go after several hours.

"Don't be so stubborn; eat your jello, Abby," Mother commanded, putting another large spoonful on Abby's plate. "Waste not, want not. You should be grateful you have food in front of you; lots of children around the world don't."

Abby saw no choice and skimmed her teeth atop a small spoonful.

It was mushy and impossible to chew. *It was like trying to swallow raw eggs, like they did on the extreme reality shows,* Abby thought, which nearly made her retch. Only the fear of being spanked in front of everybody at the rest stop made her fight down the rising tide of her other lunch and try to swallow the jello.

When Abby finally managed to swallow the one bite and thought it might all stay down, Mother said, "Eat it all, Abby."

Abby sank on her bench. It was not possible. Jenn looked at her own jello-free plate; Abby knew she was trying to think of a way to eat Abby's jello without Mother noticing.

A remnant of sandwich on Abby's plate suggested alternating bites. She took another teeny bite of jello and then a small bite of sandwich. Abby ate as slowly as she dared, hoping to run out of time, or that Mother would drop her vigil so that Abby and Jenn could think of something else when Mother's back was turned. But Mother showed no signs of lowering her guard.

Each bit of jello threatened to evict all of the sandwich. She managed to tip a bit onto the ground while Mother packed the snacks but other than that, she had to eat the whole thing. She felt wretched.

At last, Jenn jumped up to collect the disposables and throw them away. Abby turned slowly on the bench, the contents of her stomach threatening to mutiny. She stood up gradually and quickly lost the struggle. She rushed after Jenn, leaned over the trash can swarming with flies and bees, and threw up her lunch, as well as what was left of her breakfast. It burned her nose as it came back up, and she had to taste the jello yet again, which triggered more heaving. Her nose and mouth streamed with goo. When she finally opened her eyes, she saw Jenn standing beside her, methodically tapping the food off the paper plates, precisely folding each one, and tucking them just-so into the barrel. Jenn blocked Mother's view with her body, taking the longest possible time. Jenn had saved the cleanest paper napkins and handed them to Abby one at a time to swab her nose and mouth with.

Jenn timed her folding and tucking so as to push the last utensil into the trash can just as Abby straightened up. Jenn gathered Abby's hair back and smoothed the heat-induced frizzies in a meaningful gesture of concern and care. Abby sent her an appreciative glance, pushed a hoarse "thanks" through a sore throat, and glanced over her shoulder. The parental units carried the remains of lunch back to the car, apparently not noticing anything.

"We'll say we were watching the bees, Abs," Jenn said quietly, twisting Abby's hair into a short rope so it would stay back.

"Yeah, good," Abby croaked. At least one person stood by her, she thought grimly. She would truly be sunk without Jenn.

"Next time, pretend that you have to go to the bathroom, and call to Mother when you're going; I'll switch plates with you."

It was a perfect plan. Too late to do her any good, but perfect. Abby only wished she could guess everything Mother was going to do and have plans for all of it.

Jenn and Abby approached the picnic table, awaiting orders.

"Go to the bathroom, then we'll leave," Mother said, looking their clothes up and down but missing their faces, which they attempted to arrange into neutral masks. Abby's was still slightly pale, but she was right in guessing Mother wouldn't notice it.

As the family climbed into the car, Mother spied an overweight couple walking their little wiener dog, on the way to the pet area.

"Girls, *never* let yourselves go like that," she hissed. "Stomachs hanging over their pants; they can hardly walk. It's revolting."

The girls knew better than to say anything. Abby thought it might be hard to do things, being that overweight. Walking did seem to be quite an effort for them. But they seemed far happier together and with their dog than she did at the moment, and she fantasized about trading places with them if it meant she could be happy. Perhaps if she gained a lot of weight, her mother would hate her enough to leave her alone. No, that would surely backfire, she quickly decided. Mother would hound Abby around the clock.

In the car, Abby's bra was unbearable. The trip was just as horrendous as she figured it would be, and she had no chance of being hit by lightning on this hot, sunny, clear August day. She just wanted to escape everything and everyone. She took a pillow from its corner on the back window ledge and leaned against the side of the car for a nap, waking only briefly when Jenn nudged her and pointed to the Amish horse and buggy on one of the backroads Daddy liked to take as a shortcut. When she woke up, they were nearly to Aunt Sofia's house on the outskirts of Little Lily, North Carolina. Abby's empty stomach clenched painfully. Mother repacked her knitting and books, looked for trash to throw away, and directed Daddy, who already knew the way. He turned up the radio while nodding vaguely at Mother.

Abby made sure her space was in order, then sketched horses with the drawing pad and colored pencils from her backpack. She challenged herself to draw the unfamiliar Appaloosa horses from the quilt catalog Jenn had shown her. As the car wound through dry, tan, gently rolling hills, Abby looked for horses in fields, but saw only cows, including some blotchy, black-and-white Holsteins. That made her wonder about spotted, blotchy horses and she paused mid-stroke, finally connecting the dots on the realization that Moony was an Appaloosa, and she'd missed seeing his unusual spots even when they were inches from her eyes, always more focused on inspecting his extremities and trying to remember her lessons than on truly looking at him. She started a drawing of him, wondering what his coloring would be called, mulling over the fact that in some breeds, blotches were called spots, and in other breeds, only circles were called spots. She was just concluding that she couldn't draw him until she studied his coloring and looked up his coat patterns when the car stopped. They had pulled up to a large yard sloping gently up to a white house surrounded by big oak trees and azalea bushes suffering in the drought. The central section of the wooden house was the oldest, with two stories. To the left was a long one-story addition that Abby knew was the large family room. To the right was another, smaller, one-story box: the kitchen.

The Wizes stepped from the car into the humid warmth of the North Carolina evening. Slanting sunshine glowed on Mother as she directed the unloading.

"So-FIE-ah, they're HEE-er!" a distant voice called. The front door swung open and a dozen people streamed onto the lawn, smiling, calling hellos, and yelling at the last one to shut the door so the bugs didn't get in the house nor the air conditioning out.

Chapter 7 Sofia

Abby recognized several people in the crowd now streaming down the golden hill, its brown grass gilded by the last rays of sun. Mother's older sister, Sofia Holsworth, came down to the car to embrace Mother and take a bag. Mother's hair was shorter, carefully curled, and naturally dark. Sofia, the smaller and thinner of the two, had straight brown hair streaked with lighter strands; she wore it loose at shoulder length. Sofia's laugh emerged more easily than Vivian's, and she seemed more lighthearted. Both sisters were pale, dressed tastefully, and carried themselves with poise. Sofia, the divorced mother of three children, joined the throng welcoming the visitors.

The oldest, Jonathan, was almost 18, a senior this year, and stood near a girl of color whom Abby didn't know. Next was Penelope – Penny for short – 16, with two girlfriends. Then Ricky, 12 – Abby's favorite and the life of any party – with a couple of guy-friends in tow. Two dogs raced around barking at everyone; assorted cats policed the occasion with their unwavering gaze.

"You're just in time to help us destroy the pantry!" Ricky called out. "Mom's cleaned it out, and we're all human garbage disposals!"

"Make it any more appetizing and they'll run you over to get to it," Sofia retorted with a wry smile. "But there might be something edible, actually. Kids, help your Aunt Vivi with her things. Many hands make light work!"

It only took one trip when so many hands pitched in. Daddy locked the car and joined the procession into the house.

"Girls, you'll share the room all the way at the end of the upstairs hall." Sofia waved upward as the Wize sisters filed into the blue-wall-papered entryway. "The grownups have the foldout couch in the family room. Meet in the kitchen, okay?"

Abby followed Jenn and Penny up the wooden stairs. Several bed-room doors led off the upstairs hallway, some open, some closed. The last one was the smallest, a plain room with a single bed against the right-hand wall and a low trundle bed next to it.[8] An Oriental carpet peeked around the edges of the beds, leaving a narrow strip of wooden floor visible. Penny scooped an open box off the trundle.

"More antique junk … this time from Granny," she said. "We don't sell jewelry, only furniture, so actually, take whatever you want out of here." Abby shrugged and picked an old watch, figuring it would be fun to play with. Jenn chose a vintage brooch and pinned it on her tank top, amusingly out of synch. The sisters parked their luggage and followed

Penny back downstairs, turning left at the bottom of the stairs, heading through the formal dining room to the kitchen to join the line. A relaxed bunch of friends and family picked plates from a stack of mismatches, helped themselves from the many bowls of food on the counters, and sat at tables in the kitchen or dining room.

Jon maneuvered his plate past Abby and Jenn, introducing Melissa on the way to the kitchen table next to the dinner line. Although Jon didn't describe their relationship, Melissa seemed to be more than a friend. Abby saw an intelligent, lively expression on Melissa's plain but welcoming features.

Jon probably regretting introducing Melissa to Mother and asking if they could sit by her when she pointedly turned away from Melissa's friendly outstretched hand, looking for the nearest diversion and finding her younger daughter. She yanked Abby out of line and made her stand next to Jon, like a shield against this affront. Abby's face distorted in proportion to the damage Mother dished out, starting with the slight Mother inflicted on Melissa, growing with the wrist pain, and solidifying with Mother's words. "Nice to meet you, Melinda. Did you meet my second daughter, Abigail? She's the one who insists on marching to her own drummer."

Melissa's face nearly mirrored Abby's by the end of the exchange; she quickly took the seat farthest from Mother and kept her head down. Abby saw that Melissa understood how to survive an encounter with Mother; Abby tried to throw her a sympathetic look like Jenn would, but Melissa had already shut down.

Purpose served, Mother let Abby get back in line, now behind Penny and her two friends, Barb and Carol. Barb's unusual appearance stood out: she was shorter and wider than the other two but her dyed, choppy hair, black eyeliner and black clothes contrasted markedly with Penny's classic wardrobe and tidy bun. Slender, tall, quiet Carol wore a faded t-shirt and baggy knit basketball shorts with her straight, waist-length, auburn hair.

"Penny tells me you're into horses?" Barb asked, tattoos peeking out from below her sleeve as she served herself from the buffet.

"Sure am," Abby replied, looking at Barb with new interest.

"So's my sister Angie," Barb said with a funny look at Penny and an equally strange little move of her hand.

"Oh?" Abby said, wondering what this was all about, spooning up samples of several dishes.

"Yeah, she does this horse whispering stuff. It's kind of … kooky."

"What does she do?" Abby pictured a horse draped in silk scarves, surrounded by lighted candles and warily eyeing a barefoot girl in a long dress dancing around it, softly chanting strange words and showering the horse with handfuls of flower petals.

"She wiggles ropes at the horse, waves an orange stick at it, talks about its 'horse-anality.' Nutty stuff like that."

Abby didn't know what to think. She remembered seeing an orange stick in The Ride Place's lost and found corner, but she didn't know who owned it or if they used it. She could not imagine the managers at The Ride Place allowing anything actually kooky. But Barb obviously thought her sister was off her rocker.

They stood there regarding each other uncomfortably. Finally, curiosity overcoming her, Abby asked, "Will I get to meet her?"

Barb shrugged. "If you want to, I s'pose."

"Well, if it works out, it might be interesting. Good for some laughs if nothing else, I guess."

To Abby's relief, that seemed the right thing to say. Barb smiled, nodded, and said she'd check. Abby smiled and, glad there was no livermush, tended to her aching insides.

After cleaning up the meal, everyone went to the family room. Jenn chatted with Jon and his apparent girlfriend, the adults gossiped, and Ricky and his friends played *Magic: The Gathering* cards in a corner.

Penny and her girlfriends channel-surfed. *Oprah Winfrey* featured women who had married wife-beaters. Abby thought their lives sounded even worse than hers.

"They're so stupid," Barb commented to Carol and Penny. Pointing to one woman, she added, "Anyone could see that guy was trash. Why did she marry him?"

The girls agreed that the men's drinking and low-paying jobs – if they were employed at all – should have been a good clue. Mother and Aunt Sofia nodded approvingly at these assessments.

Penny pointed the remote at the TV and the downtrodden wives gave way to an interview of Vanessa Anne Hudgens and Zac Efron about the new *High School Musical 2*.

"They're going out together in real life, you know," Penny said to no one in particular. She sized them up on the screen. "He's kind of cute but not my type. She seems okay, nothing special," she decided.

"They lip-synched it all, you know," Barb said.

Abby felt very out of touch. She hadn't seen the sequel, and had not paid much attention to the first movie. The shelves next to the TV held dozens of new titles that she had only heard about: *Pirates of the Caribbean*, all three DVDs; all the *Shreks*; *Bridge to Tarabithia*; and several *Harry Potter* movies, the last of which she had not yet seen. Maybe, if she was lucky, she would see it while she was here.

She realized that, compared to Penny and friends and maybe most teens, she spent a lot of time hiding in her room reading. Her bookshelves contained mainly horse books: all the Walter Farley and Marguerite Henry books, several beginner riding books, the breed books, and some comprehensive books like *Horses for Dummies.*[9] Most of them had been gifts on birthdays and Christmases, having so little spending money herself.

She toyed with her watch, noticing it was the battery-powered kind, and, surprisingly, keeping the correct time.

"Let's go look at somebody who's really hot," Penny leered to her friends, dumping a cat off her lap and disturbing a dog as she nodded to Abby in silent invitation and led a procession to her room, just to the left of the sisters' guest room.

Quality antiques furnished the room styled in what Mother might have called "Early American Teen Disorder." Sofia, a realtor and antiques dealer, kept many of her best finds. Clothes draped over most available surfaces, shoes littered the floor, jewelry spilled over the top of the dresser, childhood mementos hung crookedly from the walls, and trinkets escaped from baskets on the shelves and in corners. Mother would have pitched a fit.

Penny slid into a wooden chair in front of the computer table at the window, and the other three girls arranged themselves around her. Penny found the YouTube page in her Favorites and clicked on it. Hakene Bodant, the famous young actor so many of Abby's friends talked about, appeared on the monitor. Apparently Penny had spent a lot of time searching the internet for photos and video clips of him, because a long list of sites popped up when she selected another picture.

Again Abby saw how behind she was. The sisters were not often allowed to use Mother's computer. Mother didn't want the girls visiting inappropriate sites or messing up her Crafters Circle party information.

Abby had never seen any interviews with Hakene Bodant and was completely captivated by his bubbling energy, his wicked humor, his infectious grin, even the way his lower lip wiggled when he was deciding what to say. She watched the video avidly.

"I don't mind signing autographs, really," he said in his attractive British accent. "Except the professional autograph sellers, they really get to me. Like, when I know it's, sort of, about the 20th time I've signed for the same guy, I might finally tell him I'm not going to give him another one to sell on eBay."

Wow, the issues famous people have to deal with, Abby thought.

Another site showed him in a snapshot with an Asian girl who'd posted the photo. Her friend was in a play he'd come to see and they'd met backstage. She said he was "very sweet." One of the comments under the picture called the girl a nasty name and screamed in rude capitals: "DON'T YOU KNOW WHAT I WOULD DO, WHAT I WOULD GIVE TO MEET HIM, LET ALONE GET A HUG FROM HIM?? I ADORE HIM!!!!!"

The girls called her a ranting lunatic. "Duh, we don't know, 'cuz we don't know you!" "What a groupie!" "Get a life!"

Hakene was very serious in an interview with Larry King from CNN Live. Martha Stewart hosted him, teasing him about shaving, which he handled gracefully. A Brit, Jonathan Ross, said shocking things to and about him, which he again handled very professionally.

The only question Hakene did not answer was a question about a play he'd been in. Penny and her friends leaned closer for the next screens. Parts of the play apparently featured Hakene in the nude. Actually naked. In front of a live audience. Abby was flabbergasted. He was so … normal! … in his movies. Wasn't he embarrassed? Why did he do this? He certainly wouldn't have to for the money; he was rolling in dough from the movies.

Someone had snuck a camera into the play and then put the photos up on the internet. Abby didn't know whether to hide her eyes or lean closer. It was very strange, feeling fascinated and repulsed at the same moment; and she stayed stuck, looking sideways with her mouth open. Abby wasn't at all sure what to think about looking at Hakene Bodant's naked behind. Certainly he seemed to have a nice body; but Penny and the girls were leering at it and making comments about going to see the play just to see him naked, as Jonathan Ross had encouraged people to do. The girls suggested Hakene could try again with them after failing with the barn girl. This was too much for Abby. She muttered, "Bathroom," and slid out the door.

She stood in the hallway for a minute, thoughts jammed, not ready to go downstairs and put on a polite face for company. She sought refuge in her room, as she did so often at home. Without a nook to retreat into, she laid down on the low pullout bed, wincing as she bumped a forgotten bruise. She squirmed to get her bra straightened around; it had not shifted with her when she laid down. Her pinky finger chose that inconvenient moment to ache again. Abby sucked on it, feeling stupid. Her *HP* #7 book stared at her from her open backpack, but she couldn't focus enough to read. She pulled the pillow over her head and tried to sort it out.

No doubt Hakene thought that as an actor he should do these things. She had read interviews in *Reader's Digest* with different actors who talked about stretching themselves as artists, but how many of them stripped for the world to see? Even Madonna, famous for her suggestive acts and lyrics, had worn a bikini in the old show Abby had seen briefly on a neighbor's TV, while going door-to-door for her school fundraiser.

Voices intruded on her contemplations, growing louder. Someone yelled. Were they yelling at her? Abby took the pillow off her head and promptly sneezed. The cat had snuck in and laid down on the floor right under her nose. She searched for a tissue, hearing Ricky and Penny argue.

"You can't look at stuff like that. I'm telling Mom!" Ricky fired.

"I can look at anything I want; it's my computer in my room!" Penny retorted.

"Doesn't matter, you're not allowed! How would you like it if I was looking at naked *girls* on a computer?"

"You wouldn't dare!" Penny lit into her brother.

"Yeah, I would too dare. My friends even find porno sites, too; so if you can, I can!"

"That's disgusting. I'll tell Mom!"

"And I'll tell her about your dear Hakene!"

They were sword-fighting with words. Stab, recoil, slash, block … then a mutual silent retreat. After a moment, Penny's voice, although low, reached Abby's ears.

"If you don't tell, I won't tell."

"Deal. Pinky swear."

Abby could almost hear them hooking pinkies and shaking on it. This only added to her confusion. They both thought it disgusting for the other to look at nude pictures of the opposite gender, but wanted the right to do so themselves. That was a double standard, maybe even hypocritical. It was messed up, almost as messed up as Asst. Rev. Gottle's fling with Mrs. Talinda. Maybe he started his downward slide by looking at pornography.

Abby just couldn't try to be polite to people downstairs now. Cat evicted, nose cleared, door shut, she searched her backpack for something to do until bedtime, shoving aside the troublesome book. Half-started horse drawings peeked out at her. She dug out her little pouch of colored pencils and allowed her drawing to carry her to calmer places.

"Hey, why are you in here alone? I was looking for you," Jenn asked, peeking in the room.

"Um …" Abby said.

They understood each other so well. Abby knew that Jenn could tell something had happened that was too big to easily put into words.

And they both knew that the best way to solve this was for Jenn to come in and sit patiently near Abby while she tried to put it into words.

"Well, you know Hakene Bodant?"

"Yeah," Jenn said in a quiet, neutral voice, thankfully avoiding adding "doesn't everyone?" or giving her own opinion about him. They'd never talked about him, only said that they both liked the movies but preferred the books, as usual.

"Penny had a bunch of interviews and pictures of him on her computer, and some of them were of him naked," Abby blurted.

Jenn raised an eyebrow but waited, soon looking away to better allow Abby to grapple with her thoughts.

"Well I did think he was sexy, especially some of the pictures of him from last spring." Abby dwelt on one early shot of him in bleachers at a polo game. Seated, he glanced over his left shoulder, flashing a fun-loving, high-energy, toothy smile. His hair was especially sexy in that shot, and his eyes were electric. Later, his strange wispy facial hair and expression made him too serious and too moody to connect with.

"He handled adults and autograph sessions and crowds of photographers and screaming fans – no way I could do that – and he was really great, I really envy him that way. I wish I were that confident.

"And it was fun to imagine him with less clothes on. But when he actually was naked, it was kind of disgusting."

Abby half-expected her sister to contradict her or even make fun of her now that she'd said it. To Jenn's eternal credit, she did neither. She sat quietly and battled with what to say.

"I know what you mean," she finally agreed.

Abby realized that, as close as they were, they'd never talked about boys, bodies or sex. Mother had forbidden dating until after they turned 16. Jenn was old enough, but hadn't found anyone she was interested in. They struggled silently with this strange new topic.

"Maybe we shouldn't—"

"If you think that—"

They grinned at each other, re-establishing their close, comfortable bond. Affection grew between them, easing the tension and softening their hearts. The warmth in the room created an openness that loosened Jenn's tongue and tuned Abby's ears.

"Children don't have sexual feelings," Jenn said kindly, accurately pinpointing Abby's underlying concerns. "At some point, right about your age, their hormones start waking up and they start turning into adults, getting interested in sexual things."

Abby did feel like some things were waking up.

"So maybe it's new to you to have sexy feelings at all." Jenn looked at Abby to see if this was correct. Abby allowed that maybe it was.

"And then there's the fact that very few of us walk around naked," Jenn added gently, "so seeing nakedness is a new thing."

That seemed about right to Abby.

"Come to think of it, we see ourselves naked the most, but that's from a different viewpoint than seeing others," Jenn mused, tipping her head and staring vacantly. Abby sat patiently until Jenn came to. "We'll figure it out together. Let me know if you have other questions."

"Of *course* I do, tons of them, and I can't exactly go to Mother!" Abby protested. "She buys me awful bras and forces me to shave."

"Yeah, it's hard enough without Mother."

"This horrible bra – I hate it. I can't get it comfortable. Why is it called a training bra, anyway? Do boobs need to be trained?" Abby's questions tumbled out.

"I don't know why they call it that, Abs. Breasts can be squeezed or lifted, but they are the shape genetics – or God – gives you," Jenn replied, smiling. Abby figured she knew what she was talking about, judging by her curves.

Jenn offered to look, and after Abby said yes, gently lifted her shirt and showed her the adjustments on the straps. She also suggested making the hooks looser.

"The seams do kind of dig in," she shared. "Like on your socks. A sports bra, you could turn inside out; but these, I doubt it." Jenn studied the bra and concluded that turning it inside out would be worse. She did help Abby let out the shoulder straps and settle the rib band lower. That helped some.

"What's a sports bra? And how am I supposed to reach behind me to hook this thing?"

Jenn drew a long breath. Mother hadn't said or shown her anything, and Abby didn't even know what she didn't know.

"A sports bra is super-stretchy, no hooks. You slide it over your head. You might really like them for riding. We could go find a kind you like. I could get the money from Mother. A bra with hooks, you hook in front of you, inside out, then slide the hooks around to your back and turn it right side out. After the hooks are behind you, then you stick your arms through the shoulder straps." She took a spare bra from her own suitcase and demonstrated on the outside of her shirt.

That way would definitely work better, Abby thought. And a bra-shopping trip sounded like a little bit of fun, actually. A kind of secret girl thing to do together. Plus, Jenn was braver than Abby, so surely she could get the money.

"When will I get my period? Is it going to hurt?" Abby asked. She hadn't intended to ask, didn't even realize it was on her mind.

"Not for me, usually. Sometimes you get a sort of twinge when the egg releases, but the blood flows a couple weeks later; and unless you get cramps, it isn't so much painful as ... a *pain*."

Jenn smiled at her joke. So did Abby, bolstered and comforted by Jenn's patient, soul-to-soul help.

"Maybe I'd better show you the, er, equipment before you need it. I remember a girl in sixth grade who stood up to hand in her test and was soaked in blood. I was just really glad I wasn't her."

Abby was horrified. "How embarrassing!"

"Yeah," Jenn agreed, "and you can't control it, so we're at its mercy. At least we can afford supplies; lots of *femmes* around the world have to cancel their lives and sit home one week out of every month; there's a club at school that helps make pads to send overseas and some here. Gee, I never thought about sewing with them until just now. Thanks for the great idea, Abs!"[10]

Abby appreciated the light moment. "When will mine start?"

"I don't think there's any way to predict exactly. Hopefully, it starts out light and you'll see it on toilet paper or on your underwear. Could be anytime, anywhere, so let me show you pads and tampons. I'll give you a couple, and you can get a purse and start carrying them. A good former Girl Scout is always prepared, right?"

Jenn got the supplies from her suitcase, laid them out on the bed, told Abby how to use them, and answered all her questions.

Afterward, Abby got into the trundle with a jumble of thoughts and emotions, the strongest one being appreciation of her cherished sister. Her other one was that her body would gang up on her soon, in league with Mother and Jesus, all of them crouched, hiding, waiting to pounce on her and make her already-hard life even more difficult. Jenn was her only defense against a world out to get her.

Chapter 8 Vacation

Sleep erased yesterday's confusion and most of the aches. Abby woke with a gentle sense of being ready for whatever the day would bring. The capris and shirt she chose hid the bruises and the adjusted bra. She carefully applied the deodorant to avoid the healing cuts and decided to try going without the limiting bandaid on her pinky.

In the kitchen, Jon glanced up from making coffee.

"Good morning," he said.

"Morning," she replied. He was so much older than she, they had never really connected, so she was cautious. He seemed perfectly friendly and relaxed, though.

"What would you like for breakfast?" he asked without looking up from stirring artificial creamer into his coffee cup.

"I usually have cereal," she murmured shyly.

"Over there in the cabinet," he said, waving his dripping spoon and hastily catching the drops.

Abby opened the upper cabinet door and chose the Wiggy Jiggys from among the Happy O's and some high-fiber cereals, then fetched milk. Jon brought her a bowl and spoon and joined her at the table.

"Sleep well?" he asked comfortably.

"Yes," she answered, wondering if yesterday's travel fatigue and lack of food had caused her to be extra-sensitive last night. "When did everyone else go to bed?"

"Oh, not that late. Around 9:30, I guess."

"And Melissa is your girlfriend?"

"Um, yes … possibly a bit more serious than girlfriend," he said with a definite Look In His Eyes.

Abby didn't know what to say to this so she offered a small "oh" between bites of brightly colored cereal.

"We've known each other for more than a year. She just gets more and more interesting," he said.

He seemed willing to share, and Abby took a chance.

"Um, like what?"

"Her heritage," he responded quickly. "Her mother is Native American, European, and Hawaiian; and her father is African American and Asian. She says wherever she goes, people think she's native-born." He smiled, apparently recalling some interesting stories about her travels.

Abby attempted to imagine anyone embodying more than two continents, but couldn't. "Interesting" would be an understatement for a heritage like that!

47

"She's also a member of the Bahá'í Faith," he added, then seemed to get lost in his own thoughts. He said it *bah-HI.* Abby tried to repeat it in a voiceless whisper; but it wasn't easy to say. A strange word, in any case. Probably a strange cult. But Abby felt safe enough to reply.

"What is that?" she asked.

He looked at her, unsure. "Uh, well, it's a really interesting religion she's been teaching me about. I don't feel like I know much about it yet myself, but, ah…" He trailed off, wrestling with how to voice what was unclear to him. "At first, see, I thought it was some kind of a communal thing, like the Jewish communes in Israel, but it's not physical or geographical like that."

Abby must have looked blank, because he tried again.

"They don't live in communes or gather in one place like, say, the Israeli Jews in kibbutzes, or the Utah Latter-Day Saints," he clarified. Abby nodded her understanding.

"It's definitely a religion. There is a Prophet they follow who seems too good to be true. I mean, not to criticize, but I sure can't understand someone who did the things this Bahá'u'lláh did. He was either really from God or they're all lying about how forgiving He was…even to His brother who kept trying to kill Him for, like, 20 years. Also, how everyone seemed to just lose their minds … I mean, not go crazy but, like, go blank whenever they were in the same room as Him …"

Abby carefully repeated *bah-HAW-oh-LAW* to herself as she waited for Jon to sort out his thoughts. She could almost hear Mother's insistence that she repeat words, especially names, until she pronounced and them correctly.

"And if Bahá'u'lláh isn't enough to impress us, we've got His son, 'Abdu'l-Bahá … so humble, so loving and funny … and wise …"

AB-dool-bah-HAW, Abby rehearsed silently while she finished her cereal, trying to smile encouragingly at Jon without dribbling her milk down her chin.

"You know those bracelets with WWJD? What Would Jesus Do?"

Abby nodded.

"Well it's not really fair, is it?"

"What do you mean?"

Jon unabashedly shared his thoughts, and Abby was interested and honored.

"Well, according to the Bible and the Christians, Jesus was the son of God and even seems to be God Himself at times. So how could we possibly figure out what God Himself would do in a tough situation? We're not God, for God's sake!"

Abby smiled, not knowing if he realized his own joke. Jon saw her, realized what he'd said, and smiled with her.

"But 'Abdu'l-Bahá never claimed to be a prophet. He was just ... well not 'just,' but ... well anyway, he was raised by Bahá'u'lláh, who *was* directly plugged in to God, you know, so it's a lot more reasonable, we could say, to study 'Abdu'l-Bahá's life and try to be like him. And actually, he said we could. Or should."

"Should what?"

"Try to be like him. Do like he did. Follow his example."

"Are you?"

"I'm thinking about it. Well, I guess I already have, haven't I?" He laughed, his baffled look replaced by certainty. Abby saw that he had cleared up something that had been gnawing at him.

"Hey, thanks!" he said.

"What for?" She was quite surprised. All she'd done was eat breakfast.

"For listening, for asking honest questions. It really helped. Wow," his voice dropped, "one of the Bahá'í months is named Questions. That must be pretty important if they named a month after it, huh? Sure helped me." He put his dishes in the dishwasher. "She gave me a book. I think I'll go look at it now," he said. "See you later." He was gone, carried by a private whirlwind.

Abby was putting her own bowl and spoon in the dishwasher when Ricky came down to the kitchen, saw her, and grinned his goofy grin. His slightly curly, light-brown hair was combed. He wore a polo shirt and clean jeans.

"Hey!" he said. "Whatcha doin'?"

"Nothin'," she tossed back with the same smile he'd thrown at her.

He went to the fridge and got out a bag of English muffins, a jar of jelly, and a new stick of butter. Abby sat down again.

"I'm kinda in a hurry this morning," he said, ripping apart the muffin with his usual zeal and pushing the two halves into the toaster.

"Why's that?"

"Gonna go on a ride-along," he said.

"A what?"

"Ya know, ride along with the police. Or one policeman, anyway," he explained as he took a knife out of the drawer and peeled the paper off the end of the butter.

"Wow, really?" Abby was genuinely impressed.

"Yeah. I'm s'posed to meet a policeman at the station, and then we will go patrol for a few hours."

"I'd be scared of someone shooting at me," Abby confided.

"Oh, I think that'd be cool. I'd get down low in my seat and watch.

Waaayy better than watching it on TV!" Ricky enthused.

Abby watched him, dumbstruck for a moment. He grabbed the hot muffin halves out of the toaster, tossed them onto a paper napkin, sliced off thin squares of hard butter, and spread it on the hot halves.

"I might be a cop when I ... you know, for my career."

"You would *want* to be a policeman?"

Ricky paused his jelly-loading to look at her.

"Yeah, why not?"

Abby wasn't sure she should explain. Getting shot at, being in a rather low-status job according to Mother, having to handle everything from loose dogs to murders ... it creeped her out. But he seemed very keen about it. She tried to gloss over any hard feelings with a small smile and a shrug. She hoped the shiver she felt didn't show.

Ricky fished a can of soda pop out of the fridge and brought it and the muffin to the table. He bit into his muffin, gulped soda, then burped the ABCs for Abby.

She couldn't help but laugh.

"Pop for breakfast?" she said, still giggling. Mother only allowed carbonated drinks for special occasions like birthdays.

"Absolutely," Ricky declared, puffing out his chest. "Starts the day off with a bang ... or at least a lot of fizz!"

Abby admired his spirit if not his choice of foods, and they chatted about their upcoming school years while he ate. As he finished, Penny and Jenn came into the kitchen. Sofia soon joined them. Abby slid to the seat furthest in the corner. She found her willingness to speak shrinking with each person who came into the room.

The kitchen bustled as everyone wished Ricky a fun ride-along and got food for themselves. Abby had not heard any prospective plans for the day; it seemed no one had decided. Options included shopping, swimming at the public pool, a trip to the coast – which Abby silently favored – and having the neighbors over. Sofia turned to Abby.

"Penny says you might like to go riding."

"Oh! Um..."

"Vivi says you've been riding for several years now."

"Yes, I have," Abby said with a touch of pride.

"Well, there's a stable not too far from here that rents out horses. Perhaps you'd like to go on a trail ride or whatever it is they do," Sofia said, watching Abby for a response.

"Um, I didn't bring my boots," Abby said, once again bitterly resenting her mother, who seemed to thwart her at every turn.

"I think they take people in tennis shoes," Sofia said.

"Well, if it works out, um, I ..." Abby trailed off as she wandered down mental pathways of horse smell, dusty trails, and scenes from movies with herself as the star. Her chin rested in her hands, elbows on the table, index fingers fiddling with the small gold hoops she'd so often worn since Mother had allowed her to get her ears pierced a few days after her 12th birthday. She dismissed the nagging detail of no boots, and had trouble imagining her fantasy horse because she didn't know what it would look like. But she drew great courage from the idea of doing something so wonderful.

She came back to earth to ask Sofia, "When would I go, please ... if it all works out?"

"We'll have to check with everyone to make sure, but maybe even this afternoon," Sofia said with a smile. She seemed to understand that, although Abby didn't show it much on the outside, she loved riding. Abby liked Sofia, and she found herself wishing she'd been born into Sofia's family instead of Vivian's.

After breakfast, Abby followed Jenn into the dining room.

"You okay?" Jenn asked Abby softly, giving her that coded look that meant: "Way down deep are you okay?"

"Yes, I am," Abby was able to answer truthfully. Boosted by the successful breakfast conversations with two of her cousins and the promise of riding soon, she was quite well indeed.

Chapter 9 Horseplay

Between grocery shopping and neighbors coming over that night, Abby's horsing-around had to wait until the next day, and even then it wasn't trail riding. Penny's friend Barb had arranged for them to see her sister "wiggle ropes and wave sticks" at her horse.

Penny drove Abby over to the stable, where they met Barb and her older sister, Angie. Abby wasn't sure why Barb had come if she thought the whole thing was so kooky, but hoped the girl wouldn't criticize so much as to make a scene.

Abby felt strange in her tennis shoes and capris as she followed the older girls inside to sign legal releases and read the ranch rules, but they were the best she could do, and everything else was very familiar and comforting. The dingy barn, dirty and brimming with things Abby treasured. Horses and halters and hay that made her sneeze. Leather and sweat and manure she had to carefully step around to keep her tennies clean. She even saw a chunk of hoof paring and picked it up, feeling the familiar hardness and noting that it must have been recently cut because it was not yet dried and curled.

Angie leased her horse from an owner who required her to use this training. She carried an orange stick and a long white lead rope clipped to a thin green rope halter. A red string stuck out of her back pocket.

Why the different equipment? Abby didn't know how many questions Angie would tolerate and decided she'd better wait to see.

Angie led the group down the lane toward the paddocks. Abby expected Angie to go in and catch her horse, but she stopped at the gate and whistled. A medium-sized bay lifted its head and stared at Angie for a moment, then continued to nibble at sparse blades of brown grass.

"Ah," Angie said softly with a small smile. "The game is on."

Why did Angie seem to be happy about this disobedience? Weren't horses supposed to obey right away?

Angie slipped between the strands of twisted wire fencing, then ambled not toward the horse but in front of it, leisurely threading the red string into the leather loop at the tip of the stick. *This* was different! Abby was used to walking in a firm – hopefully boss-like – manner right up to the horse and catching it as soon as possible.

Angie bypassed her horse who gazed steadily at her, forgoing grazing. Angie changed direction, aiming beyond the horse's hindquarters. The horse lifted its head and took one step toward Angie, who stopped and began to back up. This was really bizarre. Abby was starting to agree with Barb, who whispered, "Told you she was nuts."

The horse dropped its head again, and Abby began to feel frustrated with its lack of cooperation. Abby felt like hollering that Angie should go right to the horse and catch it. She was glad she hesitated, because the horse took another step toward Angie and she backed up another step. It almost seemed like the horse was in charge of being caught, and Angie was dancing with it in some kind of catching dance. Abby had certainly never seen anything like it.

The horse stepped again, and again, then walked steadily toward Angie, who laughed, her outstretched hand holding out the halter and lead rope like a treat. Soon Angie was running backward, the horse trotting toward her. For a second, it looked like a game of tag, the horse catching Angie. Soon the game was over, with Angie laughing and out of breath at the gate, and the horse – a mare, Abby saw – looking alive and happy. Abby was totally dumbfounded. What *was* this?

Angie began to stroke and hug the mare, explaining that Beauty and she played the Catching Game, part of the Parelli program of horse whispering, or natural horsemanship.[11] Abby repeated, *pa-RELL-ee*. Angie rubbed Beauty all over with the halter and lead rope. She examined the mare while giving her a massage and satisfying any itchy spots that Beauty wanted scratched, such as an apparent favorite under Beauty's belly. Angie scratched it with the bundled halter, laughing when Beauty stretched out her neck and upper lip and nodded her head like a dog. It looked like an oft-rehearsed and beloved ritual.

Angie stroked Beauty some more, but now it looked like an ordinary check of Beauty's legs and skin. Abby kept expecting the mare to leave, but she showed no sign of wanting to. One time, Beauty scooted backward and then stopped.

"Oh, the old favorite, huh?" Angie said with a smile, scratching in the hollow in front of the shoulder. Beauty leaned into Angie's hands, asking her to scratch harder.

Abby fretted that Beauty was still not haltered. Any moment now, the mare would push her way past Angie and escape back to her buddies at the other end of the paddock.

After what felt like eons, Angie knelt and held the halter open. When Beauty plunged her head into the halter, Angie quickly tied a knot. No fighting, no crownpiece slapping. Abby started wondering if this equipment was better and if she should use it. Perhaps on her knees. But how would you get a horse like Moony to stick around? She would look for the right time to ask. Abby began to feel that if catching and haltering was this different, the rest was going to be *really* different.

Angie stood up. She held a horse treat by Beauty's tail, stretching the tail forward. Beauty bent nearly in half to reach the tidbit. It looked like horse gymnastics.

"Isn't she crazy?" Barb said, but now Abby detected a hint of pride in her voice. Finally Abby understood: Barb showed her admiration with teasing that sounded like criticism.

Angie bantered with Barb good-naturedly. "Yup, crazy as a dizzy duck!" "Crazy as a three-legged dog finding a corner in a round room!" "Crazy as a long-tailed cat at a rocking chair convention!"

Angie unlatched the gate while they joked, stood tall, looked at Beauty, then pointed toward the opening. Beauty exited, turned and waited quietly while Angie shut the gate. What, no dragging the horse? No barging through gates?

Angie sent her down the lane, pointing with the hand that held the lead rope. When Beauty didn't move, Angie wiggled the orange stick behind the mare, which made her walk on. Abby noticed that Angie hadn't actually hit Beauty with the stick, just sort of threatened her with it, but more as a cue than an angry confrontation. Angie walked next to the mare's belly ... on Beauty's right side. Weren't you supposed to do everything from the horse's left side?

This was all so smooth and pleasant, so different from Abby's usual struggle with the horses she had to chase down, trick into a halter, and drag to the barn. This way might actually be useful.

Beauty's nose arrived first at the cluster of sheds Angie had aimed at. Instead of tying her to one of the rails, Angie pointed Beauty around the rails, even backing her between two posts by wiggling her finger like she was scolding the mare, then hugging her and lavishing love on her after Beauty backed smoothly. Abby began to feel that the surprises might never end.

Barb held the lead rope while Angie fetched a grooming bucket and bareback pad from one of the sheds. Abby had never seen anyone ride with a bareback pad. It seemed dangerous yet glamorous. Sometimes boarders at The Ride Place rode their horses in from the pasture bareback, tying their lead ropes in a loop to make reins. But no one did anything very fancy riding bareback, nor for very long. Saddles seemed much safer. And where was the bridle?

Angie brushed Beauty, holding the middle of the long lead rope in the crook of her elbow. Beauty pinned her ears once, swinging her head around at Angie. Angie actually apologized, looked at the spot nearly underneath the mare, and found a swollen bug bite.

"Hmm, well, it's right under the cinch area. I guess no bareback pad today. I'll ride naked then!" She grinned mischievously at Barb, who reliably started in with jokes about Lady Godiva and how uncomfortable and risqué that would be.

Heart sinking, Abby recalled Moony turning to bite at his sides. He'd probably had an itch, maybe a burr from the debris in the cinch, and she'd *slapped* him for it. He'd pinned his ears at her because she'd been unfair. She hadn't meant to be; she just hadn't understood, hadn't been taught this more fair approach. Abby was beginning to realize there might be a *lot* she didn't understand about horses.

Angie stowed the grooming tub and bareback pad in the shed and pointed Beauty down a path between pens, followed by the three other girls. Horses in the pens approached, ready to make trouble with Beauty, but Angie whirled her string and stick over her head like a helicopter, making a whistling sound that kept the rascals back. Beauty walked calmly under the singing string, seeming to rely on Angie to protect her from the threats and bites from the other horses.

They reached a round, pipe-panel pen. This time, Abby was not surprised to see Angie back Beauty through the gate, wiggling her finger. Barb latched the gate as Penny and Abby leaned on the rails of the fence to watch.

Angie led Beauty to the middle of the round pen, scratched the mare's itchy spots again, and cued Beauty's front legs and then hind end to glide away … first with a touch and next with just a look. It was so smooth, yet so fancy! Angie rubbed Beauty, cooed encouragement, and hugged her neck. It looked nothing like Abby's usual sessions – it looked safer, and a lot more fun.

"How about Circle Game?" Angie asked Beauty, then waited as if the calm, attentive mare might voice a reply.

Beauty pressed her head into Angie's chest, perhaps as an answer. Misty-eyed, Angie caressed Beauty's ears, jaw, and cheeks, murmuring rapturously. Abby felt it was the most beautiful thing she'd ever seen. She couldn't imagine a horse ever giving its head to her, and envied their love. A matchstick of desire flicked against the grit of envy in her heart, caught, and began to burn. She *so* wanted that kind of relationship with horses!

Angie stroked the mare tenderly for as long as Beauty touched her. "Put my heart in my hand and rub her all over with my love," Angie said softly.

When Beauty drew away, Angie stood tall, finger-scolded her back, and pointed to her right. Beauty walked in a circle around Angie as the girl passed the rope around her, leaning on her stick. Abby had seen horse owners at The Ride Place lunging their horses, keeping a close eye on them, whips ready to cue or smack the horse. Abby had assumed that was because the horses would stop if you didn't keep after them.

Yet Beauty continued to walk with no prodding at all.

After two laps, Angie tipped her head to one side, smiled, and reeled in the lead rope. Beauty came in to Angie for more praise, rubbing, and hugs. Abby's hand twitched, wishing to clap the mare heartily for its good work, but Angie only stroked or scratched her.

She sent the mare out the opposite way for another two circles and brought her in again. Beauty came in faster than Angie could reel in the lead rope, creating a loose loop of rope that Beauty accidently stepped on. Abby held her breath, waiting for the explosion. Horses panicked when they felt their heads trapped like that. But when Beauty felt the tug on her halter, she calmly stepped off the rope. Abby wondered if Angie even noticed what Beauty had done; she'd been busy rubbing and praising the mare.

Next, Angie sent her to face the pipes. When Angie faced Beauty's side, stood tall, and pointed her stick at Beauty's shoulder, the mare glided sideways halfway around the pen.

It all looked like a conversation … not just love, but almost some kind of language between them. Once in a while, Angie would make some little comment to Beauty like "Good one!" or "No, move your hindquarters more!" She reminded Abby of a teacher leading a class. *Love, language, and leadership all together,* Abby mused. Angie was doing stuff Abby had never even dreamed of … and she dreamed about horses a lot!

After cueing Beauty sideways from each side, Angie softly mused, "Hmm, what to squeeze her between?" Looking around, she spied a discarded cardboard box. Barb fetched it, and Penny helped her lift it over the pipe panel. Angie carried it a few feet away from the fence, stood next to it, and pointed to the gap.

Beauty seemed unsure about this request. Instead of smacking her or yelling at her, Angie stroked her and talked with her. Beauty's head bobbed up and down as if she were wearing bifocals and trying to read small print. Angie waited. Beauty poked her nose toward the box. Angie praised and stroked her one more time, then finger-scolded her backward, away from the box.

Abby gave up trying to predict what Angie was going to do; Angie did the opposite of pretty much everything Abby had been taught to do with horses. But Abby loved it all!

When Angie again sent Beauty into the narrow space between the box and the panel, Beauty panicked halfway through and rushed forward. Angie was ready for it, though, and wiggled the rope hard, then aimed her stick at Beauty's hindquarters, getting the mare to face her. The confident, relaxed horse whisperer again praised Beauty and pulled another treat from her jeans pocket, this time asking the bay mare to bend way down between her front legs while Angie held the morsel just in front of Beauty's seeking mouth.

"That's to help her stretch, and maybe one day to bow," Angie said to the trio of watching girls.

Although stretching sounded boring, bowing sounded awesome! But why was she rewarding Beauty for bolting through the opening?

Angie sent Beauty back the other way. That at least was becoming predictable: Angie wanted Beauty to do everything from both sides, not just the left. This time, when Beauty went more willingly and did not rush through quite so fast, Angie gave her another treat. *Hmm, maybe she was thanking the mare for trying.* It seemed like Angie could see Beauty's thoughts and change them.

Angie asked the mare to go through the narrow space again, and Beauty went completely calmly. Angie stopped the mare in her tracks with just a little shake of the rope and turned away, a telltale grin spreading on her delighted face, only turning back to Beauty at sounds of licking and chewing.

"She's processing that success," Angie said, stroking and cuddling the oversized baby girl. "Licking, chewing and yawning mean relaxing into a new thought, a new mode."

"Pick me up!" Angie told Beauty, climbing up the pipe panel to the highest rail. Nothing happened. Angie waved the stick at the mare's far-side hindquarters, bringing Beauty close enough to slide a leg smoothly over her back. She was going to ride the mare using that same skimpy rope halter and that same lead rope, not even tied in a loop!

Angie looked ahead, lifted her rope-holding hand, and smiled; Beauty obediently stepped forward toward her audience. Where was the kicking that Abby thought was required? The repeated clucking? Angie looked to her left, toward the middle of the pen, and as the pair passed in front of the girls, Abby thought she saw a slight movement of Angie's right leg. Beauty turned left into the middle of the pen. Angie seemed to slump, and Beauty stopped. Angie hadn't even moved her hand, let alone pull back hard on both reins.

"What did you do to stop?" Abby finally asked her first question.

"Well, where Beauty and I are at in the levels, I let my energy down and then block her forward motion. But we're working on me thinking stop and she stops," Angie responded, twisting around on the mare's smooth brown back to answer.

Abby had been hoping for something a bit more useable, like "Pull the rein this way and give this cue."

"A truly Zen answer," Barb commented.

"What are 'levels'?" Abby ventured to Barb.

"In Parelli, there are levels of study. You can do the first three at home with the DVD kits. She has graduated Level 1 with Beauty and is doing her Level 2."

"Oh," Abby replied absently, watching Angie bend Beauty's head to both sides with some special rein cues. "Why are you doing that?" she couldn't help asking.

"This is my emergency stop," Angie replied, rubbing the mare. "If she ever gets scared and runs off, I'll bend her with one rein like this. I should have done it when I first got on, but we were next to the fence, so I brought her into the middle. We did it at the halt, and I also do it at the walk and trot. When we get up to cantering, I'll do it at the canter."

Abby realized this is how she could have handled Moony running away during the Rescue Race. This was valuable information!

Angie asked Beauty to move her front and back feet with cues that Abby couldn't decipher but that the team seemed to know completely.

The duo began to walk around the pen's perimeter. Angie seemed to be turning Beauty with invisible cues from her body or legs, because the rope-rein never moved. They changed directions a few times. Then Angie asked Beauty, "Well, should I try trotting bareback?"

"*Try* is not a four-letter word!" Barb replied impishly.

Angie set Beauty ambling around the pen again. Angie seemed to be focused on something only she could see or feel. After a while, she lifted the rope, breathed in, sat tall, and seemed to expect Beauty to go faster. At first, Beauty did not respond. After another moment, Angie made a kissing sound, then began to slap her own thigh. At this, the mare broke into a slow trot. Angie bounced and slid off-center.

Beauty slowed down to a walk again and seemed willing to stop, but Angie told her, "No, I've got it now," and sent her into a trot again while leaning back a little further. This made a big difference; Angie stayed on much better. Even Angie's brown ponytail barely bounced. After one circuit of the round pen, Angie shrank down again. The mare stopped and received her rider's thanks with a quiet grace that reflected her name.

Angie asked her to trot going the other way, improving as she went, ending by changing directions while the rope lay on Beauty's neck.

Stopping elegantly, Angie laughed in appreciative delight. Barb clapped and Abby and Penny soon joined in. Abby overflowed with admiration for everything she'd seen. She hadn't even known that such a willing, harmonious time was possible with horses. What she thought was right and normal was backward compared to the cooperation and acceptance this happy pair enjoyed.

Barb opened the round pen gate and Angie rode Beauty out. *Going forward for a change,* Abby thought, catching the playful spirit. Angie chatted, happy and relaxed, as the complacent bay moseyed to her paddock, Angie swinging her stick and string like a modified cowgirl high over her and Beauty's heads on the path between the pens. The horse world looked so free and easy to Abby now, with no tack to undo and no struggling against the horse. What couldn't you do with boxes and fences and nearly invisible cues and a simple halter, lead, stick, and string? And a horse that seemed just as happy to do whatever you asked as to be back with its buddies?

Barb and Angie recounted how Beauty had used to be, before they started Parelli with her. Abby was amazed to hear of a completely different mare. One who could not be caught in less than an hour. Who could not be ridden without a harsh bit, big spurs, and a riding crop or two. Who – even with a shed full of special tack and supplements – was unpredictably spooky.

This challenged basic horse lore: "A horse's nature is set: it's unchangeable." "If a horse is a bolter, it will always be inclined to bolt." "If a horse is hard to catch, that's the way it is." People at The Ride Place always said things like that. Did this Parelli thing claim the ability to change how a horse *is*? Abby waited for a break in the conversation and asked.

"Oh yes, definitely," Angie asserted. "Of course, the human has to learn horse language first. But eventually, yes, we can help to change horses' minds and hearts so they're better with things that they're not naturally okay with."

"Is there anything that can't be changed? Like, what about a horse that bites?" Abby had heard that once a horse has learned to bite people, it had best be sold, possibly to the killer-buyers, because that habit was impossible to break.

"I don't know if there are any horses that are hopeless, I'm not an expert," Angie said. "But Pat – Pat Parelli – says backing a horse away cures biting. I can't speak from personal experience, because that's one thing Beauty didn't used to do. But beating horses into submission will backfire, and they ignore us if we beg them to behave. We need to be firm, fair, and friendly as the situation requires."

She slid off Beauty's back at the bay's pasture gate, motioned her in, turned her around, gave her one last hug and kiss, and undid the halter knot. Beauty sashayed off sedately, first to get a drink and then to sniff her buddies.

Angie's explanations sounded so reasonable, so true! Abby just needed to learn how to do it. She decided she was going to. Somehow.

Chapter 10 Bookstore

Abby climbed into the Holsworth's trundle bed early, tired and happy from spending time with horses. She fell asleep right away and dreamt …

∞ ∞ ∞ ∞ ∞ ∞ ∞ ∞

… spotted and painted horses swirl around her … they have no fear … she feels no fear … she stands smiling in their midst and they come to her … she hugs their necks and they hug her against their chests with their heads … smells them and they sniff her … laughs and they neigh in response … rides them sure-seated and they chase the wind … wondrous … glorious … magical …

∞ ∞ ∞ ∞ ∞ ∞ ∞ ∞

The magic stuck with her when she woke up. Dressing, she pondered how to get hold of the Level 1 study kit and equipment. Angie had said the Parelli halter and rope was worth it. She also said the first study pack plus equipment cost about $230, an impossible amount of money to Abby. Maybe when she got back home, she could find the owner of the orange stick at the ranch and see if they would share equipment or videos with her. Perhaps she could do chores in exchange.

Mulling it over, she entered the kitchen and jumped backward to avoid running into Jon.

"Oh! Hi," she blurted out.

"Good morning," he said lightly, appearing unoffended by her inattentiveness.

They fetched breakfast – she a glass of milk and a toaster pastry, he a cup of coffee – and sat down together.

"What are your plans today?" Jon asked.

"Don't have any," Abby replied, stowing a bite of Toasty Tart in her cheek before speaking. Mother would be all over her like a bad rash if she was impolite while a guest in the Holsworth's home.

"Do you want to come with us?" he invited. "Melissa and I are going to go to a couple of shops. One is a coffee shop we like, the other is a new bookstore. And maybe we'll hit some last-of-summer sales."

"I probably could. I'll have to check with Mother," she said, flattered at the invitation.

Jon mentioned needing to check the mouse traps in the pantry, as there'd been a funny smell. He mentioned a large disgusting roach one of the cats had caught in the kitchen, and they traded revolting house-vermin stories, Jon wondering if he'd already caught all the stupid, filthy mice, leaving only the smart, disgusting ones who warned each other away from any new traps. Ricky walked in and Jon asked him how Tuesday's ride-along had gone. Abby also nodded her interest.

"It was cool!" Ricky enthused, getting the last two Toasty Tarts and a can of soda pop. They had documented a fight between two special-ed kids at the high school. The teacher had said the kids taunted each other all summer session, one kid calling the other an "ass pee," which Ricky assumed was some kind of new insult.

They had also investigated a report of a motorcyclist trespassing on someone's vacant land. Neighborhood Watch members had been trying to catch bikers who'd been roaring around the field. Ricky had watched the officer gather descriptions of the motorcycle and its rider.

"Well, I'm off to Brent's house," Ricky bubbled, tossing his empty can across the kitchen into the trash by the back door. "Three points!" He jerked the full trash bag out of the wastebasket and clanged outside.

Abby finished her milk and tart, cleaned up, and excused herself. As she left the kitchen, she changed mental gears. She might have to break a cardinal rule: Don't Wake Mother! The door to the family room was closed. Abby tested the knob, then opened it carefully.

Daddy sat on the edge of the bed, taking earplugs out of his ears. Mother was lying down, her arm crooked over her eyes as she often did when "just resting." Daddy beckoned to her, putting his finger to his lips. Abby tiptoed to him and haltingly asked how he'd slept.

"It could always be better," he murmured, smiling sadly. His genial face looked haggard and he had bad breath. She felt sorry for him.

She whispered her request to go with Jon. Daddy whispered back that Abby could go where she liked today. He asked that Jon take his cell phone, then gave her a sleepy smile as she whispered her okay. She left the room quietly and went upstairs to get ready.

Jenn was just getting up. She said she would probably go shopping for school stuff with Penny and her friends, maybe check out some new CDs, hit the closest mall. She'd be back in time for dinner and would show Abby whatever she bought. Abby shared her newfound passion about Angie's "craziness" with her horse. Jenn gave her a quiet high-five and said it sounded really neat.

Grabbing the backpack that often served as a purse, Abby found Jon waiting for her in the front hallway.

Jon worked at a burger place, Abby knew, in order to afford his car. Either the job didn't pay much or the multicolored, shabby car was too costly for him. Holes marked missing plaques, and dents and scratches competed with the rust. Jon wrenched the passenger door open for Abby and held the glove box shut so she could slide in. Duct tape and staples barely restrained the flopping fabric headliner, upholstery gave way to bulging foam, and bags of cans filled the hatchback.

"Morc welcomes you," Jon said.

"Pardon?" she asked, noticing that. "N" was a hard sound to make with a plugged nose; she'd have to switch to "Excuse me."

"Morc – M-O-R-C, my Mobile Office and Recycling Center – welcomes you," Jon said louder. "Robin Williams would never be caught dead in here!"

It took a moment to figure it out, then Abby connected the famous comedian and his first famous role, the alien Mork, which had played in old reruns on cable. The last movie she had seen him in was *Night at the Museum*. He had played a serious part for a change, but he had jabbered away like Mork in one part of it. She had liked that movie enough to watch it a second time with the director's comments.

Jon coaxed the reluctant ignition and they chugged off, emitting clouds of blue smoke. Rattles, squeaks, the loud engine and the laboring air conditioning made talking too hard, so Abby simply looked at Little Lily's parched, tree-lined neighborhoods and stark strip malls. It was promising to be a cooker today, as usual.

Melissa waited for them on a bench outside her family's apartment building, working on something in her lap. Abby switched to the back seat, covering the protruding seat springs with the cushion Jon gave her. Melissa expertly held the floppy glove-box door shut as she slid into the front. When Abby asked what she'd been working on, she showed Abby a small piece of fabric and some colored thread.

"It's counted cross-stitch," she said. "It's a simple design I made. 'No Hate' with the red line across the HATE." Melissa showed Abby the attractive hand-stitched design.[12]

"What will you do with it when they're done?"

"Probably a bookmark," Melissa explained in her soft Southern accent. Mother had trained Abby and Jenn to speak in an educated, slightly European way. Sometimes it took Abby a minute to understand accents, as when "I" sounded like "Ah."

"I've done some sewing, but never counted-stitching," Abby said.

"It's not too hard," Melissa said. "I learned from the directions in the little kits I got at the mall. I bet you could, too, if you wanted. I can show you, if you want."

She showed Abby the chart and the thread symbols. True, it didn't look too hard, but Melissa's stitches were incredibly smooth. Abby knew it took skill to make it look that good.

Melissa tucked the project away as they parked at the coffee shop.

"Y'all didn't have any breakfast yet, did you?" Melissa asked.

64

"Oh, uh, yeah, I did," Abby responded.

"I left room for a muffin," Jon allowed, got out, and then held the door open for the girls, first at the car and then at the coffee shop.

Abby had never been in a coffee shop this hippie, this back-to-nature. Mother would have instantly disapproved. Battered tile floors and mismatched wooden chairs crowded between tan walls hung with artwork. Wooden windowsills supported a jumble of terracotta pots holding herbs and flowers pressing against the front windows in wild profusion. The relaxed, friendly expressions on the young adults suggested they were regulars. Some of them studied laptops. Others chatted or ate. Jon and Melissa bought muffins and juice to share, settling with Abby at a small table near the back of the shop.

Abby gazed at the art on the walls as the others ate. A small white card explained each work. Drawings, paintings, photographs, stained glass, wooden plaques. Children, still-lifes, nature scenes, sayings, geometric patterns … the art was as varied as the décor.

By itself on the back wall, a large, black-and-white, framed picture of a smiling old man seated in front of a plant caught her eye, looking at her with the most intriguing expression she had ever seen. At first he looked happy, even jovial, but as she looked more, she saw a touch of sadness, followed by resignation and a large dash of wisdom. She got the impression he'd endured a lot, yet found reasons to continue. Maybe it was Albus Dumbledore, Abby thought. This man's eyes twinkled as J.K. Rowling described, but he lacked half-moon glasses. He definitely had the flowing white hair and beard, though, and the robes. On second thought, this wasn't a drawing of an imaginary person, or a photograph of the actor who played Dumbledore.

Melissa and Jon turned to see what had drawn her prolonged attention and prompted her wavering smile.

"That's 'Abdu'l-Bahá," Melissa said, smiling in comradery.

"Who?"

"He's the one Jon was telling you about, the son of the founder of my Faith, the one who was a man we can try to be like," she explained.

"Oh. Yeah, uh…" Abby struggled to remember what Jon had said. "I like that he waves his hands, kind of like waving me to go there."

"I like that too," Melissa said. "I wish I could go to him, too. That picture was taken in New Hampshire, so he came to us."

"He was in America?" His robes and hat were definitely a Middle-Eastern style.

"Yes, coast to coast. People recorded what he said and did, took his picture, and even made some movies. The closest he came to here was Washington, D.C. They celebrate it every year."

"The owners of this café are Bahá'ís, that's why the picture is here," Jon clarified. "Sometimes they have Bahá'í discussions and music here."

Abby looked around. Melissa intuited her question and said that the owners would be in later.

"Are the workers all Bahá'ís?" Abby asked.

"I think right now only one or two are; the rest are not," Melissa replied.

Abby wondered if any of the employees she could see were Bahá'í. They all looked normal. Maybe Bahá'ís looked regular, like Melissa.

They finished their food and got up to go, stopping several times to let people pass in the crowded aisles. Now Abby saw that the art depicted Bahá'í themes of unity, justice, and the like. One photo entitled "Children of the Half-Light" showed three children – white, dark black, and in-between – holding hands and passing under an archway toward the sun. An abstract painting entitled "Order Out of Chaos" featured bright blocks of color. A stained glass star was called simply "Nine-Pointed Star." They seemed harmless enough.

She followed Melissa and Jon down the street toward the bookstore, encountering a bubbling fountain on the way.

Melissa and Jon searched through their pockets for coins to toss in the fountain, combined them, and divvied the kitty three ways.

Careful not to spill her coins, Melissa crossed all her fingers, two sets on each hand, then crossed her legs and arms. Giggling with Abby and Jon, Melissa tossed all her coins high. They flashed, then splashed. Jon made his coins spin before hitting the water. Abby threw hers in low and straight.

"Rats!" she said.

"Whatsamatta?" Melissa said, still happy.

"Forgot to make a wish!"

"You can share mine. I've prayed for it so often there's probably some left over!" Melissa grinned.

"Yeah?" Abby rejoined.

"Yeah, for world peace. Hurry up, Golden Age!"

Melissa sat on the edge of the cement basin and crossed her fingers, arms and legs again.

"C'mon, Jon, cross everything and then cross them over me! C'mon, Abby!" Melissa invited.

Chuckling, they piled crossed body parts on top of each other, making a human pretzel. Jon suddenly burst out guffawing.

"Whazzo funny?" Melissa asked, half-guffawing herself.

"Who's got any coins left? And who can throw it?"

"Oh!" Melissa gasped for breath between laughs. "Okay, time for some creativity. We'll toss imaginary coins with our tongues; I think it's the only thing I can still move!"

Jon responded by crossing his eyes, making the girls laugh so hard they could barely keep *anything* crossed. Then they each pretended to throw in a coin with their tongue, the act made even harder because the fountain was behind them.

"Did anyone remember to wish?" Jon gasped between bouts of laughter.

Groans and more shouts of laughter answered him. But Abby had made her own wish: to have more fun times like this. She had precious few, and loved every second.

They broke apart, holding their sides and rubbing bits that were not used to bending that way. Slowly they stood up and walked on to the bookstore, still smiling and giggling.

Jon's phone rang. He answered it, then listened intently. His face grew more and more serious. When he closed his phone, he was grim.

"It was Mom. A fire started burning yesterday. Now it's spreading toward home."

The girls reacted instantly, blurting out concerns and questions.

"It's about 20 miles from our house, at the edge of town, and they're concerned about all that dry grass and brush catching fire. Right now it's headed toward us and, well, everyone is worried."

The trio had stopped to huddle on the sidewalk. Jon said they had enough time to go to the bookstore, but after that they should go home. If they had to evacuate, they'd have enough notice.

Abby had never been in a fire. She worried about what effect it would have on Sofia's house and family, and on her own family's visit. Maybe the Wizes should leave North Carolina early ... but Abby was counting on that horseback ride Sofia had offered.

Absorbed in her anxious thoughts, she followed Jon and Melissa. To her surprise, the cement sidewalk became new, green laminate flooring. Her friends were already out of sight, tracking down books.

Abby stood for a moment, unsure. Something sparkled next to the cash register: a tiny rack of beaded strings that caught the light beautifully. A little sign said they were bookmarks, but they were so pretty they could have been jewelry, with three or four beads on each end of a colored string. She fingered them for a moment, then drifted to a collection of miniature books at the end of the counter.

On the cover of *Zen Cowboy*, a cartoon outlaw sat in the full-lotus position in front of a cow and a cactus. A built-in bookmark ribbon ended in a tiny gold metal boot. Abby flipped through the pages and read clever jokes about Moo and Mu, Cowboys and Taoboys, Koans and Cow-ans. It was only $4.95, but Abby had only about two dollars. She put the cute book down reluctantly and eyed another even-smaller book, *Native American Wisdom*. Historic old photos of Native Americans (and even a few horses) were paired with quotes, one of which seemed meant especially for her:

> I have noticed in my life that all men have a liking for some special animal, tree, plant or spot of earth. If men would pay more attention to these preferences and seek what is best to do in order to make themselves worthy of that toward which they are so attracted, they might have dreams which would purify their lives. Let a man decide upon his favorite animal and make a study of it, learning its innocent ways. Let him learn to understand its sounds and motions. The animals want to communicate with man, but Wakantanka does not intend they shall do so directly – man must do the greater part in securing an understanding.
>
> Brave Buffalo (late 19th century)
> Teton Sioux medicine man[13]

Abby read this twice, stunned. Of course, she instantly knew what her chosen animal would be … had been for as long as she could remember. And she had just seen that there could be actual communication between horses and humans, thanks to Angie the Angel. This wise man said we *should* study an appealing animal or place and learn from it. Abby vowed to try.

She wanted the book badly, yet after she'd emptied every last coin in her coin purse, and even dug into all the corners of her backpack, she still had less than half of its $4.95 purchase price. Plus tax. Yet she knew she would need the affirmation the little book provided her. She carefully folded the front cover flap onto that page and carried it in front of her. She didn't want anyone to think she was stealing it, but was unable to put it down.

Jon seemed occupied with the military books and Melissa browsed in the history section. Abby looked for the animal books, finding equines shelved among the pets. She carefully put her little book on the edge of the bookshelf and examined the titles, delighted that she owned several. She picked up her small treasure and ambled through more rows, looking for anything interesting.

The magazine racks held several horse titles. Some were familiar: *Horse & Rider*, *Western Horseman*, *Horse Illustrated*, and *Young Rider*. But several she didn't know: *Cowboys & Indians*, *Western Cowboy*, and others. She squatted and looked at the ones on the bottom rack, then leafed through the *Horse Illustrated*. She always enjoyed the foldout, a tear-out poster of the month's featured breed: this month, the familiar Missouri Fox Trotter.[14] It was like the Tennessee Walker that was so popular in her home state. Hmmm. Missouri, Tennessee, both gaited breeds ... she wondered if the breeds were closely related, maybe like cousins.

Nothing else appealed to her amongst the ads for horses, saddles, and sprays, nor in the articles about building arenas, barrel racing, small horse properties, or flying lead changes (whatever they were; something about cantering, it seemed).

She put it back and picked up the unfamiliar *Cowboys & Indians*. After a few pages, she understood why she'd never seen it before. It featured some of the fanciest furniture, clothes, and jewelry she'd ever seen, all Western-themed. She'd probably never in her whole life get to put on – much less own – the expensive strands of turquoise and silver; or see – let alone live with – the antler-and-leather chairs. Every page overwhelmed her more, so she began to turn several at once, past the wine and restaurant reviews and articles about luxury resorts. Then her eyes stopped dead at the golden word "Parelli."[15]

Several small photos hooked her. Somebody – Mrs. Parelli? – sat smiling in front of a horse she worked with, holding an orange stick. A man – maybe Mr. Parelli – worked with horses in front of a crowd. Abby's nose nearly touched the page as she scrutinized the miniatures, mining them for information. The halters were the same as Angie's, and the horses did even neater things than she had: playing with a big green ball, standing on a platform, jumping barrels. The ad said they had actually been in Memphis, Tennessee last February. But they weren't going to be anywhere close to her for the rest of the year. Abby's heart plummeted as fast as it had soared, then rebounded with the thought that maybe they'd be back somewhere close next year, and maybe she could figure out how to go.

If she "learned horses' innocent ways" through the connection Angie had ignited in her, maybe her dreams would be beautiful *and* useful. She *had* to learn this Parelli thing. Somehow it had to work out, it just had to. She stood praying desperately to God, wherever God was, to please, please hear her ... *Have to get hold of this stuff to learn this ... money or no money ... somehow ... please ... please! ... oh!*

She jumped when she felt a hand on her shoulder. Jon and Melissa looked quizzically at her.

"We're ready to check out. Are you buying anything?" Jon asked.

"Oh man, I, uh ..." Abby blushed, embarrassed about not having the money to buy these two things she wanted so badly. And now she was ashamed about being embarrassed! She looked down at her treasures, mumbling, "Don't have enough money."

"How much money would you need?" Jon asked after a questioning glance at Melissa and her quick answering nod.

"Um…" Abby totaled up the two items. "About $9 more."

Another signal passed between the pair.

"Bring 'em," Jon said. "We're buying."

Abby stood rooted to the floor, mouth open, stupefied. She'd never wanted anything so badly in her life, and had never had someone give her a treasure just when she needed it, for no reason. Embarrassment, relief, and gratitude flooded through her in turns. She was also ready to be ridiculed for it, darn it! Mother's wonderful training …

But the pair waited patiently, encouragingly, until she stammered a heartfelt, nearly tearful, "Thanks! Thanks *so* much!" Smiling with her, they approached the register.

As Abby laid her two prizes on the counter next to Jon's military career book and Melissa's Bahá'í book, a breeze from the open door blew the jeweled strings about. Without thinking, she touched them.

"Which one would you like?" the cashier asked her.

"Uh … I like all of them," Abby replied, mind elsewhere.

"Well, please pick one. Your purchase qualifies you. It's our grand opening this week," the cashier said.

Abby could not believe a word she was hearing. It was almost as if the heavens had opened up and admitted her to the select company of the blessed – today, now, right here. As Jon and Melissa smiled over her, she dazedly chose a light-green string with clear blue and bright green beads at both ends. The cashier quickly wrapped it in rustling tissue, taped it shut, put it and the books in a sack, and gave everything to Jon, who had paid. To the assistant, it was a simple sale. To Abby, it was her personal blessing – a little whisper from the universe saying, *You're on the right track.*

Chapter 11 News

The teens drove home singing. Melissa started the old "Titanic" camp song, which begged to be shouted at the top of their lungs.

Normally, singing about doomed lifeboats would not make Abby happy, but today she was joyous about it. They all were. They dallied in the Holsworth driveway during the final chorus, Jon's deeper voice repeating "sea" and the two girls belting out the higher refrain of the families lost.

They found Sofia, Vivian and Paul in the kitchen, eating a quick, tense lunch together.

"What's the news?" Jon asked, sombering.

The adults took turns describing the looming emergency. The fire was officially out of control, burning steadily toward them but still a distance away. Fire fighters from all over the region battled it, especially near houses. Some residents had been evacuated, but no houses had been lost yet.

They complained about the lack of news on the radio and TV. They wanted continual coverage and more information, but neighbors knew more. The phone rang often as the neighborhood connections revved up, debating how the fire started and why it got so big so fast. It might have been some punk kid, a pyromaniac juvenile delinquent. Seemed like most years about this time, right before school, fires sprang up. The bigger overgrown fields could hide a kid and give a fire enough time to flare out of control. Sofia griped that no one needed extra stress from this threat. One neighbor had just learned she had cancer, another cared for his elderly mother afflicted with Alzheimer's. The wave of woes flowed.

Ricky breezed in to grab a bite. As he heard them talk, he stopped dead in his tracks, his face white and his jaw open. Abby noticed him first. Gradually the room fell silent, everyone staring at him. He continued to stand, frozen.

"What's the matter, Ricky?" Sofia finally asked her youngest son.

It was a minute before he finally closed his mouth, swallowed hard, and murmured, "I heard about the guy who set the fire."

Everyone pelted Ricky with questions.

"On the ride-along," he answered. "We took the report about a motorcyclist roaring into a field – that field the neighbors say it started in. They've been having trouble with trespassers, with bikers being noisy. I bet anything the guys were scouting it out so one of them could go in there and set the fire, way in the middle. They could get it going in the daytime when it would be harder to see."

This added hours to the debate. Had the police gone back to look? Could someone have seen smoke? If the police had this information, why didn't they get the media to broadcast the biker's description so the public could help track down the rider or bike? Homes could burn down because of some arsonist on the loose!

Fear of what could happen to their own home – and if not theirs, to others – fueled radical talk about what should be done to arsonists. The adults favored jail at the very least ... and more, if possible. It reminded Abby of Daddy's ranting radio talk shows. She thought they were riling themselves up, but still, setting fires for "fun" was very, very bad.

When the adults started repeating themselves, Abby edged from the room, taking her books and beaded bookmark from the forgotten bag on the counter. The family room was empty, the stairs vacant, the upstairs rooms silent. Good. Penny had offered her computer to Abby, and now she definitely had something she wanted to look up. Her little Native American book slid onto Penny's computer table as she laid down her valuables. She opened it and read:

> Conversation was never begun at once, nor in a hurried manner. No one was quick with a question, no matter how important, and no one was pressed for an answer. A pause giving time for thought was the truly courteous way of beginning and conducting a conversation. Silence was meaningful with the Lakota, and his granting a space of silence to the speech-maker and his own moment of silence before talking was done in the practice of true politeness and regard for the rule that "thought comes before speech."
>
> Luther Standing Bear, 1868?-1939
> Oglala Sioux Chief[16]

Abby imagined the boring conversations she'd have to endure, waiting around all the time for people to ask or answer.

Taking a deep breath, she carefully typed *parelli.com* into the ADDRESS field. Dazzling horse photos and bunches of subpages greeted her. Classes, instructors, an annual Colorado conference, equipment, and rotating pictures of Pat and Linda Parelli beckoned. Tempted to cross her fingers and maybe her eyes, she yielded to her burning desire and clicked on Tour Stops. The last event listed was in November of the current year, dashing her hopes of finding out if she could go to one nearby next year. She consoled herself by clicking on photos and reading testimonials.

At first, when she wanted a new page, she shut down the whole site and re-entered it. After a bit, she remembered Penny's techniques and began using the BACK arrow, sliding scroll buttons, and more. Not being skilled at computers, especially the internet, she was proud of herself. School computer class had covered only basic typing, clicking, and saving. They couldn't even print anything because paper and ink cost too much. Successfully connecting with the Parelli website and lucking into navigating it proficiently boosted her hopes that she could progress with her dream.

She pined after the Level 1 kit in its beckoning red box and envied the happy people adoring their horses in clinics and courses. She studied the banners that said the Parellis wanted to help horse owners' dreams come true. When she felt she would become bitter with longing, she clicked on the little X-for-exit. Her wish kept threatening to burst like a bubble; it was beautiful, special, and in danger of floating beyond her grasp at any moment. She vowed not to let Mother find out. God only knew how Vivian would use this desire against Abby.

Which reminded her … Abby logged back on and, copying the name she'd seen on the book Melissa bought, entered "Baha'i" in the SEARCH field. She didn't know how to make the little marks over the two letters, but apparently didn't need them. In the first listing, Bahai.org, pictures of happy people popped up. No horses, but more skin colors than on the all-Causasian Parelli site. *Hmm, wouldn't people with darker skin want to do Parelli? What about the Native Americans? They were experts with horses!*

Sympathy germinated in Abby's heart for anyone who couldn't connect with their special animal or place, because of skin color or any other reason. She was certain her life would be worse without horses; she flew on their backs, away from everything sad and bad. *Fly from sad and bad, ride to glad!* A babyish rhyme, but meaningful to her.

Photos of racially mixed groups on the Bahá'í site showed them studying booklets, praying, singing, discussing earnestly, and working with children. She read quotations from Bahá'u'lláh about the earth being one country and mankind its citizens; about the world reaching peace and security through the unity of all people. It seemed to be serious business, and yet the people looked seriously happy … like Melissa. She seemed cheerful and enviably confident. Abby wished she could be more like that.

She spent the afternoon following links and reading websites, until Mother called "Dinner's ready!" up the stairs. Abby quickly closed down the computer and, taking her books to her room, found a new sports bra waiting on her cot. Apparently Jenn had bought it and dropped it off for Abby before leaving with Penny again.

Abby was almost as touched by the love and care it represented as by its usefulness. She quickly peeled off her T-shirt, took off the old bra, and slid on the new one, inside out as Jenn intended. It seemed like it would be great, including for riding. She would whisper her thanks to Jenn, the world's best sister, at dinner.

Heading downstairs and smelling the crockpot stew, she realized she hadn't had lunch and was ravenous. Everybody gathered in the kitchen to eat and complain about the lack of news on the spreading fire. Sofia and Mother passed on theories and tidbits that neighbors had embellished in a real-life game of "Telephone." Daddy blamed as many governments as he could think of.

As Abby joined the families at the expanded kitchen table, Penny and Jenn quizzed Ricky about the motorcyclist in the field. He racked his brain again, trying to remember every last little bit.

"Do you know the rider?" Penny asked. "Or think you've seen the motorcycle? One of your friends?"

No one had asked this question yet; everyone waited breathlessly for Ricky's answer.

"Hmm, well, I don't think ... or maybe ..."

His elders pelted him with questions, urging and insisting he think harder; but he frowned more and shook his head slightly.

"I guess not, no, probably not," he said, slightly irritated.

Abby thought he'd *almost* remembered something but lost it in the hubbub. Maybe if he'd been given "a space of silence" ...

While the others roundly criticized the authorities' bungling of the fire, Sofia quietly told Abby that, if everything worked out, she could take that trail ride the next morning. The adults could take her on their way to a street fair, assuming the fire didn't get worse. This was good news, and Abby began to daydream about it. She still bemoaned her boots and jeans, and wondered whether she should try to do any Parelli on the horse she was assigned, but overall, she was sure it would be wonderful.

If only she'd picked up a Harry Potter crystal ball at the bookstore, she might have seen she was wrong. Almost dead wrong.

Chapter 12 Flying

True to her word, Sofia drove with Abby, Vivian and Paul to the Pleasant View stables for a 9 a.m. trail ride. Several roads were closed due to smoke, making for slow going. That was fine with Abby; it gave her time to relive her dream from last night. She'd won a five-way coin toss for Baby Doll, the best lesson horse at The Ride Place ...

∞　∞　∞　∞　∞　∞　∞　∞

... in a big field, Baby Doll trots up ... Abby ties a string around Baby Doll's neck ... plays ground games with her on the way to the dirt track ... Tag ... Follow My Leader ... Jump This ... Tyler meets them, grins handsomely, gives Abby an orange wand ... she leaps up onto Baby Doll's bare back ... cues the mare to turn ... walk ... stop ... trot ... jump over poles ... canter ... spin ... gallop a final lap ... oh! free, sticking to Baby Doll's back, Abby flies, unified with her horse, ecstatic ... no fear ... they jump all the fences heading back to Baby Doll's pasture ... Abby jumps off, hugs Baby Doll ... the horse hugs back ... tucks Abby into her chest with her lower jaw ...

∞　∞　∞　∞　∞　∞　∞　∞

Memory of the dream's horsey hug carried Abby through the rest of the slow drive.[17] But when they arrived at the trail ride, she felt like a tourist – improperly dressed in capris and white tennies she worried about dirtying, unfamiliar with the horses and layout – rather than an experienced equestrienne. But at least her right pinky had healed so she could handle the reins, and her bruises were fading and hidden.

Her nose started to clear as they pulled up. Mother paid for the ride, signed paperwork releasing the ranch from all liability in case of accident, double-checked the pickup time, then left with Daddy and Aunt Sofia. Abby handed her backpack to the office girl to stow away during the ride. Abby had brought Jenn's loaner supplies, her own coin purse, an icy water bottle, and her *HP #7* in case the adults were delayed picking her up.

Abby met her mount, a gray horse with well-used tack. She bent to see if it was a boy or girl and saw the wedge of sheath near the back legs. She patted him ... *oops*, stroked his neck.

"We'll get along great," Abby whispered to him, smelling his wonderful, unique scent, admiring his large brown eyes, cradling his jaw through his well-worn bridle. "Ride together to glad, huh? Loan me some of your horse magic?" He evaded her hand when she tried to touch his cheek, but she was confident they'd bond soon.

Coached by the wranglers, each rider measured stirrup length by tucking the stirrup into their armpit and reaching toward the leather flap called the saddle jockey.[18] Arm length is generally a usable guide for leg length, the wranglers explained. Abby started to adjust the fender herself but stopped. She did not want to reveal what she knew. They might, if they were like Mother, ridicule her or give her a harder horse.

The wranglers helped each rider mount their horse from the left, get their feet in the stirrups, and hold the reins. "Kick your horse lightly to go," they instructed. "Pull back gently on both reins to stop. Stay well behind the horse in front of you. And don't let 'em eat on the trail."

Angie jumped to Abby's mind. Angie had never once kicked her horse to go nor pulled to stop, but Abby didn't know how to cue a horse in the new way. She decided she'd use the lightest cues she could.

Gunsmoke hadn't read the memo, though; he resisted all of Abby's cues. The other riders headed out onto the trail, going toward the hill behind the stables, but Abby couldn't convince Gunsmoke to take even one step. Her stupid tennis shoes were too soft. And the fenders irritated her bare calves. She *knew* she should've brought her riding clothes!

The last wrangler twisted a green twig off a nearby tree and gave it to Abby to use on Gunsmoke's rump. Gunsmoke reluctantly headed after the herd until he was distracted by some tasty-looking weeds.

The wrangler smacked the horse with his long reins whenever the gray head bobbed down, which was at nearly every patch of weeds. Abby tried to pull Gunsmoke's head up, but just wasn't strong enough. She braced her feet against the stirrups to pull harder. Suddenly, her left foot slipped all the way through the stirrup, and her right nearly did.

Oh no! This is deadly! She remembered all too well that riders were supposed to wear boots with heels that stopped the foot from sliding through the stirrup. If she fell off now, with her foot trapped in the stirrup, she would land on her head and be dragged! Gunsmoke ate as Abby wrestled her foot out, concentrating on keeping the balls of her feet on the stirrups while trying to get Gunsmoke moving. She used her stick so long and so hard that her arm started to give out. This wasn't the ride she had hoped for at all. The wrangler picked a green stick for himself and rode right behind Gunsmoke, smacking him often, causing him to shamble down the path halfheartedly. Once the wrangler smacked too hard and Gunsmoke jumped forward several steps, nearly unseating Abby, until a delicious patch of brown grass stopped him. The rising heat sapped what little energy Abby had to beat him.

The wrangler nagged Gunsmoke until he was nearly caught up with the group. A cluster of wilting trees grew into the path, and the riders had to slow down while ducking and leaning. This allowed Gunsmoke and the wrangler to catch up as the trail started up a steeper hill.

"Just gotta show him who's boss," the wrangler asserted.

"Yeah, cowgirl up," Abby replied with confidence she did not feel.

Minutes later, the group stopped to enjoy the view from atop a hill. Gunsmoke immediately plunged his head into some weeds by the trail. Abby tried to tug his head up, but didn't dare brace against him for fear her tennies would again slide through the stirrups. He swung around to dig into another patch of weeds. That seemed to trigger a new thought in his one-track mind, for he began to walk back down the path. Abby pulled hard with both reins. Forget gentle. Forget unity. Everything she did with this horse had to be with all her strength. It was a battle. The appeal of her dreams had tricked her into thinking she could escape disaster on a strange horse.

Oddly, hauling back on his bit didn't make Gunsmoke stop or even slow down. He broke into a rough trot. Abby bounced all over, painfully, slamming her most-private parts into the saddle, hunching, grabbing for the horn, nearly dropping the reins. She was terrified she'd fall. Bringing her worst fears to life, Gunsmoke began cantering: a choppy, hard-to-sit canter made harder by Abby's rising panic that she could not stop him.

She screamed in fear and frustration, drowning in her inability to ride this monster. Voices shouted at her to stop him, but she was already trying as hard as she could. Gunsmoke was running away!

She was living her worst nightmare, including being in desperate danger. Frightened about her shoes, she clamped her knees, leaned back with all her might, and shouted, "WHOA!!"

Gunsmoke shook his head, thrust his nose forward and seemed to gather steam the more she hauled on the reins. In sheer panic, she tried what she had seen Angie do. Clueless, she tried to pull the right rein down and back as hard as she could ... and it broke!

She wasn't sure how hard she could pull on the left rein before it also broke. Worse, the clump of trees loomed on the left. If she pulled on the left rein now, and he obeyed, he'd veer toward the trees.

But it was either that or get knocked off by the low-hanging branches. She pulled with every last bit of her strength on the left rein, fiercely trying to turn him before she hit the branches. Gunsmoke did seem to be turning. Maybe it would be all right. But a familiar, odd, unbalanced sensation grew into a sickening sliding feeling, and the horse went one way and she went another, and she was still heading toward the low branches, and oooohh this was going to hurt, this was going to...*Oh God, please, help, save me, get me out of here, nooo, God pleee...*

Chapter 13 Friend

Abby stood just past the clump of trees, blinking in the warm morning light. She was dazed. That was understandable, since she had just hit ... er, not hit ... um, how ... where was the horse? She looked around. Where were the shouting riders? Why did the trees look so different, too? The stable had shrunk, or the changing light made it look smaller. It must be that she just didn't know the layout.

But where was the horse? Had he thrown her and run off? Had the others gone after him? But hadn't that one wrangler been right behind her? She looked around the other side of the trees for Gunsmoke and the wrangler. No sign. Surely she should at least hear some shouting. No, nothing.

This was way, *way* too strange. Had she blacked out and were they all back at the stables? The stables that looked like a house from this angle? Might as well head there; it beat just standing around in the heat.

She walked past the trees and down the path; it had become a well-kept walkway rather than the rough, rocky horse path. Gunsmoke's clumps of dry grass were now silvery-green sage and yellow flowers. By the house, someone stooping in the yard glanced up. Looked again. Seemed surprised. Set their trowel down next to a bucket and straightened up. Lifted their hand to their ear. Someone wearing strange clothes. Not ranch clothes, more like earth-colored peasant clothes. Loose clothes, a loose stance, a free hand waving at her.

"I fell off!" Abby shouted.

The person – apparently a woman, or girl – didn't answer but lifted her watch, lips moving. Still, she smiled; that was something.

Abby walked further and cupped her hands to her mouth. "Where is everyone? Did the horse come back?"

The woman smiled again and called, "It ees ahkay. Come dawn!"

She must be from overseas; she had an unusual accent. But up closer, she looked a lot like Melissa – a mix of nationalities. Abby descended the last slope to the barn ... er, house ... and approached the woman. Girl. Whichever.

"Where is everyone?" Abby repeated. "Who are you?"

"I eir, is, are Dali. Dali Puerta," the lady answered. "End you eir?"

What an odd last name: *p'WHERE-tah*. "I'm Abby. Abby Wize."

"Wise?" Dali Puerta looked at her for a long moment, as if it was Abby who had a strange last name.

"Yes, Wize, with a 'z'. Well anyway, Mrs. Puerta, Miss Dollie, uh, I must've gotten lost. I fell off a horse. I mean, I was going to fall off and then, um, well, I lost everyone. And the horse. Did you see them?"

Dali Puerta held up her watch again. It seemed to whisper to her. Abby stared at the watch. She knew she was behind the times on iPods and Blackberrys and Bluetooths and all that, but she had never heard of a whispering watch.

"Help let you with all-embracing vision," Dali said nonsensically. "Coming in for now?" Her watch whispered again, and she held out her hand to Abby, clearly inviting her inside the little house with a word Abby didn't catch. They stepped through a wooden doorway, past the thick earthen walls, and into the cool living room.

The ceiling slanted up to a vent that drew air through the open windows and doors. A screen appeared across the doorway, the same kind of screen as on the open windows.

Doors led into a bedroom and bathroom. A low wall revealed the kitchen. It seemed even more back-to-nature than the coffee shop she had gone to with Jon and Melissa. Plants, yes, and wood. And some practical, beautiful decorations. Pretty rainbow-glass doorknobs, and hammered metal shelves. Mottled pottery, quilts over the furniture and weavings hanging on wall brackets.

"I like your house," she said a little guiltily when she realized she'd been peeking more than Mother would consider proper.

"I are glad that you liking it," Dali said, smiling and listening to her whispering watch. "Could you like ... no, would you like some ... thing to drink?"

"Oh, I have water back in ..." Back in where? The small house sat where the stables had been. She had ridden up that hill and just now walked down it. "Where are we?" she blurted out.

"Would you pless sat down?" Dali asked politely. She held out a stained glass tumbler of what looked like cool water. Abby accepted the water and, still standing, sipped from it appreciatively.

Her capris passed a quick inspection for dirt. She apparently hadn't been on Gunsmoke long enough to get very dirty. She blushed, ducked her head, gingerly sat down, and pretended to look at her chair.

"Are you all right?" her hostess asked, concerned.

"Ye ... um, I'm, uh, not sure. I'm not hurt anyway, that's good. But I have to say I'm very confused. You weren't here when I came before. Are your parents home?"

"Ah ... is different ..."

"Um, well then, where am I?"

Dali took a deep breath and seemed to be deciding what to say. Her whispering watch stayed silent.

"You are ... where you were ... before."

"I'm in the same place I was?"

"Yes, I have belief so."

Abby could tell her hostess was worried that this would be unhappy news for Abby. Somehow Abby did not think this was a joke or a lie. Hesitant to make a fool of herself, she asked Dali to explain. The watch began whispering again.

"I not sure, but you come a long way from where you were."

It seemed to Abby that Dali's English was getting better by the minute. The whispering watch, no doubt. Some kind of translator she wore? While she was ... weeding?

"I thought you just said I am where I was before. Which means I didn't come very far at all!"

"I'm much sorry. I mean, you came a long way in time. How would you call that?"

"I don't know, yeah, far, I guess. How far, do you think?"

Dali looked at Abby, again seeming to decide something. Silence from her watch. Dali was on her own for this one, whatever it was.

"What year ... is it ... from when you came?"

"Year? 2007, why?"

"2007? In what calendar?"

"What do you mean, 'what calendar'?" Abby was getting frustrated. Her confusion was growing, not lessening, with the discussion.

"I am so sorry. Do you need to ... take a break?"

"Break? No, I need to know where I am, where everybody went, that's all." Abby began to change her opinion about Dali. She'd seemed a fast learner, but now she appeared rather slow.

Dali smiled and stood up smoothly. When Mother came to pick Abby up and met Dali, Mother would at least approve of her graciousness and gracefulness.

First, though, Abby would need to figure out how to meet the car, regardless of where the wranglers and horses had gone. Mother would never let her forget it if she was off lost somewhere.

Dali opened a wooden box on a wooden table, touched something inside, and shut it gently. Several beautiful painted horses next to the wooden box reminded Abby of the TRAIL OF PAINTED PONIES statues she often admired in horse catalogs.[19] The sound of drumbeats began to fill the small house. They became hoofbeats, and loud nickering. Brassy bugles sounded, blending into neighs. Other instruments followed, and other horse voices ... a little foal answered a happy clarinet ...

Dali had glided off somewhere. Abby had nothing to do but sit in this soft, comfy chair and listen to the horse music, remembering playing clarinet and hearing other instruments in grade-school band class back in New York. She rested her heavy head on the back of the chair, which seemed to adjust instantly to hold her head just right … just right …

∞   ∞   ∞   ∞   ∞   ∞   ∞   ∞

… and horses … her favorite escape … sunshine on their shiny coats … their smell … oneness with them … beautiful, majestic horses obey her very thoughts … no reins, no saddles needed … cantering up and down hills … a bunch of trees in the path …

∞   ∞   ∞   ∞   ∞   ∞   ∞   ∞

Her eyes flew open to reveal Dali sitting opposite her again, regarding her while the watch whispered away. Abby relaxed again.

"Feel better now?" Dali asked, smiling slightly. "You were getting upset. Thought that help you calm down."

"I do feel better, thanks. I was just confused."

Dali looked at her a long moment, then shrugged.

"Do you want to talk about your … situation … again? Or would it be too … confusing?"

"Um…" Honestly, even thinking about her situation was upsetting; who knew if talking about it would send Dali to her little sound-box again? She was supposed to have crashed into that tree and didn't – and now the stables were gone and she had traveled a long way … in time?

"How about if we talk about you for a while, Dali?"

"All right, Abby, I will tell you what I th … what I can," Dali said earnestly.[20] "Told you my name: Dali Puerta. And my age is 18. This my aunt's house that is now mine. I work … um, part-time. My bliss is grow plants like you saw on the hill."

"And where are we now? Are we in North Carolina?"

The watch whispered again on Dali's wrist. She had propped up her elbow on the arm of the couch, the better to keep the watch by her ear.

"We are in the, ah, area of North Carolina, yes."

Abby wasn't sure why her hostess said it like that, but at least she was where she was supposed to be. Just not when.

"For me, it's Friday, August 17, 2007. What … um, what year is it here?" Abby's statement had set the watch to whispering again.

"I think you use Gregorian calendar. Middle 2nd century, our calendar."[21]

Abby felt stupid. She knew about other calendars in the world: the Chinese New Year, and Muslim lunar months. Jon Holsworth had mentioned a Bahá'í month called "Questions." But to not even know what her own calendar was called, that was just plain pitiful. She hadn't even thought to say she was from 2007 *AD*.

Dali didn't seem to think Abby was stupid. On the contrary, she was smiling as if she'd solved a hard puzzle. Her watch whispered nonstop. Abby was very glad that the gizmo helped Dali to help her.

Dali looked at her seriously again, and said, "I tell you how far you traveled, but you maybe not want to hear."

"Try me."

"Pardon?"

"Yes, I would like to hear."

"Today Jalál or yours Saturday, 17 or Sultan of Kamál, 864 BE, how it falls this year. Traveled 700 years into your future."[22]

Abby stared blankly at Dali's unusual face, trying to grapple with her extraordinary announcement, twisting her watch around her own wrist. Glancing at the very unusual house and recalling the morning's unusual events, though, she realized it was probably true. She had no idea how, but the facts in front of her eyes indicated that she had left 2007 and was now in ... 2707? Wow! It explained the constantly whispering watch, anyway. She wondered a little crazily where the spaceships and jet packs were.

"Time should be same," Dali surmised, glancing at a clock that did, indeed, match the time on Abby's old watch.

But ... Jenn would never know what happened to her. She had never even thanked her sister for the sports bra she now wore; dinner had been too noisy. Jenn's face swam in front of her, gazing concernedly at her. Slowly it transformed into Dali's face, also showing deep concern. Same sisterly care, new face.

Well, if this was the face of the future, it was a good one. The dire predictions from *her* time about *this* time were apparently wrong. Best put on a good front and be glad that she had a helper while she tried to figure things out.

Abby flashed what she hoped was a winning smile, realizing that she needed this person, so she'd better be on her best behavior.

"You will have many questions. I not sure I can answer them all," Dali said, looking relieved.

"Well, I bet you'll do the best you can, and that'll have to be good enough," Abby said, trying to adopt a mature tone but surprised at how much her words sounded like Mother. "I should just be glad that I'm not dead." She lumbered on, trying to sound more like herself. "Um, I'm not, am I?"

"Oh no, *that* I can answer. You definitely not dead." Dali said, a very pretty smile emerging through her worry. It reminded Abby of something she had once read in a teen magazine back in Surely, while waiting for Jenn to get her hair cut: a smile was your best business card, and a cheap, instant beautifier.[23]

"What time is it? What are you going to do today?"

"It's coming onto noontime." Dali looked keenly at her for a few moments, saying nothing.[24] Just before Abby began to feel uncomfortable, though, Dali added, "I work some this afternoon. Tonight is scheduled a ... gathering."

"How do you get to work? And where is the gathering? Aren't you afraid to live out here all by yourself?" The last question had popped into Abby's mind as she tried to imagine Dali's living arrangements. She hoped it wasn't too personal.

But Dali smiled wide again and answered, "I'm not afraid to live out here; it is quite safe. I love it very much. The gathering is close. My work is further away, in the nearby town. We could walk or use a ... bicycle."

"Are there horses in your world? Would you ride one to work?"

"Oh yes," Dali replied instantly and thoughtfully. "We have horses and other animals, but it is rather different than in your time, I would imagine. You may like to see how we have horses. I suppose a person could ride a horse to go places, but ..." She looked doubtful. The watch whispered. "As in your world, it is not commonly done."

"If I can, yes, I would like to see," Abby wondered how the animals would be different. "Is it a horse show, or a rodeo?"

"Yes, a show with horses and other animals. What is rodeo?"

"Riding bucking horses, roping steers, you know, barrel racing, that kind of thing," Abby tried to explain, struggling to imagine pigs, sheep, goats and other livestock in a show ring competing for ribbons with horses.

Dali gazed at her for a moment, her brow slightly furrowed, then blinked long and slow. After a couple of seconds, she said, "There is no need to rope steers. Once in a while someone might ride a bucking horse if they're feeling foolish and ... ready to be injured. Racing, we sometimes have, but not in the show you'll see."

"Oh."

After another thoughtful pause, Dali said, "Do you like food?"[25]

"Um, do you mean do I like eating? Yeah, doesn't everyone? Or do you mean do I like to cook food? Well, Mother doesn't ..." Mother. If she ever got back home, Mother would probably kill her even if Gunsmoke hadn't. Better she stay here in the future until she had a really good explanation.

"Are you hungry?" Dali asked.

"A little, I guess."

"Would you like to help make our noon meal with me?"

Abby looked at Dali's face to check on meaning. Could she say no? Or did Dali expect her to help, like Mother would? It seemed that Dali was waiting for her honest answer.

"Maybe I can help. I'm not very good at fixing complicated stuff."

"I'm sure you'll do well," Dali assured her.

She led the way to the sink, where both girls washed their hands. Counters and cabinets stretched between the sink and a refrigerator-looking panel. Three chairs, two stools, and an eating table set against the low wall into the living room completed the small, tidy nook. At least Abby could identify that much, 700 years in the future.

Dali pulled open a small panel in the lower row of cabinets. Abby was enveloped in the smell of fresh-baked bread, a smell she'd never been able to resist when they passed Cinnabon in the mall ... and could not resist now. Dali straightened up with a pan of hot bread.

"It will settle while we get our salad," she said, setting the pan on a coiled, woven straw trivet in a Native American style.

She went to the biggest panel, swung it open, and took out lettuce, some colorful vegetables, and several dressings.

"The garden did well this summer. Would you like ... cucumbers on your salad? Carrots? Radishes? Lots of tomatoes this year, maybe you can help me eat them up. Well, here, choose what you wish."

Abby was not terribly fond of salads, but this would at least fill her stomach. Dali invited Abby to taste-test the vegetables while Dali shook the bread out of the pan, put the loaf into a cutting rack, cut off two slices, and put them onto two pretty pottery plates. Abby eyed it with distrust. She loved white bread and fluffy baked goods with sugar on top, not dense dark brown stuff with chunks.

"Give us this day our daily bread," Abby muttered.[26] Plain bread and salad didn't seem like a complete meal, and Abby struggled not to be rude to her solicitous hostess.

"...and grant Thine increase in the necessities of life, that we may be dependent on none other but Thee," Dali responded sincerely.[27]

"What?"

"Oh, sorry. Never mind," Dali said quickly.

Dali made her salad and showed Abby the dressings, describing one new bottle and asking if Abby would be interested in trying it too. When Abby agreed, Dali unscrewed the lid and poured. Abby noted the lack of safety seal inside the lid and asked about it.

Dali poured the dressing silently, watch murmuring. Had she not heard? Was it a rude question in this world? Abby was gathering her apology when Dali gently asked her why bottles needed safety seals.

"Well, because, um ... to show you if someone has messed with your bottle," Abby said. Bottles just had them; always had.

Again, Dali seemed to blink really slowly. "Safety seals began in your 1980s, after seven people died from poisoned pills," Dali noted quietly. "Anonymous murderers randomly poisoning totally innocent strangers.[28] It marked a milestone in America's decline."

"Oh, I see, before I was born, in '94." Abby understood. "And now you're not worried about anyone poisoning you?"

"No, we're not," Dali confirmed. "One of many good things about our time."

They sat down together. Abby watched her hostess, wondering how she should hold her fork here, leery of breaking any table rules. Dali simply squeezed Abby's hand, looked directly into her eyes, said, "I'm glad you're here," and tucked into her bread.

Abby bit into hers. The bread was moist, very flavorful and, due to the various grains and chunks, different with every bite. The salad and dressing were also easy to get used to. The lettuce was very dark-green, and not quite sweet but ... deeper. In both color and flavor, the head lettuce back home paled in comparison.

Abby was unexpectedly glad she had some clue about proper table manners. This surprise meal with a complete stranger made her feel self-conscious, even though Dali was only warm and accepting.

A clear, soft chime sounded. After three repetitions, Abby began to count, ending at 12. The last few sounded more like a wailing siren. Abby wondered if it was faulty, but Dali seemed not to notice.

"Noontime, thank God," Dali said.

"Why? Is noon special here?"

"Every time is special here," Dali replied, "but starting at noon, we can say the noontime prayer."[29]

"Oh," Abby said. She had not thought about the spiritual practices here. "Why is every time special?"

"I will try to show you the answer to that," Dali said. "I'm just afraid of ... overwhelming you."

It was Abby's turn to look at Dali searchingly. She was not used to someone being so concerned about her mental state. And emotional state. Even physical state, for that matter. Come to think of it, she should probably add spiritual state. She had traveled to the future, where she was being completely cared for by a total stranger. How much stranger would it get?

Chapter 14 Town

"I usually ride my bike to work. But I only have one bike, so we'll walk. Is that all right?" Dali asked as they cleaned up from lunch.

"I guess so. Is it far?"

"About five times as far as you walked this morning, I think."

Abby looked sharply at Dali. How did Dali know how far she had walked? Dali wouldn't have been able to see her that far away. Abby did not want to argue, however, and let it slide.

"We may be able to borrow a bike for the return trip. You'll be tired by then, probably. Unless you already feel tired and would rather rest here at home."

"No, I'll go," Abby replied quickly. She couldn't imagine hanging out alone, and was a little surprised that Dali would consider leaving a stranger alone with her whole house and all its possessions.

"Good. Let me just get my bag. Do you think you'll need anything before we go?"

"Not that I know of." In truth, Abby had no idea how to prepare for their afternoon, because she had no idea what it would be like. So she added, "But if you can think of anything ..."

Dali studied her. "You might want to visit the restroom first." She held her watch up to her ear and it whispered again. "Yes," she added decisively, "let's show you the bathroom."

Past a wooden door painted red stood a boxy toilet and a combination shower and bathub. The far wall featured fluffy towels on a rack and a tall wooden cabinet with festive floral tile shelves holding more Native-looking woven baskets. On the wall, a color photograph of a pair of pretty, bright, brown eyes in a light-brown face supervised the sink opposite. Dali's face? Abby looked away from it lest she fall into Dali's eyes as she had into her own.

"In your time, toilets have water and pipes going in and out of the house, yes?" Dali asked.

"Right."

"Most of our houses collect their own water, and our toilets have no water. When you ... go, swing the little door out of the way, like this," she said, pressing a lever. "Everything will drop down the hole."

"Like a porta-potty then," Abby said. "With no water."[30]

"Maybe so," Dali said. Abby noted that the watch was silent about porta-potties. "After, press this button to start the waste breakdown. Except for, er, men-stral products. For those, the instructions are printed ... oh."

"What's the matter?"

"The words are in UL. I'm afraid you won't understand it."

"What's, um, *yule*?"

"U-L, the universal language. It's the worldwide secondary language that we all learn in school." Her watch coached her quietly. "It includes a lot of English, but it's not close enough to your American for you to read. Even my American is very different from yours, just as your 2000s English is very different from the 1300s."

Abby had seen some of the English from the Middle Ages. It was indeed nearly unreadable. She'd just have to try her best, *try* not being a four-letter word. Dali left, shutting the door softly.

Abby thought she figured it all out pretty well. She washed her hands and, glancing in the mirror above the sink, decided to wash her face to erase the last traces of the recent/long-ago trail ride. The soap pump was a work of art in itself. As she admired it, Mother's voice called it *cloisonné* in Abby's head. Dali tapped on the door just as Abby was drying her hands on a soft, rust-colored towel.

"I'd like to offer you some clothes before we go," Dali said, handing her some folded garments. "You'll be more comfortable in these. I kept some favorites from when I was your height, and it would be so pleasant to have someone enjoy them again."

"All right," Abby replied, admiring the tan slip-on shirt and embroidered and stamped golden stretch-waist pants. They were loose, cool, and flowed and swirled against her skin delightfully. Abby had thought the woven fabric would be stiff like her mother's linen suits.

She found Dali in the clean, simple, pleasantly natural-smelling bedroom, retrieving something from a bureau drawer.

"Uh, I don't have any deodorant, or spare underwear," Abby said.

Dali pondered this, with her watch whispering away. "You should be able to get along without deodorant here," she finally said.[31] "We can wash your underwear whenever you wish, or I can loan you some.

"Oh, and I used to wear these gold butterflies in my hair with that outfit, would you like to try them? I think they will look even better in your brown hair than my black. Such a pretty color of hair!"

Abby admired the barrettes but, knowing only how to braid, fumbled with them as Dali stood silently.

"Ah, would you … like some help?" Dali waited for Abby's consent, then separated a lock and clipped it to a section of hair further back. Once both barrettes were in, Dali helped Abby admire the effect in the mirror over the bureau.

Dali said she didn't have any shoes in Abby's size, and so Abby's once-white canvas sneakers had to serve. Ironically, she now wished they were dirtier, so they would blend with her new outfit better.

"If you need a bag, I have just the right one," Dali offered, pulling open a drawer in the simple low wooden bureau and pulling out a knotty, macraméd tan purse with long handles. It coordinated well with the outfit, but Abby had nothing to put in it. Embarrassed, she silently hoped that she wouldn't need the supplies Jenn had given her, which were "back home" in her backpack.

"Thanks, I don't have anything to carry right now, but I'll let you know if I do. And thanks for … all this," Abby stammered clumsily.

"It is my privilege to help you." Dali's manner was so gentle, and her smile so warm and sincere, that Abby felt like she had gained another big sister. She imagined she could muster her courage and ask Dali for anything she really needed.

The watch whispered, and Dali's face sombered.

"We're late. We'll have to take the bike," she said. "Can you … did you ever … are you okay with riding double? On a one-seat bicycle?"

"Yes." Abby noticed that Dali struggled with words too. She wondered how to avoid ruining the beautiful pants in the bike chain, even if she avoided falling off. One of the girls would stand on the pedals; the other would sit on the seat, legs hanging in midair, holding the pedaler's waist.

"Good, then it might work," Dali said.

The girls left the house, Dali murmuring a few words. The door swung shut and clicked – a carved wood door inset with a tall, clear, lead-glass panel. While Abby admired the door's shiny, textured metal doorknob and reflected on the voice-activated closing, Dali retrieved a bicycle. It looked surprisingly like a regular woman's bicycle, with baskets in front and back. Instead of a greasy, pants-leg-eating chain, though, Abby saw a clean, clear tube. Unfamiliar gadgets adorned the handlebars.

"What if you pedal and steer, and sit on my lap to rest. You're lighter."

Abby thought that Dali should steer, since Abby had no earthly – or other-earthly – idea where they were going. Before she could say anything, though, Dali added, "I'll give you directions. It's not hard."

After a few false starts, they arranged themselves and lurched down the road. Soon they were both laughing.

"I knew I should've gotten the seat to fit across the back baskets," Dali said after they'd wobbled to a stop for the 10th time. She strained to touch her tippy-toes to the ground, balancing the bike for Abby, who prepared to simultaneously jump onto the pedals, pedal off, and steer straight. "I'm trying to get better at listening to those divine promptings."

"Can you still get a seat? If we have to come home like this ..."

"I've already, er, borrowed another bike," Dali said. "Wait!" Reaching down, she unfolded the top bars of the pedals, making them twice as long. "Now we can both pedal. I forgot I had those."

Abby was glad for the pedaling help, but wondered silently when Dali had phoned anyone about another bike. Abby hadn't seen or heard anything like a phone.

Once they were truly coordinated, Dali sang a song Abby did not understand – a biking song, she supposed. Dali directed her down the road that could have led to the stables hundreds of years ago. It sure looked different; the plants were more orderly, the road better tended. It had been plain brown dirt before. Now it was paved with a surface that seemed cooler than the familiar black asphalt and let the bicycle tires roll easily. And the fire had been raging just over *there*, she thought, looking left toward where Little Lily should have lain. She didn't see any smoke, but caught an alarming whiff of the smell.

Some 20 minutes later, topping a hill, she saw more houses. The only other traffic was a couple of bicycles and a small, canopied tricycle. Dali waved at all of them, calling out a greeting in her own language – New American, Abby supposed. A woman sat in a porch chair, working with something in a large pot. A man hung up laundry outside. Dali waved at them, too.

Everyone waved back warmly, gazed wonderingly at Abby, then went on with their business. After the fifth time, Abby asked why they were staring. She'd put on the clothes of the time – what was wrong?

"They're just curious. They don't know you, and I didn't tell anyone I was expecting a visitor. Also, most everyone has darker skin than you. So they're trying to figure out where you came from and who you are. Everyone knows everyone around here. It's a small town."

"What's this town called, anyway?"

"Lodlan." She pronounced it *LOAD-lun*. "L-O-D-L-A-N."

"And most people are darker than me?"

"Yes. Through the generations, all the skin colors started to genetically mix. But there are always some people with darker or lighter skin, and, er, other differences. Once in a while, someone has skin as light as yours or as dark as, say, my Uncle Arno's. People notice these variations and think they're rare and beautiful."

Surprised, Abby pondered the concept that she – as well as a really dark-skinned person – would be rare and noticeable. She was used to her skin color being unremarkable.

Most of the houses they passed were similar to Dali's, with some variations and less land around them. Several were U-shaped, a few were many-sided, some were two-storied, and a couple had a double yard. Like Dali's, all of them looked made of earth and wood, and most looked rounded and natural. The attention to plants and beauty was obvious. Each home had a pleasing variety of flowers, gardens, trees, tidy fences, benches, attractive statues, or strings of lights. Cats and dogs watched the pair cycle by; Abby was glad to know that pets still accompanied people in the far future.

In the yard of a wide, three-storied house with a wraparound porch, Abby saw a pair of teenagers standing with about 10 adults, two of them holding babies, all pointing and looking at the roof. As Abby pedaled herself and Dali past the house, she saw another half dozen kids in the side yard, playing a gentle ball game. She glimpsed a wheelchair, cast, bandages and a variety of skin tones. *A special school? Foster home? A very diverse family of many adopted kids?* She wondered if extended families here lived all together in one house – something Daddy had told her often happened in bygone days. Did these people want to share a house, or could they not afford separate homes? How did they get any privacy?

All the houses and streets were very clean. One small house, however, was not as well-kept as the others. The yard was mostly dirt, and the house had no decorations. Kids and dogs roamed the bare yard, shouting and playing.

Several small, slow, nearly silent, enclosed four-wheeled vehicles shared the road with a few small trucks and trikes, both canopied and not. Empty strips of land bordered the edges of the road.

"What are those shiny lines?" Abby gestured toward the gleaming strands peeking through the road surface.

"Those are the, ah, let's say, 'guidance channels' for when someone drives a wreckless," Dali replied, pointing to one of the small vehicles.

"What are 'guidance channels'? And are they reckless a lot?"

Dali listened to her watch for a moment before replying.

"Are you familiar with trolleys that run on tracks in the road?"

"Yes. I've seen pictures, anyway."

"These wires guide our wrecklesses – oh, you call them autos or cars, right? – like trolleys on tracks, or maybe like train tracks. Those wires … monitor all the cars in the area and prevent collisions, running off the road, or going too fast. Drivers see a display panel of all the necessary information."

That was some kind of cruise control, Abby thought.

"Our cars are gyroscopically stable, expandable, have air-pressure bumpers all around, and can be powered from several sources, including recycled, ahh … plastics. Not the same plastics as from your time, though." Dali's watch whispered a short list of features.

"They're expandable? How?"

"We make them bigger or smaller by sliding out panels and beams. Most of them hold two to six people, or the same amount of … what do you call it … stuff."

Abby smiled to hear such slang coming from Dali.

Tall trees blocked a large, unusual building from Abby's view until they pedaled almost right up to it. It presided over the large gardens that surrounded it, much the way small-town courthouses reigned over their town squares. This, too, looked to be in the center of town – but this building didn't look like any courthouse she'd ever seen. It had more sides and an arched roof, and, astonishingly, reflected the sky all the way to its base.

"Turn counterclockwise at the House of Worship, then right again onto School Street," Dali instructed, pointing past the building.

Abby looked around while she pedaled down School Street, with its indecipherable sign. The traffic was light, and the cars very small compared to her world. She saw several buildings that looked like businesses, but didn't see what they were selling.

"The Dependencies," Dali said, pointing to them.

"The what?" Abby said.

"Oh, sorry. Hospital, medical clinic, university, traveler's hospice, orphans' facility, home for the elderly, and such."**[32]**

"All in one building?"

Dali smiled. "Well, in small towns like ours, some are combined and some are even shared between towns. And see that separate building with the big windows pointing northeast? The Local House of Justice and Lodlan's town council have offices there. They often meet together to discuss local issues."

"Where do you work? Where are we going?"

"I work at a school – in the library and sometimes the office. See up ahead? With the student artwork?" Dali pointed down the street to the right, at a building festooned with colorful murals. Abby told Dali she was impressed with the quality of the art – landscapes, fantasies, and what looked like favorite teachers and important events.

"I'm glad you like it. The students repaint sections once in a while. It is always something interesting, uplifting."

"Don't you worry about graffiti?"

Dali consulted her watch again. This time, it didn't help her.

"Would you please explain who are graffiti?"

"Not who – what. Like, someone paints their name real big all over the artwork, or a big moustache on the face of one of the people. You know, graffiti. To be mean or flashy or they just don't care."

"People do this in your time?"

"Uh, yeah." Abby had a hard time not sounding like a Valley Girl, and nearly added "duh!" to it. *Do they do graffiti in 2007? Is rain wet?*

"No one would think to do such a thing now. It is an outrageous idea and would cause a great deal of hurt."

"Yeah, it does."

A local artist in Surely had painted a fabulous landscape on a store wall, Abby remembered. Within a month, it was defaced by graffiti. As soon as they saw the artist start painting, everyone knew what would happen. Its predictability didn't make it any more welcome.

Dali directed Abby to the bike rack, which held two other bikes. They coasted smoothly to the rack, and Dali dismounted, then Abby.

"School starts this week. I choose to work five half-days a week. I use Thursdays for long personal projects, or for something fun. Friday, yesterday, was our primary day of rest. We learned, partly from your time, what too much work and no play can do." Dali smiled gently.

"But don't you need the money?" Abby's father had once said that people worked to pay for houses, furniture, cars, clothes, food, utilities, health care, college, vacations, and on and on.

Dali consulted her watch as she parked the bike, got her bag from the rear baskets, and headed toward the door. She didn't lock the bike, Abby noticed, nor were the others locked. It would be cool not to worry about everything getting stolen all the time!

"And what *is* that watch?" Abby finally blurted.

"Watch? For what?"

"No, your watch."

"I need to watch?"

They both stopped, realizing they were speaking from two very different worlds. Abby knew from her experience with Jenn that the best solution was to wait. Dali pulled open one of the doors, turned into the room to the right, pressed her finger to an electronic pad, and greeted the other office workers. They walked back out into the hallway and headed down the second corridor to the right.

The watch whispered.

"Oh, you think this is a wristwatch?" Dali finally said, relief flooding her face.

"Isn't it?"

"Well, it does tell me the time, but it is soooo much more than a mere timepiece," Dali said with conviction. The girls walked as Dali listened to the watch. "We call them yuters."

"*What?* Uterus?" It felt obscene to even say it.

"Just a yuter." Dali carefully repeated it for Abby. "*YOU-ter.* Originally, it meant the Old American word *computer*. Now, it delivers almost all our knowledge in this world, so I think it is fitting that it also sounds – as you said – like the old word *uterus*." Smiling, Dali checked to see if Abby was still with her, mentally and physically.

She was, but just barely. "Go on," Abby said.

"Your computers had internet, e-mail, games, pictures, documents, dictionaries, calculators, and so on, right?"

"Yeah," Abby replied, momentarily and unhappily reminded of some computer pictures she didn't want to see.

"Imagine a computer that can do much, *much* more ... and fits on your wrist. Of course, the bigger yuters serve groups and buildings, but this model – the Wristlet Anagojal Esthezic Recoursive Yuter, or WaerY – this wrist-yuter serves individuals."

"Oh." Abby thought about this while repeating the strange words to herself: *an-ah-GO-jell ess-THEEZ-ic ree-CORE-sive.* "So when your *WARE-ee* whispers, it's ..."

"Answering my questions, mainly from a global database."

"How do you ask it?"

"Out loud. Or mentally. I can ask it something in my mind and it can understand, and it looks it up and answers back in my mind. But I prefer to speak out loud with it, especially when I need to clearly hear how to pronounce some of your words."

"Wow, cool!"

"Is it too chilly for you in here?"

"No, cool means it's really neat ... um ..." all the words Abby could think of to define 'cool' were just as unhelpful as the original. Groovy, neat, boss, hot, tight, sweet, phat, rad ... what a strange thing, not to be able to define this basic concept. "It means I like it a lot."

The watch whispered again and Dali said, "In UL we say bonega."

"*Boe-NAY-gah?* Your watch told you that?"

"It told me what you were trying to say."

"Man, that would be handy! Does everyone have one?"

"Almost everyone. But they are not free, and some people who are very poor cannot afford one."

"You have poor people?"

"Yes, differences in material wealth mean we look out for whoever needs help – that is our trust."**[33]**

"Of course," Abby echoed, clueless.

"My work," Dali announced, turning and pushing through swinging wooden doors into what appeared to be the library.

Chapter 15 Library

"Anyway, we are careful to live so as not to need lots of money," Dali said, putting her bag into a cabinet. "We also learned this from your time. Wasn't there a saying: 'Don't let your possessions own you'?"

"Yeah, something like that," Abby replied, noticing unusual cubicles housing expensive-looking screens. The plentiful bookshelves looked familiar until she noticed they were made of beautiful, heavy, carved wood. Dali led her across high-quality, clean carpet and past comfortable upholstered furniture. All the framed artwork on the walls gave the library – and the school – an upscale, inviting appearance. Abby wondered whether kids were still kids here. Didn't some juvie ever wreck stuff, pull the fire alarm, steal the paintings?

"What age of kids go here?" Abby asked haltingly.

"This is a regular secondary school, so about 11 to 15 in normal studies," Dali said, looking at color-coded notes in a work room. "Higher-level studies are at another school. While I gather presentation and discussion materials for the teachers, would you like to look at the library displays, or would you prefer to spend some time on a yuter?"

"Um ... which is the best one to see what this world is like?"

"The yuter," Dali said firmly. "You could start with Local Events."

Dali led Abby to a cubicle and invited her to sit in an ordinary-looking chair that gradually molded itself to her body. Dali's WaerY whispered constantly, coaching her as she worked with a large, transparent, wire-framed rectangle mounted on the cubicle wall.

"There, that's as good as I can get it," Dali eventually said after pressing and murmuring to the rectangle. "We don't have many people asking for translation into the Old American of the mid-2nd century." Dali smiled gently. "Remember I told you about larger yuters? This screen is part of the school's ALLY, just like I have a household ALLY. The name originally came from the term "ALL-purpose yuter", but it's such a blessing to have this kind of helper that people started calling it *AL-eye* instead of *ALL-ee*.

"Anyway, I've made this as close as I can to your computers, and opened the local shows." Dali showed Abby where and how to touch the screen to command it, then left her to explore Lodlan in 2707.

The first screen showed videos, text, links, two articles, and a TV schedule. So it was still called TV? Oh, maybe not: the words were translated into her antiquated lingo. Abby tried to picture Dali's living room and didn't remember an ALLY screen, despite Dali saying she had one. Maybe people now didn't watch TV like in Abby's time … hometime.

She saw shows on food, gardening, news, drama, and live cameras, but noticed an absence of sports, talk shows, or reality TV. She surveyed listings for Consultation, Games, Homebuilding, Gathering Ideas, Feast Results (what could the result of a feast be? indigestion?), Holy Day Suggestions, Travel Offers, Looking For, BrainBank, and more. Was there a Horse Channel? She saw an animal channel, but not one specifically for horses.

Abby chose Games, and touched its icon. She had not necessarily been expecting Solitaire, but she was surprised to see a video of a recent local celebration. Laughing children and clapping adults played a game that looked like a cross between Musical Chairs and Country Line Dancing. When the music started, the kids stood up and danced almost gracefully between their chairs, retrieved something small from the laughing adults dancing around them, then dodged and spun back to the chairs. When the music stopped, everyone froze, an announcer gave results. Everyone unfroze, laughed and clapped.

It looked like a lot of fun, whatever it was, and no one seemed to lose and leave, either. Abby had always disliked games that eliminated people, mainly because she was not the pushy type, which usually eliminated her early.

The people of the future loved to laugh and have fun, Abby thought. Did away with the Spock-like portrayals, for sure. Not a pointy ear in sight! A whole garden variety of colors, though: eyes, hair, skin. But probably nobody with green blood, Abby joked to herself.

She meant to select Homebuilding, wondering whether it would detail building a house like Dali's or contain clues to a peaceful home life. Instead, she accidentally opened Consultation. A wheel of words rotated and swelled on the screen:

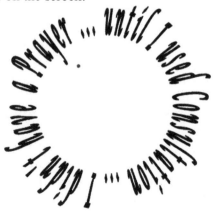

The words circled around and around, then shrank and faded to the growing title:

Next, a gray-haired man appeared, wearing tighter-fitting, more formal-looking clothes than Dali's. He was darker-skinned than Dali, too, and had almond-shaped blue eyes and an appealing humble, loving manner with a pleasant, carrying voice. When he spoke, the translated words didn't match his mouth movements. Abby suspected she was somehow hearing his real voice, though.

"Welcome to Consultation Today. I'm your host, Ling Modderay."

The camera zoomed out to show several people in soft chairs, looking very relaxed, smiling at Mr. Modderay. *His name sounded just like* moderator, *minus the final syllable. Coincidence?*

"Today we have a very promising topic for our consulters to dig into," he said eagerly. "The topic posed is 'My child talks about being unhappy in school, but won't say why. What should I do?'

"So, group, let us get started, then. A child is unhappy in school. Please begin."

All five consulters settled into their chairs, bowed their heads, and closed their eyes. Silence reigned for long moments, surprising Abby; talk-TV in 2007 would never allow such a lull. She was also surprised that the consulters hadn't been introduced. Were they that famous? Or did they just not care about personal fame?

After a short while, the second consulter from the left, a woman, sang a short song. When it was done, again no one moved. Translation was perfect, but Abby hadn't understood several words and, while trying to sort them out, lost others. The bits she did get were "God...above all things, and nothing in the heavens or in the earth but God...Himself the Knower..."**[34]**

The camera did not zoom in, replay, inset smaller shots, use a split-screen, or do anything dramatic at all. It continued to show five consultants, sitting quietly. One of them began humming something, and the others seemed to join in. Then that stopped. One by one, they opened their eyes, but remained quiet until the last one opened his eyes. They all smiled at each other, more relaxed than ever.

"I'm remembering," said the woman on the far right, "that 'Abdu'l-Bahá wrote—"

Abby gasped. She knew who 'Abdu'l-Bahá was! Melissa had told Jon! And Dumbledore's picture in the coffee shop! She'd lost part of what the woman was saying and dragged her focus back to the screen.

"...must give him learning, and at the same time rear him to have a spiritual nature. Let the teacher be a doctor to the character of the child, thus will he heal the spiritual ailments of the children of men."[35] The woman was reading from what could be an ALLY screen. They all seemed to have one. Abby bet the ALLYs had lots of things they could pull up for their consultation.

"It is commendable that the parent is so concerned about sia child. We all agree that the parent is to be commended for caring for sia little one so well?"

The yuter was translating just fine, but Abby was pretty sure she'd heard "see ya" twice from the man second from the right. Must have meant *his*, with some unusual accent.

Everyone murmured agreement. A smaller inset shot appeared, with a man who seemed to be the secretary for the occasion sitting at a kitchen table and showing an attractive painting to the camera.

Wait, that didn't look like a TV studio. It looked like somebody's real home. Abby quickly reviewed her meager understanding of TV production. Didn't they need room for the big cameras, lights, wires, and people? Apparently, they'd figured out how to make it all fit into regular spaces. No wonder they appeared so relaxed.

A woman's voiceover broke in quietly. "If you're viewing this program live, you're welcome to yuter words of support for the back of the painting the consultants will send. Key to episode 864-22. You may also use Key 864-22-PF to yuter us post-program feedback."

The man on the far left spoke.

"One other Writing that may help in this instance is, 'How wonderful will it be if the teachers are faithful, attracted and assured, educated and refined Bahá'ís well-grounded in the science of pedagogy and familiar with child psychology; thus may they train the children with the fragrance of God. In the scheme of human life the teacher and his system of teaching plays the most important role, carrying with it the heaviest responsibilities and most subtle influences.'

"That was 'Abdu'l-Bahá, quoted in Star of the West, Volume 17, on page 55," he concluded.

The panel sank into silence. Abby almost selected something else, thinking the clip was finished, but then the woman second from the left spoke up.

"Has the parent already consulted with the teachers about sia unhappy child?"

Several others nodded their heads, and one said, "I was thinking the same thing. More fact-finding."

One of the women said, "It may be something simple, if everyone will come together for the good of the child."

"Yes, has the parent consulted with everyone who interacts with the child?" another asked.

"How about checking on how well the child is sleeping? It could be something physical."

"Has sia voiced the reason to a playmate who could be encouraged to share?"

Words flowed so quickly Abby couldn't follow who was talking. She'd thought no one was coming up with any answers. Now, they were happily offering solutions left and right. It again reminded her of the Native American quote about allowing time. Pauses might mean that great realizations were hatching.

The secretary touched spots on an ALLY screen that Abby couldn't quite see. Abby's screen now dwelled half on the secretary's collection of the suggestions and half on the consultants themselves, shifting from one bright, excited face to another.

Silence fell again. Ideas seemed to have run out. Each consultant looked like they were listening to a voice from within. When no one had a new idea, they looked at each other with satisfied expressions.

"The final thought I have," second-from-right man said at last, "is that perhaps the school the child attends is not a good match for sia, and that sia may find happiness in a different school. After all, unhappiness in a school is grounds for transfer."

Abby was amazed. If a kid was unhappy in school, they called a meeting, put it on TV, and talked about automatic transfer?

Every kid she *knew* didn't like school. A lot of them only went because they had to. Some talked about dropping out just as soon as they could. The hard-core cases dabbled in failure by repeatedly skipping school. What did the Lodlan schools do to make things so different?

Chapter 16 Pollution

Watching a few hours of ALLY programs messed with Abby's head. They hinted at a radically different worldview. Few of these shows would have secured broadcast slots in Abby's hometime. Leaning back in her chair, overloaded, she realized the programming was so different because the people were different. It seemed that most people in 2707 were Bahá'ís and had a new set of priorities about what to air. Fortunately, Dali appeared.

"Almost 4 o'clock," she announced. "Almost time to leave."

"Good," Abby said, standing and stretching. "Where do we go now?"

"Well, I was going to a gathering at a neighbor's tonight, but I am thinking I should get you to bed. You must be exhausted."

Abby's only response was her biggest yawn ever.

"I thought so." Dali led the way out the door, flashing her pretty smile again. Abby could get used to making her smile. "Let's get dinner when we pick up your borrowed bike."

Dali chatted with several departing teachers as they all headed outside. She tried to include her guest, but since Abby didn't speak their version of American, she was unable to participate. At least when they reached the bike rack, they doubled up easily and pedaled smoothly back down School Street toward the business district.

Abby caught a better look at the House of Worship as they biked toward it. Each of its many sides featured a large, clear glass door surrounded by glossy, carved wood. The edifice was built of the same earth as most of the local structures, but with additional wooden accents. It looked to Abby like a grand fairy-tale cottage; both welcoming and otherworldly. As they biked nearer, beams of lustrous brown appeared like ribs between sections, reaching to the peak of the building. What had Mother called them? Timber something? Half-timbered, Abby thought; she could almost hear Mother's voice.

Up closer, some of the burnished wood looked like actual branches coated with protective gloss. Surrounding gardens offered glimpses of lush bushes, grassy patches, and bright flowers. The garden had been cleverly planned to show the ripening fruits and tall drying grass clumps to full advantage, even in the August drought. Jutting branches of huge evergreen trees briefly framed a simple stone fountain's cascading water.

The heat brought out the appealing scent of the pine trees that the girls passed. Birds flew and chirped lazily. Several people walked on the garden pathways. Two people sat talking on a bench under a tree.

"What goes on in the House of Worship?" Abby asked.

"Dawn prayers every morning; anyone can go. On workdays, we see many of the Bahá'ís who are elected to governing councils. All the Bahá'í Holy Days are observed here. We use the holy words of every religion. Voices only, no instruments or recordings. You feel ... like ... like the angel choir carries you away." Dali's voice quivered, her eyes shining with tears, remembering.

Abby doubted that listening to prayers and hymns here would be much different from her boring church in Surely, wonderful acoustics or not. But to be polite, she didn't say so.

"Do you see that it has nine sides?" Dali asked as Abby pedaled by.

"I wondered how many."

"Nine is a special number.[36] It is the last number before you have to start reusing the single digits to make higher numbers."

"How did the world come to be Bahá'í? I'd never heard of it before this week."

Dali directed Abby to steer around the House of Worship and turn onto another street, then asked, "What's your religion?"

"Episcopalian."

"Is that Buddhist, Zoroastrian, Hindu ...?"

"Christian."

"Oh, I'm glad I studied the Bible! If you're familiar with the Hebrew Bible, the first half of the Christian Bible, you might remember Moses promising to return as the Messiah?"

"Um, I guess so."

Dali pondered her next words while Abby pedaled.

"And are you familiar with the statements in the Hebrew Bible that Moses Himself was the return of Abraham, in a spiritual sense?"

"Um ... not really, but I've heard of Abraham."

"You may have heard that Jesus said He was the return of Moses?"

"I think so."

"And in the second half of the Christian Bible, your New Testament, did Jesus promise that *He* would return?"

"Yes." Rev. Davison had definitely said that.

"We might notice that these Spokesmen from God came, went away, and returned, in spirit. We might accept that God has always sent Messengers to guide us.[37] Sia changes the *social* teachings each time ... like diet or marriage laws. But the *spiritual* teachings are the same, like the Golden Rule, how to pray, that souls are eternal, the importance of meditating, and such ... even if some of the teachings are less-emphasized in some religions."

"What does 'sia' mean?"

"He or she. His or hers. One or one's. God has no gender, having no body. You would say *He*, though, right?"

"Right." Always so much to think about here. "Go on."

"Well ... I could mention that all religions promise an age of world peace. My favorite Christian promise is in the Lord's Prayer."

Abby could not recall such a promise, so she rushed through the prayer robotically, as usual.

> Our Father, who art in heaven,
> hallowed be thy name.
> Thy kingdom come,
> thy will be done,
> on earth as it is in heaven.
> Give us this day our daily bread.
> And forgive us our trespasses,
> as we forgive those who trespass against us.
> And lead us not into temptation,
> but deliver us from evil.
> For thine is the kingdom, and the power, and the glory,
> for ever and ever. Amen.[38]

Had she missed it? She began again in time with her pedaling, trying to find the promise in the mindless, singsong chant.

Abby had only repeated a few words when Dali said, "It's in 'Thy kingdom come ... on earth as it is in heaven.' Asking God to make Earth like heaven – full of love, peace, joy, and all."

Abby pedaled aggressively, head down and feeling stupid, like she should have known this, but Dali said soothingly, "It's not very obvious, but it's my favorite Christian peace promise. World peace wasn't even possible until about your time, when people – the world – was connected enough. Then, people *had* to learn to get along, yes?"

Abby flashed on 9/11 terrorists, poverty, wars, starvation, pollution, climate change ... so many huge problems needing immediate solutions. "Well, yes, those big issues are going to need everyone's help, sure; but in my own little world" But she battled with Mother ... lost money to thieves at the ranch ... faced a fire some punk had started. She could almost smell the smoke and felt vulnerable and scared. But here in Lodlan everyone got along and things worked nicely. Didn't they? Wasn't she safe here? She frowned as Dali directed her to stop in front of a restaurant.

"Good, here's the spare bike," Dali said, patting a silver bike.

They dismounted, Abby turning troubled eyes to Dali.

"So, does it end? I mean, I guess we didn't actually blow up the world, because here you are, in the future; but ..."

"Please know, it was a close thing," Dali said. "And we are still cleaning up ...er ... toxic waste from your time, and physical and mental illness in the ... gene pool."

"*Mental* illness from toxics? Toxic stuff?"

Dali's WaerY continued to whisper.[39]

"Is there something in your time," Dali ventured as she parked her bike, "about, say, autism increasing?"

"Yeah, there is. Every year I've seen a couple more autistic kids in school. Daddy's radio program talked about it growing."

"Yes, even back then, people connected increasing pollution and worsening health.[40] 'Better living through chemistry,' Americans said starting in the 1930s, but First Nation cultures warned that we should live in harmony with our God-given biology. By your time, poisons were everywhere, changing their genes, affecting their children.[41] And when we don't help our health – like feeding babies formula instead of breastfeeding ... oh, I can really get going."[42]

Dali tried to calm down as Abby trailed her finger thoughtfully along the wrought iron bike rack, remembering that she hadn't been breastfed at all. Did that cause some of her health issues?

"One of the worst effects of all this internal pollution was that many people started ... disconnecting ... from each other emotionally. Autistic or not, many people seemed unable to give or receive love." Dali looked at Abby piercingly as she spoke, seeming to give Abby a message of some kind, but Abby didn't get it.

"Parents," Dali added, "might appear not to love their children."

Comprehension dawned. Abby had long thought that Mother hated Jenn and herself. Dali was saying that pollution cut off Vivian's ability to show love. Maybe Daddy's, too. That explained it! The girls were nurtured physically, sure ... they always had a house, and enough food and clothes – rather nice clothes compared to some. But beyond that, it was criticism and coldness.

Abby didn't know what pollution her mother's family might have. Granny was always catty, starting fights, and had had polio. Mother's father had died of liver failure ... from drinking! Did they pollute the genes they gave to Mother? It was too hard to figure it all out now.

Dali saw Abby's befuddlement and held open the restaurant door.

It looked very much like the coffee shop back in Little Lily. Wood floors, plants, some tables, friendly people. Even large artwork on the walls. After the hostess showed them to their table, Dali translated the menu, which was in UL.

"Steamed veggies on brown rice with your choice of sauce; spinach pizza; falafels; soy loaf and gravy; baked potatoes with different toppings; stir-fry; curried green peas with bread; salad—"

"Are you guys vegetarians?" Abby blurted, then worried she may have been too blunt.

Dali smiled at her comprehension, blinked slowly, and seemed to repeat the WaerY. "In 1907 AD, 800 years ago, 'Abdu'l-Bahá is said to have described the food of the future, saying, 'Medical science is only in its infancy, yet it has shown that our natural diet is that which grows out of the ground.'[43] He also wrote that meat wasn't forbidden and was even needed in certain cases, but that our bodies weren't actually suited for animal products, and it was better to be content with earth-grown foods.[44] Like vegetables, fruits, grains, nuts, and herbs. What you might call *vegan*. So," Dali finished, tilting her head playfully, "what veganish dish would you like to try?"

"Maybe the soy loaf, but I don't have any money."

"I know, and I'll buy," Dali said. "I'm enjoying this a lot, and the food is affordable. You'd also like the mashed potatoes, yes?"

How did Dali always know? Abby had just been feeling like a burden when Dali said she liked hanging out. And Abby *did* want mashed potatoes with her fake meat loaf!

Dali tapped two pictures on the menu and closed it. "We can learn to understand others' inner realities when we try to become like the Master."

She was doing it again! "How? Who's the Master?" Abby asked.

" 'Abdu'l-Bahá."

"Oh, I've heard of him! But I only know that we're supposed to follow his example for how to live and be happy … right?"

"Good for you!" Dali was genuinely pleased. "I like how he could read hearts and intuit people's deepest feelings and needs. [45]

"Oh, like you've done about five times so far today."

Dali laughed with Abby, long and delightedly.

"Well, I use my WaerY and lots of spiritual guidance."[46]

"Yeah, I should be able to do that in about 700 years," Abby grinned as the server brought their food. "Why do you call him 'the Master'? It sounds kind of like, uh, like a dictator … or a slave-owner."

Dali seemed taken aback as she listened to her WaerY.

"Oh no, not like that," Dali answered, toying with the concept. "I agree, that would be terrible. No, it's more like when you say a person gets a Master's degree, or how a master key opens all doors. It's because 'Abdu'l-Bahá had a masterly understanding of his Father's teachings. He fully mastered the skill – the *art* – of living the Bahá'í life. That's why we should try to be like him. Oh, and, actually, Bahá'u'lláh Himself called His teen-aged son 'the Master.'"[47]

"Hmmm," Abby murmured around a mouthful of food. The soy loaf tasted almost like Mother's, but less greasy. The vegetable gravy was great. Abby peered near a small rack of seasonings, looking for something to put on the potatoes.

"We have butter-like vegetable spreads," Dali said. "They're good. I'll get you some." Smiling, Dali signaled the server, who came back with a small bowl. "There's your, erm, *vutter* to go with your deep-dish questions."

Abby replied with a wide grin. She was catching on to Dali's quick, dry sense of humor.

"Which question were we on?" Abby tossed out.

"Originally? The one about how the world got to be Bahá'í."

"Still?"

"We'd just got started." Dali shook soy sauce on her stir-fry.

"If you say so." Abby listened as she ate.

"Each of the special Prophets promised that Sia – er, They would return and bring peace to earth. But since They had passed away centuries previously, how could Their decayed bodies return? They couldn't. It was a spiritual return, not a physical one."

Abby paused mid-bite. She realized she had always imagined Jesus physically floating up from the earth into the clouds, and that He was still there, watching, biding His time until He returned. But that wasn't very logical, even accounting for miracles. People in Jesus's time thought that heaven was an actual place above the clouds and that He'd gone there. But science showed that heaven is not in outer space.

If Jesus's ascension was spiritual and not physical, though, that explained it, Abby thought. *His soul went with everyone else's soul, to someplace we can't see with our physical eyes – a sort of invisible, parallel universe you can only see spiritually, somehow.*

Dali chose a snow pea with her chopsticks as Abby's mind worked.

"This might be the first time you have considered that science and religion can be – are – in harmony," Dali ventured, and Abby nodded. "Let me know if it gets too much," Dali added gently. Mouth full, Abby gestured with her spoon; the biking and the meal were reviving her.

Dali continued, "God has promised to keep sending us these special Messengers, like authors of a book that's still being written."

Abby was pleased to finally understand a spiritual metaphor.

"In the Year One BE – 1844 AD," Dali explained, "finally the age of world unity was born. By the time Bahá'u'lláh had outlined how to achieve unity, then peace,[48] He had been attacked many times; the same treatment almost all the Blessed Founders of the world religions have endured. But He and His son, 'Abdu'l-Bahá, both lived into old age and left many Writings to guide us.

"After people tried everything else, sia saw the need for morals and religion, and looked for one that covered modern issues. Bahá'u'lláh's principles are so broadly accepted by people of any and no faith, it drew them together. The Bahá'í principles are such a useful blend of practical and mystical."

"Yeah? Like what?" Abby asked, finishing her savory meal.

"Educating all children ... whether sia want to go or not." Dali grinned quickly at Abby, who mustered a smile around her fork. "Having a secondary language that everyone in the world can speak. Treating men and women fairly. Eliminating prejudices, and also the extremes of wealth and poverty. Our world government helps the nations solve differences and work together on world issues – like your United States government involves the states."[49]

Dali seemed to be gaining new insights into her own faith as she spoke; her face glowed with the excitement of discovery and sharing.

"Spiritual values are the real basis of getting along, though. And we all learn them early. Those, and spiritual consultation, stop corruption, greed, laziness, and so on."

"And who started this faith?" The name was so different, Abby hadn't memorized it yet.

"Bahá'u'lláh. It's Arabic for *Glory of God*. He fulfilled the promises of the Other Spokesmen: He brought God's teachings for the Golden Age of World Peace, which you're now ... visiting."

"No way!"

Dali listened to her WaerY, then beamed. "Way!"

Abby was too stunned to smile back. Questions banged into each other and exploded before she could give voice to any. Dali's face fell as she spoke.

"I'm afraid I may have gotten carried away. I'm sorry. I'll be quiet now." Meal over, Dali led the way out of the restaurant.

They mounted their bikes and pedaled home in near-silence and near-dark. Overloaded, Abby simply enjoyed the cool, noticing the bike's clear tube now glowing, mirroring the fireflies also beginning to glimmer. Crickets started to chirrup, soothingly singing one unsettled soul homeward.

Chapter 17 Dream

Dali made up a bed on the sofa, gave Abby some PJs and showed her how to press a button on a teardrop-shaped device pointed into her mouth to clean her teeth. As Abby drifted off, exhausted by all the new ideas, she heard Dali murmuring in her room. Soon deeply asleep, she dreamed Dali was calling Mother ...

∞   ∞   ∞   ∞   ∞   ∞   ∞   ∞

... telling her how to get to the earthen house ... 'Prank call!' Vivian sneers, hangs up ... **ZZP** *... in a courtyard, boys climb down from a tree-house ... younger kids wait for wisdom below ... some of them file chaotically into a classroom-amphitheater with chairs parked on cement tiers ... class stops while everyone discusses seating ... some kids say they can't concentrate ... Abby climbs up the tiers to stand near the complaining kids and, surprised, hears distracting noises from two directions ... realizes the noises are inaudible in other parts of the room ... explains this to the teachers, who encourage the kids to move ... watches the kids yammer and shove chairs ... wonders why the teachers calmly ignore the noise and lack of learning ... and lo, the kids make order out of chaos ... amiably find new seats ... shuffle their belongings ... quiet down and focus on a teacher who resumes the lesson. Teaching took second place to consulting and honoring others' needs ... must be a dream ... would never happen in real life ... Abby walks out ...* **ZZP** *... under the tree again ... the boys, grown into men, come down again from the treehouse with a problem ... head off in different directions ... several of them head into a meeting room ... beckon Abby to come with them ... say they need to* clarify *(whatever that means) ... a loose-ranging discussion on an unexplained issue ... a newborn baby? a fellow student? an elder? ... she cannot hear a word, and yet ... they all show potent abilities to discover truth and inner realities just by focusing ... they are confident ... determined ... beautiful ... spiritual lightning rods channeling divine energies into divinely-inspired suggestions ... the group finds an agreeable solution ... pledges to implement it ... streams out the door to undertake their mission ...* **ZZP** *... though Abby knows no details, she soars with the feeling of working together ... honoring each other... seeking the best, the brightest way ...*

∞   ∞   ∞   ∞   ∞   ∞   ∞   ∞

Abby resisted waking from the buoyancy of her dream. She'd been one of these ideal humans for just a while, even if only in her head, and she wanted to hang on to it. This new way of being touched her deeply, awake or asleep.

If only she could be like those mature, capable, relaxed kids – so real just a moment ago. She envied their confidence, their powerful oratory, made more impressive by their young age. Was there any hope that she could have their advanced perception, or was she building more castles in the air, as Mother accused her of so often?

Abby's eyes flew open. Dreams *can* come true! Parelli promised it with horses and Angie had shown it! 'Abdu'l-Bahá *wanted* us to be like him: a superbly perceptive, balanced person ... and Dali had such powerful, usable intuition!

Abby clung to the last bits of dream-feeling, yearning to keep those spiritual capabilities. Speaking truth, honoring basic needs instead of suffering over the task at hand, working out problems together, being open to heavenly guidance ... it was all beyond her now, but maybe she could copy their tone of voice, or actions. She smiled. "Fake it till you feel it," the saying went. She might see more inroads after she'd imitated them for a while. She moaned softly with longing, imagining being able to solve difficult problems easily and happily, like on *Consultation Today*. To find hidden truths within people's hearts, for good purposes only, of course.

Living like that might show her how to understand the high-level abilities and ideas Dali had described with such delight last night.

She chortled, thinking of video games where the quest made you hunt down keys and find information to rack up points. She'd never wanted to play a video game like she now wanted to play this spiritual adventure. If only she could figure out *how* to unearth the clues and learn the powerful abilities she wanted so badly!

Where to start? She pondered, and, unexpectedly, her beaded bookmark popped into her mind. It brought back the memory of that gift, unknown and lying in wait for her. "Maybe if there's one, there's more," she speculated. Maybe she could look for hints and grab onto them ... maybe ideas that Dali or the yuter offered.

Studying the ceiling glowing with the soft morning light, Abby reminded herself that there would be missteps, resistance from her family, and missed opportunities, because that was life. But if she kept at it, kept up her *try*, she should eventually make some progress.

Pleased with her plan, she sat up. Today was Sunday. Dali had to work again. Abby's agenda was to rack up real-life, hidden assets and enjoy the age awaited by everyone for thousands of years: Peace On Earth. She wondered if lions actually did lie down with the lambs, as she'd heard they would when heaven came to earth. If they did, maybe she would see it when she went to the animal show.[50]

Chapter 18 Service

"Good morning!" Dali chirped at Abby, who sat on the couch, not knowing how to start the day. "Oh, you can put on the same clothes as yesterday," Dali answered Abby's unspoken question. "The clothes, erm, refresh themselves overnight."

At breakfast, the only cereal on offer was whole-grain with non-dairy milk ... different but acceptable-tasting.

"We have a few hours before my work today," Dali said as they cleared the simple breakfast. "Want to go with me again or stay home?"

"Uh, well," Abby stammered, afraid of offending her hostess by treading on possibly dangerous territory, "I, mmm ... wouldn't know what to do all by myself in your house. Could, I mean, would it be okay ... if I go with you? Yesterday was, er, nice?" Abby glanced at Dali, not sure if this had offended her as it likely would have triggered Mother, but Dali began to wash their breakfast settings.

"You'd be very welcome to come and spend more time on the school ALLY," she said cheerfully. "Care to rinse these?"

"You have to wash your dishes by hand? Don't machines do everything for you?" Abby asked, rinsing soap off a bowl. Depictions of the future usually showed people doing the least work possible.

"Simpler is usually better. Machines cost, and not just to buy them. Besides, it's just me here, and it's not many dishes." Dali's mouth twitched. Was she trying not to laugh? "I am sorry, but your fantasy is a little unrealistic," Dali chuckled.

"Well, it's not wrong to want a break from too much work, is it?" Abby defended the fantasy, a little miffed.

"Yes, too much work is bad. Or unhealthy or demeaning work," Dali was amused as she soaped the spoons. "But your fantasy would have to end with overweight, out-of-shape – what do you call them? uh, potatoes people? Moderate work gives us skills, and perseverance. Myself, I have great meditations ... realizations ... during these mindless little tasks."

"I suppose," Abby grumbled, rinsing the spoons and laying them to dry on an absorbent pad. It was just hard to have all your basic assumptions wiped out overnight. Or wait, was this wiping part of her new wish? "And it's 'couch potatoes.' " Abby peered at Dali through her hair, wondering too late if this was too forward.[51] But Dali was more like Jenn than Mother, and replied without irritation as she finished tidying the kitchen.

"Oh. Thank you! So, we could garden, walk up the hill ... oh!

Today is a Public Service Day!"

"Can I do that, too?"

"Yes, of course. Let me just check something." Dali approached a large framed photograph of a sunset in a corner of the living room. Abby finally noticed that the picture changed, now to a cluster of colorful flowers, maybe ones Dali had grown.

"Oh, is that is your ALLY?" Abby surmised.

"What? Yes." Distracted, Dali murmured to it, studied what became a yuter display, and touched the screen. "Today's Service is at Mr. Sawqui's house." Another strange name … *SAW-kwee.* "That's good, it's close to the school, for my work afterward. Let's take our lunch and water, and ride the bikes," Dali planned aloud. "Oh, and tonight after work, some of my friends are getting together at The Draggin' Dragon. If only you could understand them … ah! Yes! That could work!"

Dali scurried into the bedroom, where Abby heard her rummaging.

Wanting to be helpful, Abby searched the kitchen for portable food, discovering helpful pictures on most packages and cans. She saw a small can of bean salad. Were there crackers? And throwaway utensils? Though they probably would not be actual plastic. Or would they need to pack the metal spoons and then bring them home? She contemplated the innards of the silverware drawer.

"Oh, balela!" Dali agreed with Abby's choice of food and fetched crackers from a wall cabinet. "Yes, we have recyclable utensils. They're in the back." Dali groped behind the metal utensils.

Abby put two small cans, two spoons and several napkins into the plastic bag Dali held out. Actually, it felt like a mix of plastic and fabric.[52]

"It's sure to be hot today." Dali added bottles of juice and water to the lunch bag and brought spare clothes for both of them. "By the time we're done biking and working at the Service Day, the clothes will be sweaty and dirty. Refreshing takes overnight, and it takes us to not be in them." She tipped her head in her quizzical way, seeing if Abby caught the small joke. Abby smiled back.

Picking up their bags, they left the house and found their bikes heating up in the mounting Lodlan sun.

Biking down the country road, Dali's song sounded like yesterday's tune. Abby asked her about it when she finished singing.

"A Traveling Prayer," Dali said, obviously glad Abby had asked. "We learn a lot of song-prayers when we're children. Then we spend the rest of our lives figuring out how to live them." She chortled, chin high and hair blowing. "I wonder if we're still using some of the same tunes from your time. Shall I sing it again? In your Old American?"

"Sure," said Abby.

Dali began to sing with the WaerY ...

♫I have risen this morning
by Thy grace, O my God,
and left my home trusting wholly in Thee,
and committing myself to Thy care.
Send down, then, upon me,
out of the heaven of Thy mercy,
a blessing from Thy side,
and enable me to return home in safety
even as Thou didst enable me to set out
under Thy protection with my thoughts
fixed steadfastly upon Thee.
There is none other God but Thee,
the One, the Incomparable,
the All-Knowing, the All-Wise.♫ [53]

It was a quick tune and the girls both pedaled in time to it, Abby's mood lifting too, noticing how different it felt to pray for little things, not just for the big formal times inside churches.

"What are some of the other things you have prayers for?" Abby asked as they approached the edge of town. She sensed a trace of something to investigate.

"Oh, my!" Dali rattled off. "For help, healing, families, children and youth, safety, spiritual insight, unity, Divine Guidance, meetings, detachment from everything *except* God, praise *to* God, Holy Days, the obligatory prayers—"

"The what?"

"The Bahá'í obligatory prayers. To say one of three special prayers every day, plus any other prayers we want. And a ... special verse."

"Really? Outside church, I only say a prayer to bless the food."

Dali fell quiet as she biked steadily, perhaps thinking how best to answer. Abby remembered the quote from her *Native American Wisdom* book about not pressing for a response. Now it didn't seem boring at all, but helpful to everyone. Less frantic. Ricky's train of thought was sidetracked by badgering and interrupting. Getting uptight just cut off the Divine. Oooohh, this was a solid clue on how to stay in the spiritual, insightful mode!

Dali slowed to stay even with Abby, who lagged a little on the uphill slopes, muscles protesting the unusual exercise, rising heat burnishing her bare face and hands.

"Did you ever have a time when you wished you were more clear about something? Or needed to stand firm? Ever had to handle something really difficult?"

"Well ... yes." Abby was a little embarrassed to admit it.

"We all have," Dali hastened to say encouragingly as they passed the first houses at the edge of Lodlan. "The Bahá'í teachings offer guidance on how to think, and believe, and live. So we read from the Bahá'í Writings every morning and evening. That, with praying and meditating, leads us to become ... centered. Strong inside."

"Centered," Abby repeated. It sounded and felt like a watchword she could use – a mini-motto. She thought she could figure out how to pray without being in church, though meditating seemed completely foreign. "What should we pray and meditate *about*?"

"Great question," Dali replied warmly, "and many correct answers. Maybe pray to handle a difficulty you face. Or meditate on something you wish you were better at. People can meditate on some virtue sia think sia need. I like to ponder signs God might be giving me, and see if I can guess what my current test is ... and why I'm getting it. These days, I meditate on: 'God hath never burdened any soul beyond its power.' "[54] Dali waved at townspeople as Abby wrestled with these new thoughts.

The words made sense, but she felt the concepts slipping out of her mind as quickly as she heard them, try as she might to collect them. Wryly, she thought of TV shows that said "Don't try this at home," and wished Rev. Davison had urged her with, "*Do* try this at home." Grace at meals didn't seem to count; like the Lord's Prayer, it felt like just rattling off empty words.

"What do you mean, 'tests'? Not tests on paper, like in school ..."

"God sends us tests, challenges, hurdles, whatever word you like. They make us grow. Oh, here we are!"

They came upon the run-down house Abby had seen the previous morning. Other volunteers arrived on foot, by bike, and in the little cars, greeting each other and heading to the side yard.

As they parked their bikes at the curb, Dali held out her hand and told Abby to put it in her ear. Abby's old world mind heard "stick it in your ear." She stared at Dali, taken aback by the rudeness, but saw only the usual sisterly expression.

Dali repeated herself, showed Abby a tiny, nearly transparent bud, and helped Abby insert it in her ear. It hovered, unfelt, in – but not touching – her ear canal. Dali tested the ear-yuter, speaking New American, then UL. The earbud translated Dali into Old American in one ear, while Abby saw and heard something rather different come out of Dali's mouth.

The lips and voice finally matched when Dali ended the test by saying, in Old American, " 'Let us encourage each other, and set all in motion.' "[55] Abby threw her a thumbs-up, and Dali replied with the soul-happy smile Abby had grown so fond of.

"This is an AerY" – Dali pronounced it *AIR-ee* – "the Audile Essential Reference Yuter. I've set it to only translate into Old American, so you'll understand everyone but won't have to learn any of the other commands. Even though it's the standard one we were issued in first grade, it should still work. When I got a WaerY, I just stashed it away and didn't think about it."

"Oh. How come you learned to speak, um, Old American?"

"In language class I chose Old American because it's one of my heritages. But now I think God wanted me to, so I could speak with you! The yuter helped me at first, because I was out of practice. But now Old American feels very natural."

It blew Abby's mind to think that God had prepared Dali for her. Unlike the remote God she was used to, this God was all around you, at your fingertips, even inside you. *Living with a constant connection to a God like that would make me pay more attention to what I do*, Abby mused, following Dali up the walkway to the sign-up table. Was this what Rev. Davison meant when he spoke about living as if Jesus might come back and see everything you did?

Only, Rev. Davison's vision felt different from the new one. Back home, Mother and the church overrode Abby's voice, ignoring her merit, her very person. The view here was….loving. Here, her thoughts might actually be welcome.

A lively, silent conversation sprang up in Abby's head and she stood near the sign-up table, staring at nothing. In her old world, people might exclude God for fear of punishment for doing – or being – wrong. Here, people seemed to constantly check in with Him … Sia … before, during, and after everything. And they seemed to feel … secure. They must be sure their mistakes would be forgiven. Wow, that would change *everything*. Her mind went blank, trying to imagine life with support instead of criticism, love instead of coldness. Nope, she couldn't picture it. *Should I meditate on this? Am I meditating now? Or do I have to sit cross-legged with candles in a quiet, dark room for it to count?*

Abby looked around the plain yard, concerned she'd been "woolgathering," but she needn't have worried. Since Abby didn't care what job they did, Dali had signed them both up for digging, and was now reading messages on an ALLY screen on the table. The front door of the weathered house opened, and an ancient man emerged.

Abby had never seen anyone this old, though he was no doubt even older than he looked. His gentle eyes peered out from under his snow-white, wooly hair. Two well-used canes and a young man helped him navigate the three steps down into the front yard.

"Mr. Sawqui takes cares of himself and the house, pet-sits, and helps raise several generations of children," Dali explained quietly. A woman set a chair in the shade at the bottom of the steps. Another clapped her hands and called everyone over.

"Thank you so much for coming today for Service," she said. The AerY translated almost as fast as the woman talked. Abby recognized some familiar-sounding words, but was glad for the translation.

"We helped Grandfather repair his house last year, and he says the repairs are lasting quite well." Cheering and clapping greeted the leader's announcement. Abby guessed that some of these workers had helped last year. "This year, we'll help him with his yard. He said he would love to have some roses, if only the kids didn't tear everything up, so we'll start with a strong, decorative fence for flowers, and a bench. We're also going—"

"May I?" Mr. Sawqui interrupted. The woman bowed and helped him stand.

"I'd like to fence in the back yard," he said, kindly but firmly. "The roses will go here, and the bench will sit here," he said, as a sketch of the front yard appeared on the ALLY screen a helper held. "We'll plant the roses in the fall, when the weather cools and rains return."

The crowd nodded and murmured.

"Stakes mark where fence posts go," he continued, pointing to markers in the front yard and on the ALLY. "We need to do both fences first. The cement, wheelbarrows, shovels, and everything else are ready over there." He pointed to the supplies. "Any questions?"

There were none, and Mr. Sawqui sat down as the leader said, "You've each signed up for a task. If you'll gather your supplies, we can get started."

"Hooray for digging!" Dali exclaimed while others cheered. She and Abby picked up shovels and joined the front yard workers. Diggers, post holders, cement mixers and cement pourers discussed their work, sometimes sounding like the consulters on the yuter show.

Surprisingly, someone volunteered to play music. Abby grappled with why she thought that was strange, reasoning that back home, there'd almost certainly be a radio. Live music had the advantage of no commercials, and it would be, well, live! The workers ribbed the musician, asking him if he knew any dirt-digging songs, setting a joking atmosphere.

Dali and Abby took turns shoveling while two other teams dug close by. Abby didn't know any of the songs, but everybody else was humming or singing along to the mandolin-sounding instrument. It was almost fun, at least until the shade vanished.

"Anyone for a spray?" A smiling, middle-aged, bronzed man pointed a sprinkler-headed hose at them, ready to wet down anyone who said the word.

Half the group, including the musician, moved out of the way; the other half stood like scarecrows. Abby stepped up to get sprayed, and her squeals joined the others as a light, cold spray hit their warm bodies.

"Stop, stop, we're making mud!!" one of the ladies shrieked, shoes squishing as she stepped out of the damp dirt. Workers bandied good-natured threats about a mud fight, agreeing on a good one next workday, unless the grass had grown in by then.

Dali and Abby gladly handed over their spot to the two volunteers who stopped in during their morning walk. The girls found a bit of shade by the house and shared one of their bottles of cool water.

"How old is Mr. Sawqui, anyway?" Abby asked.

"Mmmm, you know, I'm not sure. I think I heard he celebrated his 125th birthday about 10 years ago by going on pilgrimage," Dali answered, watching the slender, deeply-lined elder thoroughly enjoying his morning.

"So he's 135? You're joking, right? And where's pilgrimage to?"

"Israel, and I'm not joking. Since we learned so much from your bad example – " Dali nudged Abby with an exaggerated grin to emphasize her polite teasing " – oldens often live to 150.[56] But most choose to live in an olden-aid home after they reach 130.

"Mr. Sawqui's wife passed away a few years ago, but he has a lot of family around here. They gather here, at his house, for dinners and celebrations, and visit him often, not just when they pick up or drop off their little ones. The lady who organized us is Sue Lee Sawqui, his granddaughter."

Amazed, Abby watched the patriarch happily chatting with volunteers who came over to connect with him for a few minutes. She'd be doing well to even draw breath at that age, let alone live in her own house and host a big project! Perhaps because she hadn't grown up close to her grandparents, she felt a great fondness for him, and it seemed others did too, judging by the jovial, nice-sized group that came to help. He was a treasure just by living here, she thought, as she went to mix cement.

By noon, most of the fence posts were in. People breaking for lunch rinsed themselves off using the hose at the front of the house, some turning east and murmuring. Abby tried not to stare, but it was so odd that she couldn't help but peek.

"The Medium Obligatory Prayer," Dali whispered. "One of the three I mentioned; that one is for morning, noon and evening. At the start, we rinse our hands and face with clean water."

"Which one do you say?" Abby whispered back as they fetched their lunch sack and a thin, shiny, blue cloth that they spread on the dirt under a parched tree by the side of the house.

"I usually say the long one before I go to bed. We say that one once a day. You may have heard me saying it last night."

"Why don't you say it silently?"

"Well, we know how powerful words are. So I believe that saying a prayer out loud just increases this power and carries my voice and intentions further."[57]

Thinking about Dali's words, Abby absently brushed Dali's picnic blanket and eventually noticed how soft, even plushy, it felt … not at all the thin, plasticky feel one would expect from looking at it. She fingered an edge and peeked at the underside, noticing that dirt and grass didn't stick to it.

Dali showed her how to pop open the top of her chilled balela and eat it straight out of the can.

"I like this cold," Dali commented, scooping up a spoonful of black beans, celery, small tomatoes and garbanzo beans in flavorful marinade. "It's even better than gazpacho because it's more hearty."

"I've never had anything like this. It's great! How did it get cold when it's so hot today?" Abby wondered.

"I gave it plenty of time to cool down … or do you mean … this spot I pressed before we left the house?" Dali showed her the can's blue cooling spot, and also the red heating spot. Abby dipped her whole-grain crackers into the marinade and savored rich, tasty spoonfuls while watching the other volunteers and half-listening to Mr. Sawqui's socializing.

A young man came over and asked to join them. Abby almost choked, gulping with worry. What should she do? At least she could understand him, thanks to the invisible AerY, but it wouldn't help her know how to speak, or how to act with someone who didn't know … who she was.

"Please, join us," Dali said, arranging the little group into a triangle on the blanket. "Abby, this is Tonba Sayre. Tonba, this is Abby."

"Alláh-u-Abhá, Sister Abby," Tonba said, bowing slightly, kneeling and settling down onto his feet.

Abby didn't know what *ah-LAU-oo-ab-HAW* meant, and the AerY was silent. She nodded, repeated his name – *TONE-bah SAY-er* – and smiled at him.

"How are you? It's very good to see you," Dali said respectfully, formally.

"I'm doing very well, thank you. My walk has been full of beauty lately," Tonba replied. Abby recalled, from her little wisdom book, an Indian describing walking in beauty. An *American* Indian, she mentally corrected herself. Here, everyone had ancestors from all over the world and might have come from anywhere in the world, including the Indian subcontinent ... whatever they called it now.

"I would be pleased to hear whatever you wish to share," Dali said.

"This past Honor, I traveled to the Land of Tá to help celebrate my gee-four parents' 100th anniversary. It was very fitting they were married in Honor, as that virtue was much in evidence during my entire time there. We also made our pilgrimage to the Holy Houses; and I made many supplications for the health and welfare of my family and friends, including yourself."

The AerY was working just fine, but Abby still didn't understand half of what Tonba was saying. She looked to Dali and was alarmed to see her mentor paralyzed with emotion, teardrops tracing paths down her face.

Dali took Tonba's hand in both her own. Tonba also struggled to contain his emotions, and Abby felt completely left out of whatever important event was transpiring. When the tricky moment had passed, Dali patted his hand, let it go, and whispered with some emotion, "I'm sure you felt aweful."

It might have been a lot of things, but *awful* was not what Abby would have guessed about Tonba's pilgrimage ... and wasn't that supposed to be in Israel, not Tá?

She was completely confused, and gave up trying to understand. Feeling strange about it, she surreptitiously rubbed her too-white sneakers in the bare dirt, trying to cover as much of the white as she could without taking them off. With Dali and Tonba still deeply engrossed in a baffling conversation, she fiddled absently with the nearly-empty lunch can, pulling at a loose corner of the label to see how it was fastened.

Suddenly, the can was a limp, wet film in her hand. The last bits of marinade and beans spilled onto her pants and the blanket. She yelped and scooted back. Dali and Tonba jumped too, not knowing what was wrong. Dali saw the dripping label in Abby's hand and laughed.

"Never mind, Abby, no real damage done. We'll just shake out the cloth. It's time to go anyway."

They all got up, Abby wiping her pants clean, surprisingly, with a napkin. Turning to Tonba, Dali bowed to him as he had to her, and said, "I will carry with gladness the blessing you have brought me."

He bowed back and replied, "The gladness is mine. I will look forward to telling you more if the time becomes convenient."

They wished each other *god-BEE*. which the AerY translated as "goodbye."[58] Dali turned to Abby.

"I'm so sorry you were left out. I'll explain now.

"The Bahá'í calendar has 19 months, with Arabic names. Last winter, in the month of S͟haraf, or *honor*, Tonba went to the Land of Tá – to Tihrán, the capital of what you call Iran – for his great-great-great-grandparents' 100th wedding anniversary.[59] And it was all very honorable … er, full of honor for them and everyone."

Abby nodded her understanding, and for Dali to continue.

"Bahá'u'lláh was born and reared in Tihrán, but He was exiled to Bag͟hdád, the capital of what you call Iraq. His house in Bag͟hdád, and the House of the Báb in Shiraz, are both holy places of pilgrimage for Bahá'ís.[60] In your time, Iraq was a country of great turmoil, yes?"

"Oh yes, it's a real garbage pit right now … oh, I mean …" Abby was embarrassed at her bluntness. This was not how the eloquent young men in this morning's dream had created cohesion and insight, but the Iraq and Afghanistan wars were the hottest topic on Daddy's talk-shows. Men in Surely sometimes spit on the ground – or worse – when Iraq was mentioned.

"Tonba's heritage is Middle Eastern, American Indian and, er, subcontinental Indian. Some of my family were neighbors with his family years ago. His sisters live here, so I see him once in a while. He's such a noble spirit, almost like the brother I wish I'd had. But we're all 40th cousins anyway," she ended lightly.

"And the can?"

"Yes, the can. Once the lid is off, if you press this other spot here," she demonstrated with her own can, "and pull the ripcord on the label, it pre-decomposes. I forgot to tell you to watch out for that."

"And what did he say when he greeted me?"

"Hm … Yuter, please repeat Tonba's greeting."

"*Alláh-u-Abhá,* Sister Abby."

"Right. Bahá'ís say this as a greeting – 'God is All-Glorious.' I like to remember the similar phrase, *Alláh-u-Akbar* – God is Greatest – in the Islamic call to prayer, and think about how the Bahá'í Faith was born in an Islamic country, as Christianity arose in a Jewish environment. "

"And he said his time was awful?"

"Yes, he did."

"But he'd been saying it was so honorable, and then it was awful?"

Dali stared at her, then asked her WaerY, "Yuter, can you answer?" A voice spoke softly in Abby's ear and from Dali's wrist, "One: A-W-E-F-U-L, AWE-ful: full of awe; a reaction to something awesome. Two: A-W-F-U-L, AW-ful: full of distress; a reaction to something very unpleasant."[61]

"Homophones!" Dali exclaimed cheerfully. "Words that are spelled differently and mean something different, but sound the same. Well, that clears *that* up."

As lunch break ended, some volunteers left, bidding the workers who stayed a heartfelt "Godbee." Abby followed Dali to their bikes, pausing at the simple shade canopy Mr. Sawqui's family had erected in the front yard for him and the workers, and under which Tonba performed a cultural dance with colorful hoops. The solemn, respectful group handed him the hoops as he reached for them.[62]

Perhaps because he danced intently to the Native American drumbeat and chanting the musician and his WaerY provided, Tonba didn't grace the audience with his eloquence. Instead, the dance and the beautiful hoops – streaked with black, red, white, yellow and brown on a white background – spoke for him. As Tonba gathered hoops, hopping on one foot or the other, spinning and twirling the hoops faster, the colors blended into a pleasant tan, almost exactly matching him, Dali and the other mixed-race onlookers.

"It's his famous Racial Unity in Diversity dance," Dali said as she tugged Abby away. "If you want to see all of it, with his narration, we can pull it up on the Yuter when we get to my work today." The girls loaded their picnic gear, mounted their bikes and began pedaling toward the school.

"I liked it, thanks for taking me!" Abby exclaimed. "And thanks for the AerY!"

"You're welcome. I just love when I can receive divine inspiration *when* I need it instead of *after* I need it," Dali remarked.

At school, Dali led Abby to the staff bathroom to clean up and change.

"Oh, before I forget," Dali said from her changing room, "Tomorrow afternoon is a performance of the animals. I reserved two seats for us."

"Sounds great! Wow, I could really get used to life here!"

"And I could get used to having a little sister to boss around," Dali answered with tender affection. Abby was too grateful for Dali's overwhelming care to say anything, but she assumed Dali could divine her feelings.

Chapter 19 Creation

"See that white blower thing on the wall of your changing room?" Dali asked. "Blow it on yourself. Before you put your spare clothes on."

Abby lifted down the cordless blow dryer and pointed it at herself. Nothing happened. "How do I ... does it turn on?"

"Ah, yes, press the green dot on the handle. You'll know it's on if you feel it."

Abby pushed the dot. Wherever she pointed it, she felt cleansed, refreshed. It created the most wonderful feeling of a silent wind or invisible shower carrying away the dirt and sweat, stimulating her skin and the spirit inside that skin.

Dali interjected, "You know, I just figured out something."

"What?" Abby replied, relishing the sensations the blower created as it cleaned the back of her sweaty neck.

"You know how we got confused over 'full of awe' and 'terrible' when Tonba was talking? Telling homophones apart? I was just remembering when you asked me about wrecklesses. I meant wreckless with a 'w,' because they don't wreck, and you thought I said reckless without a 'w,' meaning dangerously!"

"Yup, I did! Thanks for clearing that up!"

"The Yuter told me."

"Thanks, Yuter!"

Finished with her cleansing, Abby pressed the blower's red OFF dot, hung it back up, and got dressed. She rolled up her dirty clothes and brought the blower out to Dali.

"Did you like the Cleansing Wind? The staff bathroom is pleasant, isn't it?" Dali asked, hanging the device back up in Abby's changing room. The bathroom was astonishingly clean, with fragrant soap in decorative containers, low carpeting and plush chairs in a lounge area, and fresh wildflowers ... a stark contrast to the grungy, graffitied school bathrooms Abby was used to.

"Schools have top priority for money, of course," Dali said gently. "Children are the most important."

This was so opposite her usual invisible, third-class-citizen status that she felt something both break and bloom inside her. That was how it *should* be, she knew down deep. But would it take 700 years before children would be provided with what they *really* needed?

Dali saw the emotions tangling in her, and waited patiently.

Abby worked through it and was finally able to look into Dali's pretty brown eyes, noticing for the first time that Dali wore little if any makeup. She realized with surprise that, although Dali did not primp like the old world supermodels, she seemed beautiful with a radiance that came from her heart and showed in her face. *So the more spiritual you got, the prettier you got? Was this another clue?*

"Ready? Good. I thought you could either ... how do you say? ... cruise the Yuter again, or I could find some crafts."

"Browse or build, hmmm? Surf or shape?" Abby surprised herself by suggesting better wording without giving in to Mother's faint voice in her head automatically criticizing the less-than-perfect phrasing. "Maybe some of both?" she ventured, momentarily reminding herself of the kids in her dream.

"Excellent!" Dali clapped. "Let me get you started on the Yuter, and then I'll get some crafts."

Dali led her to the same table as the day before and started the ALLY.

"What should I look up today?" Abby asked.

"I think you might enjoy Auntie Zoray," Dali opined. "She's funny; I always laugh."

"Who's Auntie *ZOR-ray*? Never mind. Whatever you think," Abby said. She trusted Dali with her life, so letting her pick the computer programs was a no-brainer.

Dali pulled up a page touting "Auntie Zoray" in big, zany letters across the top. A realistic cartoon of a Middle-Eastern-looking woman peeked out of the 'o' in Zoray, showing a brightly patterned shirt and coordinating head scarf, shiny black hair, big hoop earrings, and a welcoming white smile. She waved from under the 'r' next to her head, her fingers and wrist clanking with rings and bracelets. It was hard not to smile just looking at her, so Abby smiled back, feeling happier already.

Dali reminded Abby how to select shows and, satisfied she was all set, left to do her work.

Still grinning, Abby chose the first topic, noticing that the screen felt like very sensitive plexiglass. As she watched, the text of the article switched from New American to Old American.

Dear Auntie Zoray,

I'm in university. I'm a neatnik and my roommate is a slob. I tried consulting with him. He said he'd try; but it's no better. I finally put a line of tape down the middle of the room. I'm just about to put up screens so that I don't have to look at his books, sports gear, clean and dirty clothes, just *stuff* spreading all over his half of the room and creeping into mine. But I'm not sure if this will do any good. It bothers me to see mess. 'Abdu'l-Bahá said: "The home should be orderly and well-organized."[63] And Bahá'u'lláh said: "Wash ye every soiled thing" and "Be ye the very essence of cleanliness amongst mankind."[64] I'm at a complete loss! What can I do?

~ ~ Bothered Brother

Oh brother, Brother,

You do have a problem, and you are right about what the Master and the Blessed Beauty said. Some people really don't care how messy their place is, and reminding them is like the harmless twittering of birds outside their dirty windows. So let's roll up our mental sleeves and think creatively. Can you get another roommate? Or can you move out? Declare a day that cleanup will happen, even if it's only once a month? Clean it yourself, if he'll let you? Trash out your side of the room and see how he likes it? (Just kidding; what if he *likes* it??!!) Consult with your Resident Assistant? Keep your back turned, and buy yourself some eyeglasses that will block your peripheral vision? Say a bunch of prayers to not be bothered anymore? (Those would be in the prayer book under "Detachment.") Good luck, and let me know what happens!

~ ~ A't Z

Abby chuckled. Auntie Zoray was a hoot and a holler, as they would say back in Tennessee. Home … her room, the ranch, Jenn. Her breath caught in her throat; tears welled up from a stab of homesickness. How would she get back home? What if she never got back? She could almost see Jenn's cherished face in front of her. She closed her eyes and saw it more clearly before it faded. Maybe her hormones were making her more emotional these days; she had to wipe her eyes and take deep breaths before she could click on another letter.

Dear Auntie Zoray,

About ten years ago, we planted a fruit tree in our yard. We knew it would grow large enough to hang over our neighbor's yard and maybe drop leaves and fruit there, so we got permission from them to plant it. They said they'd be happy to have us plant it, because it was a ManyFruit tree, with grafts of different fruits all growing on the same trunk.[65]

But those neighbors moved, and our new neighbors are not happy with what they call "trash" dropping into their yard. We like our tree, and so do all the other neighbors who come over and pick the peaches, plums, and apricots when they are ripe. We make tasty jelly.

We've tried to consult with our new neighbors, but they just don't want to talk. Do you have any suggestions?

~ ~ Fruitless Strife

Dear Fruitless,

Too bad you're not growing cucumbers; then you could be in a pickle instead of a jam. So you have some sour neighbors? Maybe they wish you'd planted a lemon-lime tree so they could suck on lemons. Or maybe they already do! How about growing a sugar tree to sweeten them up?

Okay, more seriously, might they give you permission to come on their side and get the fruit they don't want, and rake those leaves? And you offer them some jelly in exchange? Or how about if you install a net, so the fruit either collects without dropping or rolls back onto your land? It usually works better if you can approach people with a proposal ready to go, instead of asking them to solve your problem – or one they think is yours. However it turns out, do enjoy the fruits of your labor!

~ ~ A't Z

Abby read a couple more and enjoyed Auntie Zoray's wacky sense of humor. It could not be said that the people of the future had no fun!

She scanned the local newspaper online and saw a small notice about the get-together Dali had mentioned that night at The Draggin' Dragon, near the Temple. It was to "Celebrate The Declaration Of Elle Tulia," whatever that was.

Glancing around, she saw that Dali had left small bags on a nearby table. One looked like a baggie of clay; another was a sack of fabrics. The third looked like wood, possibly to carve; and the last held colored stones and a large tile.

Dali was still nowhere to be seen, so Abby pulled out the wood and studied it. She pressed it with a fingernail, and it seemed to be soft wood but nothing more. She shook the bag; it was definitely empty. No burning or carving tools, nor any instructions. Even if there were, she wouldn't be able to read them.

She put the wood down and spread out the stones. With no plan in mind, she placed the stones on the tile, then accidentally knocked the wood onto it ... and why not? She arranged the stones around the wood. There seemed to be room left over, so she rolled the clay into snakes and balls, adding them to the tile. What would the fabric do? Loose threads around the edges of the fabric invited pulling. They came off in her fingers and, without thinking, she dropped them on top of the design. She liked it and pulled off more threads, dropping and poking them here and there. Some nestled down on the tile, some lay over the chunk of wood, some poked up between the stones. She was thoroughly absorbed in her design when she heard a soft sound next to her.

"This is awesome!" Dali said, awefully.

"Is it?" Abby replied, coming out of a dreamlike place of creating. "I'm just messing around."

"I'd never have thought of combining everything."

"Am I not supposed to?"

"No need to limit your creating with a 'supposed to.' The important thing is, have you enjoyed it?"

"No, not at all," Abby said with a straight face.

"I can tell," Dali matched her without missing a beat. "We elevate ourselves when we create. God's main name is Creator, and whenever we ... participate? ... in one of God's attributes, we feel closer to Sia."

"What do you mean?" Abby inquired, sprinkling the last threads on her creation.

"Let's take another of God's attributes or qualities. Give it a try; name one."

"Knows everything?" Abby ventured.

"All-Knowing, yes, bonega. We can't be, mmm, omniscient, but don't you feel *more* when you learn something? Not just increasing your knowledge; it also somehow increases your spirit."

Abby turned toward Dali, considering the new, spiritually appealing idea that art brought out God's attributes in her own soul.

"I'll have to ... um ... meditate on it," Abby finished lamely.

Dali smiled brilliantly, patted her arm and beckoned her to a workroom, where they sprayed the assemblage and parked it to dry.

They mounted their bikes in the welcome late afternoon cool and rode around the left side of the House of Worship. A couple of blocks down a new street, Dali led her to a crowded bike rack in front of their restaurant, The Draggin' Dragon.

"You have the AerY to interpret for you," Dali said as they dismounted, "but let me teach you a few words in UL. There may be people from other countries here, so UL will be safer than teaching you our current American."

At Dali's prompting, Abby carefully repeated words like "Jes" (it sounded exactly like what it meant: *yes*), "Saluton" (*sah-LUTE-own*, meaning *hello*), and "Kiel vi fartas" (*KEE-ell vee FARR-tahs*, meaning *how are you*).[66] But Abby couldn't stop laughing after the last one. She was just glad Dali didn't ask her why, and busied herself with parking her bike next to Dali's.

"Oh, and if people ask your name," Dali advised, "maybe don't say your second name, your family name."

"Why not?" Abby asked, still giggling.

"Usually when people discover their calling, sia change their last name to reflect that." Dali tugged her purse out of the bike basket and slung the long strap over her head.

"What do you mean, 'calling'?"

Dali cleared her throat and sang the quotations. "The Bahá'í Writings say, 'True reliance is for the servant to pursue his profession and calling in this world.'[67] Also: 'The best of men are they that earn a livelihood by their calling.'[68] Calling is like a job, but with the, um, added meaning of the work God has in mind for you."

Dali checked Abby's face for signs of understanding. Abby smiled and Dali continued, "My last name is Puerta. After I turned 15, I realized my calling is opening doors for people who want to learn. That's why I chose to work in a school."

"Like you've been helping me. Puerta means *door*?"

"Yes, in Old Spanish. I liked the sound of it."

"So do I." Then Mr. Modderay's name hadn't been a coincidence after all. "What's so important about turning 15?"

"In the Bahá'í Faith, the beginning of spiritual maturity is 15. Tonight's party is because one of my friends turned 15 a few days ago. She wants to reaffirm her faith publicly, with a public declaration."

"Why would you reaffirm your faith?" Abby asked, noting the faint glow in her bike's drive tube fading the longer the bike sat in the growing shadow of the restaurant.

"The Bahá'í Faith urges us to investigate important things like our religion, instead of accepting whatever faith our parents hand down to us. Most of us are raised Bahá'í, but we decide whether we accept it or not. And there are laws to follow, and some 15-year-olds don't feel ready to sign up for the responsibility to follow them yet. Before 15, we can sin as much as we like. Just kidding!"[69]

"What laws?" Abby managed to hold her thought through the joke.

Dali's WaerY helped her elucidate the handful of prescriptions. "Say one Obligatory Prayer and 95 Alláh-u-Abhá's every day; read the Writings every morning and evening; observe the Fast; contribute to the Fund; attend the Feast; avoid alcohol and other drugs except for medical need; have a Bahá'í burial, don't have sexual relations except in marriage, shun gossip—"[70]

"No gossiping? That's different."

"Gossip in the sense of backbiting – speaking ill of someone who's not there. In your time, people not only gossiped but enjoyed it?"

"Yeah, that's an understatement," Abby muttered, ducking her head and folding her arms across her chest defensively, remembering the rumors at the ranch.

"It must have been hurtful. It's very damaging, as I guess you know, so Bahá'u'lláh banned it," Dali said kindly, touching Abby's arm sympathetically. "Beyond the handful of laws, the Writings have lots of guidance for our daily lives. How closely we obey all this is up to us. No prayer police throw anyone in prayer jail if we mess up." Dali's joke caught Abby by surprise. It took her a second to summon a smile, loosen her protective stance and find a reply in kind.

"Oh, so no one will smack you down if you sneak a bite during Fast?"

"No one will smack you down even if you totally skip fasting," Dali rejoined.

"Cool, um, but back to the names thing. That man at Service today, what was his last name again?"

"Sayre."

"Is that his calling name?"

"Yes. He is an eloquent speaker. He *says* many marvelous things, you see." Dali laid a patient hand on her bike seat, gently exploring the fabric as she waited for Abby.

"And your friend tonight?"

"Elle Tulia? She hasn't chosen another name yet. And she doesn't have to. But your last name, Wize? People may not know if you're 15 and chose your name, which is quite a claim, or … well, it would be easier if you don't mention it, since you won't be able to answer their questions, because you haven't learned any of our languages yet."

"But Wize is spelled with a 'z;' it's not Wise with an 's.' Daddy says that Wize doesn't come from wisdom."[71]

"Of course," Dali acknowledged. "Although I hope someday it will, because wisdom is the mother of all other virtues.[on wisdom] But a listener can't tell the difference, and I image you'll speak your name tonight, not write it. I just don't want you to have any misunderstandings, so maybe you can avoid mentioning it."

"You're saying people in the Golden Age lie? And won't they find out my name anyway?"

"I'm not asking you to lie. We can simply steer the conversation away from awkward topics," Dali said, turning to open the restaurant door. "And the Yuter doesn't reveal personal details that you don't want it to."

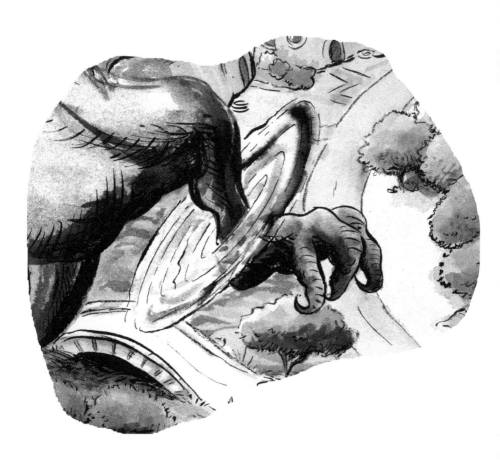

Chapter 20 Party

Once inside the Draggin' Dragon, Abby's mind snapped, untethered, between déjà vu and presque vu. The strange and the known leapt out at her in turn, defying her to place herself in time and space.

While Dali waved at friends who called to her, Abby tried to anchor herself by naming the familiar and unfamiliar elements.

Wood, and plants, and a homey, clean impression, for the third time. A long counter stretched to the left, like the first restaurant Dali had taken her to just yesterday. If they had been wood instead of an unidentifiable blend, the tables and chairs in the middle of the room could have been those in Jon and Melissa's coffee shop. But unlike either of those eateries, on one end of the main room, several machines with control pads, screens and tall, blank wall panels dominated nearby vacant floor space. A large, bare room lay beyond the main room, but Abby's eye was caught, held and disoriented by the very lifelike, scenic wallpaper running around the top third of the main room. No ordinary wallpaper strip, this was animated. One section depicted large trees bordering a grand, sunny meadow dotted with couples and groups of people and animals ... meandering, meeting, greeting, dancing, riding, wrestling, playing tug-of-war.

Horses cavorted with sheep and goats. There, in the trees, several sinuous Asian dragons – wingless, yet flying – played a gliding game of hide-and-seek with valkyries astride soaring cloud-horses and medieval knights on mailed chargers. Here, on a low knoll, maidens in kente-cloth kaftans, embroidered kimonos, flowing gowns or long-fringed buckskin read to grazing zebras and a pair of lazing, winged, European dragons as friendly as their Asian cousins. Elsewhere, samurai collected frangipani flowers by a stream, which girls twisted into leis and tossed in a nimble game with ebon warriors and spirited unicorns.[72]

Abby pivoted slowly in place, drawn in and staggered by the new, unexpected ways the many vignettes blended races and cultures.

Dali's name continued to ring out from several directions and Abby forced herself back to the present, catching up with Dali at the end of the counter. The growing crowd of young singles impressed Abby with their blended cultures and facial traits, not to mention the wide varieties of color and style in hair, dress, and jewelry. Abby was pleased that she was not the youngest. Several little kids left older siblings or young parents to play in the big adjacent room.

"Dali!" squealed a girl from a nearby table. Dali immediately hello'd back – or rather, *saluton*'d and *kiel vi fartas*'d – while Abby tried hard not to laugh again.

"Good practice to keep a straight face, Abby," Dali murmured while waiting for her friend to weave her way closer. "Useful when people tell you their unusual names."

"Yeah, like what?"

"I knew a young man in professions training whose first name was Metric. That seemed odd, but who was I to say?"[73]

"Oh. Okay, I'll add that to my meditations: how to keep a straight face when people have odd names or when languages sound silly," Abby said.

Dali's possible answer was cut off by a long, loving hug with the delighted girl.

"Abby, this is Elle Tulia, my close friend since forever," Dali glowed. "Elle, this is Abby."

Abby nodded, smiled, and echoed *ELL too-LEE-ah* with a "Saluton, Kiel vi fartas?"

"I'm very well, thank you. And you? Where are you from?" Elle's question was translated through Abby's AerY.

Dali came to her rescue, speaking to Elle in New American. "Abby's my distant cousin from North Europe. She has an AerY to translate our words, but is shy to speak UL."

Abby thought those were excellent white lies – er, cover stories. Actually, it didn't seem a lie or story at all. Dali had said everyone was related, however distantly. And Abby's family tree did originate in Europe. Although she'd become a little bolder with today's progress, she still withdrew in tonight's crowd and was grateful, once again, to Dali. Abby added harmless white lies and cover stories to steering conversations as possible techniques for building the spiritual speech of the advanced youth she wanted to emulate, thinking vaguely of new ways to handle Mother.

"Ah, okay," said Elle. "Well, hungry yet? Just come from work?"

"Uh huh," Dali said, linking arms with Elle and getting in line to order. Abby followed, looking in vain for a display board of the choices, hoping for pictures.

"Do you know what you want yet?" asked a voice behind her. It belonged to a shortish, good-looking, polite young man in loose purple pants and an embroidered, yellow zip-up shirt. They studied each other, Abby surveying the intricate tattoos around his ears and eyes, he taking in her unusually light skin. Sparkles drew her eyes to shiny beads dotting his thick, wavy, dark-brown hair gathered in a short ponytail. She'd never seen anyone like him, but found him and his adornments attractive. He handed her a menu from a stack on the counter.

"I'm sorry, but I don't read UL," she said, then panicked. He would not understand her. She looked at Dali, whose back was turned, engrossed in conversation with Elle.

The young man, though, saw that Abby did not even look at the menu, read her face, and asked, "Your AerY is translating?"

"Jes," said Abby, heart racing, palms sweating, feeling caught.

"Would you allow me to read the menu to you, and you can tell me what you'd like?"

"Jes, um, please," said Abby, heartily wishing she hadn't fallen apart so soon into her UL lesson.

This guy seemed to be as intuitively gifted as Dali, though, because he said, "You're doing great. The UL word is plaĉi. *PLAH-chee*. But I understood you just fine anyway."

She was very grateful.

"My name is Kreshi, pleased to meet you," Kreshi said expectantly.

Kreshi? Like *FRESH-he*? Cute, like him! "Me, too. Oh, I'm Abby. What's your last name?" For once she spoke up, regardless of the large crowd, but instantly feared she'd been too forward. Kreshi looked at her thoughtfully, snapped his fingers and unhooked his WaerY. He pressed a couple of places on its case and deftly wrapped it around his ear.

"There! I find it takes a lot of concentration to communicate mentally with the Yuter, and with this noise my wrist is too far away to hear. This will whisper closer," he said, smiling for the first time. Even his teeth were tattooed! Abby had read about unusual ways to beautify oneself, but to meet such a person took it to a new, vivid level.

"What did you ask?" Kreshi lifted his gaze from her small gold pierced-earring hoops. Was piercing weird? Didn't people here do that? She hadn't noticed.

"I was wondering about your last name," Abby replied, trying to be her most polite and yet eager to know his calling name.

"Ah. It is Tender," he said. "And yours?"

Abby's face fell. She'd walked right into that one! Now what?

"Abby, what do you want to order?" Dali was going to have to change her name to whatever the UL was for Rescuer. Bless her heart, she rescued Abby thrice a day every day. "Do you want something substantial or light? They have tacos, would you like that? That's medium-heavy," Dali prattled on, steering the conversation.

"Sure. Do they have fried rice, too?" Abby asked on a whim.

Dali smiled. "That's fun, mix and match cultures through food!"

The AerY translated as Elle bubbled, "Oh, yeah! Are you going to have them season the taco so it goes with the Asian rice, or keep the taco Mexican and do the rice like it? Or leave them original?"

"If I order Italian, and you keep the seasonings traditional, we can have an international feast!" Kreshi proposed to Abby, taking over Abby-saving duties from Dali.

Elle peered over Abby's shoulder at the menu she had memorized with other criteria in mind. "Oh, how about a Russian beet soup?"

The little group stepped up to the counter and ordered through the Draggin' Dragon's ALLY. Elle and Kreshi paid through their Yuters, while Dali paid for Abby with several small, colorful bills. Scanners above each cubby of the cash drawer sitting on the counter read the value of the money Dali put in and also of the coins she took as change. Dali pointed out the holes in the middle of the coins, enjoying Abby's cry of amazement at seeing a tiny, real feather encased in the center. Another coin contained a bit of green.

"Those are the current Kingdom coins," Kreshi explained while the foursome found a spot in which to stand and wait for their food.

"I'm sorry, I haven't seen them before. Could you please explain?" Abby hoped her flimsy story would work, avoiding looking at Kreshi lest he see through the … er, pretense.

"Well, you know, the Kingdoms of Creation. Coins with bits from each Kingdom." He pulled coins from his pocket and sorted through them for ones that matched Dali's.[74] "Yes, here's a mineral kingdom coin, the red volcanic soil from Hawaii; they even dye shirts with it. And here's a vegetable kingdom; I think this one's got a bit from the world's oldest living thing, the bristlecone pine in California. Then for the animals, this one's a molted feather from the world's smallest bird; let me see if I can read … yup, the bee hummingbird of Cuba. For the human kingdom, here's one with a bit of hair from Marta Kair; she's a Teacher of the Year. The kingdom of the spirit is always represented by light. This one has a micro light bulb powered by the warmth of your hand, see? That one's tiny prism makes a rainbow in bright light."[75]

Abby enjoyed his easy rambling as much as the beautiful coins. She thought them the coolest thing in numismatics since the time she read in *Muse* about some islanders using huge stones as money.[76]

"Hey, there's Kwan!" Elle interrupted her nonstop yakking with Dali to call out to the latest newcomers. "Kwan! Penda! Over here!"

"Oh, food's ready," Kreshi observed to Dali. "How about I get the food, you and Abby get the drinks, and Elle grabs a table, if she makes it that far?" Dali laughed in agreement and snuck a few words into Elle's ear, busy as she was with more friends.

They met up at a table in the middle of the room and started to set up four chairs, which quickly became eight, which allowed only half of them to eat at the table, but no one seemed to mind as most were too busy talking to eat, though everyone offered a different dish to share. The Spanish rice looked just like Abby's fried rice but with different seasonings, which explained her friends specifying the spices. Two mushroom dishes confirmed it: a Creole-tasting dish varied from a Polynesian one by using different spices and additions. Abby tasted everything, to be polite, then settled down to her crispy, scrumptious tacos, which stayed tidy due to an almost invisible and obviously edible wrapper. Abby wondered why no one on Earth had thought of this.

Dali whispered, "I ordered your taco twrapped. Or maybe you like your tacos messy?" She tipped her head mischievously, grinned, and turned back to her conversation. She had said *twoo-RAPT*, like wrapped plus "t." Abby practiced it in her mind, enjoying the word more than the fall-apartness of an untwrapped taco.

As the others gabbed about strange topics,[77] Abby's eyes fell on the animated wallpaper closest to their table. This section showed people and animals at a seashore, some of them picnicking on the sand, others resting on rocks or playing tag. A group played monarch-of-the-mountain among grassy dunes.

Bathers in modest, artistic swimwear splashed, surfed, and rode playful dolphins and frisky sea serpents – maybe another variation on the dragon theme. One rider on a black horse pranced across wave tops. Abby decided it must be a friendly kelpie – a Celtic water horse not depicted so kindly in Abby's hometime.[78] It pranced over to a nearby dragon trapped under a rollicking whale and hauled it to safety. *Was this the Dragging of the Dragon?* she wondered as she spooned up the last grains of rice and taco crumbs.

"Would you like to play a game?" Kreshi interrupted her daydreaming.

"I don't have any money," she replied, caught off guard.

"And no credit, either, I'm guessing? That's okay, I'll pay," he said graciously, listening to his WaerY's translation. Abby could hear her own voice in a language she'd never spoken.

Dali and Elle were still talking so much they hadn't finished eating. Kreshi invited Abby to copy him as he cleaned his place, carried his tray to the sorting station, and sorted organic scraps, recyclables, and washables into their designated bins.

Going to the bathroom to, um, wash her hands, Abby paused by the large room at the back of the restaurant to watch a rambunctious game. It looked like martial arts group-fighting, except all the moves were stylized and set to music. While the toddlers watched and played, a circle of five people "fought" back-to-back. Other dance-fighters approached them regularly, sparred symbolically, then backed off.

Someone might have been softly calling out the moves, but if so, it blended too closely with the clapping, laughing and chatting to hear.

Again Abby's mind whipped between the familiar and the unknown. Memories of watching Daddy's bowling team vied with the dance ... er, fight ... uh, dight? fance? in progress in front of her eyes.

Shrinking against a wall, dizzy with brain-spin, she forced herself to compare the wavering flashbacks with the here-and-now.

In both scenes, a chattering crowd watched and cheered. In both worlds, watchers and doers represented all ages, races and genders, although Lodlan's event-goers were much more racially diverse and creatively decked out than would be the bowlers in Surely.

The actual activities were different, too, although both involved dozens of players, yet the action, and even the rooms had a different feel. Finally Abby realized that she had expected to be assaulted by a toxic cloud of cigarette smoke and the deafening arguing that would accompany the drinking in a busy bowling alley. At this *fance*, as in the Musical Chairs game she'd seen on the school ALLY, the partiers still whooped it up but avoided the pollutants and skipped the arguing.

"Then, pollution, disunity, pain," Abby murmured, surprised at her last word. "Now, purity, togetherness, joy. I'll take now, thank you!"

Kreshi loitered near one of the blank wall panels.

"Do you like to dance?" he asked Abby.

"Um ..." Abby wondered how that translated. Her face must have carried the message, though, because Kreshi said, "This is easy to learn. Here, watch me."

"Yuter, please ... aw, forget it." He took his WaerY off his ear long enough to hold it up to a small scanner by the floor-length screen. The screen lit up with a human silhouette, black with a green outline, which pointed to the floor. Kreshi stood on the indicated spot and flexed his knees. "*Waves I*, please," he said to the figure. It nodded and started to dance to slow, pulsing music.

To Abby, it looked like a futuristic DDR – Dance Dance Revolution game – but without a footpad, with arm movements, and following the figure instead of arrows. The first song ended and Kreshi asked for *Waves II*, which was slightly faster, with a few musical flourishes and extra moves. By the time Kreshi finished *Waves IV* and offered Abby a turn, she'd nearly memorized the song despite its steady increase in tempo, difficulty, and flourishes. With each increase, the figure glowed brighter and acquired more detail and Kreshi improvised his own moves more often.

Abby had not felt very successful at her last dance, a square-dance in grade school gym class, so she hesitated when Kreshi offered her the floor. She took a deep breath and stepped up. Kreshi called encouragement. She mimicked the figure, relieved when the song ended without the figure dimming or giving her a thumbs-down. Even better, Kreshi clapped and cheered for her.

"That was fun! Thank you very much." Abby curtseyed.

"Such courage!" Kreshi said. "And persistence!"

"Persistent, yeah, if you mean stubborn," Abby said ruefully, remembering Mother's accusations. "Courage, not so much; I was a little scared, actually."

"Courage means pursuing right action even *when* you're scared," Kreshi imparted. "I see courage, persistence, and willingness; great qualities that make Abby uniquely Abby!"

Abby had never been complimented with such precision. "Sure never heard that before," she muttered.

"Pity; you deserve support for your soul."

She blushed and found she could not look at him. She also felt her stomach give a funny lurch. She knew then that she liked him, but immediately thought that it could never work.

Attraction mixed with regret and must have created a strange expression on her face, because Kreshi asked, "Would you like to dance again, or do you need to sit down?"

"It might be good to sit for a minute before I try something else," Abby said, thinking perhaps she could balance her thoughts again.

"Okay, here's an empty table. And would you like a drink?"

"No, I'm not old enou … oh! I mean, sure. I'll have whatever you choose," she said, sitting down. She really needed to get her worlds separated better, she thought. Drinking never meant alcohol here. If she continued putting herself in spots like this, she would be writing Auntie Zoray with the strangest story that jovial woman had ever read.

Kreshi brought an orange-colored iced drink with a straw that spit colorful sparks, and a scarlet cup sporting a wedge of bright-red tomato sprinkled with dark seasoning. He laid several spoons on the table.

"Here, taste each one and then choose whichever you like."

Now, along with her stomach flipping, her heart was melting. If everyone was so eternally polite in this world, how could you tell the difference between regular manners and flirting? Dali couldn't help with that question because she was now several tables away, jabbering with the friends who kept arriving. The restaurant was now quite full, although it didn't seem to be any noisier than earlier. For once, she felt glad to be part of a large celebration, feeling her confidence grow with the support and understanding.

Kreshi sat companionably with Abby as she spooned up one

concoction and then the other, sipping water and waiting a bit between them to clear her palate, as Mother did when tasting wine.

Abby closed her eyes to better savor the orange drink again. She felt special; she felt calm, included, accepted. A bell of deep knowing rang in her soul, alerting her to the realization that, now awake, she was living her version of that morning's special dream. She marveled that in just one day, she'd gathered enough clues and, however inexpertly, brushed up against enough spiritual things that she'd become more centered, more aware, and perhaps even wiser.

The red drink was more vegetable-ish, but the fruitier orange one appealed to her more. She watched the straw-sparkler until it fizzled out while Kreshi savored the spiced tomato and sipped his vegetable juice.

"Are you employed?" Abby had had to work out the most polite way to ask him what he did with his time.

"My calling is to tend things, including plants, animals, children, families, ideas, conversations, and projects," he recited. "Right now, I lead unifying, low-impact outdoor expeditions for families and groups, usually in the mountains. I've just been leading tours in the Appalachians. I'm a friend of Elle's – of Dali's, too – and was close enough to take a train for Elle's party."

"Is it too rude of me to ask how old you are?"

"Not to me. I'm 16."

"And you're out on your own?"

"Why not? I reached the age of decision last year," he said.

She would have to stop sticking her foot in her mouth. Dali had told her that age 15 was the beginning of maturity here.

"And is turnabout fair play?" he continued. "May I ask how old you are, what you do, and what your last name is? Or will Dali leap to your rescue again?"

With her newfound courage, she took a deep breath and plunged in.

"I'm 13, I'm still in school; my passion is horses, and my last name is Wize, W-I-Z-E, but I didn't choose it, it's a family name," she responded in one breathless rush.

"A very 'Wize' answer, however, Abby." Kreshi smiled and raised two fingers to his temple. "And I salute your courage in telling me when you weren't sure if I'd like it."

Will I ever get used to having my mind read? Abby wondered.

Chapter 21 Dragons

Just then, another young man joined them. He was thin and toted many little cases in the small pockets of his net vest.

Kreshi stood up to hug the new arrival. "Saluton, Rykeir!"

After they'd hugged warmly, the new fellow turned to Abby. "Hi! I'm Rykeir Gamero. And you are?" he inquired politely, touching the heel of his hand to his forehead and presenting his palm. As he did, Abby noticed that his black hair, braided close to his head, was entwined with tiny blinking lights.

"Abby," she said. "Saluton, *RYE-keer gay-MARE-oh.*"

"Abby is Dali's cousin from … your family's from Northern Europe, did she say?" Kreshi asked, frowning slightly.

"Yep," Abby said.

"Kio?" asked Rykeir. Abby heard him say *KEE-oh*, which came through her AerY as "What?"

"Oh, she's a bit shy with UL," Kreshi intervened. "She has an AerY and, as you can see, I'm using my WaerY in this attractive new fashion." He turned his head so Rykeir could see the thin strap wrapped around his tattooed right ear. "Do you think?"

"Sure, love it!" said Rykeir adventurously. He touched a couple of places on his WaerY and, with Kreshi's help, strapped it to his ear. "Soooo stylish, don't you think?" he grinned, modeling exaggeratedly.

Abby noted the difference a smile made for Rykeir. Though he hadn't seemed at all good-looking, his cheek and his bright smile caused her to recall Jenn's explanation about bodies God gives people, adding that a spiritual outlook created an inner warmth that could prettify a plain face; Rykeir, Dali and even Melissa proved that.

"What are y'all up to?" Rykeir asked.

"I was about to invite Abby to accompany me on her first dragon-guided tour of Dál Riata," Kreshi replied. His *DOLL ree-AH-tah* drew a blank look from Abby and he added, "A Gaelic overkingdom covering much of Scotland and a bit of Ireland 2,000 years ago."

"Excellent! May I come along?" Rykeir asked, lifting his eyebrows and bugging his eyes at his two companions.

"Only if you tell me how you got those fabulous lights in your hair," Abby claimed, feeling as impish as the two young men acted.

Both guys burst out laughing at her chutzpah, and Rykeir said, "I'll tell you if you don't fall off your dragon. Deal?"

"Deal," Abby said, trusting they wouldn't purposely set up a game that would humiliate her.

"Three-player format it is," Rykeir said. "Give me just a second to retrieve the table diagnostic I came to get, and I'll start the game. I also have a new game to install, but I'll do that after we finish, okay?"

"Okay," Kreshi and Abby chorused; and almost before they were done speaking, a 3D grass field popped up on the table surface.

It was way better than anything Abby could have dreamed. It looked real – really real. Even more real than the wallpaper border. She reached into the image to touch the grass, but it was without form.

"The beginners all do that, don't they? Tsk tsk tsk," Kreshi declared with fake sadness, shaking his head and cueing controls on the table.

"Every last one," Rykeir solemnly intoned, rummaging in pockets.

"Would either of you would like a pierced ear? You'd be my first, so I might get your nose or eyebrow instead. I think I have a stapler right here." Abby fought to keep a straight face as she patted her pockets, amazed at her own gall, as Mother might've put it, but thrilled to keep up with them.

"I have been thinking I'd get something pierced, but not just now, thanks," Kreshi parried lightly, signaling Rykeir with a nod.

"Yuter, Dál Riata Dragon Tour," Rykeir commanded. "Three dragons. Beginner level, please."

A long-necked, pearly gray animal appeared directly under Abby. For an instant, she thought it was a horse, but as it turned to look at her, she saw that, no, it was a square-headed dragon. To her right, a black reptilian creature emitted smoke from large nostrils.

Kreshi appeared on her left astride a stout, mottled tan dragon. She turned to get a better look at the pair and felt her dragon's body turn. She looked down and the dragon looked down. She looked right and the dragon looked right; she twisted right and it swung to the right. On a hunch, she leaned back in her chair – which now felt like a saddle – and sure enough, her dragon backed up. While she tested out several more maneuvers, the scene grew until the restaurant disappeared behind the guys and became the hills of Dál Riata. Her only wish was …

"A horse instead of a dragon?" Rykeir smirked.

Abby ducked her head in sudden embarrassment, which made her mount sink into the grass. "Oops!" She got it to stand again by sitting up straight. "Sorry, yes, I did wish that … no offense to Sir – or is it Lady? – Pearl, here." She reached down to pat its neck and felt a mane! Not daring to incline her head, she cast her eyes down and, to her utter delight, saw she was now astride …

"A pegasus!" she exclaimed.

"Actually, a pterippus," Kreshi clarified. "Pegasus is a specific Greek character; it's a proper noun for that creature."

Abby wasn't listening. She stroked her mount's lustrous coat; the pearly scales were now hair. Her comfortable, specially cut saddle accommodated powerful, pearly-feathered wings coming out of its shoulders. It turned to eye her, showing a capable, proud face that humbled her with its willingness to partner her, even for a game.[79]

"Might as well all ride variations of your favorite theme." Kreshi's grin threatened to take over his face as he adjusted his seat on the dazzling golden unicorn he now rode. Its pointed brown horn was smooth, not spiraled as she'd sometimes seen. Its darker legs, muzzle, mane, and tail reminded her of a buckskin's coloring.

Rykeir now rode a dragon-horse, its sturdy black body covered with saucer-sized, diamond-shaped scales. Pores on its neck and thin snake-tail spouted smoke instead of hair. It tossed its head, flapped long black batwings, and pawed the air with black hooves.[80]

"Everyone ready? Everyone's earrings firmly in?" Kreshi asked, smirking and winking at Abby. Her tacos and orange drink flipped. He was irresistible. Did he know how she was falling for him?

She nodded, not trusting herself to speak.

"Okay, Longma, lift off," Rykeir told his hybrid creature, whose glistening wings took over from its galloping hooves, trailing a magnificent stream of smoke. Kreshi's unicorn did not have wings, but simply rose into the air behind Rykeir. It wasn't a dream but, like her own dreams, it seemed entirely real. Thrilled, Abby looked skyward. Her pegasus ... er, pterippus ... also looked upward, but did not rise.

"How ... ?" She saw no joystick, reins, or other means of control.

"Just think it," the guys both said.

"Your intention," Kreshi added.

Now she understood. Harry's thestrals. Angie's Parelli session. Her riding dreams in new form. She envisioned her goal, willed herself to lift off, and expressed in her body what she wanted her *TARE-uh-puss* to do. They soared high, and hovered exactly where she'd planned. She could see far ahead now. She looked right with only her eyes, without willing to go right, and saw low hills and irregular outlines of farmers' fields. Careful of her body movements and her intention, she looked to the left and saw cliffs and ocean.

"Oooo, the little mutilator learns fast," Rykeir said.

"This is fantastic!" Abby's cheeks hurt from smiling so broadly.

"All the first-timers say that," Kreshi said.

"And all the 10th-timers, if I've done my job right," Rykeir said.

Abby turned her head toward Rykeir, causing the pterippus to rotate slowly toward him too. "Why, what's your job?"

"Three guesses, and the first two don't count."

"You make games? You made this one?!"

"Helped make it," Rykeir corrected amid wisps of smoke.

"What's your last name again?" Abby asked.

"Gamero," Rykeir said, all the lights in his hair blinking at once.

"Ahhhhh," Abby breathed, understanding ... and glad for that. She smiled and looked ahead as Rykeir said, "Shall we tour the coastline? Or the mountains? Ladies first."

Abby reveled in the adventure. She willed her steed forward along the coastline, accompanied by hyper-real sound effects of wind, birds, and ocean. Willing correctly, she turned her head to check on her companions; her steed's head turned, too, but not its body. If she wanted the pterippus to turn, to change direction, she twisted slightly in her saddle with the intention of turning. If she wanted to go faster, she sat up a little taller and thought of more speed. If she looked, thought, and leaned down, the pterippus descended. If up, it climbed. Eventually, she found that her lower back was stiff. Trying to relieve the ache, she scooched back in her saddle ... and her steed skidded to a halt in midair – she'd forgotten to turn off her willpower.

"Hah, first near-wreck at time code 06:23," Rykeir said. "You didn't fall off, though, so that's saying something. You *sure* you never played this before?"

"Not this game," Abby answered. "Honest." She saw Rykeir's raised eyebrow. "I swear!"

"Oh, so if you tell me three times, then it's true?"[78]

"Yep, absolutely, fer shur," Abby retorted, grinning.

"So *you* say!" Rykeir waggled his fingers at her. "Kreshi, I'm detecting an accomplished fibbulist who needs further testing!"

"Definitely! Yuter, game course 4C, please," Kreshi requested.

Obstacles appeared. A line of blinking lights showed Abby how to navigate them.

"Whenever you're ready, go ahead. I'll be right behind you," Rykeir added grandly, "to pick up the pieces."

Abby set off at a moderate pace, carefully watching the route as her magnificent steed approached the first obstacle: five horizontal poles about 16 feet apart, hovering some four feet off the ground. The guide lights showed touching down before the first pole, jumping it and landing after the first, second, third and fourth poles, and soaring away after the fifth.[82]

Could she do all that without touching any of the poles? She had never jumped with a horse, and certainly never flown one. Summoning her courage, she decided on slow and easy. As she descended toward the first pole, following the arcing lights, she saw the initial touchdown spot. Her pterippus would have to furl its wings and jump without them immediately after landing, then unfurl them during the last jump. This was going to be tricky. But if she could match her body's signals to the suggestions of the lights, she might just make it.

Easy now ... the first landing was a little bumpy, but she stayed on well. She leaned forward slightly, willing the pterippus to jump the first pole, and firmly hunkered down to land. Her mount's massive muscles bunched and rippled under her as it alternately coiled and released its mighty frame to do her bidding. Never once did she fear for her safety; they were united in thought and motion. After nailing the fourth and final landing, they soared off again, a whoop of ecstatic delight gushing up from her soul and out through her mouth.

The game's sounds told her that Rykeir and Kreshi were just behind her. When she heard them reach her height, she twisted left, leaned back, and threw out her arms as she came to a tidy halt.

"Yup, you're a certified fabulous fibber," Kreshi said. "I'd put her at the intermediate-plus level. What say you, Rykeir?"

"I say if you ever need a job testing games, Abby, let me know," Rykeir said admiringly. "*Nicely* done, fibulosity notwithstanding."

Neither boy could know how much good that little bit of praise did for Abby. She felt on top of both of her worlds. "Aweful game, Rykeir. I'll test any riding game you make!"

The rest of the game was just as phenomenal. They tackled stationary, then moving, then flaming hoops. Squeezed through empty, then caving-in, then exploding tunnels. Outran arrows, then cannon balls, then flying saucers. Abby, using a technique she had seen in an old movie, led the saucers into each other.[83] Finally, they enjoyed flying over the mountains, her two friends pointing out pretty lakes and historic castles. Her steed never tired, never balked, always obeyed her slightest cue. Abby felt she would burst with euphoria.

"Touch down near that little town," Rykeir suggested. As they did, the game ended; the restaurant and their table and chairs reappeared. The three players grinned like idiots, bonded as close friends. They sat smiling at each other, reliving the experience delightedly, silently.

Finally, Abby turned to Rykeir. "So what brought a world-class game maker to ... Lowland? What's the name of this town?"

"Lodlan," Rykeir answered lazily. "I travel all over checking on games. It's great; I have BFFs everywhere."

"And now you have to tell me," Abby commanded him.

"Tell you what?"

"How you did those lights in your hair. I might want some."

"Ha! You'll have to tell me if you're ever in the same city, because two makes a trend, which we might not want to start," Rykeir said. "But okay, it's just white micro-lights in thin strands of solar wire."

"Can I get the lights from you?" Abby asked. "I would want peach-colored, though."

"Um, I'll have to work on that," Rykeir said. "Next year's Ayyám-i-Há present, probably."

"A Yamaha? What's motorcycles got to do with it?"

Both guys blinked long and slow, then laughed so long and loud that everyone nearby looked over, including Dali, holding a charming little girl on her lap. She threw Abby a big grin and clapped briefly, acknowledging that Abby was having a great time.

"The Days of Há, the days in between the calendar, *eye-YAWM-ee-HAW*," Kreshi said. "A bit like your Christmas season, I'd think, but actually completely different."

"Now that's clear as mud, Kreshi. Good job explaining," Rykeir growled. "Yuter, please explain Ayyám-i-Há."

Into Abby's ear came a soothing female voice.

"Ayyám-i-Há, also called Intercalary Days. The four or five days before the last month of the Bahá'í year, the month of fasting. In your culture, using the Gregorian calendar, this festival runs from sundown to sundown, approximately February 25 to March 1, thus aligning the Bahá'í year with the solar year. The believers feast, show hospitality, hold charitable events, give small gifts, and prepare for the Fast.[84] Say 'repeat' to repeat."

"Repeat," Abby requested, as the guys sat watching her with small, silly smiles fixed on their unself-conscious faces.

The definition repeated. Abby could see how it was like Christmas but totally different. The feasting and gift-giving were the same on the surface. Only, it said *small* gifts. She would bet they didn't overindulge now as they did in 2007. Then, people groused about the Christmas spirit ... of excess. Ads showed unrealistic, completely redecorated holiday houses with mounds of absurdly expensive presents under picture-perfect trees. Parents punched each other over Tickle-Me-Elmos. Guilt tricked people into overspending. And not just money – Abby struggled to comprehend – but time, energy, and emotions. Too much eating, too much drinking, too much of everything, really. It all seemed ridiculous from this vantage point.

"How do I get the yuter to tell me other things?"

"The yuter is always listening and looking, unless you tell it not to, but to be clear, it's best to start by saying, 'Yuter.' To practice our courtesy, we try to say 'please,' and when we get our answer, to say 'thank you.' But you'll still get your answer even if you don't do any of that, as long as your intention is to ask it."

"And it scans my mind? Or I speak silently to it?" Abby inquired.

The guys glanced at each other.

"It's complicated. Entire fields of research dig into this." Rykeir shifted in his seat. "At some point a few hundred years ago, artificial intelligence developed to where it could detect human neurons firing, let alone people silently mouthing words or eye patterns that indicate intention. Basically, Yuters can speak to us very quietly, and we can speak to them silently, and it usually works great."

"Abby, the yuter database goes way back. You could ask it to compare two cultures and translate any language, including Old American," Kreshi offered.

"Thanks. But ... how did you know ..." Abby trailed off, concerned that her fragile cover was blown.

"Knew it all along," and "We can read minds!" they said.

"Not!" Abby retorted. She was sure they were pulling her leg. "Seriously, can you read minds? Without the yuters? Dali said something about 'spiritual intuition.'" Intrigued, affronted and joking in equal measure, Abby relied on her sense that they actually were trying to help her.

They looked serious for a change. "We have limits in the physical realm," Rykeir finally offered.

"At which point the spiritual realm can inform us," Kreshi added.

"We've been asking our yuters to pick up what yours was telling you," Rykeir backtracked. "They can do great stuff, like take pictures, pull up information on any subject, find people or animals, take notes—"

"Aaaahhh." Abby suddenly understood how Dali knew that she'd appeared by the tree. That was one smart girl. She'd been weeding when Abby had dropped in from nowhere, looking and talking totally out of place and jabbering about horses, no less. The WaerY had helped her figure it all out. She'd said she preferred to converse out loud with it; that's why it whispered.

Abby slumped in her chair, dumbfounded with the memory and a new understanding of how hard and fast Dali had scrambled to speak reassuringly with her, quickly deciding what questions to ask both her and the WaerY while conveying empathy. Abby remembered how frustrated she'd felt, and how Dali had defused it, picking up on Abby's mention of horses and playing calming horse music, removing herself to give Abby time and space to regroup. Abby blushed and ducked her head when she remembered how she'd denied she was upset. She'd been plenty upset, especially compared with the fine-tuned awareness and consummate control she now knew the people in this time had.

Abby glanced up at Rykeir and Kreshi. They smiled warmly at her and at Dali, still at the other table. Unused to having this much support, Abby found herself withdrawing, needing to be alone with her own thoughts for a bit.

"Why don't you take some time to absorb all this?" Kreshi said softly. "This is a lot for you, but we only wish you to be happy. 'Abdu'l-Bahá placed great importance on being happy. He often asked people if they were happy. Try asking your yuter to pull up the 'for what age are you waiting' quote."

This escape seemed as good as her usual ones.

"Yuter, please pull up the 'Abdu'l-Bahá quote on 'what age are you waiting for.' "

After a brief silence, the AerY responded.

"Sorry, that function is blocked. See Dali Puerta for access."

Rykeir waved at Dali and spoke into the WaerY still strapped to his ear. "Dali, can you unblock Abby's AerY? We're going to show her how to use it."

Dali nodded and spoke into her WaerY.

"So, have you ever asked the Yuter for anything?" Rykeir asked.

"No," Abby replied. "It's only been talking to me."

"Okay, two hands to start with," Rykeir said, rubbing his hands together and shaking out his arms. "Asking great questions requires even more skill than riding mythical equines. Watch … or rather, listen, closely. Yuter, please give us the quote on 'what age are you waiting for' by the Master."

"Quoting: 'Do ye know in what cycle ye are created and in what age ye exist? This is the age of the Blessed Perfection … and the beautiful springtime of His Holiness the Eternal One!

"The earth is in motion and growth; the mountains, hills and prairies are green and pleasant; the bounty is overflowing; the mercy universal …. Lift the hem of thy garment in order to receive it.

"If we are not happy and joyous at this season, for what other season shall we wait and for what other time shall we look? End quote. From a letter by 'Abdu'l-Bahá to the Spiritual Assembly of Samarkand, Russia; in *Tablets of 'Abdu'l-Bahá*, page 641."

"Referring to Bahá'u'lláh, in that first part," Kreshi explained. "If she wants to hear more, what are her options, Yuter?"

"Say 'more' to hear more at this time. Say 'hourly' to hear a quote on happiness every hour. Say 'daily' to hear a quote on happiness once a day. Say 'other' to hear quotes on other topics."

"Hourly." Abby wanted more of the elevated feeling she got listening to the quote.

"Seeing as you catch on fast, you can practice speaking to the Yuter silently," Rykeir suggested. "It's all about intention, so the riding game warmed you up. Eyes closed for beginners, which is all of us.

Abby closed her eyes to focus her thoughts, then said —*Hourly*— to the Yuter with her mind. It gave a subvocal response so natural and familiar that it was like hearing her own internal voice.

—Making the usual exceptions for sleep, other necessities, and preoccupations.—

—*Uh, yeah, sure. Thank you.*—

—You are welcome.—

"Wow, I need a yuter of my own!" Abby exclaimed.

"Spoken like a true air dean," said Kreshi.

"A what? Oh, wait!" Again, Abby briefly closed her eyes to begin concentrating. She didn't have to keep them closed this time, though.

—*Yuter, please translate ... that ... into Old American.*—

—AIR-dee-yen, E-R-D-E-A-N. It is already translated from New American. It is a citizen of AIR-den, E-R-D-E-N, your planet Earth after the Most Great Peace.—

—*Explain Most Great Peace, please.*—

—Caution: response to this request will be long. Say 'later' if you prefer to hear it later.—

—*Later, thank you.*—

The guys clapped and whistled softly. "Well done!" "Brava!"

"It seems so much easier here ... now," Abby mused.

"That's good to hear," Kreshi said. "All that emphasis on learning and purity really is making a difference."

"Purity? Sorry, I don't understand," Abby queried, forgetting the purity quote Dali had shared with her.

"In your time, major inequalities and lack of moral direction were pretty widespread, right? People sometimes acted unethically – stealing, selling drugs or abusing their bodies, right?"

"Oh yeah, big-time, roger on that one," Abby said somberly.

"Here, everyone is taken care of, and virtually no one is negatively addicted to anything."

Abby wondered why he said "negatively addicted" with its suggestion that you could be addicted to something in a positive way, but decided not to ask. And yet it was an intriguing question.

—Would you like me to hold that thought for you?—

—*Yes, please!*—

—Noted.—

Way, way too cool. Abby wondered what this gadget would cost back home. Millions, no doubt, if it were even possible. But it wasn't; the technology didn't exist yet. She sighed and turned back to Kreshi.

"Right, purity. Similarly, no one has bad intent. No one is going to try to steal things, or cheat someone else, or flout laws," he said, Tending the conversation deftly.

"No one at all *ever*?"

"Well, once in a great while someone does, but it's rare. Of course, children might do wrong, but their yuter will pick up on it."

"Don't the kids just take off the Yuters?"

Both guys looked at her strangely.

"We tell each other that if you don't want anyone to see, it's probably wrong," Kreshi replied slowly. "You're giving us a great example of the thinking of your time."

"So why would you want to hang out with me?" Abby retorted, a little miffed.

"We're all products of our culture, but we all can start to make decisions about things we want to improve, right about age 13," Kreshi replied evenly. "My WaerY told me you were speaking Old American to Dali. You sounded open-minded and thoughtful, a little deeper-focused than I imagined someone from the second century would be, so I got in line behind you and found a chance to speak with you. Independent investigation of time-travelers, you know."

"And me being a time traveler, does that weird you out?"

"No, that's the best part. As foretold, we've seen life on other planets for centuries now.[85] And lots of stories and scientific ruminations have been written about time travel. At least you're human, not an alien species, so you're easy to talk with!"

"Of *course* I'm not an alien!" Abby pretended to take offense but was laughing too hard to pull it off.

"Back to purity, though." Kreshi embodied his calling name again.

"In my time, when kids want to do something wrong, like steal candy, they'll figure out how not to get caught," Abby explained. "If a yuter monitored them, they'd try to take it off."

"Sneaky little fiends, huh? In our time, we go at it differently," Rykeir explained. "Now, everyone helps everyone, especially with kids. If a kid, let's say, steals fruit – we really don't have much sugar-based candy – and their parents don't see it, someone else might step in, or alert a parent, who will lovingly counsel the child. If no one does, the yuter will either talk with the child or bring the parent into the loop. It's about love and education, not punishment and catching people doing badly."

Abby paused, trying to wrap her head around it. "It still sounds too much like spying on the kids."

Rykeir arched his eyebrows. "Have you ever tried to actually watch a toddler every waking moment, for years? Tried to help a teen when sia won't actually talk to you?"

"Well, no, I'm the youngest in my family," Abby admitted. "But still ..."

"Let's talk after you've had some skin in that game, the hardest game of all," Rykeir retorted. "It's easy to be high-minded when we haven't done it. We need all the help we can get when it's really real."

"Kids now have what they need," Kreshi added softly. "And they are very much loved and well-taught. It'd only be a childish impulse that would make them misbehave. But the thing to remember is, yuters are observers; parents and adults are in charge, and they're reasonable."

Abby slowly rubbed the edge of her simple wooden chair, thinking. Kreshi blinked, absorbed in thought. Rykeir fiddled with wires and bits in his pockets.

After another slow blink, Kreshi said, "All that was background for why it's easier to learn and live now. I think of our society now as being like a large tropical basket; loosely woven for good circulation of air, meaning the spirit of God but woven, meaning, interconnected, sturdily enough to hold the fruit of the age; the people."

"Plus I have to say, the yuter is essential to ... well, in your simile, the yuter would be the cushioning between the papayas so they don't squish each other and bruise!" Rykeir snorted.

"Which makes it easier for you to read my mind." Abby couldn't resist getting in a dig.

"Honestly, it's not like that. Divine promptings are the most helpful, even more than a yuter," Kreshi revealed.

"Please explain," Abby invited. Dali had mentioned something like this, too, but Abby wanted to hear it from them.

At a nod from Kreshi, Rykeir explained as he twisted wires into a tidy circle, "We all have a piece of the Divine. We might call it our eternal soul, our inner knowing. Like when Bahá'u'lláh wrote: 'O Son of Being! Thy heart is My home; sanctify it for My descent. Thy spirit is My place of revelation; cleanse it for My manifestation.'[86] Yes?"

"I guess so," Abby replied.

"The Master, 'Abdu'l-Bahá, said we can develop the qualities he had. He was so connected to the Divine that he had really advanced spiritual insight, suasion of the spirit, whatever you call it," Rykeir continued, spreading out tiny electronic parts on the table.[87] "It was almost like he had an invisible crystal ball for knowing things, including knowing things about people.[88] We should strive – do strive – to have that kind of connection."

"Did he – do your scriptures – say how we should do that?" Abby asked Rykeir, seeing a big clue to the mode she wanted.

"Through prayer, meditation, prescribed fasting, studying God's word, obeying God's law as brought to us by the current Divine Messenger, working on ourselves and our virtues, being of service ..." Rykeir's voice faded as he ducked under the table.

"Dali said that, too. It seems easy to understand," Abby murmured, "but I'm sure it's very hard to do."

Kreshi took over as Rykeir crouched on the floor, opening a small access panel in the table pedestal. "The hardest thing ever. Islam has a hadith, a tradition, that all souls must cross the Sirat al-Jahim, the Bridge of Hell, which is hair-thin and razor-sharp, and from which the wicked will fall into hell.[89] And His Holiness Jesus said it was harder to do than fitting a camel through the eye of a needle."

"But wasn't that just about rich people getting into heaven?" Abby surprised herself by injecting. "Rev. Davison said something about that. Um, Yuter, do you have a Bible? That you could look it up?"

"In the King James version of the Holy Bible, the New Testament, there are two versions of the quotation you request.

"First, quoting: 'Then said Jesus unto his disciples, Verily I say unto you, That a rich man shall hardly enter into the kingdom of heaven. And again I say unto you, It is easier for a camel to go through the eye of a needle than for a rich man to enter into the kingdom of God. When his disciples heard it, they were exceedingly amazed, saying, Who then can be saved? But Jesus beheld them, and said unto them, With men this is impossible, but with God all things are possible.' End quote. That was Matthew 19:23 through 26.

"The second is Mark 10:23 through 27 and is very similar, though it makes the additional point that it is hard for those who *trust* in riches. Special note available."

"Huh, that's all new to me!" Kreshi said cheerfully. "Yuter, please provide special note."

"Special note: The original word gamla – G-A-M-L-A, GAM-lah – can be translated in two ways. One is rope. It was not easy to thread and pull a hawser through a ship's mooring ring or a sturdy rope through the harness rings of a beast of burden, never mind through the eye of a sewing needle, even the large needles they had then for heavy work. The other meaning is camel. It was also not easy, upon arrival at a walled city at night, to unload a camel, lead it through the small doorway in the closed gate, and reload it. Both the ring and the doorway might be called a 'needle's eye.' Perhaps Jesus intentionally means both, so that the analogy would make sense to those who travel by land, those who travel by or work on the sea, and anyone who knows how to sew. In any case, such tasks were very difficult but not impossible, especially with help."

"Interesting. Difficult but not impossible. Help needed. With *God's* help, *all* things are possible. And Jesus did have at least a few wealthy disciples." Kreshi obviously enjoyed the discussion, learning from it, not at all upset at being corrected, picking out the key words with joy.

From under the table, Rykeir's muffled voice added, "Yuter, please, how do the Bahá'í Writings compare?"

"They affirm and elucidate. Quoting: 'O Ye That Pride Yourselves On Mortal Riches! Know ye in truth that wealth is a mighty barrier between the seeker and his desire, the lover and his beloved. The rich, but for a few, shall in no wise attain the court of His presence nor enter the city of content and resignation. Well is it then with him, who, being rich, is not hindered by his riches from the eternal kingdom, nor deprived by them of imperishable dominion. By the Most Great Name! The splendor of such a wealthy man shall illuminate the dwellers of heaven even as the sun enlightens the people of the earth!' End quote. From *The Hidden Words of Bahá'u'lláh*, Persian number 53."

"Thank you so much, Abby, for bringing it up. Okay, not rich people, but for a few," Kreshi summarized as Rykeir regained his chair and rubbed his hands over a job well done. "But can we all agree Jesus Christ did drop many hints that it's not easy to become or stay spiritual, regardless of finances?"

Abby remembered her last time in St. Zosimo's and her fear that she would not be one of the chosen when Jesus returned. She nodded, glad to be asked and included instead of lectured at and frightened.

"But we have an advantage now," Kreshi finished. "It was much harder for the people of your time, with so many negative influences all around you. Staying emotionally positive and spiritually connected must have been very hard."

"Yeah, impossible sometimes," Abby said thoughtfully. *Only*, she wondered, *maybe not impossible with God?*

Chapter 22 Happiness

After a meditative interval, Rykeir whispered loudly, "We may not have as much candy as your time, but we do have chocolate."

"You have *chocolate*?" Abby eagerly snapped back to the moment.

Both boys jumped back in their chairs and warded her away with ludicrous hand motions, making Abby giggle.

"Of course," Rykeir continued, "One of the positive addictions, in my very humble, very addicted opinion."

"Oooohhh, I sure could go for some, too. But I don't have ..."

"We're buying," Kreshi consoled her. "We know time travelers don't come with exact change."

Rykeir went to place an order. Abby's mouth watered in anticipation of digging into a decadent chocolate something. Kreshi briefly consulted his WaerY, then leaned in.

"Do sia have a 12-step program for chocolate addicts back home?" Kreshi asked in a low, funereal voice. "Only 'cuz if sia do, you should join."

She acted offended, slapped at his arm, missed on purpose, and wound up laughing. "It's just been a ... very sudden switch, from my usual diet to a total health-freak diet. Actually, my diet isn't as bad as some," she recalled Ricky's dubious breakfast. "Mother doesn't allow ..." But she didn't want to discuss Mother on the best night of her entire life, so she tried to find something else to think about. Her AerY immediately prompted her.

"Let's think about being addicted to positive things. It's 'later' now."

"Everyone's the comic here. Even your computers are a laugh."

"Yes they are, thank God and the programmers! Okay, so, positive addictions ... you could say we're addicted to happiness, joy, laughter, learning, unity, peace ... I could go on but I think you get the idea," Kreshi contributed.

"Yeah, I might. Yuter? I thi..." Abby's voice faded away as she blinked and switched to silent mode.

—*...nk I understand that I can be strongly drawn to good things but, if the attraction gets out of control, then it's bad. Okay; anything else I'm supposed to think about, please?*—

—Good work, Abby; well thought out. Many Erdeans have said essentially the same thing. As for something else to think about: a happiness quote, if you would like that.—

—*Sure.*—

—In honor of your successful game, here is one by the Master.

153

Quoting: 'Supreme happiness is man's, and he beholds the signs of God in the world and in the human soul, if he urges on the steed of high endeavor in the arena of civilization and justice.' End quote. From The Secret of Divine Civilization, page 4.—

As she listened, Abby began to mentally construct ...

∞   ∞   ∞   ∞   ∞   ∞   ∞   ∞

... an arena fenced in slats spelling out "civilization" and "justice" ... supremely happy, she rides a tall steed named Endeavor ... cues it magically through a flowing dance ... singing birds call her attention to the flowering trees, distant majestic mountains and fragrant hedges basking in honeyed sunshine bordering the arena ... she notices the joy and harmonious ease of the other riders ... adds a scoreboard accumulating Happiness Points, for each rider and for the group ... urges Endeavor to even greater effort ...

∞   ∞   ∞   ∞   ∞   ∞   ∞   ∞

The smell of Rykeir's desserts brought her out of her Scripture-based fantasy. Three plates held different desserts: cake, ice cream, and six pieces of candy.

"No, *no*. Not candy. Belgian truffles!" The young men chorused in feigned umbrage. Rykeir added, "Created, we believe, in honor of the imminence of the Bahá'í Revelation."

"What do you mean?" Abby asked.

"Belgian chocolate was invented about four years before the Bahá'í Faith began. A fitting invention, along with many other fitting inventions for this era. Everyone want some of everything?" Rykeir asked and, at their nods, dividing the desserts.

It'd be impossible not to be happy here, Abby mused. *Everyone is so kind and caring, everything is so beautiful, so carefully arranged.*

"Oh, we still have lots of unhappiness. I have some I could spare if you're running out," Rykeir said, making a goofy face and handing her a chocolate collection.

"What could make anyone unhappy? It's so perfect!"

"You're just on vacation. Everybody loves wherever sia are on vacation," he teased, passing Kreshi the third sampler plate.

"Not when you nearly get killed crashing into a tree," Abby retorted defensively. She sought to soothe her ruffled feathers with a truffle. It worked: rich chocolate medicine.

"Okay, granted, but when real life sets in wherever you are, then the bliss fades some. The bike breaks, you lose your job, it rains too much, or doesn't rain at all, you get sick—" Rykeir vented.

"I thought y'all were so healthy here."

"We still have illness. Not as much as in your time, but some. And people still get hurt, disabled, or killed in accidents. Of course, we can repair or replace almost every body part, if we can get to people soon enough. But there are definitely still tests and difficulties. For a complete account of our petty woes, visit Auntie Zoray," Kreshi said.

Abby smiled, happy to know about Auntie Zoray. "I thought there wouldn't be any sorrow at all when earth becomes heaven," Abby said around a bite of what must be chocolate soy ice cream, the most luscious ice cream she'd ever had.

"Yuter? Any input, please?" Kreshi asked.

All three yuters relayed the answer.

"When asked about attaining happiness without suffering, 'Abdu'l-Bahá answered, 'To attain eternal happiness one must suffer. He who has reached the state of self-sacrifice has true joy.' From *Paris Talks*, page 179. When asked if a person who had attained development through suffering should then fear happiness, he answered, quoting: 'Through suffering, he will attain to an eternal happiness which nothing can take from him. The apostles of Christ suffered: they attained eternal happiness.' From *Paris Talks*, page 178".

While Kreshi leaned back in his chair and tended, Rykeir explained, "God has assured us that to be prepared for the next world, we need to grow strong in the positive attributes, here in this world. So Sia sends us trials and tribulations – which, by the way, I'm developing into a card game – but in real life, it might be managing our finances, or not offending people, or controlling anger. In fact, developing any of the godly attributes is what it all boils down to. Patience is a huge one."

"I keep hearing about attributes and virtues. What are those?"

"Yuter, please list some virtues for Abby."

"Attentive, assertive, brave, calm, careful, caring, cheerful, clean, compassionate, confident, cooperative, considerate, courteous, creative, curious, detached, determined, enthusiastic, excellent, fair, faithful, flexible, focused, forgiving, friendly, full of awe, full of pity, generous, gentle, graceful, happy, helpful, honest—"

Abby got the idea. "Yuter, please stop. Thank you."

"Huh, you weren't even halfway through! You didn't get close to your *own* virtue!" Rykeir kibitzed.

"Ha ha, I get it! Wise."

"And somehow, the list never includes *my* favorite," Rykeir bandied.

"Let me guess. Smart … alec," Abby nailed it.

"Who's reading minds now?" Kreshi grinned.

"Just a lucky guess." Abby enjoyed the banter as much as the chocolate, which was almost gone.

Dali appeared at their table and asked Abby if she was about ready to head home.

Abby took a long time to answer, sure that everyone could hear, but she wanted them to. Did yuters convey feelings? She didn't know if the others could feel her joy at being part of this precious event. Tearing herself away might be one of the most difficult things she'd ever had to force herself to do.

"O Courageous One, you can do what you need to do," Kreshi murmured to her.

She felt her courage rise with his benediction.

"I guess all good times must come to an end," she said regretfully, modifying the saying from her era and steeling herself for what she knew she had to do.

"Come back around any time," Rykeir ventured, "when you want another walloping."

"Beat you at riding games? Sure!" Abby retorted quickly. "Or pierce your ears, or any other body part. Or learn more yutering. Or argue religion."

"Arguing about religion is taboo for Bahá'ís ... you weren't really arguing, were you?" Dali fixed the boys with a firm stare.

"Were too," Rykeir responded resolutely.

"Doubt it," Dali rejoined.

"You're right. Hey, didn't you have somewhere, or somewhen, to go?" Kreshi motioned Dali toward the door and winked at Abby.

"Yeah, get out of here, before we make you stay longer!" Rykeir parried, his hair lights all blinking.

"Okay, okay, we're going, we're going!" Dali laughed. Abby copied the other three as they pressed their right hands over their hearts and nodded a God-bee.

"See you later, we hope! Namaste! Great to see you! Ciao! Adios!" Everyone called as Dali steered Abby by the elbow to maneuver her through the thinning crowd.

"Oh, but I didn't even thank the hostess!" Abby exclaimed, Mother's etiquette exhortations sounding in her head.

"She's there, if you still want to," Dali said, pointing out an older sister of Elle's. "Also, this is the aunt who gave me her house," Dali explained, inviting Abby over to meet a thin-faced, khaki-toned, inviting-looking woman standing next to an ebony-skinned, very fit, energetic man. "Her name is Polska Homer. This is her husband, Uncle Franco Ardent; we call him Arno. Go ahead, I finally realized their yuters will translate you to them; it's not important if you speak Old American."

"I'm very glad to meet you," Abby said to the middle-aged … no, she'd be a young woman in this world where a lifespan was a century and a half. "I'm staying in the house you gave Dali. It's very nice."

As Arno looked on supportively, Polska grasped both her hands warmly. Polska's face and dark-brown, puffy hair framed an attractive smile and searching, warm, blue eyes. Abby was not ready to be x-rayed by Polska's eyes, though, and found herself looking down at the lean woman's clean, loose, orange dress and low-heeled brown shoes next to her own worryingly-dirty-yet-not-dirty-enough tennies.

"I'm so glad you found that house," Polska said. "I had a feeling it would play host to a very special visitor someday. I think it is you. Welcome. I trust you've been comfortable."

Abby was uncomfortable with Polska's spiritual vision flooding her. She stammered her thanks and then nudged Dali along toward the evening's hostess, Tuanay, to whom Abby offered her hand.

"Thank you for a wonderful evening," Abby said as sincerely as she could. "I had a terrific time."

The muscular young woman smiled warmly, gripped Abby's hand firmly, and said she was really glad Abby had come, and even more glad she'd had so much fun.

"I saw you with Rykeir and Kreshi," Tuanay said. "They are such great company, *jes*? I hoped they'd come enliven our gathering."

"*Yes, too-ah-nay.*" Abby was careful not to stress any syllable.

"You're a very lucky girl to have had the undivided attentions of two such exceptional young men at the same time." Not one iota of judgment or jealousy flashed in Tuanay's words or tone. Copying Dali's *DON-cone*, Abby also told Tuanay, "Dankon. Thank you."

As they turned to leave, a large group filed in the door: several young couples with a passel of youngsters … here, it seemed, to celebrate a 5-year-old boy's achievement: finding a weakness in some fruit harvesting machine engines and designing a fix, just in time for the upcoming harvests. Abby wondered if the boy would be back in 10 years to celebrate another milestone.

As she waited for the doorway to empty, she gazed one last time at the wallpaper border. This section showed a low, ragged mountain, dotted with hikers and mountain climbers as well as zebras and other zoo animals. Monkeys climbed trees to play with giraffes. A few companions formed a camp circle, sitting on logs and roasting marshmallows near the gently flaming mouth of an obliging dragon.

A small gaggle of dragons, winged and not, circled the peak in great swoops, joined now by several pterappi from both East and West. Three figures broke off and flew in a smaller group toward a broad ledge where a lone teenaged girl stood admiring the view.

As Abby watched, she noticed that the girl looked like herself, in distinctive shirt and pants, her light skin standing out. The three figures drew closer and landed: a buckskin unicorn, a pearly pterippus, and a black Longma swirling in gray smoke.

Abby's wallpaper doppelgänger greeted and caressed each of the creatures, then stepped back, stood tall, held up her hands and spoke authoritatively. The three animals slid together, blending into a new, single creature: a pterippus-unicorn-dragon.

Its horn protruded from a golden horse head. Pearly feathered wings beat powerfully from its shoulders. A pearlized patch of hair between the wings seemed to mark a rider's spot. The golden front end blended gradually into black hair patterned in scales over its ribs and hindquarters. Black legs led to strong black hooves. A black mane waved in the wallpaper wind, smoke dripping off the tips. The magnificent tail resembled a burning flame in the wind.

"Wow, that's ... what is that?" Abby stammered softly, thunderstruck.

"Let's make a new name for your new creation. Part winged creature – ala ... part Longma – ma ... part unicorn – corn. Almacorn?" the yuter offered.

"Almacorn!" Abby breathed, watching herself climb on the new creature and fly off.[90] The wallpaper continued to create scenes around real restaurant patrons: miniature Kreshi and Rykeir mirrored each other in a dance reminiscent of the DDR Abby had tried; tiny Dali peered out over the railing of a lighthouse. Abby spied Elle ... and the birthday boy who'd just come in ... and three defenders from the martial-arts dance ... and—

"Oh, doorway's clear," Dali said. Abby tore her eyes away from the tableau and followed Dali out of the restaurant. Mind blown, heart swelled, she really, *really* hoped she could come back, and soon.

It needed a new name, she reflected. It was not a restaurant in the usual sense, but a place to find fun and eats. What would the right word be? Featery? *I performed a few unique feats there!*

Her AerY said pleasantly, *"Featery is cute, Abby. We usually call them 'foodles,' though."*

As Abby pedaled home with Dali, Tuanay's comments echoed in her head. She did feel lucky, very lucky ... and something more. Again, her stomach tingled in that funny way when she thought about Kreshi. He was definitely special. She liked him. A lot. *Was this love?* She wondered what he felt about her. They were three years apart, and she must have seemed like just a kid sister to him. But perhaps when she got older, three years might not be so much. But they were also many hundreds of years apart, and even though he knew it, they could not erase the fact that she was from a different world. If he were ever interested. Which she hoped he was.

"Are you ok?" Dali asked quietly.

"Sure would be nice to have some secrets," Abby retorted.

"That's possible, but usually you have to block your Yuter," Dali half-joked, smiling to lighten the mood.

Abby couldn't stay irritated, with Dali sounding so much like Jenn. And she could really use a sympathetic ear right now. Here was a boy … man … what's between a boy and a man? A moy? Okay, here was a moy Abby liked but shouldn't. What to do?

Dali glanced at Abby but said nothing more as they pedaled down the bike lane, passing the House of Worship. Lights shone in the fountain, along the wood beams, and by the walkways. *Just as pretty as in the daylight,* Abby mused, *but in a different way.*

Perhaps it was the loving space Dali gave her, or maybe the infusion the House of Worship created, but eventually Abby's thoughts gelled. "I've never liked a moy before. I don't think I can do anything about it, though, with our time and age differences. Even if dating is allowed, and even if I was 16. And I bet you Erdeans don't look at dating like we do."

"I bet you're right," Dali said seriously. "Didn't your media create the impression it's okay to be sexy … have sex … with people you're not married to?"

"No duh." Abby flashed on obscene songs and stripping celebrities.

They passed Mr. Sawqui's house, where an expanded car full of smiling, familiar faces hummed away from the curb. Everyone waved and called to each other.

"Well, here, or, now, it's different," Dali answered. "It's a huge topic, because once we feel that attraction, it's hard to remember how to manage it. We remind each other and ourselves that, 'Chastity is only hell if you forget the heaven of a fortress well-built.' "

"Meaning, you have to check out the other person really well first?"

"Yes! It's smart to make sure all the bricks are in place before moving in."

"That sounds like it could take a while."

"That's right. Which is good, because if love is blind, time takes the blindfold off! Oh, and since the beginning of maturity is 15, people can marry then, so they practice assessing each other when they start maturing sexually, like at about your age."

"Wow, so people start having kids at age 15? No wonder so many of the parents at the Draggin' Dragon looked so young."

"We usually wait until we're more mature to have any children. In our early 20's."

Speaking of the foodle brought back images of the evening: a roomful of friends, the wallpaper, the potluck tasting, dancing and fancing. Again she felt very lucky indeed. As they wheeled their bikes up to the house, humbleness and gladness also washed over her. She felt like giving thanks, but didn't know how. Her questing thought was timid.

—*Yuter, please, what is a suitable prayer of thanksgiving?—*

—Perhaps you will like this one, Abby. Quoting: 'In the Name of God, the Most High! Lauded and glorified art Thou, Lord, God Omnipotent! Thou before Whose wisdom the wise falleth short ...'—

Abby startled at the surprisingly apt choice of words.

—'... and faileth, before Whose knowledge the learned confesseth his ignorance, ... toward the shrine of Whose knowledge turneth the essence of all understanding and around the sanctuary of Whose presence circle the souls of all mankind.

—'How then can I sing and tell of Thine Essence, which the wisdom of the wise and the learning of the learned have failed to comprehend, inasmuch as ...'—

Abby sighed. Could the wisdom of the Wize learn to comprehend?

—'...no man can sing that which he understandeth not, nor recount that unto which he cannot attain, whilst Thou hast been from everlasting the Inaccessible, the Unsearchable. Powerless though I be to rise to the heavens of Thy glory and soar in the realms of Thy knowledge, I can but recount Thy tokens that tell of Thy glorious handiwork....

—'All praise and glory be to Thee, Thou of Whom all things have testified that Thou art one and there is none other God but Thee, Who hast been from everlasting exalted above all peer or likeness and to everlasting shalt remain the same. All kings are but Thy servants and all beings, visible and invisible, as naught before Thee. There is none other God but Thee, the Gracious, the Powerful, the Most High.' From Bahá'í Prayers, pages 136 to 138.—

Abby was grateful for so much just now. Standing in Dali's yard after parking the bikes, drinking in the fresh air and the night sky accented with a whippoorwill call, her spirit soaring with swooping bats and a fleeting, white, owl-like shadow. Blessings, all of them. Being here, experiencing a sublime world. Using an intuitive device to explain it to her. And whatever that didn't handle, well, the world's best guide had adopted her and helped her in every way humanly possible.

"Thank you, Yuter. And thank you so much for helping me, Dali," Abby said humbly.

"It is my very greatest pleasure, Abby," Dali replied. "And now I must ask your forgiveness."

"For what?!"

"For, uh, abandoning you at the Draggin' Dragon. I should have stayed with you. I got carried away, seeing my friends. Also, I thought you were doing just fine; I knew Kreshi and Rykeir would take excellent care of you. But still …" She exhaled loudly. "It may surprise you to find out that we are still human, and we still make mistakes."

"Oh dear, I, uh …" Abby was totally surprised. She had very little experience handling personal apologies. "Well, I forgive you, if you forgive me for being irritated about listening to my thoughts about Kreshi."

"Of course I do. I understand how difficult this must be for you."

"You understand? Really?" Abby wondered how Dali could see things from Abby's perspective, different as it was.

"Ah, my secret is exposed," Dali said in a mock-mysterious voice, leading the way into the house. "As part of my Old American History class, I studied your culture." Dali frowned, then glanced at Abby and seemed to steer the conversation away from the flaws of Old America. "I enjoyed studying the languages of your time, including Esperanto and Old American. They went into UL, along with special words included from unrelated languages like Arabic, Bantu, and Chinese."

"Is that how you were able to speak with me so quickly?"

"Yes, and of course with my WaerY."

"And Rykeir and Kreshi did take awesome care of me, but was any of that more than big-brother caring?" Abby asked.

"That is a deep, complicated question," Dali said. "More than we can cover tonight. But I will say that I think Kreshi liked you more than a little."

"Really?" Abby's head snapped toward this tidbit. "How can you tell?"

"He's actually fairly quiet. I was surprised that he struck up a con-versation with you. I've never seen him smile so much. And every time I've asked him to dance, he's told me he isn't into dancing. I've never seen him dance with anyone else, either. But maybe he's just taken up dancing since then."

More food for meditating … and to hold close to her heart.

Getting ready for bed again felt like the second night of an extended slumber party. When Dali came out of the bathroom, Abby asked her, "Should I take the AerY out?"

"You don't have to; you can leave it in if it's comfortable," Dali replied.

It was, so Abby left it in and slid into her couch-bed. Abby heard Dali murmur her Long Obligatory Prayer in the little bedroom, thanks to the AerY. She felt so welcomed, encouraged, looked after. And, just possibly, loved ...

∞   ∞   ∞   ∞   ∞   ∞   ∞   ∞

... she's a child in a swing ... **ZZP** *... a baby in a tree-borne cradle ... the wind blows, hard, harder, hurricane-strong ... breaks the branch, tumbles her out of the cradle and into Dali's protective arms ...* **ZZP** *... a teenager, she dances away from Dali ... mounts a dappled horse ... it grows wings and carries her aloft 'round the mountain peak of a lush tropical islet ... she looks down ... laughs ... leaps from the pterippus deep into the sea ... lands on a gigantic seahorse ... it changes from luminous yellow to fiery orange and sweeps her up to the surface and in to shore ... she skips happily across the wet sand ...* **ZZP** *... in a grassy meadow, she slows to catch her breath ... sees a handsome centaur quietly looking at her through big glasses ... opens his huge book ... strikes a teacher's pose ... grins, and she recognizes Kreshi ...*

∞   ∞   ∞   ∞   ∞   ∞   ∞   ∞

"Happy Monday," crooned the AerY as she opened her eyes to the morning light with the pterippus, seahorse and centaur still coursing happily through her mind.[91] "In the words of the Master, 'It is demonstrable that in this life, both outwardly and inwardly the mightiest of structures, the most solidly established, the most enduring, standing guard over the world, assuring both the spiritual and the material perfections of mankind, and protecting the happiness and the civilization of society – is religion.' From *The Secret of Divine Civilization*, pages 71 and 72."

Even though the Bahá'í Writings had first struck Abby like a taco-flavored, fried-rice, chocolate loaf, she could now see the similarities with the Bible she'd grown up with. Different religions had their own unique flavors, and tasting them was expanding Abby's palate.

Licking and chewing on that tasty thought, she arose to greet her Monday.

Chapter 23 Deepening

"Care for a shower this morning?" Dali invited. "I've been spot-bathing and making sure I do my feet, but we have time before the deepening to do a more thorough job."

"Should I be spot-cleaning my feet, too?" Abby asked, wondering about a hidden rule or some physical danger.

"If you want to," Dali said, pulling plush towels off the bathroom wicker shelves and checking the soap. "Anyone can opt to follow Bahá'í laws and teachings, whether or not they're a declared Bahá'í. Bahá'u'lláh asks us to wash our feet every day in the summer."

After, as Dali sipped her lemon water at the breakfast table, Abby asked, "What's on tap for today, boss?"

Dali frowned, got up, fetched her WaerY from the bedroom, and put it on the table between them. It whispered as she carried it.

Abby was pleased that her Erdean enculturation now enabled her to see that Dali sometimes did not understand Old American, especially slang. Dali started to sit, then smacked herself on the forehead in the universal, apparently timeless, sign for, "Ack, I missed it!"

She fetched the ALLY from the living room and pressed it onto the low wall next to the kitchen table, touching its frame three times.

"There! Full access for both of us! If only we used all our resources to full capacity! We're so rich, so blessed, we forget what we have!"

Dali settled into her chair and began to eat her nut-buttered toast. Abby realized that toast was sliced from a loaf made less than two days before; two days packed with learning, love and growth. Her own tolerable scrambled tofu and sweet onion breakfast wrap went nicely with her mint tea.

"You asked about today's schedule. Maybe you'd like to go with me to Spiritual School this morning? And the animal show is this afternoon," Dali said.

"Oh! The animals! Where? What time?" Abby asked.

"It's all within biking distance," Dali said, pointing to a map on the ALLY. "The 'Ilm Academy gets over in time to have lunch and then get to the animals, which starts at, uh, three."

"Okay. Just let me know what I need to do," Abby said, watching virtual green lines lead from the you-are-here symbol to a dot labeled SPIRITA LERNEJO and on to BESTMONTREJO.[92] A stray thought floated across Abby's consciousness about doing laundry sometime soon. She did not want to stink. Humiliation over that issue swelled within her, and she did her best to squelch it.

"I'm about to put in some laundry; it'll be done by the time we get back tonight," Dali said. "If you wish, I can loan you some underwear while yours are washing." Dear Dali. Practical yet always considerate, even with touchy issues. Abby would take Dali's way of handling intimate matters any day.

Dali's loaner bra was worth writing home about, if only Abby could send Jenn a letter back in time. It looked like a cotton camisole but as Abby's body warmed it, it shrank to hug her. The fabric of the boxer-cut panties was similar. Both were extremely comfortable and, Abby noticed most of all, completely seamless.

Abby gathered her Earther clothes and Dali's loaners, meeting Dali at the machine sitting behind a low wall off the far corner of the living room. Dali's washing machine looked like one from Abby's time. She supposed washing machines could've changed only so much, even in seven centuries, but something made her double-check her assumption.

Remembering Kreshi's tip, she ventured a new request with the yuter. "Yuter, please compare washing machines between my time and now."

"Washing machines now are better described as washing, drying, mending, and folding machines. They are called clothers."

Abby stood corrected. A *KLOE-ther* was way better. Everyone in her time would want one. Probably everyone here already had one.

"Not everyone," Dali shared, smiling. "They cost money and have to be maintained. Some people don't get their clothes dirty enough to need the deep cleaning, but I am often out digging in the dirt, like when you first saw me."

"It's a pretty cool machine, though!" Abby replied, holding out her clothes.

"We do have some very bonega machines," Dali replied, gesturing in wordless invitation for Abby to load her clothes into the clother. "Healers use a lot of machines, and the outer space professions have very advanced equipment. But most of us keep our machinery to a minimum, because of problems like exploiting Mother Earth for the raw materials. We're still rebuilding the world from the ravages of your time."

"That sounds bad!"

"We're almost there. People eventually realized that happiness means owning less, instead of working more to buy more, pay for places to store it all, and afford repairs. And trashing out the planet to throw the broken machines away … tchuh!" Dali made a sound of disgust, then shook her head. "When people went lower-tech to spare the planet and free up time for playing and service, they knew that would mean a bit of extra work, but that's a Glad Tiding. [93] Once their health improved enough, of course."

Abby's brow wrinkled as she tried to imagine how work could be a glad tiding. Playing with it, though, she thought that work being worship made more sense than worship turning into work.

"Puttering through chores counts as gentle exercise," Dali continued, adding her own clothes to the clother, "but I like them because I have good meditations when my hands are busy and my mind is free. Some chores, like fixing things, bring their own reward, too. Or my gardening gives me tasty food I can share, and helps whoever is following the Master's diet."

"What's that?"

"Simple foods such as the Master ate: fresh vegetables and fruits, bread, broths, rice, teas. He did have a sweet tooth, too," Dali smiled as she added soap, "but he didn't let it control him. Often his friends gave him candy, but he shared instead of hogging out."[94]

Abby copied Dali's gentle manner. "You mean *hogging them all*, or *pigging out*." She paused to gather her thoughts. "I am surprised at how low-tech Erden is, but it makes sense."

"We have high-tech, too, when it's the best answer – the yuters, for example. Or the Natural Disaster Prevention Division's machines.

"What do they do?"

"Oh, let's see … relieve fault lines to prevent major earthquakes, and nudge comets away … and steer hurricanes away from people and onto empty land … wildfire control …."

Dali started the clother and headed for the kitchen, Abby following. "We have finally learned that it's best to live simply, spiritually, er, would you call it *close to nature*?" Abby nodded. Dali continued, listening to her WaerY, "It's less expensive, more, um … you called it sustainable; we just call it wise."

The girls packed two lunches: packages of soy sticks, veggie wedges and an "aweful sauce" with paper napkins and energy bars. Dali showed Abby where to press the water bottles so the inside self-cooled while the outside stayed at room temperature and therefore dry.

When they left the house, Abby asked if Dali would teach her how to command the door shut, and was delighted when her own carefully repeated *"POR-doe, sh'low-SEE-jew"* caused the artistically carved wooden door to swing shut and click.[95] They loaded their bags into the bicycle baskets and rode off down the familiar lane. Abby opened her senses to the beauty around her, inhaling the fresh morning air. Wait. Smelling? In the morning? She had never been able to smell in the morning; her nose was always plugged up. Why did it work now?

—Yuter, please, why can I smell now and I never could before?—

—Stuffy noses that are not linked to illness are usually allergies. Common food allergens from your time included citrus, corn, wheat, soy, nuts, dairy, and shellfish, as well as many toxins.—

Food allergies could make a stuffy nose? That was news.

—Yuter, please, how would I figure out which food was making my nose stuffy every morning?—

—Eat a diet of inoffensive foods for a week or two, then add in one thing at a time and see if it gives you symptoms.—

That sounded like a huge pain.

—Is there any other way, please?—

—Some people have found the following practices helpful: Read or consult with others about it. Find a skilled healer to work with and test you. Pray and meditate about different foods; then see if God suggests anything, or pass your hand over different foods to see how their energy interacts with yours. A variation is to hold the item while someone tests your strength, which is called muscle testing or energy reading.—[96]

That just sounds fruity, Yuter, pardon the pun, Abby thought. She didn't want the yuter to respond, so she didn't think "Yuter ... please."

The girls pedaled up to the community center a few streets away from the Lodlan House of Worship, where the 'Ilm Academy Spiritual School was held. Its plain front lawn invited the students into its spacious, cool interior. The littlest pupils scampered through its one large room, heading for the fenced play area in back. Bright balls, hula-hoops, and other toys peeked through wire mesh cages under the extended roof. The girls parked their bikes and wandered closer to the kids as Abby asked questions.

"You leave toys out?"

"They're not out. They're put away."

"But they're not locked up; anyone could steal them."

"No one would steal them. Well, highly unlikely, anyway."[97]

"Oh, right, no crime. I keep forgetting. But didn't we just lock your house?"

"Yes, because animals smell the food and could open the door and help themselves," Dali said, smiling. "Raccoons are extremely clever, with their little hands. Goats are the worst. They have no fear and no manners, but are drawn to food like pilgrims to a shrine."

Abby laughed, thinking of John Wayne's drawling use of that word. His pilgrims might have honed in on a corral or a bar, but not a shrine.

"And I suppose if the door isn't closed tight and locked, bugs and mice would get in," Abby supplied, watching the children take toys out of the wire cages.

"No, we have … ah … energy fields around houses that keep the smaller creatures out."[98]

"No crime, no illness, *and* no bugs in the house? I hope I never leave!" Abby breathed.

"Well now, sometimes we do have crime, as Kreshi and Rykeir mentioned," Dali amended. "Once in a while someone will intentionally harm someone else, steal something valuable, set fire to something, wreck something big … a few years ago, someone attempted to hijack an ocean freighter. *Had* to be insane to try that." Dali turned slowly toward the community center front doors.

"So they get a lot of counseling," Abby parroted Kreshi and Rykeir.

"Hmm, well, there is capital punishment for killing and arson, and severe punishments for theft and—"

"I thought you were so focused on educating people into correct behavior."

"Yes, we are. We prevent crime through education, and counsel wrong-doers in the early stages, but we do have punishments. Yuter, what's that quote about putting to death an arsonist?"

"Bahá'u'lláh wrote, 'Should anyone intentionally destroy a house by fire, him also shall ye burn; should anyone deliberately take another's life, him also shall ye put to death.'[99] Of course, justice is carried out by the proper authorities, not by individuals. And the death of the murderer or arsonist is the maximum punishment … no abuse or torture, no 'justice killing' of family members or confiscating lawful possessions, no revenge."

Dali waited for a moment before offering her thoughts. Abby waited, always interested in anything she had to say.

"Please remember that Bahá'u'lláh's laws of crime and punishment only fully apply to now, when the justice system is, well, *just*. He also allowed for life imprisonment or lesser punishment, and admonished criminals to sincerely regret and pay for their crimes, because the scales will be balanced in the next life. My reading gives me the feeling that wrong-doers would *really* regret trying to escape punishment in this life. Yearning to be closer to the Eternally Loving God but held at a distance would be much worse than whatever just sentence they'd get on this earth."

As they walked slowly to the main door of the community center, Abby contrasted Dali's description of eternal punishment to Rev. Davison's sermons on the fire and brimstone of hell, thinking that the former was much fairer … more just … even though she caught a whiff of smoke just thinking about hell. She looked around to see if anyone was burning trash nearby. As she entered the building's large central room, the burning smell faded, replaced by soft clanging noises from a small kitchen off to one side.

"We take turns cooking the noon meal after class," Dali said, "for whoever wants to stay and eat together."

As Dali looked for a pair of chairs, Abby mentally predicted that they would be shouting over the kitchen noises. Unconsciously, she found herself muttering a question.

—Like the Draggin' Dragon, this building is sound-programmed. Today, the room will dampen all sounds but adult voices, except for emergencies.—

She hadn't even addressed the yuter, and it still helped her.

—Now, in the words of the Master, quoting: 'Happiness consists of two kinds; physical and spiritual. The physical happiness is limited; its utmost duration is one day, one month, one year. It hath no result. Spiritual happiness is eternal and unfathomable. This kind of happiness appeareth in one's soul with the love of God and suffereth one to attain to the virtues and perfections of the world of humanity. Therefore, endeavor as much as thou art able in order to illuminate the lamp of thy heart by the light of love.' End quote. From *Tablets of 'Abdu'l-Bahá*, volume 3, pages 673 to 674.—

—*Thank you, Yuter.*— Abby appreciated the hope this quote gave her. She felt that if she developed her spiritual self, she could wind up nearer to God in the next world.

—You are very welcome. Have a wonderful deepening.—

Not for the first time, Abby felt awash with gratitude for the super-useful yuter. Maybe it was her polluted Earther thinking, but she began imagining the evil ends people in her hometime would put it to.

"Dali, what prevents people from using the yuter in bad ways?"

Dali stopped greeting people and looked deep into Abby's eyes to intuit her intent. Abby tried to look back steadily, and almost made it.

"Here, we're trained not to do bad things, no matter what the opportunity or tool. Since anything can become a weapon, it is the training and beliefs that matter, not the tool."

"What do you mean, 'anything can become a weapon'?"

"A pillow is very nice, is it not?"

"Of course."

"It has also been used to suffocate people."

"True."

"Everything can become a weapon, Abby. A hug can crush. A kiss marked the Blessed Christ for death. Shall we ban pillows, kisses, or hugs? Coffee mugs and power cords? Babies and old people?"

"What have babies and old people got to do with it?"

"In the very worst of times, they have also been used as weapons.

Like, bombs were tucked inside a baby's clothes. And when somebody picked the baby up, the bomb exploded, killing everyone around."[100]

Oh no, that was too horrible to think of. She wished that Dali hadn't said it. She shook her head, trying to rid herself of the appalling images now swirling in her mind, trying to distract herself by intensely examining the people chatting and choosing chairs.

"I am so sorry, Abby. Perhaps I shouldn't have answered your last question that way. In our time, we're aware of some of the worst things from your time, but we have the blessing of being far from it. It is remote for us. But I can see it is very tangible for you."

"I was six years old when 9/11 happened." Abby trusted the yuter to help Dali understand what she meant. "The footage ran on TV for three days. School was cancelled. People didn't know what to do. One of my schoolmates, his uncle-in-law was killed in it. I will never forget it. And you know, the war on terrorism is still—" Abby stopped. Wait ... a *war* to stop terrorism? How was more fighting going to stop the killing? Wouldn't it mean people were just keeping the cycle of retaliation and death going? It was still death and misery and horror ....

"When did it end?" Abby pleaded.

"Unfortunately, not for quite a while." Dali laid a sympathetic hand on Abby's shoulder to soften the blow. "Bahá'u'lláh wrote about two simultaneous processes. One was the building up of new, unifying practices, which He mostly explained in His Writings. The other process was the sweeping away of anything not built on spiritual, sustainable, peace-oriented practices. Wrong-minded things that really could not be fixed needed to go. But the hardest part was getting to the point where people finally saw the real answer: they had to be willing to begin the change within themselves. So, not until things got *really* awful, in your sense of that word."

This was super-bad news. As bad as Abby's world was, it was going to get worse? How she could possibly handle it?

"These processes eventually led to the Most Great Peace," Dali explained compassionately, holding Abby's hand. "First came the Lesser Peace, when all the nations signed a cease-fire treaty, and started working together on vital issues and discussing a world commonwealth. But we have only recently reached true, lasting peace ... peace written not just on paper, but in the hearts of the people."

The room was getting crowded. Several people squeezed by Abby and Dali, interrupting the discussion, giving Abby a moment to think.

So Bahá'ís knew about the two processes from the early days; her days? Knew it would get worse? How could Melissa be so happy? She had even influenced Jon to her way of thinking! If Abby ever got back to her own time, she'd have to ask Melissa how she coped.

A soft tone sounded: the class facilitator ceremonially struck a small gong twice more with a small wooden mallet.

Dali, Abby and at least 100 other people seated themselves at tables arranged in two concentric circles around a large empty space in the middle of the room. Abby faintly heard the youngest children playing in back and the older ones on the front lawn in a more structured activity. The noise faded, but still the adults could monitor their little ones in case they were threatened by, say, an ill-mannered goat.

An elegantly-dressed, dignified, older woman stood, opened her small book, composed herself, closed her eyes, and chanted in a rich, melodious, authoritative voice, translated by her trusty AerY.

—*This sounds different from UL or New American, Yuter.*—

—Correct, Abby; it's in the original Arabic.—

—*It's really beautiful! Arabic, huh? One of the languages that went into UL?*—

—Actually, one of the languages we use words from, unaltered.—

—*Oh, that's right. OK, please continue with the translation.*—

—Translating the words of Bahá'u'lláh: 'Verily, this is that Most Great Beauty, foretold in the Books of the Messengers, through Whom truth shall be distinguished from error and the wisdom of every command shall be tested. Verily He is the Tree of Life that bringeth forth the fruits of God, the Exalted, the Powerful, the Great.'—

The translation continued but Abby drifted away with the thought that Christ and Bahá'u'lláh sounded so much alike because They *were* so much alike. Different times, same message. Different voices, same Source. Bahá'u'lláh, the return of Christ and apparently the other great Prophets, had returned over a century before Abby was born. Rev. Davison had even listed the signs that had already happened, and so must have other clergy, but still almost everyone had missed it. Bahá'u'lláh had indeed come like a thief in the night. But such an unusual Thief, coming to claim only hearts.

—'He is God and there is no God but Him, the King, the Protector, the Incomparable, the Omnipotent.'—

The words reverberated in Abby's mind like the great trumpet blast Rev. Davison described: warning, inviting, urging, enfolding. She felt fortunate beyond measure to hear and respond. As she continued to listen, certain phrases resonated in her heart, in her soul.

— ... be obedient to the ordinances of God ... whosoever desireth let him choose the path to his Lord ... be not thou troubled ... rely upon God ... for the people are wandering in the paths of delusion, bereft of discernment....—

Even though she didn't understand some of the words, the import became clear: God was calling. If she responded, wouldn't she gain some of the serenity she saw in the gentle faces of the gifted people surrounding her?

The chanting ended and a short silence ensued.

"Thank you, Ms. Bahiyyih," the facilitator said softly. She pronounced her name *Bah-hee-yah.*[101]

"We are continuing today with our program on the Central Figures of the Bahá'í Faith. We have several newcomers this time, so let me begin with a brief review.

"We've studied the Báb. His name was Siyyid 'Alí-Muhammad. Siyyid means a direct descendant of the Prophet Muhammad. He was born in Persia, later called Iran, on October 20, 1819. The Arabic word Báb is a title and means 'Gate'. He was the spiritual gate to Bahá'u'lláh, Who was also born in Persia, on November 12, 1817 as Husayn-'Alí Núrí. The Arabic title Bahá'u'lláh means 'Glory of God'."

Abby thought the Báb sounded similar to John the Baptist.

"Last week," the woman continued, "we deepened our knowledge about Bahá'u'lláh's eldest son and heir, 'Abbás Effendi. He chose for himself the title 'Abdu'l-Bahá, which means 'Servant of Bahá', declaring servitude to be his dearest ambition.[102]

Abby carefully repeated the new names in her mind: The *BAWB, sih-YIHD ah-lee moe-HAH-mahd, who-SANE ah-lee NEW-ree,* and *AB-buss eh-FEN-dee.*

"The Bahá'í Faith is the first religion to solve the big problem of splits among its followers. Bahá'u'lláh wrote that His son, 'Abdu'l-Bahá, should lead the Faith after He passed from this mortal life. 'Abdu'l-Bahá in turn wrote that Bahá'ís should follow his grandson, Shoghi Effendi, whose ministry was dedicated to developing the Faith so it could establish the governing councils also dictated in the Master's will. After 'Abdu'l-Bahá's death, his sister, Bahiyyih Khanum, continued to help lead the faith as she had whenever 'Abdu'l-Bahá traveled, then assisting Shoghi Effendi in many capacities." The moderator glanced at this illustrious figure's seated namesake with a small smile as Abby marveled at the striking idea that a Manifestation of God was married and had children, and that a daughter had been so instrumental in such an important endeavor. It elevated her ideas of what a daughter like herself might be able to do.

"When Shoghi Effendi, titled the Guardian, passed away with no children and no will, his faithful assistants, the Hands of the Cause of God, realized it was time for the Bahá'ís of the world to fulfill that provision of the Writings and elect the Universal House of Justice. Elected every five years, that most esteemed assemblage has guided us ever since. This continuity has made all the difference in being able to put into practice the wonderful teachings our Founding Figures left us in their thousands of letters and books."

Abby practiced that unfamiliar name: *SHOW-ghee*.

"We are extremely fortunate to live in the time for which They, and countless other Prophets and believers, worked ceaselessly: true world peace and unity. We all have the *ma'rifat* that we are world citizens.

—Yuter, please, I didn't catch that word.—

—It is *ma-rih-FAHT*, an Arabic word connoting true spiritual understanding, deep recognition, and profound knowledge.—

Remembering a science fiction book Jenn had read and told her about, Abby thought that *ma'rifat* sounded gentler than *grok*.

"This week we have a marvelous dramatic presentation that I think we'll all enjoy. Yuter, please, lights low. Thank you."

The lights gradually dimmed. In the center of the room in the empty space, a three-dimensional image appeared and grew brighter. When the Erdean woman in Victorian garb spoke, the yuter translated in her voice. Abby soon realized she was a talented Erdean actress speaking as if she had personally met the Master.[103]

"I am Ramona Allen Brown, the daughter in one of the first Bahá'í families in California. I was blessed to have met 'Abdu'l-Bahá several times when he visited America, and I attended many of his West Coast events. It was such a magical time, such a mystical experience, that I've done my best to share it with everyone I could.

"How can I help you see his dignity, his wisdom and spiritual insight, his elevated position, yet his ready humor and, most of all, how he showered his love on everyone he met?"

The actress portraying Mrs. Brown walked gracefully past antique furniture to a tapestried chair and sat down smoothly.

"Let me try to help you fall in love with 'Abdu'l-Bahá, as so many did. In fact, even a few of his enemies loved him. 'Once a redoubtable enemy of Bahá'u'lláh remarked that had He no other proof to substantiate His exceptional powers, it were sufficient that He had reared such a son as Abbas Effendi.'[104]

"When he spoke to the poor, he gave coins as well as messages of hope. He told them he knew what it was like to be penniless and in danger of dying. He'd been forced to walk over frigid mountains one bitter winter, causing him a lifetime of great pain in his feet and legs. When the small band of Bahá'í exiles first arrived in the filthy prison city of 'Akká, every day brought fresh misery. Overcrowding, foul water, starvation, and disease killed them steadily. Townspeople and officials hated them because of lies they'd heard. However, like everywhere else, the people of 'Akká gradually saw for themselves the Holy Family's superb attributes. They changed their minds and came to ask advice, pay respects, and request permission to do good deeds.

"The Master was not a strong man when He arrived in America in 1912 at the age of 67. He came to nurture the infant American community, mainly through love, but also with knowledge. He spread the message of His Father's Faith far and wide to those who had never heard of it, speaking to many huge crowds who had learned of his heavenly abilities, though he had no training for public speaking. He talked with reporters, many of whom wrote articles, some more accurate than others. He allowed photographs and audio and film recordings of himself.

"In public addresses, he might speak forcefully or humbly, in generalities or using the news of the day. He knew the spirit of his audience and addressed it. In individual appointments, he listened to everybody with such attentiveness that no matter how silly their arguments seemed, sia felt respected and understood. The Master might then gently pose questions or introduce another way of thinking, often making connections relevant to that person's life, striking a remarkable balance between humor and gravity, deep messages and lightheartedness.

"To the weapons manufacturer, he spoke of building the machinery of love. With the Arctic explorer, he encouraged personal exploration of the invisibilities of the Kingdom of God.

"Near the Old American heartland city of Chicago, he laid the dedication stone for the first Bahá'í Temple in the Western Hemisphere, which for some seven and a half centuries has been the oldest one standing.

"For 239 days, he kept such a full schedule traveling throughout Canada and the United States that he was quite exhausted and sometimes unwell. His Father, Bahá'u'lláh, had once remarked that if 'Abdu'l-Bahá wasn't careful, he would use himself up, and many were concerned when sia saw how he gave of himself unceasingly. Sia were concerned that he was indeed using himself up, and sia needed him to continue to be the guide and example to the infant Bahá'í community. [105]

"Though he made it clear he was a man, not a Manifestation of God like his Father, he displayed many highly developed virtues that we can try to emulate. Often we can see his many facets in his pictures."

The actress was replaced by a series of glowing, life-sized pictures.

"Noble," her voiceover accompanied a photo of 'Abdu'l-Bahá looking majestic. "Humorous." Abby gleefully recognized the first picture she'd ever seen of him, smiling. "Stern. Lordly. Powerful. Fatherly. Welcoming. Humble." Picture after rotating picture appeared.

"In public and private talks, he used the approach he felt would touch the hearts best. Many people related that when he looked at them, he saw their souls and knew their secret fears, their unspoken wishes.

"To increase your *ma'rifat* of him and his vital role in establishing the Golden Age we now enjoy, please prepare yourselves to reverently hear his voice."

The men and women around Abby settled themselves comfortably, many closing their eyes. One young man clasped his hands prayerfully in front of him.

In a moment, a nasal Persian voice began chanting a prayer, as a photo montage showed him speaking, greeting, walking, sitting, and standing.

♫ Praise be to God that ye are present in this radiant assemblage and have turned your faces toward the Kingdom of Abhá! That which ye behold is from the grace and bounty of the Blessed Perfection. We are as atoms and He is the Sun of Truth. We are as drops and He is the Most Great Ocean. Poor are we, yet the outpouring of the treasury of the Kingdom is boundless. Weak are we, yet the confirmation of the Supreme Concourse is abundant. Helpless are we, yet our refuge and shelter is Bahá'u'lláh.
Praise be to God! His signs are evident.
Praise be to God! His light...♫ **[106]**

Abby soared into her own reverie as the chanting continued. Phrases drifted through her mind: *breath of the holy spirit ... perfume the nostrils ... divine promptings.* The prayer ended and the scent of flowers wrapped around her, heightening her awakening. Was this *ma'rifat*, the Holy Ghost, or something else?

The elegant actress reappeared. "Always 'Abdu'l-Bahá urged people to rise to a higher spiritual level ... to increased tolerance, greater service, loftier standards, purer motives. All done with such love, such happiness, such joy; never with blame or fear.

"During his sojourn in the US, Abdu'l-Baha made clear that he is the Center of Bahá'u'lláh's Covenant. This stunned American believers, as many had not understood his station fully. He also declared New York City as the City of the Covenant."

Abby gasped, unnoticed. She knew there was something special about her birth state of New York, and especially the city which had witnessed so much suffering during and after the terrorist attacks on 9/11!

"A silent film was made of him in America, which is shown with utmost respect and reverence. The film hasn't been shown in Lodlan for more than 50 years, and your local House of Justice has requested of the National House of Justice that your community be given the bounty of seeing it at your Day of the Covenant celebration this year."[107]

Unlike anyone else in the room, Abby had lived on earth when world peace was a faraway dream, not long after 'Abdu'l-Bahá had used himself up for her, for her world and for her future. She had no trouble imagining him; his love felt so real to her. His care seeped into her heart, warming her, uplifting her, giving her direction and guidance.

"The Master often asked people if they were happy," the actress continued. "He explained, 'The purpose of all the divine religions is the establishment of the bonds of love and fellowship among men, and ... the revealed Words of God are intended to be a source of knowledge and illumination to humanity.' "[108]

Abby savored her recent happiness quotes and added to them hope and a sense of noble purpose.

The facilitator rose in the dim room as the presentation ended.

"I feel moved to add one other photo," she said, searching the room and locking eyes briefly with Abby. "Actually it is not a photograph, but a soulful sketch that the poet and artist Kahlil Gibran drew after he and 'Abdu'l-Bahá met."[109]

Abby had heard of Gibran. The drawing appeared, facing Abby. She gazed raptly at the portrait and, although he looked to the side, it was as if he looked around the room as the drawing rotated, enveloping all in his warm, serene, knowing gaze. She could almost feel 'Abdu'l-Bahá's presence, recognizing, welcoming, calling and inviting her – indeed, everyone – to join him in building heaven on earth.

She answered the call in her heart, trusting him fully; the grandfather she never had. But more ... so much more.

The sketch rotated away, but the connection stayed; the spirit of a master, and the pure, deep commitment he summoned from her. A ray of rarified light sprang from her heart – her responsive, hopeful soul – and he met it with a flash of unworldly lightning, setting her aflame.

Looking back, she would eventually see that her earlier, childish prayer at church for happiness was granted more fully than she could ever have imagined or dreamed. From this heat-struck moment forward, she would draw on these deep-seated, sublime bolts of spiritual light as she wished.

Chapter 24 Animals

Dazed by the power of her spiritual awakening, Abby stumbled behind Dali into the back yard of the community center after the deepening. Numb, a sizzling bundle of feelings, she blankly watched Dali spread the picnic blanket under a large shade tree. One small thought rose to the surface of her mind and hovered long enough to register: the blazing August heat bounced off instead of baking her.

"Your clothes," Dali said.

"Oh?" Abby was able to latch onto this simple topic, using its familiarity to spear through her mindlessness. Jenn's face and voice played in her mind's eye, babbling oddly about fabrics that wicked moisture, stayed cool in summer and warm in winter, massaged muscles, and such, but she seemed to be incongruously upset about these helpful wonders.

"This fabric balances your body temperature." Dali opened the tub of sauce and offered Abby soy sticks and cooled water.

Eating also helped Abby re-anchor to reality, which she guessed was another way Dali protected her without making a big deal of it. Abby played along, trying to keep her metaphorical feet on the ground.

"Oh, so that's why we could dig and bike in the midday heat!" Abby hadn't had to head for the A/C by noon as usual, because she hadn't been intolerably hot.

The soy sticks and sauce were delicious, as Dali had promised. The flavors blended perfectly; they were light and filling. Dali also shared some fruit that the kitchen helpers had encouraged them to take on their way out the back door.

Abby's spirit kept wanting to bound off into ethereal realms, much like the butterfly – or was it a moth? – wending its erratic way across the lawn. She looked for more.

"I know where there are lots of flutteries." Dali's sensible manner began to moor Abby. "And we can go there on our way to the animal show. Shall I follow you? To the House of Worship, please, my dear!"

They tucked the repacked lunch bags in their bike baskets and pedaled off. Dali explained that different sections of the garden were planted to attract different creatures, and led Abby to the Flutter Garden. They spread their blanket again and sat under a tree, hoping not to disrupt the aerial activity a few feet away in the bright sunshine.

Abby had never watched real hummingbirds and was dazzled by their iridescent, flashing midair antics as they vied for the most desirable flowers. Despite Dali's every effort to reground her, the deepening had opened Abby's heart so wide that every sound, every new delightful sight, seemed like the most important, most vibrant ever. Her keen awareness of the tiniest jeweled glint, the smallest chirp, caused her to brim with energy and joy like never before. Was this the spiritual rebirth that Jesus urged his followers to achieve?

"Pure joy," Dali mused, watching the flutteries.

The longer she watched them, the more Abby identified with the flitting creatures. Her own heart and soul still flashed and flew in the fresh sun of awareness. She wished she could save a memento of the midair show; she habitually collected what she could of the good moments to savor during the inevitable bad times.

"Go ahead; use the WaerY," Dali said, removing hers. She touched its face, which became a viewer. She pointed to the tiny lens spot on the outer edge and assured Abby that if she caught the fliers in the camera's eye, the photos would clearly capture the action. When asked where the GO button was, Dali smiled and gently tapped Abby's head.

"Just start," Dali said. "We'll choose size and format afterwards."

Abby stood and aimed the WaerY's lens at the airborne display with both hands. She directed a mental *Now!* at the WaerY when she saw a pretty scene. When she felt she'd done her best, she sat back down. Dali told her how to project the images against the blue blanket.

"Tell it 2D or 3D, moving or not," Dali said.

Abby asked for a 3D movie. Except for being fainter in the sun, it was an exact duplicate of the drama still unfolding a few feet away.

"If you want a 3D still, play it and tell it which moment to display. You can tell it to play slowly to see it better."

Working silently with Dali's WaerY, Abby chose a moment to freeze in 3D, like a living statue. It required a lot of concentration, but she comforted herself with the thought that Dali had grown up using the yuter and still preferred to speak out loud with it; Kreshi had also preferred to avoid mental communication at times.

She flattened the images into two dimensions to see how they might look in a slide show. By thinking it, she zoomed in and out.

"You have a real talent," Dali said, intruding on her self-absorbed art project. "Whatever you decide on, I'll upload to my ALLY. I think we need to head out now, though, or *Enotita* might leave us out."

"What does that mean?" Abby asked as they pedaled briskly through a new section of Lodlan.

"Oh, *ee-NO-tee-tah*? It means unity. And it's the name of the animal show. Sorry, it was a bad joke, made worse because I didn't remember that you wouldn't know that word."

"If you hadn't translated it, I wouldn't have known it was bad,"

Abby replied, reoriented and refreshed by the lunch, the creativity, and the breathing room, but still altered in some fundamental way. "Glad I'm not the only one who messes up jokes!"

Ribbing each other and themselves liberally, they made good time, arrived at the animal show early, parked their bikes, and walked down a covered walkway. On the left, several natural habitats lay empty.

Dali invited Abby past the habitats and the theater entrance to a large open area where trainers played with animals, preparing for the twice-monthly show. Dozens of fowl chased their trainer, the chicks all toddling after their mamas, the last ones teetering and hopping as fast as their little clawed and webbed feet could go. Ducks, chickens, crows, hawks, and many other birds pecked at the nibbles she threw for them.

Walking on, the girls saw handlers working with mammals. Several animals from the pig family did tricks for their wrangler, a teenaged girl. Nearby, a man cued a large pack of canines – coyote, domestic and wild dogs, fox, jackal, wolf, and more – to run around his legs in patterns.[110] An older man lined up felines: housecats, sand cats, a black and a spotted leopard, a male lion, a puma, two Siberian tigers, and a mid-sized red feline with huge black-tufted ears that Abby remembered had a name like *carousel*.[111] None of the animals wore a harness, leash, or even collar.

Farther on, they glimpsed two ladies with … "Horses!" Abby exclaimed. The sight of them, their smell and movement always drew her; but with her altered perceptions, they reeled her in. She peered between the diamonds of the smooth tan fence, her fingers laced through its links, her eyes drinking in every detail.

One trainer cued the bay to rear, and the other pointed her slender wand at the chestnut, who spun in circles. The women wore plain, stretchy body tights with boots, hair coiled in tidy buns at the napes of their necks. The horses' manes were long and shiny, their tails full and well-tended.

"Hey there, Xenophon!"[112] said the tall, mocha-skinned lady in the blue outfit to the bright-rust chestnut. "Feeling good today? So am I! Catch me if you can!" She ran off to the far corner of the enclosure, stopping at the fence. The horse matched her every step. She placed her hand on his mane and, side by side, they backed up.

She spun and sprang toward his tail. He hunkered down on his haunches and pirouetted to keep his place next to her, tossing his head magnificently. He mirrored her exactly as she vaulted forward, then to her right, and sank into a bow. She stepped on his bent leg and swung onto his back. He cantered forward, hustled backward, and spun and leapt just as he had when she was beside him. Abby couldn't see what cues the young woman was using; she merely looked one way and another just before the horse lunged. It was fantastic!

The other woman, somewhat older, wearing an emerald-green outfit, likewise cued her bay through maneuvers from the ground and then riding. Abby stared openmouthed as they jumped over logs, reared, and navigated a maze of poles backward and then sideways.

"Good job, Rajah!" the older handler said, hugging the horse. The bay's light-brown body almost matched the woman's skin, and her black hair blended perfectly with his black mane – visual harmony reflecting their other levels of unity. Enotita, indeed! Abby kept reminding herself that neither horse wore even a halter.

Dali nudged Abby and said they'd better find their seats, but Abby could not will herself to leave. Dali finally said the show was better, and with that promise, Abby was able to tear herself away.

Going to their seats in the main hall, they passed show-goers of all ages, styles of dress, colors – even, Abby was startled to see, a redheaded young man as light-skinned as herself, holding the hands of two auburn-haired children with milk-chocolate skin. Surprisingly, the seats were almost full. Several groups looked like whole families, even though Abby figured it to be a Monday afternoon.

Dali chose two spots on the padded benches rising up and away from a dirt-floored stage. Although the sun shone bright and hot outside, the interior was dim and cool. Onstage, nimble otters climbed a small, slick hill and slid into a pool, diving and weaving around each other in and out of the water.

An unseen announcer said, "Ladies and gentlemen, we are about to begin. We hope you find *ma'rifat* in the show."

If the afternoon's animal show was anything like the morning's deepening, Abby was quite sure she'd find *ma'rifat*. She listened for the rest of the announcement, but it had ended. *That was it? The lady was finished? No rules? No announcements about silencing phone – er, yuter – calls? About not taking videos? No grand hyperbole about how fantastic, how unique the show would be?*

"Yuters already know the rules during shows, and the viewers will decide how fantastic it is," the AerY replied quietly. "Do you prefer subaural or whispered translation?"

"Whispered," Abby murmured. She didn't feel she could watch the show while hearing the AerY's silent messages. That hunch proved true almost immediately.

Low, slow music reached over a darkened stage rolling in fog. A man's deep, measured voice rumbled over the music.[113]

In the beginning, the earth was formless and void, and darkness

was over the surface of the deep. The mist roiled. A single tone reverberated so low that Abby could feel it in her lungs, her bones. *And the Spirit of God was moving over the surface of the waters.* The fog began to swirl and streak. *Then God said, 'Let there be light' and there was light.* A blue-white light grew slowly in the middle of the stage, hovering and expanding. *And God separated the waters from the heavens.* The fog lifted to reveal the pool, now devoid of otters, dark except for a small reflection of the brightening light. *Then God said, 'Let the waters below the heavens be gathered into one place, and let the dry land appear' and it was so.* Dirt rose around the pool.

Then God said, *'Let the earth sprout vegetation, plants yielding seed, and fruit trees bearing fruit after their kind, with seed in them, on the earth' and it was so.* Waving grain stalks and large-leafed trees dotted with fruit rose up at the edges of the stage. *And God made the two great lights, the greater light to govern the day, and the lesser light to govern the night; God made the stars also.* The blue-white light broke in two and became the sun and the moon, shining on two parts of the stage.

Then God said, *'Let the waters teem with swarms of many living creatures, and let birds fly above the earth in the open expanse of the heavens.' And God created the great sea monsters, and every living creature that moves, with which the waters swarmed after their kind, and every winged bird after its kind; and God saw that it was good.* Abby leaned forward to peer into the pool and glimpsed great swimming creatures, small darting fish, eels, jellyfish, long-limbed squids, sharks, mantas, sea turtles, and dolphins becoming gradually more visible in the brightening light.

Birds began to fly all around the stage. First the smallest ones: bright hummingbirds, finches, wrens, chickadees, sparrows, parakeets, starlings, and kinds Abby didn't know. Pigeons cooed, robins called, cardinals whistled, nightingales trilled. Dazzling cockatiels and parrots joined the other flitting shapes landing in the trees, followed by majestic birds of prey. Owls and hawks and lordly eagles whirled, dove, and swept up into the trees. Lastly, two mighty condors soared in.

Then God said, *'Let the earth bring forth living creatures after their kind: cattle and creeping things and beasts of the earth after their kind' and it was so.* The pool and hillock of dirt disappeared. Four steers strode onstage, then deer, goats, and a duck and her ducklings. Roosters, hens, ferrets, roadrunners, and large rats appeared on the right side of the stage, and the two horses entered regally from the left. Donkeys entered from the back, along with two dogs, one leopard, three housecats, and a few large lizards, followed by several scampering mice. Finally, an ostrich strode in, leading a comically waddling crested penguin and a flitting bat. The animals all stood sentinel at the edges of the stage, the bat hanging from a deer antler.

Then God said, 'Let us make man in Our image, according to Our likeness; and let them rule over the fish of the sea and over the birds of the sky and over the cattle and over all the earth, and over every creeping thing that creeps on the earth.' And God created male and female. A half-dozen handlers appeared at the back of the stage and walked slowly toward the flat center. *And God blessed them; and God said to them, 'Be fruitful and multiply, and fill the earth, and be good stewards for it; and watch over the fish of the sea, and over the birds of the sky, and over every living thing that moves on the earth.'* The men and women turned outward toward the animals and raised their hands. The animals bowed to the handlers, who bowed back.

The lights dimmed except for a spotlight on one handler standing in the middle of the stage. The leopard, two housecats, a sandcat, and three goats also stepped into the light. Cued by the trainer's tiny hand motions, the three small cats jumped onto the goats' backs and rode unperturbed as the goats minced delicately around the circle and then lined up facing the audience. The cats climbed up onto the three caprine heads and sat down between their horns. The handler cued the big cat, which took a running start, leapt over the goats' backs, turned, and crawled under their bellies.[114]

"This is better than lions lying down with lambs!" Abby breathed.

The music rose rich and slow; the audience clapped as the goats and felines melted away. The four longhorn steers stepped toward a handler sitting in the middle of the stage moving her arms gracefully in what might have been ingenious cues but could also have been yoga or dance moves. Twirling and swaying around their handler, the steers reminded Abby of a kaleidoscope. Mirroring one another, they walked inwards to touch noses over the trainer's head, then stepped sideways, making a spinning bovine wheel, horns locked and clacking. They backed, turned sideways, and passed their nearest partner, tipping their horns toward each other, weaving in and out around a circle like square-dancers. Abby's opinion of cows rose as she watched the graceful spectacle. She knew that in rodeos, steers were roped and wrestled and bucking bulls were ridden, but she hadn't known they could be trained. What would it take to train and ride a tame one?

"Yuter," Abby whispered, "please remind me to research training cattle ... to be ridden. Thank you."

"Noted. And Dali wants me to remind you that now you see why we do not need to rope our cattle. As a side note, trained cattle are called oxen."[115]

Music flowed softly as stage lights picked out the oxen dancing, throwing shadows of them up on the stage backdrop.

"Oooh! The horses!" Abby whispered to Dali, who returned a sympathetic smile. Abby held her breath as the horses stepped forward.

Xenophon's chestnut coat gleamed copper in the stage lights. The tall, thin, blue-suited young woman Spanish-walked on Xenophon's far side,[116] stomping across the stage in perfect unison with his front legs. Her upper torso and head appeared at his withers, like a centaur. Then, without any cue that Abby could see, Xenophon reared up to walk on his hind legs to the middle.

Abby almost cried out. She knew it must be incredibly difficult to train a horse so well.

A woman's rich voice calmly began the second narration.[117]

Consider: Unity is necessary to existence. Love is the very cause of life; on the other hand, separation brings death. The elements that form stone, wood, or greenery are held together by the law of attraction. If this law should cease for one moment, these elements would not hold together. The trees around the stage's edge began to drop their leaves and continued to steadily deteriorate into piles of dust that whirled away, as did the rocks between the trees. The growing plants around the edge of the stage decayed to nothing.

The handler signaled Xenophon to lie down center stage. He lay on his stomach, his legs folded underneath him, relaxed. The handler beckoned Rajah, and the bay leapt cleanly over the chestnut, turned, and waited. The woman went to Xenophon, murmured to him, lovingly stroked him, swung one leg over him to sit on his back, and cued him to stand up. She beckoned Rajah to the middle of the stage and cued *him* to lie down. Xenophon backed up fast, away from Rajah, then cantered forward and jumped effortlessly over him! Perched at the edge of her seat to catch every detail, Abby couldn't help herself; she clapped loudly. Dali and a few others smiled at her.

Xenophon and his rider cantered around the stage. Rajah rose and joined them, cantering in unison, the woman lifting both her arms in a flying motion. Abby could nearly feel the wind on her face, so deeply did she identify with the rider. Still cantering, the rider motioned the bay away a little, and, with a flash of blue-clad leg and arm, wheeled off Xenophon and onto Rajah. A backdrop projection showed horses play-fighting and galloping.

Abby so lost track of herself with her exuberant clapping that her bottom slid off the bench entirely, though she caught herself before she hit the floor. Dali helped her up, her face showing concern for

Abby's safety as well as shared enthusiasm.[118]

The power of cohesion in the mineral kingdom is a form of **love.** *In the vegetable kingdom, cohesive elements make up the body of a plant, showing a higher degree of love. In the animal kingdom, the attractive power binds together single elements as in the mineral, plus the cellular bond as in the vegetable, plus the phenomena of feelings. We observe that the animals desire fellowship. This is love manifested in the animal kingdom.* The horses whirled in a full circle and continued to canter, matching footfalls exactly. After a second pirouette, their rider stood up, one foot on each horse's back, Roman-riding. The stage floor and backdrop showed beach and ocean. The horses cantered in total unity through simulated shallow surf, waves rolling under them, the woman Roman-riding easily and joyfully.[119]

Hugging herself in joy, Abby was completely beside herself, her mind blown by the show, carried away by the flow of the narrator's penetrating words.

Finally, we come to the kingdom of man, the kingdom of souls. Here, the light of love is more resplendent. In man, we find the power of attraction among the elements that compose his body, plus the harmony between his organs, but beyond these, we discover in humans the attraction of heart, the receptivity and affinities that bind people together, enabling them to live and associate in friendship and solidarity. It is therefore evident that in the world of humanity, too, the greatest king and sovereign is **love.** A fancy gallery appeared around the theater, reminding Abby of the Spanish Riding School arena in Vienna she'd seen in her horse magazines.[120] She felt as if she and the other spectators were royalty, honoring and appreciating the pageantry in front of them.

A low bar appeared near the back of the stage, in front of the cantering team. The horses jumped it and cantered on to the left, the rider still standing on their backs. When the horses reached the left side of the stage, the rider somersaulted off their backs and landed facing the far side of the stage. The horses cantered around to where she looked. They stopped, turned toward her, and bowed, sinking onto their forelegs, their chins touching the ground. She bowed back to them, and then to the audience.[121]

All the animals and their handlers came onstage for a beautifully choreographed, simultaneous bow. But instead of clapping, audience members started to hiss. This alarmed Abby; why were they expressing extreme disapproval? Soon the whole audience was hissing, and the men began to growl. Then the women, including Dali, intoned a long, low "ahhhh" that rose in pitch until they were nearly singing soprano. Suddenly, the men shouted "BOOM!" and children giggled at the verbal fireworks.

"Consultation: Do you concur with singing Honor?"

"What?" Abby had no idea what the AerY meant. But instead of an answer, she heard a musical tone in her ear. The audience stood up and started singing in complex harmonies...

> ♫We appreciate you!
> We appreciate you!
> We thank you for your service!
> We appreciate you!♫

The singing was phenomenal. It was like being inside a stereo speaker. Living music reverberated all around. When it was over the performers all bowed again and ran offstage.

As the audience members gathered their things, rustling and buzzing about the show, Abby turned and crushed Dali in a bear hug, planted a huge kiss on her cheek, and choked out a tear-filled "Thanks!"

"You kind of liked it, then, did you? You voted Honor?" Dali asked naughtily.

"It was the very, very, very best anything I've ever been to, *ever*, in *any* age," Abby gushed. They followed others into the aisle.

"You can tell them that; they'd love to hear it," Dali said.

"Who?"

"The horse trainers. The rider."

Abby stopped dead in her tracks. "You mean I get to *meet* them?"

"Didn't I tell you that?"

"*No*, you didn't!" Abby's mind reeled.

"Might have slipped by me," Dali said with a sly smile that told Abby she'd withheld this information on purpose.

"We get to *meet* them?" Abby had gone stupid with surprise.

"You're going to need a bib to catch that drool. Yes, you get to meet them, if you want." Dali nudged her playfully.

"I want! Can I get the rider's autograph?"

"Well, we usually do not do that; but if you pretend you don't know better, they will probably forgive you," Dali sniffed. Abby felt that Dali was only half joking.

"You don't do autographs?"

"Usually not. It's ... er ... about the work, not the personality. Good or bad, we focus on the deed, not the person who did the deed. We learned that from your time. Sooo many promising lives ruined by fame."

"You're saying it's bad for the soul of the rider if I go and show her how blown away I was by her riding?"

"That is it in a nutshell. Thank you for understanding. Supporting Myra normally will help her continue her dazzling performances."

Maybe that explained the absence of hype. No one whipped the audience into a frenzy. The trainers didn't milk the applause for all it was worth, and the audience knew there'd be no encores. *Always so much to think about here*, Abby mused as they walked to the warm-up area. *Why* are *we so into autographs and fan clubs in my hometime? Why do we lose it when we have the chance to meet a real celebrity?*

—Yuter, please remind me later to think about why we treat famous people like we do in my time.—

—Noted. Quoting: 'Happy is the one who hath clung unto the truth, detached from all that is in the heavens and all that is on earth.' End quote. From Bahá'u'lláh's *Epistle to the Son of the Wolf*, page 139.—

—Very appropriate, as usual, Yuter. Thanks.—

They bypassed Myra standing with the two fabulous horses, who looked quite ordinary again. Healthy, well-groomed, well-muscled, very nicely built, but otherwise ordinary, dozing behind the handlers. Abby and Dali got into a shorter line to meet the older woman.

When they reached her, Dali hugged her, kissed her cheek and said, "Hi! We loved the show. Very nicely done, even better than last time. Oh, and I've been meaning to come by for supper."

Abby stared in astonishment. Dali knew the lady?!

Dali turned toward Abby and said, "Abby, this is my mother, Farrah Chavamanta. Her last name comes from *horse lover*." Dali winked, then turned to Farrah. "Mom, meet Abby, the house guest I told you about. She has been with me for a couple of days so far, and I'm showing her around Lodlan. She's also a horse lover."

Abby barely had time to overcome this latest shock before Farrah greeted her warmly and said that, if they had time, they'd have to come back on a non-show day and stroke the horses. Her tone of voice implied that this would be a great treat, which it would be, but Vivian's voice played in Abby's head, criticizing Abby for "just wanting to stand around and pet the horses." Abby's enthusiasm dampened.

"All creatures, especially mammals, need some degree of love. Including horses," Farrah said gently. "It's one of the main messages of our show. Showing the horses love by stroking and hugging them is one of the most important things you can do with – and for – them."

"I'd really enjoy that, Mrs. *chah-vah-MAHN-tah*" Abby replied, deeply grateful again for the understanding and validation she received in this world. The three exchanged hugs and parting sentiments, then Abby and Dali went on to meet Myra. Abby refrained from asking for an autograph, but she could not help wanting some souvenir of the show that had rung the bell of her soul, especially because she had no memento from the deepening at the 'Ilm Academy. She asked Dali to record her in front of the dozing horses when they got close enough.

Myra was indeed a human being like everybody else. Not fantastically beautiful, but smiling and taking time with each fan. A notably strong hand clasp revealed her tremendous physical fitness. Her warm brown eyes regarded Abby calmly while Abby wobbled through her thanks, trying to find words to express the depth of her appreciation.

"I, uh, really loved your riding, and, um, everything you did with the horses," Abby floundered. She fished quickly through vocabulary gleaned from reading. "It was a, uh, riv … riveting performance," she stammered, never having had occasion to speak those words before. Myra smiled genuinely and replied that it was her delight to inspire people with her performance.

As Dali and Abby slowly pedaled home in the easing evening heat, Abby's AerY offered another happiness quotation.

"In the words of 'Abdu'l-Bahá, quoting: 'And the honor and distinction of the individual consists in this, that he among all the world's multitudes should become a source of social good. Is there any larger bounty conceivable than this, that an individual, looking within himself, should find that by the confirming grace of God he has become the cause of peace and well-being, of happiness and advantage to his fellow men? No, by the one true God, there is no greater bliss, no more complete delight.' End quote. From *The Secret of Divine Civilization*, pages 2 and 3."

"You just have perfect quotes, Yuter," sighed Abby as they arrived home, content and tired. For dinner, Dali spooned leftover brown rice with a creamy vegetable sauce onto two special plates, covered them with glass-like lids, and put them on the stovetop. In a few minutes, the hot, delicious meal was ready. Dali handed Abby her plate; it was cool to the touch and felt like a blend of metal, pottery, and plastic.

After dinner cleanup and Abby's shower, Dali asked the ALLY to retrieve the day's images from the WaerY. Abby settled onto the couch on top of the bedding she'd tried to tidy in the morning and they relived the day through images, especially treasuring one video that beautifully captured several butterflies and two hummingbirds. Abby prized the shot of her with the horses, and asked for it in 3D. The horses must've been trained to come awake for cameras, because they were both alert and – Abby could have sworn – smiling.

"It's been a rich day for you, hasn't it?" Dali asked.

"Yeah, richer than yesterday at the Draggin' Dragon, and I thought I couldn't top that! Although today was more spiritual, and yesterday was more ...." Abby trailed off, unable to voice her tentative sentiment. "I wish I had all the pictures, or videos, to, um, meditate on."

"Sure, what would you like pictures of?"

"Mmmm ... would it be possible to have some of those pictures of 'Abdu'l-Bahá? Or at least that last one by Gibran? Or if I can't have those, maybe the actress talking?"

"No reason you can't have all of them. Yuter, please give Abby the images she wants."

Immediately images began to display in rotation against the wood of Dali's coffee table.

"Yes please, that one! And that one! And that! Ok, I'll take them all," Abby conceded. "Would it be wrong of me to want a picture of something from the Draggin' Dragon too?"

"Not at all," Dali said. "Glad you asked."

"They're all the best times of my whole life, but in different ways," Abby murmured, avidly studying the new images of the Draggin' Dragon the ALLY projected.

"Today was more spiritual, with the 'Ilm School and then the Enotita Show," Dali supplied. "Would you say that yesterday was more of a social high point?"

"Yes, that's it, thanks!" Abby applauded, appreciating Dali naming these slippery concepts.

Dali thoughtfully directed the images to rotate in a visual feast, then retrieved the clothes from the clother. The laundry area lit up as Dali approached it, catching Abby's attention. She studied it closely, noting the growing light emanating from the ceiling and upper walls. Yet Dali had not flicked on a switch and indeed, Abby hadn't seen switches in any of the rooms.

Dali carried the clean, folded clothes through the living room and toward the bedroom. As Abby's eyes followed Dali, her gaze fell upon the artistic horses next to the wooden sound-box.

"What are those horses?" Abby asked, pointing.

Dali paused and looked.

"They're from the STEEDS OF FAITH series," she said. Realizing Dali was trying to decide how to explain it further, Abby waited.

"There are different ... places? No ... um, *mentions* of horses in scripture, and some talented people, like my mother, wanted to create sculptures from them. The writing is part of the design painted on the horse, see?" Dali picked up a bright, multicolored horse and pointed to calligraphic UL words worked into the design.

"Your mother made this?" Abby asked, floored.

"She and a ... yuter network of other horse-lovers."

"What does it say?"

"This one is a Steed of the Valley of Search, a Bahá'í quote. 'The steed of this Valley is patience; without patience the wayfarer on this journey will reach nowhere and attain no goal.'"[122]

Abby thought the sculpture and its message were incredible, and told Dali so.

"Mom will be delighted to hear that you liked it," Dali said sincerely. "I will yuter her soon and let her know."

Dali went to shower while Abby snuggled into the couch's bedding, happily watching her images rotate between 3D, 2D, moving, and stationary.

She wanted to enjoy and meditate on her new art, but kept drifting off. Several times she jolted awake to see the pictures that still rotated and videos that still played.

After several of these surprises, she realized she had grown up seeing white people in her images, yet here the people were almost all a lovely, deeper, richer shade, including, she was glad to realize, the women of color who loved horses and expressed that love in the most talented and elegant terms.

Chapter 25 School

Summer vacation for Dali's school ended and the new school year started the next morning, Tuesday, August 20, 2707, or Fiḍál (Grace), 19 'Alá' (Loftiness), 864 B.E.

Dali had arranged for Abby to attend classes with Petra, a cousin who lived in Lodlan and was the same age and, since kindergarten started at age five in both times, in the same grade.[123] All Lodlan students wore uniforms,[124] but since Dali couldn't obtain one on such short notice, she suggested Abby wear a visitor's badge and simply say, with all honesty, that she did not live in Lodlan.

They got up at dawn, wafted themselves with the Cleansing Wind device, and dressed. Abby's sports bra felt almost comfortable after its first washing. And Dali had been right: Abby didn't seem to need underarm deodorant. She didn't know why; she was just relieved that she wasn't leaving stinky spots on Dali's clothes. As she headed to their breakfast of plums, quinoa, and green tea, Abby's AerY greeted her.

"Joyful Fiḍál, Abby. The Master tells us, quoting now from mid-sentence: '... the happiness and greatness, the rank and station, the pleasure and peace, of an individual have never consisted in his personal wealth, but rather in his excellent character, his high resolve, the breadth of his learning, and his ability to solve difficult problems.' End quote. From *The Secret of Divine Civilization*, pages 23 and 24."

"Thanks, yuter; perfect as usual."

"Thank you, Abby. Have a perfect day, as usual."

After helping Dali pack some veggie bars, dried fruit, and juice, the girls put their bags into their bike baskets and pedaled off, Abby leading the way to the school and enjoying the cool morning. Mr. Sawqui, sitting on a new bench beside his new garden fence, waved and smiled warmly at them and other passersby. Abby peered at the Dependencies, down the street toward the Draggin' Dragon, and at the Flutter Garden, pleased to feel a part of it all. The yuter was right; her days in Erden were usually perfect.

As they biked, Dali explained that after secondary school like Saĝo Supera came Service Year or Job Surveying; then often work for a year or two before any higher education – university or technical training – and maybe getting married. Dali had already known what she wanted to do, though, so she had taken a year of professions training right after her Service Year, and was now apprenticing in education.

The Erdean Service Year sounded like the Peace Corps but a little more mandatory. Giving something back for being a citizen and getting paid to help.

"A lot of teens find their calling during their YoS ... Year of Service," Dali elaborated, "because the administrators do their best to match up the teens with work sia can handle and enjoy."

"I wish Earth had something like that for teens," Abby replied.

"I'm not trying to make you more jealous, but it's a good place to find a spouse, too."

"Yeah?"

"Yeah, because we get to see each other in stressful situations. We see each other when things aren't fun, or easy, or pretty," Dali grinned.

As the girls biked through Lodlan in the cool late-summer morning, Abby thought the YoS would solve the dilemma of Jenn's older friends, who said that they couldn't get a job without experience, and couldn't get experience without a job. And Abby had long thought that dating in her hometime was fake. Plus, wouldn't people gain new, broader perspectives if their YoS took them away from home, maybe far away? Just as Abby felt so much more awake and aware during her time in Erden, away from home. YoS was starting to sound aweful!

As Dali hummed the familiar Traveling Prayer, Abby imagined ...

∞   ∞   ∞   ∞   ∞   ∞   ∞   ∞

... standing at a large video game console labeled YES YES YOS *... on the screen's playing field, an icon looks like her, invites her to begin ... she wills her icon to enter the* Bestmontrejo *gates of service ... her icon mucks out the pen ... forks in fresh hay ... fills the food and water troughs ... on the scoreboard, points accumulate ... smiling, she finishes that level of the game ... a chime rings ... 3D words* Sense of Accomplishment *jump out from the backdrop ... she notices a broken fence rail ... wills her icon to tie it back up safely ... points ring up and the 3D words flash* Initiative *...* **ZZP** *... in the playfield watching several horses and their handlers, Abby yearns to do this all the time ... chime, more points, words* Career Choice *over her head ... decides which unified, graceful pair she'd like to work with ...* **ZZP** *... dictates notes to her yuter after her mentor reveals many advanced riding secrets ... bells and points add up ... Words bloom ...* Self-Esteem, Worldview, Life Skills, Patience, *and* Confidence *... Abby ends the game with a flourish ... bells peal ... fireworks rise up from the backdrop ... oh yes, yes! ...*

∞   ∞   ∞   ∞   ∞   ∞   ∞   ∞

Today, the school bike rack was nearly full. Youth wheeled up on bicycles built for one, two, even three, and walked into the yard, hailing friends. Teens climbed out of all sizes of cars. It all looked and felt so normal, even familiar. Abby had to remind herself she wasn't at the first day of middle school in Surely.

Several students called out to Dali as she and Abby reached the front doors of the school. Waiting for them to finish talking, Abby noticed a new sign mounted next to the entryway. She could not read it, though, as it was in UL. Dali handed her the WaerY and whispered, "Capture the image, as you did at the gardens, then ask for a translation of it through your AerY." Abby gazed at the carved and painted wooden sign as her AerY whispered.

> Regard man as a mine rich in gems
> of inestimable value. Education can,
> alone, cause it to reveal its
> treasures,
> and enable mankind to benefit
> therefrom.

That was quite a school motto, and a suitable one. The kids back in Surely might disagree, but she liked discovering her "gems."

Another beautifully carved new sign above the door said *Saĝo Supera Lernejo*, which the WaerY conveyed to the AerY as "*SAH-jo su-PAIR-ah lair-NAY-oh*, 'Wisdom Upper School'."

"A school just for you, O Wize One," the yuter joked. "Thank you for coming to Enotopia and gracing our Wisdom School."

"Eno-what?" Abby sassed back, following Dali inside.

"This age: Enotopia. Greek for Unity-Place."

Dali registered them in the office, then hugged Abby and said she would hear all about the morning's classes at lunch. Abby hugged Dali back, thanked her, and sat down to wait for Petra.

Soon a very pretty girl with short, wavy black hair, medium-brown skin, and big brown eyes that matched her shorts approached Abby, introduced herself, and invited her to the cafeteria. They walked down the halls as Petra introduced herself and listened to Abby's halting introductions politely.

Petra seemed very straightforward, asking and answering questions evenly. Surprisingly, she wore dozens of strands of tiny, variously-colored beads around her neck, wrists, and even fingers.[125] Abby hadn't seen much jewelry in Erden. The uniform – brown shorts, pants or skirts and a mottled knit shirt with *Saĝo Supera* stitched around the collar – looked comfortable yet stylish. Short socks, walking shoes, and a maroon book bag completed her outfit.

—Yuter, please, can I ask you something that Petra won't hear?—

—Of course. What is it?—

—*All her beads...um...*— Abby paused to formulate her thought clearly. —*No one wears much jewelry. Is it okay? For Bahá'ís? Uh, is there a ... rule ... uh, can you give me the guidance on that, please?*—

—Interesting question. Quoting: 'Should a man wish to adorn himself with the ornaments of the earth, to wear its apparels, or partake of the benefits it can bestow, no harm can befall him, if he alloweth nothing whatever to intervene between him and God, for God hath ordained every good thing, whether created in the heavens or in the earth, for such of His servants as truly believe in Him.' End quote. From *Gleanings from the Writings of Bahá'u'lláh*, page 276.—

So, adorn yourself as much as you wanted, as long as it didn't come between you and God. Of course, if you were off track, wouldn't you be the last to know? So maybe it was better to stay away from too much ... stuff. Was that why the poor could have, or build, God's Kingdom on earth? They had fewer distractions?[126]

This school cafeteria was much nicer than Becknay Middle's in Surely. A homey wood floor held inviting wooden tables and chairs. A patio with flowering vines overhead afforded outside seating. Full-length windows along one side of the cafeteria let in soft light through rainbow-generating crystals. Mobiles of origami animals rotated slowly in corners. Stations offered food and drinks that diners purchased by pausing with their selections in front of an ALLY. Abby surmised that the ALLY photographed, or in some other way identified, the individuals and their purchases for later billing. Perhaps the walls dampened noise superbly, or maybe some advanced technology kept the room clean, but Abby registered the clear impression of a clean, well-organized space populated with pleasant, mature students. Auntie Zoray's Bothered Brother would have been gratified.

Unlike Abby, Petra hadn't had breakfast at home. She chose a fruit plate and led Abby to a vacant table near a corner full of potted plants.

"Having something light helps learning, doesn't it?" Petra opined. "I would normally sit with friends, but this gives me a chance to get to know you a little bit before the first class starts."[127]

She glanced to see if Abby wanted to say anything, then sat down facing the window. Abby sat next to Petra at the round table so she could see out the tall windows framing the patio and early-morning grass and dew. In one section of the grounds, rows of plants formed a garden. Several students worked among the rows; others talked, seeming to plan. Trying to interpret the scene, Angie reading Beauty's body language came to Abby's mind, and she pretended the gardeners were horses and she the body-language-reader. She guessed they were working for fun, like the volunteers at Mr. Sawqui's Service Day.

"The first class is testing," Petra said between bites, "at eight, with Mr. Wells."

"A test on the first day?"

Petra looked at her, shook her head, listened to her WaerY, and tried again.

"The first class we're going to is Testing Lab at eight o'clock."

"Oh! I never heard of Testing Lab. What is it?"

"We test different materials, and study ourselves and spiritual qualities, to learn about strengths and breaking points."

"Wow, that's different."

"It is very interesting and very useful. Then we'll have Courtesy, Beautification and, lastly, Care of Animals."

"Care of Animals? Really?"

"Yes," Petra said, humming to warm up and then singing a verse. "The Master said, 'Train your children from their earliest days to be infinitely tender and loving to animals. If an animal be sick, let the children try to heal it, if it be hungry, let them feed it, if thirsty, let them quench its thirst, if weary, let them see that it rests.'[128]

"We start in the earliest grades just learning the different kinds of animals, watching them, grooming them, examining them, feeding them what the teacher tells us to. Later, we learn animal nutrition, healing different injuries, and so on. Upper grades learn about animal behavior, training, breeding, population control, maintaining native habitats, etc."

This was taught in school? No wonder Farrah and Myra were so fantastic. They'd had lifelong animal-training preparation!

"That's it? No science, history, social studies?"

Petra smiled and blinked slowly, unconsciously touching her WaerY, and said, "Those topics are all included in the subjects we study. We cover them all while we're studying our life skills."

Petra finished her fruit, cleaned up the table, and escorted Abby upstairs and through the hallways into a large room that did indeed look like a laboratory. The students all swiped their WaerYs or palms in front of a scanner next to the door as they went in.

"Yuter, please explain the use of the scanner."

"It is a remote 'eye' of the school's ALLY for tracking attendance and locating people when they're in rooms that are being shielded from complex electronic signals to avoid upsetting signal-sensitive classroom animals or ruining delicate laboratory experiments."

"I see," Abby said, then switched to silent mode. —*Don't students get each other to register for them, then skip school?*—

—As Rykeir and Kreshi explained to you, it is quite difficult to use a Yuter to cheat. Also, students rarely want to skip school, and then only for personal emergencies, which are excused.—

—*Huh. Okay, thank you.*—

Hometime Earther thinking was harder to amend than Abby would have thought. Abashed, she followed Petra into the room.

Testing supplies sprouted from every flat surface of the classroom. Each lab table boasted machines, meters, hand tools, and several ALLY screens. Shelves overflowed with metal pipes, tree branches, lava rocks, marble, glass, cloth, and more.

Swirling bands of colorful of paint accented with intricate characters decorated the wall next to the door. Abby didn't have a WaerY to point at it, but asked her AerY about it anyway.

"One moment, please; I will ask Petra."

Abby saw Petra look at the wall, point her WaerY at it, then look back at Abby and smile. Abby's AerY translated immediately.

"This is student artwork incorporating calligraphy of a quote from the Bahá'í Writings regarding education, rendered in the original language. It translates as, quoting: 'The Prophets and Messengers of God have been sent down for the sole purpose of guiding mankind to the straight Path of Truth. The purpose underlying Their revelation hath been to educate all men, that they may, at the hour of death, ascend, in the utmost purity and sanctity and with absolute detachment, to the throne of the Most High.' End quote. From *Gleanings from the Writings of Bahá'u'lláh*, page 156 and 157."

Abby and Petra chose two of the tall wooden stools by the lab tables. When the bell sounded – a melodious harmony instead of the jarring shriek Abby was used to – the blond-goateed teacher gave his name, Mr. Wells, and welcomed them all to the first day of class.

"We have a guest with us today, a cousin of Petra's, is that right?" Petra nodded and introduced Abby to the other students, who welcomed her each in their own way.

"Thank you. Now, the purpose of this class is to discover strength as well as weakness," the middle-aged, coppery-skinned, intense man said, pausing to let his words sink in. He wore a school shirt like the students, with woven brown pants. "Without using any Yuters, who can tell me something about the spiritual relevance of strength?"

After a pause, a student said, "Didn't the Guardian say something about the Faith getting stronger the more blows it received?"

"Good for you. One merit," Mr. Wells said. A shimmering spark launched from the wire frame of his ALLY screen. As it reached the boy, it broke into a shower of shining droplets that cascaded over his head and shoulders. The room smelled like spring air after a rain. One note sounded, clear and confident. A few students clapped. All smiled.

Mr. Wells touched his ALLY screen, and a photo of mountain peaks and valleys appeared on a blank section of the left-hand wall. Graceful letters penned themselves across the bottom of the slide. Abby glanced at Petra, who helpfully pointed her WaerY at the wall. Abby willed her yuter to connect with Petra's, and immediately heard a quiet translation.

> **Despite the blows leveled at its nascent strength, whether by the wielders of temporal and spiritual authority from without, or by black-hearted foes from within, the Faith of Bahá'u'lláh had, far from breaking or bending, gone from strength to strength, from victory to victory. Indeed its history, if read aright, may be said to resolve itself into a series of pulsations, of alternating crises and triumphs, leading it ever nearer to its divinely appointed destiny.**
>
> **Shoghi Effendi**
> ***God Passes By*, page 409**

"This pattern has been repeated throughout Bahá'í – indeed, through-out every religion's – history," the teacher noted. "Anyone else?"

"Tests increase our personal abilities," a very tall, thin girl offered.

"Yes, one merit, good job," Mr. Wells responded warmly. A bright green spark, with a sound like a little glass bell, showered its new-mown grass scent over the girl. She shivered and grinned, as more bright words appeared on the wall. Again, the Yuter translated.

> ***O Son Of Man!***
> **The true lover yearneth for tribulation even as doth the rebel for forgiveness and the sinful for mercy.**
> ***O Son Of Man!***
> **If adversity befall thee not in My path, how canst thou walk in the ways of them that are content with My pleasure? If trials afflict thee not in thy longing to meet Me, how wilt thou attain the light in thy love for My beauty?**
>
> **Bahá'u'lláh**
> ***The Hidden Words*, Arabic #49 & #50**

—Yuter, please, what do the sparks feel like?—

—As with the scent, the feel of them changes according to the de-sires of the student. Gregory doesn't mind me telling you that his spark felt like a quick splash in a summer lake.—

"For those who wish to do independent reading on this concept," Mr. Wells said, "I suggest *Fire and Gold*, originally compiled by Brian Kurzius, and added to through the centuries.

"Now, as with our spirits and bodies, it's also practical to learn how to test the capabilities of materials." He waved at the shelved supplies. "We'll be exploring all of these.

"Let's start, though, with physical strength. This month, we'll do some yoga. Next month, we'll practice tai chi. Later on, we'll explore dance, as well as some acrobatics if any of you are so inclined."

After a brief warm-up, Mr. Wells said that each student should go get a small floor mat, lay it in an empty space on the floor, remove their shoes, and stand on one end of the mat. He then willed the ALLY to play quiet music, invited everyone to begin some gentle stretching, and demonstrated several standing and sitting poses they could try.

"Just explore," he encouraged. "Do not force anything, especially any of these poses you've never done before. Yoga builds flexibility, strength, and focus. But slowly, gradually. *Kam, kam, rúz bih rúz.*"

In the quiet moments of movement that ensued, Abby silently asked the AerY to explain the last thing Mr. Wells had said.

—It translates from Persian, poetically, as little by little, day by day. A well-known and well-loved counsel of the Master's.—[129]

"It is my belief that this life is all about progress," the instructor gently began. "Wherever you are now with your physical abilities, let's call that 'one.' Your 'one' will most likely not look like anybody else's 'one.' That's all right. Over the course of this class, let's see how many bits you can advance beyond your personal 'one.' You will assess your own progress, and I will help you assign numbers to that progress. Careful, Radiance, nice and easy there."

Sitting on her mat next to Petra, Abby glanced up and saw one slightly heavier girl almost tip over, about to lose her balance and fall. Abby was glad she wasn't the only one struggling. She couldn't keep the backs of her knees on the mat while reaching for her toes. She could only do one or the other, not both at the same time. The Erdeans were so fit! Petra was about to touch her nose to her knees, her legs flat against the mat. One boy was trying out his sideways splits on the mat. Some other students looked as if they'd been doing these things for years and were moving on to fancy lotus-style sitting, interesting arm-bends, back-bends, side-bends.

"Excellent, all of you, just excellent," Mr. Wells enthused, walking among them. He seemed to be making a photo database with his WaerY, pointing it toward different students. "It might help your practice if you remember that yoga was originally Hindu-related. Keeping its religious, spiritual basis in mind can help you relax into poses; peace of mind and calm focus help your poses unfold.

"As you're ready, then, finish with any last poses you feel you need to balance out your bodies. For the studious among you, this may mean reaching up, bending back, stretching backward to counteract the bending forward and looking down you do."[130]

He walked among the students as they finished. Some blinked slowly, whispered or gave other signs of getting help from their yuters.

"When you're finished, put your mats away, please."

Abby and Petra were among the first to return to their seats after rolling and storing their mats. Petra pointed her WaerY at a wall-list that played a video after each item was fully displayed. Abby was astonished to see the many video snippets of Erdeans working athletically.

The Practice of Yoga – Some Applications & Careers
- **Care of the very young & the very old**
- **Hands-on treatment of animals**
- **Edifice cleaning & repair, especially in narrow spaces, overhead, & underneath things**
- **Machinery & wreckless repair & maintenance**
- **Outdoor endeavors, especially in caves & over rocks**
- **Gymnastic & acrobatic performances**
- **Lead activities in venues such as therapy centers, ocean-going vessels, gymnasia, & games foodles**

That one slide, probably painstakingly prepared by Dali and taking no more than a couple of minutes to absorb, made the lesson more relevant than a much longer spoken description. The last item even sounded like being paid to lead group activities in the large back room at the Draggin' Dragon!

The class ALLY suggested wording that students could use to request more on the topic from their yuters. As the last of the students reached their stools, Mr. Wells began the testing portion of the lesson.

"Now let us take a look at a simple material: paper. Each of you has some ordinary paper on your tables. Who can tell me some ways to test the qualities of paper?"

Students suggested tearing, burning, folding, crumpling, weighing down, wetting, even chewing, all of which Mr. Wells had the ALLY add to a new wall-list. He then pointed out which machines could test the attributes of paper in different ways, and said that the ALLY screen next to each machine would instruct them. He asked everyone to cooperate in twos or threes, and warned them to be especially cautious with the fire-tester and to close its doors before turning on the flames.

The students sorted themselves around the machines, commenting, testing, encouraging, observing. Although Abby was initially intimidated by the complexity of the machines and the high level of scientific rigor, Petra encouraged her through easy tasks and chose a familiar substance to test. Abby would have thought she knew paper pretty well, but discovered new properties in ordinary sheets of paper after testing it in several unfamiliar ways. The yuter logged their observations that that paper was very strong in some ways and very weak in others. One sheet held a china teacup full of water when it was dry, but disintegrated under the weight of a marble when wet. She and Petra also began to wonder about the interaction of paper and ink. Would writing in ink add molecular strength, or would it just wet and weaken the paper?

"Of course," Petra said, "we could take this as an analogy for a spiritual level of interaction."

"Come again?"

"The last Arabic Hidden Word." Petra sang the Bahá'í Scriptural verse. " 'Write all that We have revealed unto thee with the ink of light upon the tablet of thy spirit. Should this not be in thy power, then make thine ink of the essence of thy heart. If this thou canst not do, then write with that crimson ink that hath been shed in My path.'[131] Spiritual ink would give a spiritual surface a lot of spiritual strength."

Abby thought Petra's singing and the verse were very beautiful. With some meditating, she might actually be able to grasp a bit of its meaning.

Mr. Wells eventually showed the class some creative ways to use paper: pencils, pens, beads, and bows made with recycled paper; a complex paper airplane; intricate pop-up, sliding, and unfolding books; a child's paper-and-resin chair; and finally, an antique hologram of a house made of phone books, complete with paper-based furniture, countertops, and a backyard skateboard ramp.[132]

So engrossed was Abby that she was surprised when another pretty bell-tone signaled the end of class. Mr. Wells pointed to a stack of half-reams of used letter-size paper, each tied with twine.

"One of our school assistants, Dali Puerta, has prepared some paper for your further explorations," Mr. Wells said, nodding and smiling specially at Abby without putting her on the spot.

"If you like, take paper and, without yutering, build something that will hold you at least 20 centimeters off the floor for 10 seconds. Try not to use glue or tape. After you try alone, network, consult on the best solutions, and choose a spokesperson to share with the class in two weeks. Later we'll recycle them, unless someone wants to keep theirs."

Half the class, including Petra, took packets. "Fold them into little shapes," she said. "A mound of bricks or pyramids, that should work."

"How come only half of the kids took the homework? Or is it extra-credit work?" Abby asked as she and Petra left the classroom.

Petra looked confused for a moment, blinked slowly, then replied, "It's just a free challenge. We can do it if we want, to try new things, think in new ways, even help us find our profession. The students who really like this might go into construction or architecture or civil engineering. Plus, they're fun! We'll get on a yuter network and share notes and discoveries. I hope Radiance will help us test the sturdiest, most stable structure."

Abby followed Petra down the corridor, trying to figure out why the paper activity – and indeed the whole class – was so unusual. She realized she was used to pressure and criticism; in this new world, they'd eliminated both.

The next class was Courtesy. Abby had figured this would be a very dull class, but the students seemed as eager and willing to come to this one as they had to Testing Lab.

Abby lined up with the other students and held her palm in front of the ALLY scanner by the door before entering the bare classroom containing only a few posters on the walls and a collection of chairs.

This instructor was a brightly smiling middle-aged woman, which Abby reminded herself could still mean she was in her 80s. She greeted most of the dozen students by name as they sat and slid their bags onto the racks under each chair. Abby heard them warmly greet her in return as *IN-strew* or *IN-strew jenn-tee-LAH-yo*. The AerY explained that it meant something akin to *Ms. Courtesy Teacher* and added that her actual name was Ms. Reed.[133]

"Please bring your chairs into a circle," invited the freckled teacher with long honey-colored dreadlocks. Abby felt herself withdrawing warily as all those eyes circled around, able to scrutinize her.

Avoiding their glances, she noticed that on the ceiling was painted a large green tree with golden fruit sporting a painted word in each shape, arranged into clustered sentences. Petra lifted her WaerY and Abby admired the artwork as she listened to her AerY.

"Quoting: 'The learned of the day must direct the people to acquire those branches of knowledge which are of use, that both the learned themselves and the generality of mankind may derive benefits therefrom. Such academic pursuits as begin and end in words alone have never been and will never be of any worth.' End quote. From *Tablets of Bahá'u'lláh Revealed after the Kitáb-i-Aqdas*, page 169."

"Welcome to Courtesy Class," Ms. Reed said when all the students were settled. "You have been well-prepared to begin studying this topic, I expect. Who would like to outline what in your past has equipped you to learn now about courtesy, the prince of virtues?"[134]

A student raised her hand and was recognized. She said the progression of subjects during her earlier years – starting with Basic Manners, and continuing through Sharing, Giftgiving, Social Needs, and Virtues – the ongoing guidance of her family and, in fact, the influence of everybody she knew in Lodlan had prepared her to focus this year on Courtesy.

"Ah, beautifully expounded," Ms. Reed beamed. "One merit." The student's spark dissolved into singing birds and the scent of ocean.

—Yuter, please, what's with all these merits?—

—In The Advent of Divine Justice, page 83, Shoghi Effendi quotes Bahá'u'lláh as saying, 'Vie ye with each other in the service of God and of His Cause.' Students can practice for this by doing well in school, so every student tries sia best to do a good job, although it's not a competition against each other, only with yourself. One way students gain merits is answering questions thoughtfully in class. Merits increase the joy and delight of the classroom.—

They reward students for speaking up and working cooperatively? Bonega! But, a new little voice in her head offered, *if they did not like school, no reward would bribe them into changing their bad feelings.* Was this more of the Divine Guidance she hoped to develop? Another step on her spiritual evolution? *Double bonega!*

"Let us start by discussing two things," Ms. Reed went on. "First, situations in which you feel you'd like help being more courteous."

The ALLY recorded and displayed all the students' contributions, which ranged from having to deliver bad news to someone, to standing up for their rights, to losing their patience.

Petra offered an insightful contribution: "Having just come from yoga, I wonder, if I'm in a situation where speaking isn't appropriate, can I still show courtesy and respect to someone? Are there body postures we can use that convey appreciation and respect?"

"Excellent issues, everyone!" Ms. Reed enthused. "A merit to all!"

Sparks descended on Petra and the other speakers, causing a general stir of appreciation in class. Ms. Reed smiled broadly as the merits descended on individual students, then asked for "situations in which you wish others had been more courteous."

This would certainly have become a gripe-session on how rude others were if these were Abby's 21st-century schoolmates. But these students were much more reserved, removing all names or blame.

Sitting listening to how many of them had felt unheard when sharing something deep or been hurt by one thoughtless comment or action, Abby reflected on the many ways people hurt other people, even when they didn't mean to. Despite the tremendous time gap and their advanced sensibilities, she saw that she was not so different from these students who, like she, struggled to be the best they could be, despite slights or missteps from their friends and families.

"Let's take this opportunity to ponder the many sufferings of the Manifestations of God, the Founders of all the world's religions," Ms. Reed said. "Let's specifically consider Bahá'u'lláh, He being the Manifestation we know the most about. He Who saw events to come. Who knew His followers' desires before they did. Who was able to reveal superb verses faster than His secretaries could write them down. He was hurt bodily, mentally, and spiritually by attacks of all kinds from all sides, even from members of His own family, who tried more than once to kill Him. Yet He never wavered for an instant, never changed regardless of His comforts or lack thereof. This is that Being Who urged us to be unified, to strive, to achieve great spiritual victories over ourselves. His degree of sensitivity was so high that we will never fully understand it. Just think how He was hurt by even the slightest whisper of discord and how He rejoiced in even the tiniest rudiments of unity and love – the spreading of which was His purpose.

"I'm so pleased with the curriculum you have just helped me form. Thank you. We will cover courtesy when yutering, when writing, when speaking to individuals or in front of groups, on Yuter shows, when delivering bad news, when stressed, and more ... with real-life practice."

Yet another winning concept: students wrote the curriculum here. And it seemed they'd be writing letters, giving speeches, even going on TV to practice it. Amazing. Abby could have supplied them with endless examples of bad interchanges from her time. Unfortunately, she would have had to bring some people – *like Mother ... ugh, quick, think of something else* – here to show the class how bad the disunity and lack of courtesy got, because Erdeans probably wouldn't believe her if they didn't see it for themselves. Of course, the people she brought would likely argue the entire time and never take advantage of what Erden had to offer them. *It takes an open mind*, she realized, *to benefit from instruction, even if it's the best ever created.*

"You can lead a horse to wonders, but you cannot make it think," she mouthed, ducking her head so her hair slid over her face, in case anyone saw.

"This is the nature of real learning," the AerY comforted her. "Your connections and realizations would be welcomed. Making a short poem means you've really grasped a concept. No need to hide your achievement."

Through the rest of class, Abby occasionally glanced at other students and did notice ways in which they showed their engagement with the ideas. Their lips moved or they blinked slowly; they took notes and sketched ideas. None were self-conscious. None were reprimanded.

Ms. Reed had them break into small groups to role-play the first assignment of discussing ways in which the students had been hurt by someone's thoughtlessness.

"Discuss any feelings of anger or other difficult emotions that are relevant to the situation," she coached. "Emotions are markers pointing to something that needs your attention. They can be like well-trained horses that take your mind and heart to explore new and useful places. Resist the temptation to let your emotions drag your mind away like rampaging horses. Let's train your horses to partner you well."

Abby loved that analogy. She wondered if Ms. Reed had seen the animal show, too. Maybe she'd been inspired, perhaps had gained *ma'rifat* and seen a connection to her subject matter.

Before Petra, Abby and their partner could begin, one pair of students asked for full-class consultation. They vividly re-enacted the girl's younger brother dropping a chair leg on her toe. She had yelled at him most ungraciously. The girl said that she was still angry about it, because she had lost a toenail and was still limping and nursing the damaged nail bed. She could not think how to be courteous in this instance. Her role-play partner said that he, too, had no useful ideas.

Ms. Reed invited the entire class to brainstorm. Silence fell in the room, and Abby saw a number of people frowning, as if vicariously re-living the situation. At last she felt comfortable just waiting in silence, smiling as she remembered the passage from her little *Native American Wisdom* book and the scene from *Consultation Today*.

"Yell 'ouch' and get away from him? So you can calm down?" a boy finally suggested. "Or if you're too hurt to move, get him to go away? Maybe by having him go get a medi-cloth or something?"

"Call an adult to handle him as you tend to your toe?" a girl added.

"Use the time at the clinic to calm down?" said another.

A merit rewarded every thoughtful contribution. But apparently the students were so engaged that they didn't want overly dramatic distractions, because the merit sparks had become very subtle.

Finally, the class agreed that unless the brother meant it, which the sister assured them that he didn't – it was an accident, he was only six, and a good kid – the best thing to do was deal with the injury, try really hard not to blow up at the kid, perhaps by reciting a short prayer, and deal with him after the heat of hurt and anger was gone.[135]

Had Dali learned to defuse Abby by leaving the room and playing calming music in a Courtesy Class like this? It was true, it took two people to fight. When Dali left, she removed the option of fighting.

"Now, lest we think that we always need to be polite to everybody at all times, let me offer a couple of exceptions for your consideration.

"One is when we encounter someone who's truly malevolent toward other created beings. Would someone like to read this quote?"

A boy who had not made any suggestions thus far raised his hand, received a nod, and read the quotation that appeared on the wall.

> Strive ye then with all your heart to treat compassionately all humankind – except for those who have some selfish, private motive, or some disease of the soul. Kindness cannot be shown the tyrant, the deceiver, or the thief, because, far from awakening them to the error of their ways, it maketh them to continue in their perversity as before. No matter how much kindliness ye may expend upon the liar, he will but lie the more, for he believeth you to be deceived, while ye understand him but too well, and only remain silent out of your extreme compassion.
>
> 'Abdu'l-Bahá
> *Selections from the Writings of 'Abdu'l-Bahá*, page 158

"Thank you, Malik. Reverent, flawless reading. A merit. Students, feel free to ask your yuter to hold this quote for further study."

A bell rang in Abby's soul. Goosebumps sprouted on her arms and she felt tears spring to her eyes. Thank God everyone was looking at the quote displayed on the wall and the room had been dimmed. She was having "a moment" and had no idea why.

"The other situation, for similar reasons, is when you are being treated unjustly. Please silently read this story told by the Guardian's wife about the time that the Master, a Pasha who was his guest, and Shoghi Effendi arrived in Ramleh in a rented coach from Alexandria."

Petra snapped her fingers and whispered. "Yuter, can the class ALLY translate the projected quotes right into Abby's AerY?" It worked; Abby listened, comprehension dawning as her body relived a hundred memories of being slapped, cut, grabbed, and slammed. Her ears burned with humiliation at being called names, scolded, demeaned, and disrespected. She had been punished for things she had no way of knowing and that were beyond her control.

Courtesy Class now bestowed on her the *ma'rifat* that her longstanding wall of resentment was actually a castle for justice. Ms. Reed's quotes seemed to say that her tiny island of "stubborn" self-preservation was actually her spirit's innate sense of right and wrong. From the quotes, she gleaned permission to ignore the many voices that said she should submit to her unfairly dominating mother. They suggested that she didn't have to surrender herself to Mother's abuse, which changed everything, yet again.

> [When] the Master asked the strapping big coachman how much He owed him the man asked an exorbitant price; 'Abdu'l-Bahá refused to pay it, the man insisted and became abusive to such an extent that he grasped the Master by the sash around His waist and pulled Him roughly back and forth, insisting on this price. Shoghi Effendi said this scene in front of the distinguished guest embarrassed him terribly. He was too small to do anything himself to help the Master and felt horrified and humiliated. Not so 'Abdu'l-Bahá, Who remained perfectly calm and refused to give in. When the man finally released his hold the Master paid him exactly what He owed him, told him his conduct had forfeited the good tip He had planned to give him, and walked off followed by Shoghi Effendi and the Pasha! There is no doubt that such things left a lifelong imprint on the Guardian's character, who never allowed himself to be browbeaten or cheated, no matter whether or not this embarrassed or inconvenienced him, and those who were working for him.
>
> Rúhíyyih Rabbaní
> *The Priceless Pearl*, page 23

Abby didn't register Ms. Reed's homework description, nor the students reorganizing the room and leaving.

"Abby? Abby? I'll be right over there, I have to talk to Ms. Reed," Petra said, nearly waving her hand in front of Abby's unseeing eyes. Ms. Reed opened her office door while Abby sat trying to process her epiphany about her mother's viperous ways. Her thoughts collided and short-circuited each other. If she ever returned hometime, she would have to incorporate this new information, but it was too much for now.

Leaps in personal transformation were all well and good for these Erdeans and their finely tuned awareness at their highly evolved school, Abby grumped eventually, but she wasn't sure how many more of these personal bombshells she could take, blowing craters in her psyche.

She felt exhausted, disoriented, and guilty for feeling those in Erden. With that, another misconception burst. She'd subconsciously assumed that hanging out with the Erdeans would magically rub off on her and she could effortlessly become like them, but now she confronted the raw truth that everyone had to bootstrap through their own inner work themselves, whether or not they had support.

Chapter 26 Lunch

Eventually Abby sighed, resigned to the burgeoning truth that growing into an Erdean-like state of grace and accomplishment would require painful, hard, long work. Deep down, she had hoped for a shortcut, in spite of knowing nothing really great and lasting was easy.

"Would a joke help?" the yuter asked hesitantly.

"Sure, why not," Abby intoned flatly, doubtfully.

"Only wet babies like change," it ventured.

It worked. Abby snorted, guffawed and coughed, finally coming back to her surroundings. "Thanks, Yuter."

Light shone through a pretty 9-pointed stained glass star in a window. Abby moved her lone chair back with the others and went to look at the star, passing other stained glass works in other windows.

"The most popular symbol of the Bahá'í Faith," her AerY explained as she admired the star.

"… so, once we decide on the games, you'll group yuter over to Insight Upper School? Then we'll yuter the Games committee all together?" Petra asked behind Abby, translated by the AerY.

Abby peeked into Ms. Reed's darkened office and noticed, hanging from the ceiling in the nearest corner, a spiky lamp full of holes emitting light that played over the dim interior filled with curios.

"A 19-pointed star," the yuter said. "Another Bahá'í symbol. But this one is in the round; 3D."

Instead of a desk, Ms. Reed had opted for a wide chair with wide flat arms, currently loaded with open books, a half-colored-in mandala, prayer beads, and a kaleidoscope with dangling ribbons. Music played softly.

"The music is from The World Peace collection," the yuter helpfully explained. "Ms. Reed's office is a Tranquility Zone. She likes to create spaces conducive to spiritual questing."[136]

Ms. Reed's chair did look like a command center set up to explore new territory, inner and outer, surrounded as it was by overflowing bookshelves instead of control panels. Pinpoints of light from the spiky star changed color as they played over all the world's holy texts and commentaries, interspersed with carved human figures from many cultures, a small brass bowl with mallet, a dream catcher, metal brainteasers, and other games and toys of discovery.

Colored scarves hung on both sides of the chair, stirring slightly in the breeze of a small fan, which nudged the spiky star into gentle rotations but didn't disturb a perpetually spinning gyroscope trailing a small sign saying, "This is the balance" as it traversed a filament strung across a corner.[137]

Inching closer, Abby saw a ram's horn mounted on the far wall above a large, stylized painting of a tree of life.

"... the group sit game and indigenous hand games for sure.[138] May we borrow your drums and sticks?" Petra asked.

"Yes, and we'll yuter out an appeal if you need more than I have," Ms. Reed enthused.

"Great, and then we're thinking about Collective-Score MonsterBall[139] with balls of the planets; do you know who has the ones we used for the Science Pentathlon?"[140] Petra asked as Abby eyed a clear tub of simple musical instruments.

"I think so. I'll look into it and let you know. It all sounds good," Ms. Reed said. "Let me know if you need anything else. You're ahead of schedule and we have several months. Speaking of schedule, don't you want to scoot off to lunch? It's 12:30 and counting."

Abby glanced at her watch, the only thing she still wore from her hometime except her increasingly dirty tennies. She'd gotten used to it surprisingly quickly, even though it didn't do anything but tell the correct time.

They said their goodbyes and Petra led the way toward the sunny, busy cafeteria, the smell of lunch wafting down the hallway.

Abby was more than ready for a break, if not lunch. She considered begging off the two afternoon classes, fearing they might be as challenging as the previous two, but Care of Animals still intrigued her. She just wasn't sure she could handle any more personal growth today. School here was nothing like Abby's classes back home. *Back home ...* a strong wave of homesickness washed over her. She could nearly see Jenn's dear face, leaning in, singing "Itsy Bitsy Spider" ... Abby and Jenn used to pair their hands to make climbing spiders. The flashback faded, becoming unegg rolls, basil-seasoned green beans, salad with fresh-made dressings, and veggies on brown rice.

"Um, I don't have any money, should I eat the lunch I brought? But I think Dali has it, and I don't know where ..." Abby began to stammer uncertainly.

"Oh, no, don't worry, all students eat free if sia have no money. Just choose whatever you like and hold it up to the ALLY," Petra reassured her. "Or if you like, yuter Dali and see if she brought your food, if you'd rather eat that. She's going to meet us here anyway."

"Oh, right, I forgot. No, I'd rather have a hot lunch. We brought more like snacks than a meal."

"Sure, whatever you like. I'm just praying for a good seat for us today." She looked like she really was praying, instead of using a figure of speech.

"Why are you praying for a good seat? Isn't that a little ... trivial to ask God for something so petty?" Abby asked, surprised at her own forwardness.

Petra studied her for a moment. "What good is the Concourse on High if they don't help you with the small stuff in between all the big stuff?" she asked lightly.

"Concourse on high?" Abby inquired.

"Angels, in most of the world's religions, or ancestors in many Native religions."

Abby nodded and Petra turned down the line of food, holding her hand over the selections as if testing them, humming a tune. More Erdean deepery, Abby figured.

Maybe it was becoming a habit, but Abby took small portions of several foods. She held her plate in front of the ALLY and looked around. Just as she was about to ask the AerY what to do, she spied Dali waving from a corner table next to a waterfall.

"Saluton. Get what you want?" Dali asked.

"Yes, I think I'm finally getting used to this health-nut food."

Dali tried not to look surprised. "Oh? But food is really important. It's medicine *and* nourishment."

Abby was saved from a reply by Petra's arrival.

"Wouldn't you agree, Petra?" Dali switched to UL, which Abby's AerY immediately translated.

"Yes, definitely. When I fuel myself correctly, I get more done, and have good energy longer," Petra concurred.

"I mostly eat whatever's in front of me ... except for what I'm allergic to," Abby admitted, finding it hard to dig into a difficult topic. She had been "born sensitive," her newborn rash evolving into toddler eczema, then into full-blown childhood allergies magnified by periodic colds and flu. Mother often complained about living with The Princess And The Pea in real life. The doctor said these problems often went with fair skin and reddish hair like hers. Abby usually felt downright bad in the morning, except for here in Erden, but things like that just *were*; they didn't have a *cause*, or a *solution*, did they?

"I've been reading about cow's milk," Dali said pointedly to Petra. "Did you know that the dairy industry in Abby's time knew the harm it was creating for some – the allergies and congestion – and still promoted dairy as beneficial for everyone?"[141]

Abby saw that Dali was building up an indignant head of steam but found she couldn't get interested. She poked at her food, head down, but stopped when she saw that she'd blended dishes. It made her remember that Jenn never liked her foods touching.

"Well, yes, and even if you could handle it, and if the milk was pure, but you pour it on highly processed cereal for breakfast, full of chemicals and colorings, it will cause problems," Petra added. "And that's only a part of the issues to be aware of regarding food, even back then ... not to mention the other factors for health!"[142]

"The indicators were available to pinpoint many illnesses," Dali replied, puzzled. "When I watch archives about health, it really gets to me that people voluntarily ingested so many things that didn't suit the human body, then wondered why sia were sick."

Abby made a muted noise of doubt and belligerence. Surprisingly, Dali plowed on. "Did you ever wonder where allergies came from? Parkinson's? Alzheimer's? Multiple sclerosis?" Her WaerY whispered a long list to help her build her case. "Diabetes? Hay fever? PMS? Flu? Common colds, even?"

"Well, there's germs. And heredity. And age, and ..." Abby stopped, her knee-jerk list running out, knowing she could never outreason the yuter. She had never heard of a cause for many of those conditions. The doctors had always told Mother that they didn't know the cause of her allergies, but that diet changes might help,[143] which, come to think of it, might prove Dali's point, but Abby was feeling perversely peeved and didn't want to admit it. Dali listened to her WaerY, working hard to control her emotions as Petra ate, listening attentively.

"In your time, doctors incorrectly concluded that nutrition is irrelevant to health, because it wasn't included in medical school." Dali paused as the WaerY whispered. "The Master told us that when we eat complex, unhealthy foods, the result is 'diseases both violent and diverse.'[144] He advised providing children with whatever is conducive to health ... starting with breastfeeding, if possible.[145] But your food became very unhealthy, and so did your water, air, and so much more ... until illness was more prevalent than health. Would you agree?"

"No, I don't think so," Abby argued, but secretly decided that if it could make a difference, she would breastfeed her own children, if that day ever came.

"So people wake up happy, refreshed, clear-minded, and stay energetic through a long day plus one emergency?" Dali asked frankly, adding, "One of our definitions of health."

Abby tried to claim that the kids were pretty healthy – except the ones who were sick – but before she could form the words, she remembered all the adults, like Aunt Sofia's neighbors, Daddy and even Mother, who struggled. She closed her eyes, head spinning, feeling like her mouth was running ahead of her ever-more-sluggish brain. She didn't know why she couldn't be pleasant and thoughtful, like ... when *had* she last participated happily?

"I guess not, then," Abby admitted reluctantly, trying to smile and be collaborative.

"Here is another quote from 'Abdu'l-Bahá. It is very inspiring."

Dali laid her left arm on the cafeteria table and her WaerY recited a passage in a clear, soothing man's voice.

"Quoting: 'Make ye then a mighty effort, that the purity and sanctity which, above all else, are cherished by 'Abdu'l-Bahá, shall distinguish the people of Bahá; that in every kind of excellence the people of God shall surpass all other human beings; that both outwardly and inwardly they shall prove superior to the rest; that for purity, immaculacy, refinement, and the preservation of health, they shall be leaders in the vanguard of those who know. And that by their freedom from enslavement, their knowledge, their self-control, they shall be first among the pure, the free and the wise.' End quote. From *Selections from the Writings of 'Abdu'l-Bahá*, selection 129, page 150."

"When we know better, we do better. Sometimes big changes, sometimes little by little." Dali seemed to feel she'd made enough of a point about healthy food and busied herself with her (healthy) lunch.[146]

Petra changed the subject, offering to interpret for Abby the lines of colorful light playing on the bubbling surface of the small waterfall nearby, cascading into a black basin.

"The light is creating words on the water, one sentence at a time," Petra explained. She sang the actual verse. "The entire quote is: 'Although to acquire the sciences and arts is the greatest glory of mankind, this is so only on condition that man's river floweth into the mighty Sea, and draweth from God's ancient source His inspiration. When this cometh to pass, then every teacher is as a shoreless ocean, every pupil a prodigal fountain of knowledge. If, then, the pursuit of knowledge leadeth to the beauty of Him Who is the object of all knowledge, how excellent that goal; but if not, a mere drop will perhaps shut a man off from flooding grace, for with learning cometh arrogance and pride, and it bringeth on error and indifference to God.'"[147]

Abby wanted to bask in the spiritual fragrance of the quote, but fought the growing sensation that her brain was being invaded by a creeping fog which threatened to ruin her lunch.

Petra turned to Dali.

"So what were you working on this morning?"

"A unit on sex," Dali replied, glancing at her tablemates.

"Oh really?" Petra laughed. "Anything new?"

"Actually there is," Dali smiled. "After our discussion the other day, Abby, I wondered more about your time. You're causing me to do that a lot lately." She tipped her head at Abby as did when she joked. "So when this order came through to prepare some slides, I dug into it more. It's interesting but frightening."

If Dali could share anything that would tell her where she stood with Kreshi, Abby would do her best to beat back the threatening fog and participate politely.

"Anything fit for lunchtime discussion?" Petra asked.

"Maybe. Let me know if this is too … anything," Dali said, waiting for permission from the other two girls. "Just some thoughts, really, but, here we've got this deep biological urge, with these huge consequences if we mishandle it.

"I saw that your culture didn't have a reliable network to address the emotional emergency that caused people to engage in roving sex. That brought disease, unwanted pregnancy, and toxic drama, among other life-ruining problems. It was better if two people were faithful to each other, even if they weren't married, but, well, I'm puzzled over why someone would risk making a baby without making sure that there's proper support for that baby."

"What difference does being married make? Kids in my class have parents who aren't married, and it seems fine," Abby blurted out. Dang, vowing to be polite wasn't enough to overcome the growing darkness. Chagrined, she felt her stomach – and her willingness to try – shut down.

Fortunately, Dali didn't seem to be offended;[148] she seemed to be wrestling with how to ask her yuter for answers to Abby's objection. The silence was protracted until Dali burst out laughing.

"Oh! Those are good!" she wheezed, gasping for breath. "Sorry, okay. The yuter has an entertaining list of old sayings to urge girls, mainly, not to have sex outside of marriage. Like, 'Why should the farmer pay for the cow if he can get the milk for free?' "

Abby snorted in recognition and appreciation.

"On the other hand, 'Getting married just to have sex is like buying an airplane to get the peanuts free,' " Petra chortled.

"Back to your question," Dali grinned. "There's no guarantee that a family will stay together if they only wait until they're married to have sex and make babies, but there's even less chance of success if they're not married. Checking the potential mate's character and background beforehand is a safety net, you see, and needs to be constructed and fastened in place before these permanent developments, you see."

"What if I don't have kids, but he and I love each other and we're together a long time, but he doesn't want to get married?" Maybe laughing connected her to the moment a little better, but Abby felt her brain become less hijacked … less brain-jacked.

Dali blinked slowly, speaking silently with her yuter.

"It's about self-worth, that is," Dali finally said. "For eons, women debased and endangered themselves to find a man. But with no legal connection, often the woman had no claim to his estate after he passed, no financial security after all those years of dedication to him."

Petra weighed in. "Anatomy class teaches that sex is a system that excels at making babies. It sounds like in your time, people were all about the fun of sex but ignored the risk of conceiving children. And the hardships those children would have."

"When you put it like that …" Abby frowned.

"Raising children properly is the hardest job on earth, even when there's a man working to support the mother and baby. It was all worsened by the imbalance of power between men and women, then, too. So many difficulties resulting from that unfairness! How unjust it was!" Dali expounded.

"That's a lot," Petra sympathized.

"Yes, and it goes on," Dali explained passionately. "If a single mother went to work after the baby is born, it created one set of problems. If she stayed home and nursed and trained the baby, she had another set of problems. They both struggled with many hardships either way. Fatherless boys had a harder time being good fathers, not having seen models; fatherless girls had a harder time knowing how to relate to men and husbands. And children often copy the practices of their parents, so the habit of casual sex continued, with all its difficult results. It led to a lot of lost, confused, dysfunctional souls, making up floundering societies."

"So here, everyone waits till they're married? No one ever wants to have sex before?"

Abby could have predicted that her impatient, hasty and accusing question would elicit a long silence. She'd been rude; she'd oversimplified. She'd failed again to prevail against the gloom permeating her mind. Was this Satan claiming her for his evil purposes, as Rev. Davison had preached? If so, she should fight it even harder.

"Please Jesus, please, Bahá'u'lláh and everyone else, help me cast out the darkness," Abby whispered behind her hair, sketching a sign of the cross and, to cover all her bases, a crude 9-pointed star on her thigh. She couldn't think of any Buddhist, Hindu or Muslim signs and gave up trying to get the Jewish star right when Dali eventually spoke.

"Of course they might want to." Dali chose her words carefully, her voice free of anger. "We could consider several angles of your question. One is that there are no sexualized images surrounding us, egging us on, pushing that trigger, like in your time."

"Somebody tells people not to show those anymore?" A vivid mental picture of naked movie stars shocked Abby enough to override the menacing fog.

"Not quite. We understand the danger, especially to young people, of spreading that kind of imagery ... again, learning from your time. So if someone did try, the rest of us would turn away from it and someone close to them would probably ask them to stop."

So in Erden, Hakene would have no audience to play to, nor anyone to encourage him to even think about it. But in Abby's hometime, people thought either "It's a free country, he can do whatever he likes, whether I like it or not," or "Woohoo, let's go see him naked!" Abby could now see the effect that being bombarded with such images would have on people.

"Also, the human body is considered sacred now." Dali paused.

"So everyone covers it up?" A glaring, bright light targeted Abby through the window – a reflection bouncing off the windshield of an ATV that had pulled up to the gardens outside. Finding it impossible to avoid, she closed her eyes, which accented an odd ringing in her ears.

"Oh, that looks unpleasant. I'll yuter them and ask them to move the cart," Petra offered.

"Are you still interested in my answer, Abby?" Dali asked. "Yes? Okay, I was trying to explain that, yes, there are nude paintings and statues, but instead of sexualized, they're portrayed as an amazing creation of God. Which the human body is. If you ever take an anatomy class you will see what I mean."

"Why, you took anatomy, too?" The blinding light plus the effort to talk calmly was giving Abby a headache.

"Everyone here takes anatomy," Petra spoke while Dali ate. "It is quite aweful to see how intricately God designed us. It's also useful to learn how to care for one's body. This is in keeping with the quote that 'man should know his own self and recognize that which leadeth unto loftiness or lowliness, glory or abasement, wealth or poverty.'[149]

Although Petra sang the last quote in her pretty voice, Abby wasn't listening. Why did she feel so woozy? Because of this new throbbing at the top of her head? She pressed the painful spot, eyes still closed, trying to keep down her meager lunch.

"Uh, Abby? What's the matter?" Petra leaned forward, peering closely at Abby, which alerted Dali.

The young women rushed to Abby's sides, rubbing and patting her arms and shoulders. Dali gently tucked Abby's hair behind her ear and tried to peer in her face.

This helped briefly, but when they stopped, the pain surged again.

Abby pressed down on the top of her head with all her might, trying to hold in the searing pain. The room spun ... her stomach lurched ... she was spinning ... everything was white. The two friends held her hands and took turns singing to her.

The room slowly righted and the headache settled into a dull throb. Abby glanced up to see Petra looking at her with great concern.

"Let's take you to the nurse," she said, Dali agreeing. "Come on. Can you stand up?"

Abby didn't argue but allowed them to scoot her chair and guide her by the elbow down hallways into a carpeted room with plain, skinny chairs surrounded by sliding curtains. A woman wearing a white school uniform greeted them.

"One of you not feeling quite right?" she asked, adjusting a chair.

"Hello, yes, my friend visiting here, Abby, she started looking kind of ... not ... um, she doesn't feel well," Petra stood back as Dali shut the door behind them. The nurse laid a chair flat and adjusted a light.

Another attack seized Abby, worse than before. Her head felt as if it were coming apart ... she clamped her hands onto the top of her head, trying to hold it together ... the agony shot into her stomach and threatened to empty it ... her legs gave out ... they shuffled her to the bedchair and rolled her onto it.

"Abby, hold on ..."

"... Here's a bowl if you're going to throw up ..."

"... Yuter, what do you suggest?"

Abby moaned with the pain and started crying, she felt so awful.

"... She looks so pale, can we do something for her?"

"... Dali, can you tell us more about Abby's illness?"

Hands hold her as she drowns in disorientation and pain ... the nurse's shirt undulates in shades of mist ... white bubbles of angry foam pull at her ... she tumbles helplessly, thrown about in the rough surf ... threatening dots of sinister colors swirl around her as she falls ... a cord brushes against her ... it snares her, tugs at her ...guides her toward a dim, difficult shore ... spots and flecks on a suddenly familiar hide guide her, anchor her, soothe her, remind her what she's always known ... an urgent voice registers..."Abs, *Abs*, here, it'll be better, it's okay!" ... someone was talking to the nurse about falling behind on the painkiller schedule ... and slowly the pain got better, and Jenn's voice carried her through it.

But it couldn't be Jenn. Jenn was back in 2007. And Abby had Care of Animals class after the other one, if she could just figure out this stupid headache, and if she could stop the odd, mixed-up spots and circles of a heaving horse's rump swirling past her eyes as she fell ... she tried to press the top of her head but ran into something thick ... someone pulled her arm down ... Jenn and the nurse soothed her, saying that she was already better ... Jenn tenderly coated her lips with ointment on a little sponge.

No, it couldn't be Jenn ...

It *was* Jenn. It was *Jenn*! In a hospital room. With a nurse smiling consolingly, checking the IV in Abby's arm.

Tears ran down Jenn's oh-so-beloved face. Abby struggled to keep open eyes that felt gritty and unused, blurry and teary.

"What?" she whispered.

Jenn sobbed with joy and exclaimed, "Welcome back, Abs! Welcome back!"

Chapter 27 Return

Abby lay in a hospital room, struggling to come to grips with returning to Little Lily, North Carolina. Groggy, aching, and confused, she yearned for Erden the whole time Jenn held her hand and hesitantly told her what had happened three days earlier.

Abby had landed head-first in the trees and blacked out when Gunsmoke bolted for home. The wrangler called 911 on his cell phone – good thing the wranglers knew they had reception on the trail – then called the office girl and had her contact Vivian at the street fair. Needless to say, Mother absolutely blew a gasket.

The arriving paramedics had packed a stretcher up the hill, painstakingly lifted an unconscious, bleeding Abby onto it, and carried her down to the ambulance. Her breathing and heartbeat hadn't stopped, and no bones were broken, but she was scraped and bruised, with a deep and dirty cut on her abdomen and a huge bump on her head that had bled a lot both outside and in.

Now, a small hole in the top of her skull marked where they'd removed blood pooling between her skull and brain, her abdomen sported three inches of stitches, and she'd had a bunch of drugs to control bleeding, reduce swelling, combat infections, and quell pain. Since she'd finally woken up, the doctors predicted that she would come out of it in reasonably good shape.

Jenn knew that Abby would want to know, and had called the stables to ask specifically about Gunsmoke. The office girl assured her that he was now permanently retired from the dude string, since his running away with Abby had been the latest of several other incidents.

When Jenn fell silent, Abby contemplated the flowers next to her old wristwatch and a stuffed "Get Well" horse on the unused overbed table, musing that she had actually died (to her old self) and gone to heaven (on earth), but she couldn't say so. She'd gone away, come awake, and been made aware in that other time. She had arrived at the hospital late Friday morning and it was now Monday afternoon, or in Erden, she'd arrived at Dali's midday on Saturday and left the nurse's room at lunch on Tuesday. She fingered the plush pony to distract herself from the steadily growing, stabbing pain … in her heart.

"Since you still had Granny's old watch on, I kept wearing the antique brooch," Jenn murmured hesitantly. "With the IV and other lines, the nurses said you couldn't wear it, but it didn't get smashed in the accident, so I left it here, sort of connecting us." The faithful old watch was still keeping the right time, and now reminded Abby of a world she missed more than life itself.

An hour after Abby regained consciousness, Mother came in with red eyes, quite emotional, very unlike her usual self. She sat on the bed, pulled the covers too tight over Abby and leaned close, wafting bad breath in her face. Abby tried to listen calmly as Mother expounded on how worried she'd been, looking, as usual, everywhere but into her daughter's eyes. How she and Daddy considered suing the stable despite the releases she'd signed. How the vacation plans had been upset, not knowing how long Abby would be in a coma. How the Holsworths had been inconvenienced with Abby's accident on top of the fire in the neighborhood. How the fire came so close to the hospital, smoke permeating the building and making the patients restless, causing the hospital staff to consider evacuation. But the wind shifted and the fire was brought under control shortly after, so no patients had had to be moved, and the Holsworth's house had been spared.

Abby knew she was supposed to lie there, obedient and quiet and, if she could manage it, sympathetic for the difficulties her coma had brought on her mother.

Abby wished she had a yuter to explain mothers who were so self-absorbed that, as their daughters woke up from comas, they could only recite a long list of their own complaints.

An orderly wheeled Abby from the hospital the next morning. Jenn carried her sister's few belongings. Daddy, quiet and tired-looking as usual, held Abby's hand, while Mother toted two vases full of flowers and fussed about how to avoid crushing the peonies. Vivian finally wrapped the flower stems in a wet paper towel, emptied the vases, and tucked them into the corners of the trunk, harrumphing the whole time.

Abby felt by turns affection, gratitude, and irritation toward her family as she buckled her seatbelt.

At Sofia's house, all the Holsworths greeted the Wizes. Getting her worlds confused, which made her head hurt more, she wondered what the kids were doing home. School had started, right? She whispered her question to Jenn as they climbed the stairs to the little bedroom. Jenn replied that Abby was a week off; school for the Holsworth kids would start next Monday. Abby smiled behind Jenn's back: she was not one week off, but several thousand weeks off.

That night, Abby dreamed repetitious, pain-induced nightmares …

∞   ∞   ∞   ∞   ∞   ∞   ∞   ∞

… frantic hoofbeats, terrified neighs … yaps, snarls, blood-curdling laughs … in the moonless dark, huge hyenas with banefully glowing eyes chase, kill, and devour wild mustangs running in the desert …

ZZP ... *in tall cacti and rolling tumbleweeds, pistol-armed outlaws in dusty rawhide-colored coats and heavy bandoleers face off against tattooed rogue bikers in greasy, old, black leather jackets and Viking helmets who wield spears as flamethrowers against children driving police cars ...*

∞ ∞ ∞ ∞ ∞ ∞ ∞ ∞

Each time a nightmare jarred Abby awake, she was comforted knowing that Jenn slept next to her trundle bed. And she was pleasantly surprised when, at noon the next day, Jon and Melissa popped up to her room for an impromptu shut-in picnic, unaware that Abby couldn't eat the food they brought because of doctor's orders to reintroduce solid food slowly.

Abby gingerly reached out toward Melissa and Jon, checking her pain levels but wanting to show courtesy and love, however awkwardly, for these beautiful friends whom she valued so much. Melissa seemed a little surprised, but quickly returned Abby's hug. Sitting on the floor, Jon set three plates of food on Abby's suitcase.

"Melissa, can we talk?" Abby asked hesitantly. "And you can stay, Jon, if you want."

"Sure," Melissa said. She settled in against the wall next to Jon, her deep brown eyes showing interest mixed with patience. She reminded Abby so strongly of the beautifully blended, joyful Erdeans that reverse homesickness pierced her heart and threatened to overwhelm her. She'd probably never again see dear Dali, the horses, or precious Kreshi or Rykeir; never return to the Draggin' Dragon, or find out what happened in Care of Animals class. She sank, mired in her loss. She floundered, trying to grab a positive thought out of the void ... like in *Hook* ... a Happy Thought to make her fly ... a happy thought.

"Be not thou troubled," Melissa whispered, bringing Abby to tears again because she recognized it as a phrase from that long Arabic prayer in the Erdean Deepening. She intoned a gentle song:

♫Is there any Remover of Difficulties save God?
Say: Praised be God! He is God!
All are His servants, and all abide by His bidding!♫[150]

The prayer calmed Abby, steadied her, so that she could almost speak normally again. "Please sing another," she croaked through a throat so tight she could barely breathe. Melissa's voice rose again ...

♫Thy name is my healing, O my God,
and remembrance of Thee is my remedy ....♫

... Jon's voice softly joined in ...

♪Thou, verily, art the All-Bountiful,
the All-Knowing, the All-Wise.♪[151]

"All-Wise," whispered Abby hoarsely, glad that the prayer was long enough to calm herself a bit. "Wisdom, the mother of the other virtues," she echoed Dali. A soft sound of agreement rose from the friends next to her, then silence. But Abby wasn't quite ready to talk.

With a glance at Jon, Melissa picked up her plate and slowly nibbled. Jon followed suit. Abby realized they were trying to give her more time without being obvious about waiting for her to speak. When Melissa gestured that she should join them in eating, though, Abby just touched her stomach and grimaced. She was too upset to eat right now, even without the doctor's orders. Melissa nodded sympathetically. Their courteous patience revived more wrenching memories of Dali's solicitousness and dedicated problem-solving.

Thinking happy Peter Pan thoughts no longer lifted her out of her despair. Her sad, travailing spirit recalled the portrait of 'Abdu'l-Bahá and his endless offer of love and support. He was still real, and he still touched her soul. She could hold onto that in any world. But her heart kept slipping away, back to Erden.

Almost of its own accord, her hand reached out slowly to Melissa's, and found refuge and strength there. Strength ... the Testing Lab ... she herself was nearly breaking.

"That which doesn't break us makes us stronger."[152] Abby squeaked, forcing a deep breath. "Strength," she said. "Courage."

Melissa squeezed her hand, serenely supporting Abby's struggle.

"Did y'all think I'd died when I was ... gone?" Abby was finally able to ask, turning experimentally onto her side to gaze at the faces a foot above her own.

"We knew you weren't dead," Jon said, "but we wondered where your soul was. There isn't much help about comas on the web.[153] We found more about people who die and come back than about the experiences of comatose people."

"Almost everyone has heard about near-death experiences: the tunnel, and light, being stopped, reviewing your life," Melissa added in her soft Southern accent.[154] "But most people coming out of comas just say it was dark, or maybe they heard faint voices."

"I was not dead or blanked out," Abby said softly but firmly. She wasn't sure of the reception she'd get. Was this Courtesy Class material? Might as well just blurt it out. "I ... I went 700 years in the future and lived there for three days."

After a long pause, Melissa asked, "How was it?"

Abby slowly lifted her too-sensitive head, finding a willing listener. "Oh, I saw it all, Melissa, everything in your Writings ... the Most Great Peace, God's Kingdom on earth, Sia ... um, His will being done here like it is in heaven, it's all there, it's *wonderful*, it's ..."

Words failed Abby and she could only squeeze Melissa's hand in gratitude. Melissa squeezed cautiously but definitely back.

Abby lay back against her pillows, shifting carefully. She closed her eyes to better recall and describe what she could to Melissa, who would never see what she'd seen.

"They have the coolest tiny computers, called yuters, that do everything you can imagine, take pictures and remind you and translate things and look up stuff ... you wouldn't happen to know any quotes about happiness offhand, would you?"

Melissa frowned as she racked her brains. "All I can think of about happiness is one song," she replied, clearly embarrassed. She began to sing a bouncy song in a strained voice and, to Abby's confusion, a strange language – with no yuter translation.

♪*To ko za ni ni na la ba wan ki.*
Le li lan ga la ku ka na...♪

Melissa saw Abby's blank face and quickly hummed through to the last line in the foreign language, the happy beat causing her voice to be stronger and surer. Abby recognized the need to run through a familiar pattern, searching for a particular part ...

♪*Ti Yá Bahá'u'l-Abhá.*

Rejoice, rejoice, for a new day has dawned.
The whole wide world is all one fold.
Rejoice, rejoice, for a new day has dawned.
The plan of God has now been told.
The promised One by the name of *Bahá*
Came to bring a new day.
Let us be happy. Let us say:
Yá Bahá'u'l-Abhá.
Say: *Yá Bahá'u'l-Abhá.*
Say: *Yá Bahá'u'l-Abhá.*♪[155]

Melissa looked so much like Dali, as her face relaxed and her voice grew confident, that Abby felt almost as if she were back in Erden.

"What does that mean?" she asked when Melissa had finished the happy song.

"Oh, the *Yá Bahá'u'l-Abhá?*" Melissa said in her very unDali-ish southern accent, popping Abby's fantasy. "It means 'O Glory of the All-Glorious'. Arabic, I think."

"Yes, of course," said Abby, "*YAW-bah-HAH-oo-lob-HAH*. Thank you." She contemplated the blue blanket folded at the foot of the bed. It reminded her of Dali's magical blue picnic cloth. "Do you know where I can get ahold of quotes? I'll really miss them if I can't."

"Sure," said Melissa. "There are books, websites, CDs, DVDs. Just let me know."

"And do you know how I can find the Bahá'ís in Surely? For when we get back there? They might have a Spiritual School."

"Spiritual School?" Melissa sat up straight. "Like Sunday School? Or a deepening? What was it like?"

"Yeah, deepening. At 'Ilm Sunday School was it? ... they had a lady ... an actress ... a hologram ... she told about the Master in America. It had everything in it. How he was, what he did, pictures of him ... I heard his voice ..." She clung to her memory.

"Wow! Well, I really doubt you'll run into a deepening ... er, a school like that in Surely. Or anywhere right now," Melissa said. "We mainly study the Bahá'í Writings and talk about them."

"Do you have parties when someone declares? At 15 or older?"

Melissa exhaled loudly. "Whoa, you *did* do it all, didn't you?"

"Oh, it was *soooo* much *fun!*" Abby exclaimed, winced, and gently pressed her bandaged head. *If Dali or Rykeir or Kreshi were here they'd probably fix me right up, cracking jokes the whole time – Wize-cracks.* Now, she'd have to get well the old world way: slowly.

"The technology was incredible, everything worked so well ... and the *horses!* Actually, all the animals. Everything was so clean, so pretty, and everyone helped each other, really helped. They recycled, and cared for the earth and each other. And people were *united*, and everyone was a mix of everything. Most people looked like you, Melissa, and I thought of you. I thought about how hard you have it now, trying to be spiritual and build that fabulous new world even as the old one falls apart around us."

The excitement of telling an understanding listener brought Abby to life as no rest or drugs ever could.

"Thanks, Abs, I appreciate it. More than you know," Melissa's eyes glistened.

"I might have a pretty good idea of how much you appreciate it. I started to get Divine Guidance, like the Master said we should ..."

Melissa let out an astonished laugh through her tears. "You probably know more than I do, girl. And I declared 10 years ago!"

"Oh? How do you actually declare?"

"Finally, one thing *I* know about *my* Faith that *you* don't!" Melissa teased, seeing that Abby was on firmer emotional ground.

"When I know as much as you, I might declare," Abby bantered, only half-joking.

"Ah!" Melissa said, reaching into her purse, "I just saw something about that in this little book. 'You don't have to already know everything and be obeying all the principles and laws in order to become a Bahá'í. Declaring your faith is the *beginning* of your glorious journey, not the end. When you believe that Bahá'u'lláh is indeed Who He says He is, find His Word resonating in your heart and soul, want to be part of His community and help put His unifying Plan into action, and are willing to learn about and follow His Teachings to the best of your ability, you already are a Bahá'í.' "[156]

Melissa closed the little booklet and regarded Abby, who met the brown eyes for longer than she used to. Melissa smiled broadly.

"You might like this idea: being a Bahá'í could be like doing natural horsemanship. Sometimes when Angie talks about it, it reminds me of the Bahá'í Faith, because she says that horse whispering is pretty easy to understand, but we could spend a lifetime putting the teachings and principles into practice."

"So, like Parelli," Jon puzzled out, "the Bahá'í Faith is simple to understand but not easy to do, is that right, hun?"

"I'd say that sometimes it's not easy to understand, either, sugar, but yeah, one or two lifetimes would be a good start," Melissa joked.

"Well, I already know some. About putting God first, and a unified world, and how important education is," Abby allowed her mouth and brain to gear up but kept her tender head and tummy still. "And service being worship, and a universal auxiliary language, and the daily prayers. I don't drink, do drugs, have any kind of sex, and I'll try never to backbite. And isn't there also something about fasting? Did I miss anything?"

Melissa chuckled. "Well, fasting wouldn't come for a couple of years for you, after you're 15. Let's hope you won't need the burial or marriage laws any time soon, either. We often recite the "Three Onenesses: Humanity is one, no group is better or worse than any other; God is One, no matter the name, Religions are One in Essence." But honestly, Abby, you know more than a lot of people who believe in Bahá'u'lláh and declare. Just so you believe in your heart that He is God's Voice for today and want to try to follow His teachings."

"Oh, I do! And I enroll exactly how?" Abby was proud of herself for remembering her original train of thought without the indispensable, magical yuter.

"It's different in other countries, like I saw when I went to Suriname on a service project,[157] but in the U.S., there's a card that you sign, pledging your belief in Bahá'u'lláh and your willingness to try to obey the Bahá'í laws, and asking to be a member of His Faith. Someone checks with you to make sure you know you're joining a religion and then sends your card to the National Bahá'í Center, which connects you with other believers near you so they can get to know you, send you newsletters, invite you to Feast—"

"What *is* Feast?" Abby could finally find out what the yuter show was about.

"Excellent! Something else you don't know about yet. I'd love to hear how Feast in the future is. Now, it's usually in someone's home, because most of the Bahá'í communities are too small to have a Bahá'í Center. It's a spiritual meeting of the local enrolled believers. We begin with prayer, then discuss community business and administrative matters, and end with a little social time. Feast is held every 19 days."

The three friends grinned at each other in the little room. But as the silence lengthened, the adrenaline left her and Abby began to feel very tired and ill again. Her smile faded and her eyes closed.

"We'll let you sleep now," Jon said, standing up. He helped Melissa up, and she laid her hand gently and lovingly on Abby's arm.

"Thanks so much for sharing that about your … adventure. I would love to hear more, if you ever feel like it again," Melissa said longingly.

Abby responded sleepily, "I hope I can. You two are the only ones I know who'd understand."

Abby's unfocused eyes landed on her untouched plate and Jon and Melissa's emptier ones. It struck her as odd that Melissa had eaten the processed meat, jello-fluff salad, white garlic bread, and other items that – even if they existed in Erden – surely no Erdean would care to eat.

"I thought Bahá'ís ate so healthy and all," she murmured, carefully rolling onto her back.

"It's in the Writings, yes," Melissa said, looking a little guilty as she picked up the plates. "But like with so many things, we're working our way up to that. In the meantime: *kam, kam, rúz bih rúz.*"

"Oh yes," Abby murmured groggily, a tiny smile flitting across her lips, "little by little, day by day."

Chapter 28 Phonecall

Abby recuperated on the couch in the Holsworth's family room for the next several days, dozing and watching TV. Mother brought Abby soft foods, as the doctor had ordered. Vivian was not exactly affectionate, but did refrain from her usual stream of criticism. Day by day, Abby felt a little better.

Aunt Sofia obligingly played all the movies Abby asked for even though she napped often, missing large sections. This wasn't how Abby would have wished to see them. Worse still, she felt conflict coil in her stomach watching Hakene Bodant in one of his latest films and remembering the disturbing images on Penny's computer upstairs.

Jenn often sat with Abby on the couch and filled her in on events in Little Lily while she was "away." Jenn had lived at Abby's bedside in the hospital, praying fervently, reading from Abby's *Native American Wisdom* and *Cowboys and Indians* purchases, and singing anything she could think of, which seemed to rouse Abby at times. Sometimes in her sleep, Jenn relayed, she dreamt that she saw Abby far ahead, laughing.

Jenn kept repeating how relieved, how happy she was that Abby came back. Abby struggled to reply, finally realizing that although she couldn't honestly say she was glad to be back, her one shining light was her big sister, and she was grateful.

As often as she dared without making herself cry, Abby closed her eyes and watched "reruns" of Erden, trying to burn them into her memory.

The Wize family's second weekend at the Holsworths caused Abby to think of Chloë, Tyler, Moony and the others at The Ride Place and wonder if they knew of her riding accident. They probably brushed it off like all the others.

Mother and Daddy discussed which day they'd leave, causing Abby to see if Jon could bring Melissa over one last time – and bring some Bahá'í reading material.

Sunday afternoon, almost a week after she returned to her hometime, Abby convinced Mother to let her sit in the back yard with the young couple. Mother acquiesced after they promised to guard Abby, although Abby noticed that Mother only interacted with Jon.

Melissa asked for more details from the future. Abby lingered on the lessons Dali had said they'd learned from earlier times. Abby was pleased to remember to ask Melissa how she coped, knowing that the world would get worse before it got better.

Melissa mulled it over in the peaceful evening air, waving absently at gnats while Jon relit a citronella candle.

"Well, I don't think much about how hard it is, or is going to be, I guess," Melissa drawled. "It's not like I have a choice about how the world around me is. But when you put it like that, yeah, it can be rough. At least we have a lot of Writings spelling out what we should do, and showing us the world of the future, and explaining the twin processes of decay and building. That's way more than the early American Bahá'ís had," she mused, always finding the bright side. "I try to focus on building that new world, since I can't do much about the current, old one falling apart."

"You mean spread the Bahá'í Faith so more people enroll," Jon said.

"Well, that would help," Melissa answered hesitantly. "But Shoghi Effendi said that the goal of the Bahá'í Faith was also to deepen people's faith in the religion they already have.[158] The essence of all the religions is the same; I was reared to believe that deeply. The Master wrote a Tablet to a Christian lady in which he said his dearest wish is that the whole world would truly follow the teachings of Jesus Christ, because all the Prophets from God have taught the same eternal truths."[159]

"If all the religions are really the same, then why send a new one?" Jon asked.

"Great question," Melissa said warmly. "The *essence* of all religions is the same, like, the Golden Rule, and belief in God, by whatever name. They all teach praying or meditating, doing good deeds, thinking right thoughts, being helpful and serving, obeying spiritual laws and guidance, and such.[160] But there are some differences, too, because of what people in different places and times could handle. Like, cell phones and the internet, which was predicted.[161] And like, wine is permissible in the Christian faith, but in the Bahá'í Writings, drinking alcohol is not allowed because of all the social and family ills it can cause, like domestic abuse."

Melissa checked Abby for signs of comprehension. Abby nodded.

"Now, we need to sort out big, new, complicated issues, like the growing gap between people who have money, or education, or privileges, and those who don't. Environmental chaos, unethical technology and also unreasonable beliefs;[162] horrible wars with nuclear bombs ..." She wrinkled her nose, reluctant to go on with the list. "We need God's guidance and a Divine System to help us solve such complex, scary problems."[163]

"Makes sense. But I'm just a kid in school, I can't solve any of those big things."

"You can do the most important thing of all: grow your spiritual muscles for later.[164] School might be a great place to work on one of the most important laws – also the hardest and most unusual law, in my opinion."

"Oh?"

"Yes, gossip."

"You mean … what do you mean? Being gossiped about? Or not doing the gossip?" Abby asked, connecting suddenly with "What goes around comes around."

"Well, being gossiped about is really rough, for sure," Melissa began, pausing when Abby's chin quivered, remembering how mean kids could be, with hurtful nicknames and vicious rumors. Melissa laid her hand on Abby's. "Aww, I'm sorry, darlin'. Sometimes we can get justice if we've been done wrong, but sometimes we just have to take one for the team of humanity and move on. Mom and I decided to look at what hurts the most and pour the hurt into that."

She gathered an explanation when she saw Abby's quizzical expression.

"Like, when we get gossiped about and it's not true, we feel indignant, we feel truth got left behind. So we can take that hurt and the anger that comes after, and pour it into being more truthful and more dignified."

"Easy to say, hard to do, I bet," Abby offered.

"Yeah, and then of course resolving not to dish out the gossip or rumors ourselves, so we're not causing that kind of pain to someone else. Gossiping, backstabbing, and all those kinds of speech that aren't truthful, loving, helpful, moderate, and all … they cause pain.[165] And drag us into bad paths. But mainly it kills unity because it divides people."

"Even when they can't hear you?" Abby asked, remembering Penny and her friends badmouthing people on TV and their favorite celebrity's fans on the computer.

"Well, obviously that's more removed, but hurtful words get around awfully quickly," Melissa allowed. "Famous people say they can't read their fan pages because it can be so devastating."

"Yeah, famous people," Abby mused. "Or even locally famous," she murmured, thinking of Asst. Rev. Gottle and the girls reveling in juicy news at church. "I guess you're saying that even if something is true, if it's not helpful and loving and all, we shouldn't pass it on. But what do you do if someone is standing there, trying to get you to gossip about someone else? Someone you know in real life?"

"Mom and I talk about it a lot, trying to work out what words to use with a gossiper without being mean. We've come up with a couple of pretty good responses. Like, if it's a short jab at someone, I'll counter it by saying something good about that person or that quality."

"What do you mean?" Abby asked.

Melissa smiled. "Do you know about virtues?"

"I do!" Abby flashed an answering grin. "But I stopped the yuter halfway through, and I didn't memorize it, so no pop quizzes!"

"Aw shucks, and I was all ready with a quiz," Melissa joked. "So, virtues are the positive qualities of a person, but there could be good uses of negative qualities ... contra-virtues, you could say. We got the idea from a quote of 'Abdu'l-Bahá's about how negative qualities can sometimes be put to a good use, like greed can be good if you're greedy for learning, and anger can be ok if it's anger against injustice.[166] So we turned it around. Like, how could, say, stubbornness be good? It could be called persistence or not being too easily swayed from what you know is right. That's the good side of stubbornness."

Abby blanched. Why did Melissa pick stubbornness, of all the traits? A whirlwind of memories, validation, and divine breezes rolled through her soul, topped by memories of Dali indignantly complaining about the greed and injustice of Earther food industries, which seemed uncharacteristic of her then but made sense now.

"But it can be tricky, 'cuz the complainer, the gossiper, wants you to agree that the other person is bad, and I haven't found anyone yet who will separate the bad deed from the bad doer. Sometimes, I only manage to say that I think everyone's doing their best. Once, I got a gossiper to talk with the other person about her gripe; that's the most I've been able to do.

"Of course, if the gossiper is really going on and *on*, I will try to change the subject. Or see if I can distract them onto something else. My cross-stitch works well for that, actually." She grinned. "Or asking them for help with something. Just standing there looking at them seems to invite more of the same, and looking away seems to interrupt it, slow it down. If all else fails, I make an excuse to leave.

"Sometimes I have a hard time knowing the difference between gossip and confidential consulting, which we *are* supposed to do. I'm working on the thought that gossip has a nasty twist, a vengeance toward the person who's not there. So I try to encourage consultation but discourage gossip."[167]

"Wow, gossip *is* really hard." Abby saw how far she had to go in her spiritual understanding and sank, daunted, into her lawn chair.

"Well, once you start thinking things through like this, you get better at it," Melissa said soothingly, "and you can use bits of one solution for parts of another problem. It can be hard, though." She stifled a laugh, clapping her hand over her mouth.

"What?"

"Sorry, maybe it isn't the time for it, but I remembered a joke."

"I'm up for a joke."

"Jesus promised Christians the Kingdom of God on earth, and they look forward to the finished product floating down from heaven, come Judgment Day. But for Bahá'ís, piles of bricks, bags of mortar, shovels, and wheelbarrows pour down in a cloud of dust. The note floats down on top of the pile: 'Do-It-Yourself Kit.'"

Melissa glanced sidelong at Abby, saw her smile, and asked, "Seriously, though, is there anything else that worries you?"

"Yeah." Abby dropped her chin to her chest, remembering.

After patiently waiting for more and not getting it, Melissa asked if she could offer any help.

"It's my mother," Abby mumbled, always on guard about Mother.

"Is there anything I might be able to do for you?" Melissa asked so lovingly that Abby felt tears spring to her eyes.

"I ... I'm just not sure how to handle her, now that I ... I think she is, uh, she's not how she's supposed to be. It's like, she ..." Abby's voice trailed off. Mother would absolutely kill her if she ever found out Abby had said something like that. Was it gossip?

"Oh dear," Melissa said, moving close and holding her hand. Jon sat up straighter in his patio chair, looking anguished for the two girls. Women. Wirls.

"Dali said pollution can make some people not act like they should, like not loving their children," Abby choked out.

"Oh no, sweetie," Melissa whispered. "I'm so sorry."

"Yeah. I just don't know ... what to do now," Abby croaked. "It's always bad, but now that I think she has something wrong with her ..."

"Oh, darlin'." Melissa caressed Abby's hand in both of hers. "I, er, have seen first-hand some of what you're describing, so it's real. You're a noble, strong soul, no matter what. I ... I could stay in touch with you, if you like, and I can pray for you, for sure." Melissa paused, mental wheels spinning, reminding Abby strongly of Dali. "Can you confide in Jenn?"

"Oh yes, we're very tight," Abby's affirmation rushed out. "If it weren't for her, I really would be sunk."

"That's great. It only takes one caring person to keep us sane," Melissa relaxed in relief, thinking and praying.[168] "So, if you have a specific problem, we could use Bahá'í consultation, if you like. How does that sound?"

"Yes, of course. I'd like that a lot," Abby said, smiling through her tears, grateful to know that she had at least two people who cared enough to help her with her biggest trouble. A few bright lights glowed in her heart now, tiny glimmers of the lightning bolts she'd received in Erden. Goosebumps sprouted on her arms as she remembered.

Melissa got up to leave with Jon, hugging Abby tenderly.

"Oh, snap, almost forgot – here are some books and handouts for you. 'Abdu'l-Bahá is good to start with," Melissa said, motioning to Jon to hand her a tote bag he had set by his chair. "Please accept these from Mom and me. They're yours to keep if you like. Look, I wrote down my e-mail, snail mail and phone number for you."

Abby eyed the wealth of material with a wrenching mixture of greed for learning on one hand and dismay on the other. She'd never be able to sneak half a dozen big books and several small ones into her luggage, get them all home, and keep them hidden from Mother, who would have a total conniption if she found her daughter in possession of "unacceptable" books.

"Oh," Abby said, her emotions roller-coastering to teariness again. "I can't take all of that, Melissa. I wish I could. But Mother …"

"I understand, Abby, honestly I do." Melissa nodded in sympathy. "Let me pull out a couple of the smallest things for you, okay? Look, here's a little book of Prayers and Writings from Malaysia. I'll put the sticky note with my info in there. And here are the *Three Onenesses*. Remember, I read you something from this one the other day? See, they're pocket-sized. And here are some useful handouts. 'On Life' and 'On Love' and 'On Liberty'; I downloaded the three 'L' sheets … just seemed right somehow. I hope you like them, honey. Maybe you could look on the internet, too; here's the right website. And do you think you can take just one bigger book? *Paris Talks* is 'Abdu'l-Bahá's speeches in France."[169]

Abby accepted the small white volume, the even smaller beige chapbooks, and the loose pages. She studied the cover of the biggest book, which featured the Eiffel Tower. The title stood out in tall blue letters; 'Abdu'l-Bahá's name was in much smaller, muted print. If any Bahá'í book might possibly pass Mother's inspection, it was this one with its French references. Hopefully Mother would think her younger daughter was exploring their "civilized" European roots. Maybe she would assume it had something to do with Abby's schoolwork.

No, Abby was rather sure Mother would eventually find out and punish her for this transgression, but some things were worth it.

"Yes, I think that'll be just perfect," she told Melissa, accepting the big book with a shaky smile. "The best book possible. Thank you so, so, *so* much, Melissa. And please thank your mother, too."

Melissa gave the bag with the remaining books back to Jon, hugged Abby carefully again, exclaimed, "Happy reading!" and waved a cheery farewell as she and Jon left.

Abby hid the books and papers, unsure of even Jenn's reaction. When she could, though, she began reading *Paris Talks.* Eager as she was to immerse herself in the light of 'Abdu'l-Bahá's words, she found she could only read a paragraph or two before she had to stop and think … pray … prink … thay … oh heck, contemplate … about it. Otherwise, it was like eating too much of a good thing.**[170]**

Wednesday afternoon, Mother quizzed Abby about nausea, lightheadedness, and memory lapses, then called the doctor's office. A few hours later, he gave the all-clear, so the next morning, Thursday, Aug. 30, 2007, the Wizes packed their car again and left North Carolina for Tennessee. Abby watched out the window to see if anything looked familiar from the future. The route to the interstate took them close to the area where Lodlan would someday be located, but one North Carolina rolling hill looked like the next.

She read some of her *Harry Potter* book during the long drive in between bouts of dealing with pain, bandages and medications. Her fingers traced the dust cover warped by the damp ice water bottle inside her backpack at the stables. She wistfully remembered how, in the future, everyday bottles stayed tepid and dry on the outside but hot or cold on the inside. For now, the book's rippled paper was both a reminder and a promise of the future and its bonega inventions.

Reading, she was again struck by the similarities between Dumbledore and 'Abdu'l-Bahá, and not only in appearance. They both had a great sense of humor, were very wise, could see inside people, and could foretell the future. It was so cool that, as powerful and kindly as Dumbledore was, 'Abdu'l-Bahá was even better. *He* was real!

Harry and Abby had both been on a grand mission in strange lands. They were both unfamiliar with the customs of their new communities. They were both rescued unexpectedly. Just as he was totally unique in his world, so was she in hers. But while Harry's world was a fantasy, her travels were real. They weren't a dream or hallucination. She had heard, felt, tasted, *lived* every aspect of a completely real world. **[171]** Watching the withered late summer forests of the Appalachian Mountains fly past her car window, she prayed she could go back to Erden again some day … without the coma.

Mother cut her some slack, even asking her if she'd be able to eat at the same rest stop as before. Abby agreed, knowing there would be no jello. Lunch was greasy bologna and rubbery cheese sandwiches with potato chips. The white bread compressed like plastic foam as she chewed it. She pictured it plugging her guts.

Abby imagined Erdeans nibbling politely but trying to find other things that were healthier. As she slipped the rest of the sandwich to Jenn, who had nabbed the seat next to her instead of across from her, and tried some baby carrots and celery, Abby realized she had felt clearer and stronger the longer she'd stayed in Erden, maybe partly because of the healthier food. She certainly had come back a different person. Even Jenn noticed it and said Abby looked happier.

Although she couldn't yet tell Jenn why, it was true. She was more confident because she'd been nurtured and supported. She had more ways to get through the hard parts of her life. And she hoped to continue her progress.

Once home, Abby continued her slow recovery. Between naps, she pondered things such as how to contact the Surely Bahá'ís. She wished she'd had Melissa contact them for her. Their number was in the phone book, but what would she say if someone actually answered? Leaving a message on a machine was equally intimidating. If anyone ever called her back, Mother might find out, which would also be bad. Abby couldn't see a way around her problems, so she did nothing.[172]

One day, as Abby lay on the couch absentmindedly leafing through magazines, Melissa's voice floated in her memory: "Is there any Remover of difficulties save God?" Then a mental male voice added that she could "Rely upon God, Thy God and the Lord of thy fathers." Someone in Lodlan had said that.[173] Abby decided to look for those two prayers in her little prayer book, was delighted to find them, and began memorizing them, hoping that she could generate her own spiritual breezes with them, like Dali used to do for her.

School started the day after Labor Day, but Abby was still not well enough to go. With mixed feelings, she listened to Jenn get ready and leave. An hour later, Mother, dressed nicely all in black, came into Abby's bedroom, interrupting Abby's leisurely inventory of her pain.

"I have to go to a funeral," Mother said abruptly. "Funerals are not suitable for children. Will you be all right here alone?"

"Sure," Abby answered automatically, pausing the tentative explorations of the healing scar on her abdomen through the clean bandage Mother had put on the previous night.

"You have my cell phone number. If something happens, call me," Mother commanded over her shoulder as she walked down the hall, "but you'll be leaving a message."

As Mother left the house, Abby wondered what would have happened if she'd said no. Although a funeral seemed like a dreadful thing to go to, what if Abby had said she didn't feel well enough to be left alone? But Mother had already decided to go without Abby, hadn't she? Oh, what could have polluted Mother so badly?

Finally, Abby got up slowly to go to the bathroom, then eat. She shuffled along the hall, hands trailing down the wall to keep her steady. Her fingers bumped on the doorframes: Open bathroom, bump, space, bump. Closed closet, bump, drag, bump. Open basement stairs, bump, space, bump. Open kitchen, bump, space, turn.

The cereal cabinet offered her the usual choices, but today it struck her that it was all sugar and chemicals ... and required dairy, which seemed to plug her nose and throat. She fished behind the boxes and located a dusty Mason jar with old granola bars inside. Eating one, she knew they were still sweeter than they should be. Too late, she read the ingredients she'd never bothered with but that Mother fussed over. There had to be some mistake; she must be missing some secret key: the ingredients seemed to be exactly the overly processed, chemicalized, unnatural ingredients she was hoping to avoid.

With the half-eaten bar in her hand, she confronted the blank shopping list magneted to the fridge. She hoped they'd blame this wild, new weirdness on her coma. Picturing her meals with Dali, she printed:

```
From health food store
whole grain cereal x2
soy milk & rice milk
low-sugar, unprocessed
    grain bars
whole grain organic bread
whole grain crackers
organic vegetable soup - 3
    kinds
organic vegan entrees
organic nut butter
    (cheapest)
organic fruit juice - 2
    kinds
```

She exhaled loudly after taking that plunge. If that worked, it would be new for everybody. She was trying to follow her little voice and the Bahá'í teachings, along with her usual cautious evaluations.

As she sat eating at the round table in the sunroom, she noted the familiar-yet-still-strange surroundings. Piles of Mother's papers, computer, phone ... *wait!*

Computers! Phones! Everyone else was gone; she could phone the Bahá'ís now and ask about their get-togethers! She could look up stuff on the computer! She'd better ask permission first, so Mother didn't have a fit. Better call her now, before the funeral started.

She gulped the last bite, dialed Mother, and blurted, "Hi, Mother, it's Abby, I'm fine, I just wondered if I may get on your computer while you're gone."

The silence stretched unbearably. Abby crossed all her fingers, both wrists, her ankles, even her eyes. "I promise I'll go lie down when I get tired," she added, trying to think of Mother's probable objections.

"I suppose," Mother said resignedly, as if she wanted to veto the request but couldn't think of a good reason why.

"Thank you, Mother," Abby said and hung up quickly, before Mother summoned an objection after all.

She turned on the computer, clicked on the internet icon, and searched for "Surely TN Baha'i Faith."

None of the listings seemed quite right. Back at the top, it read: "Do you mean *Surely TN Bahai Faith*" with no apostrophe. She tried that, and the first listing was the right site.

Another entry showed a master website for the US: www.bahai.us, which Abby recognized from Melissa's note and her earlier search at the Holsworth's. The banner on its main page warmed Abby's heart:

Let your vision be world-embracing, rather than confined to your own self.

Bahá'u'lláh
Tablets of Bahá'u'lláh, page 86

Abby gazed at the comforting quote. The longer she looked at it, the more her brain tingled with familiarity. She could almost hear the words "world-embracing" and "vision" in Dali's voice.

Maybe she was healing or maybe she'd had time to think about it, but she felt less daunted by the enormity of the task of learning and acting on the Bahá'í teachings.

She clicked back to the Surely site and checked the listed phone number against the phonebook. The numbers matched. *Might as well call now.* She sighed nervously, feeling a headache coming on from all the thinking and especially from worrying about getting caught and chewed out by Mother. But she really wanted to grab this chance to call. She needed help ... a visitation of angels, maybe ... or maybe just the virtues they might bestow.

In a beam of morning sun falling onto Mother's desk, she linked thumbs and waved her fingers, making a shadow-puppet of an angel as she and Jenn used to do to reassure themselves that they always had angels with them. The angel fluttered back onto the keyboard, but Abby had the number she needed. Her problem now was that her impatience to make contact warred with her habitual shyness with strangers.

She needed to search for a different kind of answer; one that wasn't on a computer. She closed her eyes and called up Dali's house ... the wooden sound-box playing ... the STEEDS OF FAITH guarding it ... Farrah painting them ... *the steed of the Valley of Search was patience.* Patience was a biggie, Rykeir had said. Yes. She could use some patience for this inward search.

"Oh God, please give me enough patience to ... center myself," she prayed, "and ... confidence." She willed herself to be the right way for this call. Soon she did feel calmer, more focused. She decided on her first question. She picked up the phone, took a deep breath, and dialed. A woman answered.

"Hi, is this the right number for the Bahá'í Faith?" Abby asked.

"Yes, it is," said a female voice with a strong Black Tennessee accent. "My name is Dreamy Jefferson. How may I help you?"

"I found out about the Bahá'í Faith, just, uh, recently and ... I ... really like it. I, mmm, wanted to see if you have any meetings that I .. er, could come to," Abby stammered badly, feeling she was doing horribly.

"Yes, we sure do," Dreamy said, unperturbed. "I can send you our calendar of activities, or read you the schedule now. Which would you like?"

"Um..." Abby thought for a minute. Fortunately, Dreamy waited patiently. "Send it, please?" She gave the woman her name and address. "Are there any meetings close to me? I don't drive yet; I'm only 13."

"Not very close, no," the woman said. "But if it's all right with your parents, we could pick you up."

"Really? That would be great." Abby was relieved, and glad she'd called. She realized she'd been tense, barely breathing.

"Okay. I think LaKeesha White is closest to you; she'd probably be the one picking you up," Dreamy said. "Would you like for me to telephone you before the next event?"

"Um, no, thank you. But could I maybe have her phone number to call her?" Abby asked. "I can't come for the next few weeks. And, after that, it can only be on the weekends."

"So, Sunday School," Dreamy said. "Maybe a service project."

"Service!" said Abby, firing up, remembering.

"You sound excited about service," said Dreamy, amused.

"You have no idea!" Abby grinned.

"Well, good for you. You're ready to take down her number? Okay." Dreamy gave Abby the number and then added, "And her name again is capital-L-A-capital-K-E-E-S-H-A, *lah-KEY-shah* White."

After she hung up, Abby indulged her spirit on the US Bahá'í website, getting reconnected. She had guessed that the Faith now would be very different from Erden, but the important parts all seemed to be there: plenty of writings, lots of activities to read about or join, even an 800 number for more information. It seemed only to need lots of people to adopt and spread the teachings to arrive at peace on earth.

Happy and thankful for the chance to make that call and see the websites, she went back to bed and crashed until afternoon.

Jenn got home from school and told Abby she should be glad she missed the first day. Jenn, though a high-schooler, had heard from several neighbor kids that the hazing of the new middle-schoolers was worse than ever. One group had ambushed some of the starting 7th-graders, painted their noses red with fingernail polish, and made them sing *Rudolph the Red-Nosed Reindeer* all the way to school. If they went to the office, they were told they could call home. Otherwise, they just had to go through the rest of the day hiding, or being teased about, their noses.

Abby could relate. Last year, she had been bullied into taking off her shoes, tying them around her neck, and walking to school in a straight line with her arms out as if she was doing a drunk test. The official policy was that hazing was not tolerated. When it happened off school grounds, though, the school could do nothing about it.

Jenn's report made Abby feel powerless and afraid of the bullies, but soon her stubbornness – or persistence – made her fume about them and the adults who couldn't be bothered to stop them.

If only she could actually do something, she seethed: plant a banner of justice and unity to fight hate and ignorance. Mother would never approve of a public campaign, so anything Abby did would have to be covert; stealthy; on the sly. Maybe something would present itself if she prayed and stayed awake and aware.

Chapter 29 Reentry

Abby couldn't go to school yet because she tired easily and still had headaches, so a tutor brought her schoolwork that often drained what little concentration and energy she had. On good days, she alternated homework with reading *Harry Potter* and *Paris Talks*, in which she had carefully laid her sparkly, beaded bookmark. New daydreams and images joined the usual horse and camp ones: Dali's smile; Lodlan's tree-like House of Worship; Petra's many beaded strands; Mr. Sawqui's enchanting supervising; Melissa's sympathetic eyes; the deepening facilitator's gong; the yuter's jokes and images. As she remembered, she wrote them in her diary, sometimes using symbols and drawings instead of words, in case Mother ever read it.

Sometimes when Mother was out of the house, Abby got on the computer, trying to ask permission first. Parelli videos always buoyed her, watching people play with horses in ways she didn't know were possible.

In one of her favorites, a girl about her age cued a horse through a curtain of empty plastic jugs, on top of a platform, under a pergola, and more – in knee-deep snow, with the tackless horse cavorting as the girl talked and laughed with him. They obviously loved playing together. Abby's dreams began to include her playing like that with Moony and other ranch horses, once her drug- and pain-induced nightmares abated. They substituted for the real thing, since Abby wasn't well enough to go riding on Saturdays.

Jenn helped her save the website addresses of Parelli, Bahá'í, *Harry Potter*, and others in a half-secret folder she had created for a history report but now used for other information, knowing that Mother would never get around to cleaning out old files.

Abby's tentative prayer was answered when she intercepted the Bahá'í calendar in the mail on a day that Vivian was out. She eagerly looked through the calendar, called LaKeesha, and scheduled a ride to and from the first Sunday School she thought she could attend.

She experimented with the three different obligatory prayers, except bowing her forehead to the floor in the long one, which made her head throb. Glad to try them out before she turned 15 and was obligated to say one of them every day, she chose the short one to memorize and try to connect deeply with.

Abby considered herself a Bahá'í. She had found a registration card tucked into *Paris Talks*, signed it, and stored it and all Melissa's gifts among the things in her bottom bureau drawer. When she had written to

Melissa about it, Melissa had replied with a glittery handmade "Joy to You" card filled with supportive love and cheerful news about her senior year in Little Lily High School. She had also shared that before age 15, a believer needed a parent's permission to join the Bahá'í Faith, and it would be a registration. Once she reached 15, however, she could declare her belief independently and enroll without her parents if she wished to. Melissa included some quotes from the Bahá'í Writings on family unity that at first glance conflicted with other quotes that said no one has the right to dictate someone else's form of religious worship. Yet other quotes described the duty of the individual to find and recognize God.[174] Abby surmised that she was to make up her own mind based on all the guidance and her circumstances.

As she weighed her options, she knew without a doubt that Mother would raise Cain, whether now or in 14 months, when Abby turned 15. Still, the Bahá'í website said that even in modern-day Iran, Bahá'ís, including teenagers, were jailed, tortured and killed for their faith. Compared to that, waiting would be a breeze.[175]

Melissa's letter congratulated her on her newfound computer skills and urged her to be wary of Covenant Breakers on the internet, mentioning that safety lay in obedience to the Covenant.

Abby merged her dim memory of catechism classes with her beginning knowledge of the Bahá'í Faith and guessed that, with God's religion really being different chapters of the same unfolding book, He would want people to obey the laws – pledge to follow the Covenant – of the most current chapter they knew. The Covenant Breakers were people who said they were Bahá'ís, but fought and changed the authoritative teachings.

When Abby had first searched the web, some Bahá'í sites did not seem right. They talked about leaders and beliefs that Abby sensed were not correct. She started her next letter back to Melissa, mentioning her pleasure with her growing ability to detect the "divine fragrances" and relating that she almost wrinkled her nose at the funny smell coming from some sites, causing her to quickly click away.

She did know she should avoid Covenant Breakers entirely. They spread spiritual disease and could not catch spiritual health from the faithful.[176] Instead of accepting the authority of 'Abdu'l-Bahá, the Guardian and the Universal House of Justice, which prevents schisms and builds all-important unity, Covenant Breakers defy and oppose its central teachings and leadership.

Alternating between Bahá'í topics and *Harry Potter* eventually spawned the thought that the Death Eaters in *Harry Potter* were a lot like Covenant Breakers. Both were devoted to darkness, fighting, and resisting goodness, or maybe they were unable to tell the difference between good and bad, truth and error.

The Aurors fought the Death Eaters. In real life, appointed, trained Bahá'ís dealt with the Covenant Breakers, thank God. Reading about the Death Eaters and imagining their disease of the soul was as close as she wanted to get to any of that illness.

Contrasting with suspicious odors from dubious websites were the happy, clean scents of the sunflower bouquet sent by her neighbor-friend Grace and the spray of carnations from Tyler, the Currys, and others at The Ride Place that Mother had put next to her computer after the hospital flowers from Grandmother Lois, Daddy, and Granny wilted. Her school friend Maria and also Rev. Davison sent get-well cards, and Kat and the other girls from church sent a postcard wishing her a speedy recovery. Abby propped the cards up against the tallest horses on her windowsill and tried to ignore the fact that the flowers should have been up there, too. She did take time to enjoy them when she used the computer, even smelling them, even in the morning.

Smelling in the morning might have been from her new, healthy diet, or maybe some leftover health from Erden clung to her. She healed enough to start school in mid-September, although she still felt foggy-minded. Bemused that she'd started two schools this year, she prayed that she'd kept up adequately through the home tutor.

On her first day back at Becknay Middle, bolstered with a breakfast of organic spelt flakes and rice milk against the frequent brain hiccups, Abby picked up her class schedule in the office and stood in line to give the health aide her doctor's note excusing her from gym. Glancing around, fighting a strong déjà vu that overlaid a vision of the last health room she'd been in, she noticed a pretty poster that, had she doubted the validity of Divine Guidance, would have unnerved her. Instead it felt like Dali as well as Khalil Gibran's drawing of 'Abdu'l-Bahá – with its electrifying jolt of spiritual energy – were reaching out to her and nourishing her at the beginning of a day she was trying not to dread.

> A friend who is far away is sometimes much nearer than one who is at hand. Is not the mountain far more awe-inspiring and more clearly visible to one passing through the valley than to those who inhabit the mountain? – Khalil Gibran

She wanted to snare this thought and the spirit it gave her but had only moments to grab it. She could only start to pen "AWAY" on her arm before having to speak to the health aide and hustle to homeroom with a Mrs. Kilgore. Finding the safest seat at a worn desk in the dreary classroom, she felt the old rut reach up and try to engulf her, despite her urgent wish to stay connected to Erden and all it had shown her. She focused on inking the rest of her homemade tattoo, trying to ignore the stark, abused surroundings and the students who had already segregated themselves into the jocks and cheerleaders, the nerds, the gamers, and the Goths, viewing each other with open hostility.

The wall speaker crackled and spit during morning announcements. Just when it worked properly, Mrs. Kilgore shifted in her squeaky, falling-apart chair and drowned it out. Sliding down in her seat, hiding behind her hair, she rejected this typical moment representing everything she disliked about school. She resented having to be here and knew it was wrong, even more strongly since now, as explained by Gibran, she was the outsider observing it from a distance.

The algebra class right after homeroom was the latest Gunsmoke in Abby's stable of school difficulties, math not being her strong suit anyway. Mrs. Kilgore asked her to fill out a form noting damage to the math textbook she'd struggled with at home.

Abby looked through her book. How was she supposed to document all of the rips, doodles, rude comments, and "o" centers filled in? Fingering the letters on her arm, she wondered about Erdean books. She'd never opened one, not even in the Saĝo Supera library, but she'd bet that no one there would deface anything. Waiting for Mrs. Kilgore to finish handing out graded homework, Abby fantasized that she opened an Erdean book. Would it give her a 3D presentation? Simulated field trips? Mrs. Kilgore's chiding brought her back to Earth.

The stout, pink-skinned, gray-haired teacher lectured the students who had not done their homework. One student replied that he didn't have any paper at home. Mrs. Kilgore had no answer for that. Fleeing mentally and spiritually, Abby cast about for a suitable escape and concocted a game she would play many times: Name The Missing Erdean Solution.

She doodled a mixture of words, stick figures, and emotion-symbols as she tried to raise her volatile feelings into the realm of words. First, the underpinnings were wrong: teachers and students clashed instead of consulting. Parents clashed with both. Second, teachers and students lacked the supplies and other support they needed. Erden had solved these basic problems. Third, there was not enough agreement – unity – on the content, purpose or structure of school, resulting in a largely chaotic learning environment aimed at passing tests. Even the experts disagreed and proposed their pet theories on Daddy's radio programs. This was the hardest element because it was so vague, and yet, Abby realized, it was the most important element that Earther schools were missing.

Eventually Mrs. Kilgore wrestled the class through graphs containing X, Y and sometimes Z coordinates, negatives and positives, noting which ones were likely to be on which test. Abby did her best to keep up in spite of her often-fuzzy thinking, catching herself stealing glances at the wall next to the clock, where the yuter should be showing the cool uses of this exercise. She could only think of graphing quantities of things, and the counted cross-stitch graphs. She willed herself to imagine a bonega video showing a third application, but it failed to materialize. She wondered in which century school planners would show students the relevance of lessons.

Some students applied themselves to graphing, but a few blew it off in skillfully distracting ways. Finally, the bell shrilled. Abby half-copied one of the Asperger's kids. He cringed, whined, and covered his ears; she buried one ear in her arm under the guise of gathering her backpack. Hoisting it, she was plunged into a semi-vu of her vivid, vital dream about the noisy cement classroom and the students shuffling to better seating. *That dream ... of the boys-turned-men ... their supernatural skills and spirit ... the new way of doing things ...* that feeling jolted through her, reanimating her desire to become like them. 'Abdu'l-Bahá seemed to whisper to her on the way to art class, telling her to keep at it, no matter what obstacles rose up and delayed her.

Mr. Perez, her art teacher from last year, welcomed her in his usual loud voice. He pointed out her seat and bin and handed her a basic supply list. There'd been no art during home tutoring and she'd missed the creative outlet, but she dreaded coming in on the middle of an art project, especially if it meant asking Mother to buy something quickly. Fortunately she had the basic supplies already, and they were just starting a project for which the materials had been donated.

Over the summer, Mr. Perez had learned how to help the students find outdoor scenes in old magazines, create a pattern from the photo, color the pattern shapes, and select fabric matching the pattern. Students would cut out and assemble the cloth pieces to form the picture, then iron them in place with fusible web.

While the other students excitedly found appealing magazine landscapes, scaled them up and chose colors, Abby didn't find a picture she liked well enough to work on. She hung back after class to speak to Mr. Perez alone.

"You didn't find a picture?" he accused. Abby couldn't blame him. He never knew who was trying to get away with something.

"I didn't see anything I liked enough, Mr. Perez," Abby said politely, fighting her habit of keeping her head down and avoiding confrontation. Part of her escaped to Erden for guidance and she imitated Dali, trying to show by her attitude, words and – channeling Petra's insightful question – body language, that she was willing to comply but uninspired. Unskilled as she was, it seemed to work.

He regarded her for a minute, his mental wheels turning. Though he looked nothing like Dali, his silent, thoughtful pause was very Dali-like. As the moment stretched, Melissa's insights about coaxing or discouraging dialogue whispered in her mind, leading to the Native American quote about unhurried speech. The three ideas reinforced each other and solidified her *ma'rifat* with this new, tranquil, strong mode – a mode that felt like the model she had just vowed to keep reaching for. She tingled with the spiritual convergence and the speed with which the heavenly assistance arrived.

"Can you use a photo from home? Someplace you've been that you liked a lot? Or a drawing that can be turned into a fabric landscape?" Mr. Perez finally asked, lowering his armor a bit, sounding weary.

She allowed herself to smile and nod warmly.

"Yes, I'm thinking of a place. May I bring in something next class, sir?" Abby asked, using a tone and words so new she wondered if her divine guidance had taken over her tongue.

"Yes, but be sure you bring it," he warned, armor back up, spinning away from her. "I'll have all the fabric out for the classes to pick from."

"I will. Thank you so much," Abby replied, trying to stay spiritually centered in the face of his brusqueness and rushing off before the bell.

Entering her American History class, she passed the teacher writing on the board, "1776: The Declaration of Independence," and today's textbook pages. Before opening *Paris Talks* for her Silent Reading, Abby quickly scanned today's assigned pages to see if she was behind. One sentence leapt off the page at her, about the "unalienable Rights" of "Life, Liberty, and the pursuit of Happiness."

Less concerned now about where she sat and what other students did than with seeing what new, Godly insights would appear to her, she took her time, woolgathering behind her curtain of hair. An unformed thought nibbled at the edges of her mind again and she reviewed the page slowly, searching for hints of how to invite the thought in.

America's Founding Fathers felt that the English king extorted and also excluded them. They knew some of them would die in war in order for the rest to live in peace, but they wanted to stop unfair meddling from England. Abby tried to climb inside the minds and attitudes of the Founding Fathers and stifled a whistle of recognition when she realized she was looking back at the birth of America just as Dali had tried to imagine her world of 2007, close to the birth of the Bahá'í Revelation.

The words about Native Americans helping the colonists caught her eye. Of their own accord, passages from her little *Native American Wisdom* infused the descriptions of the Original Inhabitants helping the colonists. Delegates from the Iroquois Nation showed the colonists how best to organize and fight the king, likely mentioning their underlying noble reasoning and worthy principles. These spiritual peoples hadn't changed their beliefs much over the long centuries, maintaining their spirituality despite all obstacles, including genocide. They and their teachings deserved respect, and she felt her spirit honoring them.[177]

Her eyes bounced between the word on her arm and the history book, again drifting "away" on her own tangent, looking for insight.

The nibbling thought landed, imprinted with Dali's scent. The lofty old-style wording and references to God made the Declaration look noble-minded, yet the content focused on material and physical concerns, even at the expense of other living beings. She reasoned that it was the best they could do at the time.

Life; okay, yes, not killing or squashing each other was a great start. But the Declaration actually only included white, male landowners, who killed slaves and Natives and squashed women, so this crucial document wasn't entirely truthful even on this basic point. Prejudice, injustice and racism had bathed American society at its birth.

Liberty had been so successful that it now seemed to mean doing whatever you wanted. Abby bet that she'd find a very different view in the Bahá'í Writings.

Pursuit of happiness made her smile, because yuter quotes and Erden had amended her bitter, disenfranchised, Earther view of happiness. Abby began working on the idea, nudged by the yuter's description of Petra's beads, that having things to enjoy was fine, but expecting that objects would bring lasting happiness could only lead to disappointment, and an endless hunger for more things. Abby hatched a new Spiritual Happy Thought: she could become positively addicted to enlightenment, unity and spiritual progress instead of things.[178]

Finishing those thoughts, Abby opened *Paris Talks* and found the three unopened sheets from that night in Little Lily. She opened the "On Liberty" handout and, less surprised than she might have been at the instant confirmation, read, "Liberty must, in the end, lead to sedition, whose flames none can quench."[179]

She could almost hear Dali saying that people disliked laws, but the real solution was obedience to laws – namely, divine laws. Abby was just getting happily lost in more insights when the history teacher called for the class's attention.

At lunch, her choices were Mystery Meat, Putrid Potatoes, and Botulism Beans with a final flourish of Chemical Cake, according to the snide commentary of Jeff Wornall, who preceded Abby down the lunch line. It had to have lots of preservatives and fillers in it, Abby supposed, in order not to spoil during its trip from wherever it had started and still be cheap. Her eyes flew wide as she realized her lunch was probably full of the chemicals Dali had said caused so much illness in this world. This stuff might be worse for people than even Jeff knew!

Too late today; she was through the line. But starting tomorrow, she'd have to break out of the mold and bring her own food. She wanted to be mentally sharp and emotionally content – hard enough on Earth, and harder still after her accident. She should use Petra and Dali's wisdom and avoid polluting herself, too.

Kids sat in their cliques, jeering at and gossiping about the other cliques. The trash bins overflowed, full of wasted recycling possibilities. Everywhere, Abby saw opportunities for a better way. She was too busy being dismayed and comparing Earth to Erden to notice that she'd been pulled out of her delicate, cherished spiritual mode.

French class was taught by Ms. Black, who was white. Mother wanted Abby to learn French because Mother's father had been all-French. Mother would occasionally speak short sentences in French, which brought the language to life, but Abby always felt like a failure when she attempted to speak it back, so she rarely tried.

"Repeat after me: *Les courtesans portant les perruques*," Ms. Black said. "The courtiers wear wigs." Abby tried, but the sounds made her twist her mouth oddly. And a lot of letters were silent. She resorted to spelling French words on the invisible mental notebook she'd started to use to hold thoughts for lack of a yuter to hold them for her. What use phrases about the French kings and their ridiculous rules would be if she needed to speak French nowadays, she didn't know.

Hearing another language, though, reminded her of UL. She quickly wrote down "jes = yes" but couldn't remember hearing the word for "no". As she listened to the teacher pronounce *oui* (yes), *bien sur* (of course), and *merci* (thank you), Abby remembered other Erdean words and scribbled a list, hoping no one would see her interest and tease her. Like at her house, if you showed interest in something in school, it would be used against you.

After school she trudged home past brown lawns and early leaf litter, wiped out mentally, emotionally and spiritually and almost as tired physically. Her new safety net – reaching out to Dali and Erden when her own powers ran out – activated and she searched for a similar Erdean moment, choosing biking home with Dali. A bit of the Traveling Prayer sprang to mind and she hummed what she remembered, vowing to find that prayer and practice the melody, which was already fading from memory.

Maybe it was her extreme fatigue, but it looked impossible to fully remember Erden, let alone help build it.

But it was too wonderful to forego. She had to, absolutely *must* try to find a way to remember it ... and do what little she could to bring it about. She might be powerless and puny now, especially right now, but when she was better, and older ... maybe out of the house and away from Mother ... when she had what she needed to mount a campaign ... she *would* light a candle with a spark from Erden and hold it high against the gathering darkness.

Allowing the flame of her vow candle to burn low but not sputter out, she took a long breath, set her jaw, and turned the knob to open the front door. Beyond the kitchen entryway, Mother sat at her desk.

"Hi," Abby called.

"Come here, Abby," Mother commanded without looking up. "Do you have a headache?"

Abby put her books down in the hallway and went for inspection.

"I feel okay," Abby said in her own defense, though she did feel worn thin and did actually have a headache as well as uncomfortable pulling where the abdominal stitches had absorbed.

Mother felt Abby's forehead with the back of her hand and glanced at her face.

"You should rest, just in case," Mother decided.

"Yes, Mother." For once their plans coincided. If Mother left her alone, the house would be still until Jenn came home from high school.

Fetching her drawing tablet and colored pencils, Abby settled down in her reading nook, graced now by the old, cozy, blue blanket from the Holsworths. They'd given it to her when she thanked them for making such a comfortable recovery couch. She traced a slow circle in the soft fabric, unexpectedly remembering another blue blanket that felt but didn't look soft. This circle invited lines, and a peace symbol appeared under her fingers. The blue suggested water, leading to an image. Soon she'd sketched a crude blue-and-green world overlaid with a gold peace symbol. She had to admit, it looked and felt awesome, almost like a Girl Scout patch. Or even a logo. Why shouldn't World Peace and the Golden Age have a logo?

Erdeans probably had one, though she hadn't seen it, because Erden was bursting with art of every kind, being an enotopia.

Maybe she could get Melissa, or Jenn, or even Mother to make this sketch into a chart and then help her stitch it. She leaned against her low bureau, staring unseeing at her plastic horses, envisioning the ways she could use her finished patch, struggling to stay in the zone despite her paralyzing amazement at the ongoing waves of inspiration today. She'd half-thought she'd used up all the divine assistance she was allotted for one day, but here was more![12]

She opened up her drawing tablet and saw the unfinished drawing of Moony, waiting for her to study his unusual coloring and look him up in her breed books. Suddenly, she saw him clearly; had seen him clearly during her return to Earthtime. She was able to pencil in his Appaloosa spots on the white blanket, both peacock and not; his roan flecks, his bay points. Time traveling had taken her through a special realm of penetrating insight.

Suspecting now that since God was limitless, His assistance and inspiration was too, Abby allowed herself to be greedy for more.

Fortunately, more sat waiting. Closing her eyes, she let her mind roam over her art assignment. *Wait, I'm pondering alone in a quiet room. Is this meditating? What's the difference between thinking, meditating, planning and praying?* Was she now meditating about meditating? Grimacing, she shook her head to clear it. She had a job to do. *Can I stay tuned in to the spiritual mode while I plan? Might as well give it a shot,* she decided. *With God, the unlikely is possible.*

She knew she wanted to draw a part of Lodlan and make it into the fabric picture. A landscape should be a horizontal image of nature and the outdoors, Mr. Perez had said. That left out the Draggin' Dragon, much as she would love a wall-hanging of it … but she could still draw it! She could draw *all* of it, inexpertly or not, wallhanging or not!

Relief flooded her. Whatever she couldn't draw, she could write about. But she'd have to use some kind of code no one could read. *What had Dali said about the languages that went into UL? Like ABC … Arabic, Bantu, and Chinese? And … Essence? No, um, Aspirin something? Anyway, did it exist now?* If it did, she could learn to write it, and Mother wouldn't understand it.

It was almost like being inside her own *Consultation Today* show. Ideas and insights flowed almost faster than she could use them, energizing her in spite of feeling more scatterbrained these days.[180]

She scrambled to write down her usable new ideas, then willed herself back to the art project. *So, choosing an outdoor scene from Erden to make a fabric wallhanging of.* Going home after the Draggin' Dragon? The sky that night? The white bird? Dali's little house in front, and Gunsmoke's hill beyond? Could she fit Dali in there somehow, as part of the landscape? Maybe a small figure on a bike. She thought she would try, and see what happened … see what God inspired.

"*Try* is not a four-letter word," she whispered to herself, and began to draw.

Chapter 30 — Sunday

Abby did everything she could to be well enough to attend the Bahá'í Sunday School the last weekend in September. She felt fairly well-prepared spiritually because of her steady reading of Melissa's gifts, but predicted an uphill battle with her family when Jenn discovered her reading materials and chided her. "Jesus Is The Only Way," Jenn had sternly reproved.

Abby let it drop. He was. They were. The Founders of all the world's major religions were the way to God. Each for Their own time, each promising They'd come back. God's unfolding eternal book of faith with chapters that had each guided and inspired millions. This newest chapter appealed to Abby in ways she couldn't yet describe, but the basic message was the same.

On the Bahá'í website, she had read a letter from the Universal House of Justice to the religious leaders of the world, pointing out progress in human endeavors beside religion and urging them and their followers to build bridges instead of walls.[181] She had vowed to try not to fight with her sister and mother about religion, which was supposed to spread brotherhood and peace.

Abby liked the way the Universal House of Justice laid out delicate issues clearly and insightfully, without apologizing, finding a great balance between being honest but gentle. She could see why it was going to guide all the Bahá'ís in the future.

She'd avoided church so far this autumn, passing it off on her trauma, but she still had to get permission to go to the Bahá'í meeting. She gathered her courage, read a few prayers that seemed appropriate, and practiced some wording in her head for over a week before finally taking the plunge a couple of nights before the Sunday in question.

Mother sat knitting on the couch, Daddy was checking that the garage doors were locked, and Jenn puttered before bed.

"Someone is going to pick me up to go to another church this Sunday," Abby said, standing in front of her mother.

Vivian Wize looked at the air all around her daughter's head, as if Abby were surrounded by gnats. "What?" she asked.

"I am going to visit another church this Sunday," Abby repeated, trying to sound confident. "Some people are going to take me."

"What kind of church? Where is it? Who's picking you up?"

"Bahá'í. It's over in Partridge. Her name is ... I'm not sure how to say it." Mother probably wouldn't approve of LaKeesha's name, so Abby decided not to mention it.

Mother looked slapped in the face.

"Our church isn't good enough for you?"

"It's fine, Mother. I just want to try this one; it sounds interesting. Jon's girlfriend Melissa told me about it on vacation."

"And you listen to people like that?"

Abby knew this was a reference to Melissa's mixed racial heritage. Darker-skinned people were "less-than" in Mother's book. Abby fought that view, not only because she was now a Bahá'í, but because it was just so *mean*, which she was sensitized to from years of Mother-war.

"Please, Mother, I just want to go see how it is. Melissa had good manners and was perfectly nice."

"That's not the point. Our church is all you need. I don't know why you think you need to throw it out the window. Who knows what these … *people* … could get you into?"

"They teach all the things that our church teaches, plus more good manners," Abby said. "Honest! No drinking, no drugs, no funny stuff at all. The same kinds of things like the Ten Commandments and the Golden Rule and the Blessed Are's."

"The *Beatitudes*, Abby. And you may think you're being so clever about this, but I assure you that it will come to no good end," Mother pronounced, waving her knitting needles at Abby.

"I'll do my best to see that it doesn't, Mother," Abby said, suddenly feeling like backing away and looking down to sever the discussion. *This Divine Guidance thing is really handy*, she thought, quietly closing the door to her room.

Getting ready for bed, Abby reviewed the interchange. Normally she would have stood, sagging, full of dread, in front of Mother until Mother thought to forbid her, yell at her or hit her. Cutting it off early had short-circuited that dynamic. She'd lucked into the right approach … or maybe it wasn't luck but Melissa's useful explanation, Abby's own continuing practice, and the power of prayer.

When the others left for church on the last Sunday in September, Abby sensed the end of one era and the beginning of another. Breaking with family tradition like this felt weird, but when she thought about it, she knew she wouldn't find what she wanted in that church.

After watching them drive away from her bedroom window, Abby dressed carefully, trying for an attractive but casual look. She doubted the local Bahá'ís would expect high fashion, especially because hot, humid summer weather had returned for one last gasp. Of course, in Erden, a French courtesan gown, wig and elbow-length gloves would have kept her cooler than the polo shirt and peach skort she chose, but they would be made of that special cooling fabric that didn't exist yet.

She waited in the living room, adjusting the headband to cover the shaved spot on her head, browsing this month's selection of magazines. Near the appointed time, she heard a car pull up in front of the house; it was the green two-door she expected. She pushed the locking button on the doorknob, pulled it shut (*too bad I can't just command it to shut and lock*), and walked down to the car.

"Hi!" Abby said to the dark-skinned driver with lots of long, thin braids, some of them tinted magenta.

"Hello," the lady said in a strong southern accent.

Abby got in the front passenger seat.

"I'm LaKeesha White," the lady said. "This is Justice, my son, and Hope, my girl."

"Hi, I'm Abby," Abby said, turning to wave to the two kids, about seven and four, in the back seat. They were darker than their mother, very cute and bright-eyed. Both raised a hand in subdued greeting.

Abby buckled her seat belt and off they drove, the windows down, her hair whipping around her head in the wind.

"Sorry, the A/C is broken," LaKeesha apologized. "So we're using 240 instead." She threw Abby a quirky smile.

"Two-forty?"

"Two windows down, 40 miles an hour."

Abby couldn't help but laugh. A good joke, and funnier because it was true, though she wished her hair would stop trying to lie across her eyeballs.

"How did you hear of the Faith? If you don't mind me asking, that is," LaKeesha asked warmly.

"Oh no, I don't mind. From a friend of my cousin's in North Carolina," Abby said.

"That's nice; when was that?" LaKeesha's polite questions lasted the short trip to the modest home in the newer Partridge Glen housing subdivision. Abby just had to be careful not to let on how much she knew; she stuck to small things that she had learned from Melissa or Jon, or read in her books and on the internet.

They joined a few other cars in front of the modest white wood-framed house with young, parched trees in the dead grass. In Tim and Suzie's small living room, a dozen people fetched chairs from the kitchen or wedged themselves into the remaining spots. Tim and Suzie's adopted daughter, Florencia, greeted Justice, Hope and two other children who arrived shortly after.

Standing near the door, waiting for people to get settled, Abby spotted a row of familiar books in the tall bookcase in front of her, and, delightfully, a photo of 'Abdu'l-Bahá above the *Harry Potter* books.

She'd seen that picture in her only other deepening. Remembering that gathering brought a rush of yearning to be there again. She inhaled sharply with the longing but squashed the urge to indulge in reveries about Erden, especially because LaKeesha was whispering to her.

"It looks like the best spot for you is on the arm of the couch," she murmured. The Middle-Eastern-looking lady seated there leaned away obligingly as Abby wedged herself backward onto the couch arm as gracefully as she could.

"Everyone settled?" said a tan lady with sun-streaked hair. "Great! Let's get started. LaKeesha, will you introduce your guest?"

"Sure, Suzie. This is Abby. She phoned Dreamy a month ago."

A chorus of hi's and glad-you-came's greeted Abby. Suzie introduced everyone too quickly for Abby to remember, but she tried to acknowledge each person with a wave, nod, or smile, trying to up her social game.

"Let's sing a few songs we know, then we'll do the one we're learning, and then I'll take requests," said Suzie. "How about 'Look at Me' first."

With no hymnal and no songs posted, Abby mostly listened and sang along with the chorus, remembering Jon, and later, Dali, saying people should …

♫Look at me, follow me, be as I am.
'Abdu'l-Bahá, 'Abdu'l-Bahá.♫[182]

Next was "Magic Penny," about a penny of love – or happiness, or courtesy – that came back to you if you spent it.[183]

Suzie asked the children to lead a short prayer that started: "O God! guide me, protect me …."[184] Listening hard, trying to imagine the words on her pretend notepad, Abby stared vacantly toward the bookshelf. Fortunately no one heard her mix up a *Harry Potter* spell with the prayer, but "O God, Point Me" just might work anyway, she thought, grinning at her feet behind her curtain of hair.

Then came the children's prayer they were learning. Suzie asked little Justice to lead the song by pointing to the relevant parts of a large taped-together mural drawn in sections by the children. Abby thought it was a clever, low-tech visual aid to help learn the song …

♫O God! Educate these children. These children are the plants of Thine orchard, the flowers of Thy meadow, the roses of Thy garden. Let Thy rain fall upon them; let the Sun of Reality shine upon them with Thy love. Let Thy breeze refresh them in order that they may be trained, grow and develop, and appear in the utmost beauty. Thou art the Giver. Thou art the

Compassionate. ♫[185]

Everyone clapped when the song was over. The children clamored for "Shine Your Light on Me, Bahá'u'lláh" and were given small flashlights to shine on themselves and each other. With Suzie's proficient playing, the boisterous singing, and the children's animated flashlight waving, the group did shine.[186]

"Great job, everyone!" Suzie proclaimed after enthusiastic applause. "Okay, let's start our classes."

LaKeesha and the five children headed to the backyard with its shaded patio. Abby was the only teen and decided to stay with the adults in the living room rather than go with the little kids.

"Well, we're about midway through Ruhi Book Two," said Tim, facilitator of the study circle.[187] "You can use this today," he said to Abby, handing Abby a booklet she'd seen on the Bahá'í websites.

"What does *RUE-hee* mean, please?" she asked him quietly.

Tim, Suzie and the two others looked at the woman next to Abby.

"Peyvand, this is more your area," Tim invited.

"It's Arabic vord for *soul,* and ... mmm ... could also call your sweetheart or loving one," Peyvand said in halting English.

"And it's the name of the study classes," Suzie added, pointing to the front of the workbook. Abby's heart leapt when she saw that this workbook was about service, but as the small group worked through the Bahá'í quotations and discussion questions, trying to absorb the material about "home visits," she gradually realized that this version involved serving the Faith – and the world – by discussing the Bahá'í Faith with others.

As the session dragged on, the house got hotter, Peyvand struggled with her English more, and Robert, an Anglo man in his 30's, interjected his personal opinions and long, off-topic stories. Vihntien, the multiracial mother of two very energetic children, kept leaving to check on shrieks and shouting coming from LaKeesha's class. Every time she came back, she had to catch up. Abby peered at the name on Vihntien's workbook to get any idea how to pronounce her name, mentally whispering *vin-TYEN*, not daring to say it for fear of butchering it and causing offense.

Maybe they were different kinds of activities, but there really was no comparison between the spiritual classes in Lodlan and Surely. It was disappointing. During another rambling commentary from Robert, Abby closed her eyes and checked out mentally. She felt like she was pawing through the rubble of Melissa's do-it-yourself kit and followed that fantasy in detail. She hoped the small smile it brought would look like she was praying or enjoying the thoughts being discussed.

Aside from the adult talk, the Ruhi book itself was okay, though it could use a good batch of animated yuter presentations to really bring it to life, Abby thought, reversing her opinion of the rambling, glad it lasted long enough to kindle a few ideas about likely yuter videos.

The children returned with their new drawings: a plug and socket, a hand reaching for the hem of a long coat, a face with its nose lifted to smell wavy lines, two hands grasping a rope, and an open book floating in the clouds. LaKeesha reported that the class had discussed how to stay connected to God.[188] Then, prompted and shy, each child explained their art: drawing on God's power; holding the hem of His garment,[189] smelling the divine fragrances, clinging to the cord of His grace,[190] and seeing writings in one's mind.

LaKeesha thanked Kamál, Vihntien's younger son, for practicing the virtue of flexibility. He had started to draw a picture of Bahá'u'lláh seeing the Writings in His mind's eye after LaKeesha read passages in which Bahá'u'lláh and 'Abdu'l-Bahá described this ability,[191] but was willing to redo his art when she explained that the Writings ask Bahá'ís not to portray any Messengers in art forms because it isn't possible to do Them justice.

Abby crossed her fingers under her workbook, hoping they'd spend more time discussing plugging into God, and divine fragrances, but the children quickly became restless and Suzie asked Robert to bring trays of snacks from the little kitchen. Once they were grouped around the iced sugar cookies and bright red fruit punch, Tim was able to make his way across the crowded living room and offer the adults some sweet iced tea.

Abby was too intimidated in this room of strangers to ask that they discuss the pictures more, though she could nearly smell their latent magic. She did nod and keep eye contact with anyone who tried to bring them up, however, and was rewarded with hearing a couple of tips about how one or another believer memorized and used their favorite Bahá'í phrases as guidance. Although the passages they quoted were more sophisticated than her usual mottos, she thought that eventually she might find some Bahá'í Sacred Writings that she could grow *ma'rifat* with to add to her collection of sayings.

But the sweaty, grumpy children soon drowned out the meager conversation, first arguing over the drinks and snacks, then squabbling about who had touched or looked at whom. They seemed to be handing out pennies of discontent and irritability. Abby figured the sugar and chemicals had hit their bloodstreams, and stopped trying to get anything more out of the deepening, retreating behind her comforting, safe curtain of hair, tracing the faded "AWAY" on her left arm and drawing a new, invisible *"ma'rifat"* on her right: a poor wirl's tattoo.

When Cayha, Kamál's older brother, started crying, Abby sent up a stifled prayer to 'Abdu'l-Bahá. But at the moment, 'Abdu'l-Bahá seemed too remote to answer, though his picture smiled down on them.

Abby wanted to be here, wanted to feel some of Erden from them. She looked around at the wilted, disorganized, not-yet-unified group of Bahá'ís in the stifling living room, searching for a way to feel connected to them, sending her own timid, thread-like prayer, knowing it was inadequate. Nothing she knew helped. She was too hot, too woozy, too new to figure it out, so she gave up. In the next heartbeat, Abby felt Dali's sympathy washing over her and everyone in the room. Dali's perspective became Abby's: here were struggling souls, spiritual heroes shouldering the goal of World Peace against immense difficulties and with scant personal reward. In Dali's eyes, these beleaguered Bahá'ís were exquisitely precious, the valiant groundbreakers in an essential band of early builders.

Bathed in Dali's love, they grew illumined, radiant; Abby could almost see their glow. Her own lightning-altered soul blazed anew, enlivened by Erden's faraway solace.

Finally, Suzie suggested they all step outside to the shaded patio. Abby leaned against the white wooden siding while the half-dozen adults found spots to sit or stand, and fanned themselves.

The children got along for a moment, happy to draw on the cement patio with sidewalk chalk LaKeesha had brought and that Robert handed out. Peyvand nodded and smiled warmly, abandoning efforts to speak but exuding her nurturing approval. Tim relaxed, his job of preparing the house and leading the study circle done. Suzie apologized for the air conditioning breaking and chatted about the heat, school starting, and other easy, short topics. Vihntien admired the chalk drawings each child made. Warmed by the unity even more than the weather, Abby felt a rudimentary bridge starting to build between her and each of her fellow believers.

It was just enough like Erden that she felt truly at peace. But then Kamál and Cayha lost the plot and Vihntien rushed them off to her car, which caused LaKeesha to bustle her kids off so quickly that Abby had to shout her thanks to Tim and Suzie while running after her ride. The sun had baked LaKeesha's car and the kids whined and sweated in their insulating carseats, pushing LaKeesha into a silent funk and taking Abby with her.

Facing the hot wind coming in the open window, fighting a headache, Abby grabbed her hair to secure it, willing herself not to give in to the deadening pull of physical and emotional discomfort. She held the writhing hair in the back and twisted it as Jenn had last twisted and held it, lovingly, protectively. That sisterly care and the Happy Thought it bestowed provided Abby with a toehold out of her pit of disappointment.

The wind continued to whip her hair and she automatically began working it into two pigtails but, thwarted, could only twist two hanks, one in each hand. They felt like stiff, old, lead ropes, and generated a fantasy of holding an Almacorn's reins, sitting on its back while it carried her off a broad ledge away from sad and bad. In the next moment, she flew over Surely on her Almacorn, looking down at the special, genuine moments of her morning, like little tableaux beneath the Almacorn's pearly wings and shiny black hooves: the evocative picture of the Master; the funny blended prayer; the flashlight song energy; the two buoying thoughts from friends; the tidbits about remaining plugged in to God; Dali's love gilding the beleaguered souls; and, best of all, the Golden Moment on the patio.

It was a good tally for the first Bahá'í meeting in her hometime, but she was greedy for more. The spark of her spirit yearned to burn brightly. If only those good bits could be expanded … built upon … grown bigger … many moments put together could make a longer Golden Time, and, once solidified, those Golden Spans would lead to a lasting Golden Age.

The world had been given the vision and the guidance to enact it, only lacking people to carry it out. Even outnumbered and unpopular, believers and their friends were needed to learn the plan and start working on it. However unorganized and inexperienced they might be, all willing hands could start now to build the divine design, brick by teetering brick. As tough and slow as that task looked today, Abby knew she had to try. Dali and Erden were counting on it.

Author's Notes

While many of the events and characters portrayed in this novel are based on parts of actual events I experienced or people I met, all of the characters, events, and places are fictional as portrayed.

Equally important, the fictional elements regarding the Bahá'í Faith and future are based strictly on my own personal understanding; they are not authoritative. I invite and encourage you to investigate the Bahá'í Writings for yourself and build your own understanding from them.

I took certain controversial scientific stances for narrative purposes.

I grew up and was "confirmed" in the Episcopalian Church. I heard many sermons, like the one Abby heard, on many different topics. The emphasis on a strict observance of ritual and the seeming dearth of genuine warmth, I have to say, left my spirit out in the cold. This led me to begin exploring other faiths in my early teens.

Melissa is based on the person who impressed me with the Bahá'í Faith in the autumn of 1976.

The coffee shop in Little Lily, NC is based on a real one in Flagstaff, AZ. Called *Macy's European Coffee House & Bakery* and located at 14 S. Beaver St., it is owned by Bahá'í Tim Macy. Macy's is fancier, though, than the coffee shop I described.

My own mother, recently deceased, provided much more nutritious food than Vivian did; for that and several other things I am grateful. I have never been in a coma, and for that I am profoundly grateful.

Abby's session with Moony (a real horse) represents how my early ranch days went and, most importantly, nearly everything one should *not* do with horses. That's an urgent warning, folks! It was my arm that got broken (at age 41) falling off a horse in Rescue Race, and I who eventually found Parelli, went on to pass most of Level 4, and taught natural horsemanship based on my studies.

I dreamt many of the dreams that Abby dreams.

I'm the quilt artist that the middle school art teacher was inspired by. And my eldest son had Abby's experience in art class. It resulted in a small wall-hanging of the Shrine of the Báb, because the Bahá'í World Center in Israel was the most memorable place he'd ever been.

In giving the pronunciation of Persian and Arabic words, I used typically American pronunciation.[192]

I drew a great deal of inspiration from J.K. Rowling's *Harry Potter* series as well as her comments about the writing process. Like her, I kept notes and planned for about seven years before starting to write the first edition. Many of my thoughts were jotted down on household scratch paper and filed in a simple cardboard box. In mid-August of 2007, characters, scenes, and plots suddenly coalesced into a story.

Writing my first novels, in their original and revised versions,, has been an incredibly exciting and spiritual experience for me. Many times I sat down at the computer in great anticipation, eager to see what Abby would do. At other times I prayed, asking God for guidance on what should happen, and was quite astonished at the results.

Gathering feedback from readers and refining my own concepts led to this Revised Edition, nine years after the first.

I'd love for you to discuss the ideas in this book with me and with others. I've made an "Activity and Discussion Guide" for this book in hopes you'll form discussion groups and continue Abby's musings and explorations. Join discussions on the "Abby Wize Media" and "Abby Wize Fans" Facebook pages. Follow my happenings on the "Abby Wize" FB personal page. Email me at grow@wize.media . My website is www.wize.media ; register for my email list there, and encourage others to. My YouTube channel is "AbbyWizeMedia." **Please post reviews on Abby's Amazon and Goodreads pages and encourage other readers to.**

Share Abby! Give a copy to your local libraries (public, private, and religious). And keep an eye out for *Abby Wize – BE.*

Lisa Bradley Godward
August 2021

Endnotes

Chapter 1 Moony

[1]   Abby's whole session with Moony is a fairly true account of the author's childhood riding lessons, as well as a good representation of many things *not* to do with a horse.

[2]   The author has witnessed a horse breaking its neck fighting while being tied, and heard the shot that released it from its pain.

Chapter 4 Church

[3]   This quilt appeared in the Autumn 2007 *Keepsake Quilting* catalog, page 46, kit item #5612 for $69.99.

[4]   Abby is looking at the September 2007 issue of *National Geographic*, especially the article on the "Struggle for the Soul of Pakistan." on page 32.

[5]   Matthew 17:20 reads: And He [Jesus] said to them, "Because of the littleness of your faith; for truly I say to you, if you have faith as a mustard seed, you shall say to this mountain, 'Move from here to there,' and it shall move, and nothing shall be impossible to you."

[6]   Rev. Davison's sermon is based on actual text found at **www.FaithPresbyterian.org/sermons/robertson** from June 05, 2005 "The Second Coming of Jesus" sermon. This fairly conservative view is quite similar to sermons the author heard while growing up. Some denominations of Christianity view the end-of-days prophesies as absolutely literal.

[7]   This benediction – from the scriptures of Judaism (Bamidbar 6:24–26 in the Torah) and Christianity (Numbers 6:24–26 in the Old Testament) – was regularly given in the author's childhood church.

Chapter 7 Sofia

[8]   *The American Heritage Dictionary* describes a "trundle bed" as a low bed on casters that can be rolled under another bed for storage.

[9]   *Horses For Dummies* offers information on choosing a horse, caring for it, and buying equipment, as well as a guide to horse breeds.

[10]   The author sews these sustainable, washable, reusable sanitary pads. The designs are superior. Women and girls find them more comfortable, much more economical, and ecologically sound. Many femmes use them together with silicone menstrual cups. Find both at **www.DaysForGirls.org** .

Chapter 9 Horseplay

[11]   Natural Horsemanship is real. Look in the **Resources** section for online information.

Chapter 10 Bookstore

[12]   These two counted cross-stitch patterns and instructions by Lisa Bradley are available for your use at the end of this book. For more information about counted cross-stitch, try your local needlework store or the internet. Once you have supplies and know how, you can stitch any of the free designs readily available on the internet.

[13]   Abby is reading pages 80–81 of *Native American Wisdom*.

[14]   Abby is leafing through the September 2007 issue of *Horse Illustrated*.

[15]   Abby has come across an ad on page 98 in the September 2007 issue of *Cowboys & Indians*.

Chapter 11 News

[16]   Abby is reading pages 58–59 of *Native American Wisdom*.

Chapter 12 Flying

[17]   Horses do hug like this, and it's a great compliment when they do so with a human.

[18]   You can learn about stirrups, saddle jockeys, and the like in the online Western Saddle Guide (see **Resources**); just click on **Saddle Parts** under **THE WESTERN SADDLE**.

Chapter 13 Friend

[19]   Abby is thinking about figurines, not the big statues you see, for example, in parks. She has seen a number of TRAIL OF PAINTED PONIES figurines (see **Resources**), including realistic horses, fanciful horses, Native American horses, a pegasus, and an equine unicorn.

[20]   What Dali almost says is "What I think you are able to bear now." She is thinking about the quote on page 176 of *Gleanings from the Writings of Bahá'u'lláh*: "Not everything that a man knoweth can be disclosed, nor can everything that he can disclose be regarded as timely, nor can every timely utterance be considered as suited to the capacity of those who hear it."

[21]   In the Bahá'í calendar, Friday is called Istiqlál (*iss-tick-LAWL*), an Arabic word for "independence". The month of Kamál (*kah-MAWL*) – meaning "perfection" – begins on August 1. "BE" stands for Bahá'í Era. Year One in the Bahá'í calendar started in the Gregorian year 1844 but began switching some dates to the Badí' (wondrous or unique) calendar specified originally by the Báb in 2015. Visit **en.wikipedia.org/wiki/baha%27i_calendar** to learn more about the Bahá'í calendar.

[22]   In the Bahá'í calendar, Saturday is called *Jalál* (*jah-LAWL*), an Arabic word meaning "glory" or "splendor". The author has chosen the

dates for Abby's future based on two predictions available in the Bahá'í
Writings and one speculative idea: 1) The unfoldment of the Bahá'í
Revelation began with the Heroic Age, is now in the Formative Age, and
will proceed into the Golden Age, when the Most Great Peace will be
established. See especially selections 5 and 6 of the short compilation at
https://www.bahai.org/library/authoritative-
texts/compilations/significance-formative-age-our-faith/significance-
formative-age-our-faith.pdf?e255323a ; 2) the next Manifestation of
God will come 1000 years or later after Bahá'u'lláh's mission started in
October, 1852, therefore translating to sometime after 2852 AD. See
https://www.bahai.org/library/authoritative-texts/bahaullah/kitab-i-
aqdas/13#310032210 ; 3) while we cannot know when that will occur or
when the Golden Age will begin, the author has chosen to place this
novel at a time during the Golden Age 100 or 200 years before the
expiration of the 1000 years.

[23]   Page 51 of *Stories of Bahá'u'lláh* recounts how Bahá'u'lláh so
loved a smiling face, saying, "There are four qualities which I love to
see manifested in people: first, enthusiasm and courage; second, a face
wreathed in smiles and radiant countenance; third, that they see all things
with their own eyes and not through the eyes of others; fourth, the ability
to carry a task, once begun, through to its end." Dali and others work on
their smiles because it makes life so much better for everyone.

[24]   Dali is waiting to see if Abby is going to mention the noontime
prayer. When she doesn't, Dali figures Abby is not Bahá'í. This helps
Dali with many upcoming decisions.

[25]   Dali has only read about anorexia and bulimia, doesn't really
understand how or why they manifested, thinks they're more common
than they are in 2007, and isn't sure if Abby might have an aversion to
food, especially eating in front of someone else.

[26]   Abby is quoting from the Lord's Prayer in the New Testament.

[27]   The sentence that Dali is quoting from reads: "Give us our daily
bread, and grant Thine increase in the necessities of life, that we may be
dependent on none other but Thee, may commune wholly with Thee,
may walk in Thy ways and declare Thy mysteries." The complete
prayer by 'Abdu'l-Bahá is on pages 22–23 of the U.S. compilation of
prayers from Scripture entitled *Bahá'í Prayers*. You can read it at
https://www.bahai.org/library/authoritative-texts/prayers/bahai-
prayers/3#318634086 .

[28]   This incident is described in detail in the online article "The
Tylenol Terrorist: Death in a Bottle" by Rachel Bell. You can find a
copy at **www.FreeRepublic.com/focus/f-news/1618751/posts** .

[29]   The noon prayer is said between solar noon and sunset. This

means that in the world of 2007, Bahá'ís actually say the noon prayer after one o'clock during daylight savings time. However, the author has decided that daylight savings time is no longer practiced in 2707, in part because of articles such as the one about increased heart attacks at **www.stmarys.org/120249.cfm** and the one about increased electricity use at **www.nytimes.com/2008/11/20/opinion/20kotchen.html** .

Chapter 14 Town

[30]   You don't have to wait centuries to get a household porta-potty like this one; they already exist. Google "Composting Toilets."

[31]   Vegetarians may actually have more-attractive body odor. Read about a study of meat- and nonmeat-eaters at **chemse.oxfordjournals.org/cgi/content/abstract/31/8/747** .

[32]   Every Bahá'í House of Worship is to be a hub around which various auxiliary services – often called Dependencies – will be housed. For more information, please see "The Institution of the Mashriqu'l-Adkár," compiled by the Research Department of the Universal House of Justice: **https://www.bahai.org/library/authoritative-texts/compilations/institution-mashriqul-adhkar/institution-mashriqul-adhkar.pdf?771961d0** .

[33]   Dali is quoting from a verse on page 41 of *The Hidden Words of Bahá'u'lláh*, specifically Persian #54: "O Ye Rich Ones On Earth! The poor in your midst are My trust; guard ye My trust, and be not intent only on your own ease."

Chapter 15 Library

[34]   The whole song is "Say: God sufficeth all things above all things, and nothing in the heavens or in the earth but God sufficeth. Verily, He is in Himself the Knower, the Sustainer, the Omnipotent." It is a prayer by the Báb, and appears on page 56 of *Bahá'í Prayers*.

[35]   The complete quotation from 'Abdu'l-Bahá reads: "Therefore must the mentor be a doctor as well: that is, he must, in instructing the child, remedy its faults; must give him learning, and at the same time rear him to have a spiritual nature. Let the teacher be a doctor to the character of the child, thus will he heal the spiritual ailments of the children of men." It is part of selection 103, page 130, in *Selections from the Writings of 'Abdu'l-Bahá*. You can read the whole selection at **https://www.bahai.org/library/authoritative-texts/abdul-baha/selections-writings-abdul-baha/6#978920007** .

Chapter 16 Pollution

[36]   A letter dated July 9, 1939 and written on behalf of Shoghi Effendi explains the symbolism of the number nine: "First, regarding

the significance of the number nine: its importance as a symbol used so often in various connections by the believers lies in three facts. First, it symbolizes the nine great world religions of which we have any definite historical knowledge, including the Babí and Bahá'í Revelations; second, it represents the number of perfection, being the highest single number; third, it is the numerical value of the word 'Bahá.'" This excerpt, item 1374, appears on page 414 of the compilation *Lights of Guidance*.

[37]   For more references on Progressive Revelation from a Bahá'í perspective, see the section entitled "THE COVENANT" starting on page 110 in Volume 1 of *The Compilation of Compilations*, which is available in the *Ocean Library of World Religions*. One quotation the author considers especially enlightening is on page 167 of Bahá'u'lláh's *The Kitáb-i-Íqán*: "His creation no end hath overtaken, and it hath ever existed from the 'Beginning that hath no beginning'; and the Manifestations of His Beauty no beginning hath beheld, and they will continue to the 'End that knoweth no end.'"

[38]   The Lord's Prayer appears in two books of the New Testament: in Matthew 6:9–13 and in Luke 11:2–4. The version Abby learned is not exactly like either one of these Biblical versions.

[39]   Dali doesn't want to reveal too much specific information from Abby's future, so she asks the yuter to check its ancient archives from Abby's time for hints about toxins causing serious, long-term, even gene-affecting conditions. The yuter discovers several references from our present, including the now-new field of epigenetics and many environmental pollutants.

[40]   The author first learned about possible causes (and medically supervised solutions) to her own family's Autism Spectrum Disorders in the book, *Children With Starving Brains*, by Jacqueline McCandless, MD, ISBN 1-883647-13-4. Copyright 2007, Bramble Books. Some Bahá'í readers may find guidance to a commonly raised question after logging in to **www.bahai.us** and searching for "On the Question of Vaccination: A Compilation."

A self-treatment program the author has found helpful is presented in the first, smaller version of *The Candida Cure,* by Ann Boroch, CNC, ND, ISBN 978-0-9773446-1-1, Copyright 2009, Quintessential Healing Publishing Co.   Author Godward's own efforts at healing eventually led her to compile the ebook, *Fresh Start Anti-Candida Diet* as a meal-planning photo reference for herself and others; it can be found at **https://www.amazon.com/dp/B00NTNMWT2**

[41]   The yuter also discovers references from our present about pollutants changing peoples' genes, such as the article on the relatively new field of epigenetics found on pages 8–11 in the March 2007 issue

of *Muse*.

[42] The yuter also finds references from our present about certain problems associated with infant formula feeding, such as that found at **www.wearsthebaby.com/infantformula.htm** .

[43] Dali is quoting from a passage on pages 8–9 of *Ten Days in the Light of ʿAkká*. ʿAkká (*AH-kaw*) or Akko is now the city of Acre in Israel.

[44] Dali is referring to points ʿAbdu'l-Bahá made in letters, which you can find in the *Baháʾí Library Online* at **www.bahai-library.com** , under Primary Source Material, by clicking on **Compilations prepared by the Bahá'í World Center > 49. Health, Healing, and Nutrition** and scrolling down to items 17–18.

[45] There are many references about ʿAbdu'l-Bahá's ability to understand people's unspoken spiritual reality: on page 158 of *The Chosen Highway*, where he answered unspoken questions during his visit to London; page 36 of *Memories of ʿAbduʾl-Bahá*, recalling his visit to California; numerous places in *The Diary of Juliet Thompson*, which offers an account of her many hours with him in the Holy Land, Europe, and America; and in other such documents. The author especially likes this story from *Star of the West* magazine, volume 18, number 9, page 285:

"During one evening meal at the Master's table, a lady sat next to him listening to His words of wisdom. She looked at a glass of water which was directly in front of her place and thought, "Oh! if only ʿAbdu'l-Bahá would take my heart and empty it of every earthly desire, just as one would take this glass and empty it, and then refill it with divine love and understanding."

"Her thought was just a flashing thought, but ʿAbdu'l-Bahá seemed to read it. He was in the middle of His talk but He stopped briefly and spoke to the servant. It was just a few words in Persian, and then He continued with His conversation without anyone noticing anything. Soon, the servant came quietly to the lady's place, took away her glass from the table, emptied it, and put it back in front of her.

"As ʿAbdu'l-Bahá continued to talk, He lifted the water from the table, reached out in His most casual manner, and slowly refilled the lady's empty glass. No one had noticed what he had done – no one, that is, except the lady herself. She knew what ʿAbdu'l-Bahá was doing, and her heart was filled with great joy. Now she knew that the most private thoughts and desires of everyone present were an open book to ʿAbdu'l-Bahá and that His love included all."

[46] Readers might enjoy knowing about technology developed to read eye movements and neural activity, conduct sound through bone, and more. Internet research might come up with even more results than this: **https://www.theguardian.com/technology/2018/apr/06/researchers-develop-device-that-can-hear-your-internal-voice** . Also Google is developing technology that translates a person's voice into another language: **https://thenextweb.com/google/2019/05/16/googles-new-ai-can-help-you-speak-another-language-in-your-own-voice/** .

[47]   Dali refers to pages 13–14 in Volume 1 of *The Revelation of Bahá'u'lláh*, which says of 'Abdu'l-Bahá: "He had such spiritual insight that, as a young boy, He intuitively recognized the station of His Father. So highly did Bahá'u'lláh esteem Him that in Baghdád He used to address Him, while still in His teens, as the Master – a designation which Bahá'u'lláh had also used for His own father while in Tihran."

[48]   One major Bahá'í document outlines the critical components of a real, lasting peace. Written by the Universal House of Justice to the peoples of the world, it is one of many such blueprints of God's current plan for world peace. Others can be found in books and videos. **www.bahai.org/documents/the-universal-house-of-justice/promise-world-peace**

[49]   In *The World Order of Bahá'u'lláh*, page 203, Shoghi Effendi wrote: "The unity of the human race, as envisaged by Bahá'u'lláh, implies the establishment of a world commonwealth in which all nations, races, creeds and classes are closely and permanently united, and in which the autonomy of its state members and the personal freedom and initiative of the individuals that compose them are definitely and completely safeguarded."

Chapter 17 Dream
[50]   And maybe someday Abby will see and read the lion/lamb story at **www.NaturesCornerMagazine.com/lion_lamb.html** .

Chapter 18 Service
[51] Abby has lost some of the warmth from yesterday, and has to re-establish it. "Souls are liable to estrangement." *Tablets of Abdul-Baha Abbas,* by 'Abdu'l-Bahá. Bahá'í Publishing Committee, 1909, p. 391.

[52]   PLANTIC, which biodegrades slowly in air and faster in water, is briefly described on page 106 of the November 2007 issue of *Reader's Digest*. That article said it is available in Australia.

[53]   Dali is singing a prayer by Bahá'u'lláh, *Bahá'í Prayers,* p. 116.

[54]   Dali quotes from a passage on page 106 of *Gleanings from the Writings of Bahá'u'lláh*: "Purge your sight, that ye may perceive its glory with your own eyes, and depend not on the sight of any one except your self, for God hath never burdened any soul beyond its power." A

related passage earlier on the same page reads: "He hath endowed every soul with the capacity to recognize the signs of God. How could He, otherwise, have fulfilled His testimony unto men, if ye be of them that ponder His Cause in their hearts. He will never deal unjustly with any one, neither will He task a soul beyond its power."

[55]   Dali is quoting 'Abdu'l-Bahá from a Tablet to the Friends in the Orient, printed in *Star of the West* (available via the Ocean app).

[56]   Bahá'í Writings available to the author do not address life expectancy in the future. Years ago, she read of an experiment where a handful of people lived in a carefully purified, enclosed structure and their markers of aging were monitored. At the end of a year or so, the slowing of their aging markers indicated that they could theoretically live to about 150.

[57]   Dali doesn't mean spoken prayers reach God better; she means they have a more far-reaching effect in the world. She's remembering a passage on page 295 of *Gleanings from the Writings of Bahá'u'lláh* and on page iii of *Bahá'í Prayers*: "Intone, O My servant, the verses of God that have been received by thee, as intoned by them who have drawn nigh unto Him, that the sweetness of thy melody may kindle thine own soul, and attract the hearts of all men. Whoso reciteth, in the privacy of his chamber, the verses revealed by God, the scattering angels of the Almighty shall scatter abroad the fragrance of the words uttered by his mouth, and shall cause the heart of every righteous man to throb. Though he may, at first, remain unaware of its effect, yet the virtue of the grace vouchsafed unto him must needs sooner or later exercise its influence upon his soul. Thus have the mysteries of the Revelation of God been decreed by virtue of the Will of Him Who is the Source of power and wisdom."

The American Heritage Dictionary describes to *intone* as to speak with a singing tone, such as when reciting a chant or psalm.

[58]   The word "goodbye" originally came from the valediction "God be with ye."

[59]   The month of *Sharaf* (*shah-RAHF*) begins about December 31, depending on the particular year. *Tá* (*TAW*) or Tihrán (tih-h'RAWN) can also be transliterated as Tehran or Teheran.

[60]   Regarding Baghdád (*BAG-dad*), in paragraph 32, page 30, of *The Kitáb-i-Aqdas*, Bahá'u'lláh tells the Bahá'ís: "The Lord hath ordained that those of you who are able shall make pilgrimage to the sacred House..." In note 54, page 191, this is further explained: "Two sacred Houses are covered by this ordinance, the House of the Báb in Shíráz and the House of Bahá'u'lláh in Baghdád. Bahá'u'lláh has specified that pilgrimage to either of these two Houses fulfils the

requirement of this passage....After the passing of Bahá'u'lláh, 'Abdu'l-Bahá designated the Shrine of Bahá'u'lláh at Bahjí as a place of pilgrimage [also]."

However, those two houses were destroyed, and if they did exist, would not be accessible by the majority of Bahá'ís due to travel restrictions and difficulties within Iraq and Iran. Therefore pilgrimage currently means visiting Bahá'u'lláh's burial place near Akka, Israel, across the Bay of Haifa from the Bahá'í World Center.

[61] Erdeans know the value of awe and have incorporated it back into their language. **https://www.nbcnews.com/better/lifestyle/why-scientists-say-experiencing-awe-can-help-you-live-your-ncna961826?icid=related&sfns=xmo** .

[62] This dance is based on the one performed all over the world by noted Bahá'í Native American, Kevin Locke, Lakota tribe of South Dakota. He is available for performances. **www.kevinlocke.com** .

Chapter 19 Creation

[63] Bothered Brother quotes from a Tablet by 'Abdu'l-Bahá. An excerpt appears in *Lights of Guidance* p. 219, #733.

[64] Bothered Brother is quoting part of Bahá'u'lláh's injunction in paragraph 74, pages 46–47, of *The Kitáb-i-Aqdas*.

[65] Trees like this already exist. One example is the Fruit Cocktail Tree at **www.DirectGardening.com/detail.asp?pid=5556** .

[66] The author took many UL words in whole or in part from the Esperanto language, originally created by Dr. L.L. Zamenhof. Visit **en.wikipedia.org/wiki/esperanto** to learn about the language and about its Bahá'í connection.

[67] Dali is quoting from "Words of Wisdom" from *The Tablets of Bahá'u'lláh*: "True reliance is for the servant to pursue his profession and calling in this world, to hold fast unto the Lord, to seek naught but His grace, inasmuch as in His hands is the destiny of all His servants."

[68] Dali is quoting from a verse on page 51 of *The Hidden Words of Bahá'u'lláh*, specifically Persian #82: "O My Servant! The best of men are they that earn a livelihood by their calling and spend upon themselves and upon their kindred for the love of God, the Lord of all worlds."

[69] Here's a Bahá'í concept that Erdeans would know, influencing Dali's joke:"The hearts of all children are of the utmost purity. They are mirrors upon which no dust has fallen. But this purity is on account of weakness and innocence, not on account of any strength and testing, for as this is the early period of their childhood, their hearts and minds are unsullied by the world. They cannot display any great intelligence. They have neither hypocrisy nor deceit. This is on account of the child's

weakness, whereas the man becomes pure through his strength. Through the power of intelligence he becomes simple; through the great power of reason and understanding and not through the power of weakness he becomes sincere. When he attains to the state of perfection, he will receive these qualities; his heart becomes purified, his spirit enlightened, his soul is sensitized and tender – all through his great strength. This is the difference between the perfect man and the child. Both have the underlying qualities of simplicity and sincerity – the child through the power of weakness and the man through the power of strength. 'Abdu'l-Bahá, *The Promulgation of Universal Peace*, p. 52.

[70]   A more detailed list of laws between Bahá'ís and God – gleaned by the author from the version of *Developing Distinctive Bahá'í Communities* available in *Ocean* – includes: using one of the three Obligatory Prayers daily; reciting *Alláh-u-Abhá* (*ah-LAW-oh-ab-HAW*) 95 times daily; deepening one's knowledge of the Sacred Writings every morning and evening; annual fasting; paying debts; returning to God a small part of one's residual income after paying all necessary living expenses; going on pilgrimage; writing a will and testament; avoiding alcohol and other mood- and mind-altering drugs except under the care of a physician; obeying civil law; following Bahá'í marriage and divorce laws; being chaste outside of marriage and faithful within marriage, which is between one man and one woman; eschewing gambling; shunning gossip; and not holding membership in political parties, secret societies, or other religious organizations. Bahá'ís do not believe that their religious laws are binding on people who aren't Bahá'í, nor do they consider these laws prescriptions for public policy.

[71]   On wisdom, from the VIRTUES REFLECTION CARDS, made in several varieties by THE VIRTUES PROJECT ™ and used with permission. Available at **www.virtuesproject.com** .

"Wisdom is the guardian of our choices. It helps us to discern the right path at the right moment. It gives us clarity of thought and deeper understanding. We use our best judgment. resisting the pull of impulse and desire. Wisdom gives us maturity and patience to make sustainable decisions. We seek knowledge, enter reflection and open ourselves to inspiration. We consider carefully, then act confidently. Wisdom takes us beyond thought to deeper knowing. Wisdom grounds us in grace. Quote: 'I, Wisdom, am mistress of discretion, the inventor of lucidity of thought. Good advice and sound judgment belong to me, perception ... strength...' – Proverbs 8:12-14."

Chapter 20 Party

[72]   Asian dragons are usually considered benevolent, have thinner, serpentine bodies, and fly without wings, such as the ones depicted at **en.wikipedia.org/wiki/chinese_dragon** . European dragons are usually considered malevolent and have thicker bodies with wings, such as the ones at **en.wikipedia.org/wiki/european_dragon** . Learn more about valkyries at **en.wikipedia.org/wiki/Valkyrie** . Historically, unicorns tended to look more caprine, or goat-like, such as the one depicted at **www.BestPriceArt.com/painting/?pid=154200** . Modern unicorns tend to look more equine, or horse-like, such as the one depicted at **www.NovaReinna.com/guard/unicorn.html** .

[73]   Metric is the first name of a young Nigerian college student that the author went to college with.

[74]   In a letter written in 1936 – and quoted on pages x–xi of his "Introduction" to *The Proclamation of Bahá'u'lláh* – Shoghi Effendi noted that, in addition to a world language: "A world script, a world literature, a uniform and universal system of currency, of weights and measures, will simplify and facilitate intercourse and understanding among the nations and races of mankind." Kreshi pretends to accept her excuse about never having seen these Kingdom coins.

[75]   The October 2007 issue of *National Geographic*, page 26, show-cases collectable coins – legal tender from the Republic of Palau – with objects embedded in them. You can see Palau coins with a pearl, a tiny bit of meteorite, a bit of volcanic rock, and a four-leaf clover, as well as a working light-bulb coin from Niue and several other unusual coins, at **bizaims.com/coffee+break/curiosities+events+funny/unusual+coins** Visit **en.wikipedia.org/wiki/bristlecone_pine** to learn about bris-tlecone pines, and **en.wikipedia.org/wiki/bee_hummingbird** to learn about the bee hummingbird.

[76]   Abby read an article about giant money on pages 16–19 in the May/June 2007 issue of *Muse*, one of the Cricket group of magazines.

[77]   What might they have talked about? Eleanor Roosevelt, former First Lady of the United States, wrote, "Great minds discuss ideas; average minds discuss events; small minds discuss people." **https://www.brainyquote.com/quotes/eleanor_roosevelt_385439**

[78]   You can learn about sea serpents – including some "historical sightings" – at **en.wikipedia.org/wiki/sea_serpent**, and about kelpies at **en.wikipedia.org/wiki/kelpie** .

Chapter 21 Dragons

[79]   You can learn about the winged horse – the Pegasus or, more generically, pterippus – at **en.wikipedia.org/wiki/pegasus** .

[80]   *Lung* or *long* is the Chinese character for "dragon" and *ma* is the one for horse. Since Rykeir's dragon horse has wings, it may specifically be a *tianma*, also known as the heavenly horse or Chinese Pegasus. You can learn about the *lóngmǎ* – the vital spirit of heaven and earth – at **en.wikipedia.org/wiki/longma** .

[81]   Rykeir is referring to a humorous concept presented in Lewis Carroll's classic *The Hunting of the Snark: An Agony in Eight Fits*. His "Fit the First – The Landing" starts:

> "Just the place for a Snark!" the Bellman cried,
> As he landed his crew with care;
> Supporting each man on the top of the tide
> By a finger entwined in his hair.

> "Just the place for a Snark! I have said it twice:
> That alone should encourage the crew.
> Just the place for a Snark! I have said it thrice:
> What I tell you three times is true."

Visit **ebooks.adelaide.edu.au/c/carroll/lewis/snark** to read the whole poem, and **en.wikipedia.org/wiki/the_hunting_of_the_snark** to read *about* the poem. As a game programmer, Rykeir is also familiar with the design philosophy that any machine or computer your life depends on should have triple redundant failsafes, sometimes called the "tell you three times" protocol. To learn about other literary uses of *the rule of three*, visit **tvtropes.org/pmwiki/pmwiki.php/main/RuleOfThree** .

[82]   A horse needs around two feet for a takeoff or landing and four feet per stride at the canter. Learn about jumping events at horse shows on **en.wikipedia.org/wiki/show_jumping** . You can also find numerous slides and video clips on **www.youtube.com** using the SEARCH term **horse jumping**.

[83]   The movie is *Wild Wild West*, a 1999 "steampunk" science fiction/action comedy directed by Barry Sonnenfeld and starring Will Smith – whom Abby and Jenn adore – and Kevin Kline.

[84]   The yuter refers to a work such as *A Basic Bahá'í Dictionary* (see **Resources, Books** below) and personalizes its definition of Ayyám-i-Há for Abby.

[85]   Kreshi is thinking about the quote on page 163 of *Gleanings from the Writings of Bahá'u'lláh*: "Know thou that every fixed star hath its own planets, and every planet its own creatures, whose number no man can compute."

[86]   Rykeir is quoting a verse on page 17 of *The Hidden Words of Bahá'u'lláh*, specifically Arabic #59.

[87]   You can find numerous references by entering the words **divine**

promptings or **spiritual insight** in the SEARCH field of the *Bahá'í Reference Library*, the *Bahá'í Library Online*, or *Ocean*. One of the author's favorite such quotations appears on page 35, in the Tablet of Tarazát (Ornaments), of *Tablets of Bahá'u'lláh Revealed After the Kitáb-i-Aqdas*: "We cherish the hope that through the loving-kindness of the All-Wise, the All-Knowing, obscuring dust may be dispelled and the power of perception enhanced, that the people may discover the purpose for which they have been called into being. In this Day whatsoever serveth to reduce blindness and to increase vision is worthy of consideration. This vision acteth as the agent and guide for true knowledge. Indeed in the estimation of men of wisdom keenness of understanding is due to keenness of vision. The people of Bahá must under all circumstances observe that which is meet and seemly and exhort the people accordingly."

[88] " 'Abdu'l-Bahá, do You know everything?" Saffa Kinney is said to have asked. "No, I do not know everything. But when I need to know something, it is pictured before Me." And so 'Abdu'l-Bahá, on the occasion of His tour of the General Electric Works, knew more about electricity than did Steinmetz. Shoghi Effendi has said that intuition is a power of the soul. It was this power that was always available to 'Abdu'l-Bahá, and available in its totality. He has spoken many times of this "immediate knowledge" – this knowledge attained without the means of books or other humans, this strange intuitive power which to some degree is available to us all." Stanwood Cobb, *Memories of 'Abdu'l-Bahá*, p. 20.
https://bahai-library.com/pdf/c/cobb_memories_abdul-baha.pdf

[89] Visit **en.wikipedia.org/wiki/As-Sir%c4%81t** (that's eight one tee) to learn about the Islamic hadith (*hah-DEETH*) or tradition of the Sirat al-Jahim (*sear-RAT ahl-jah-HEEM*).

Chapter 22 Happiness

[90] The word *alicorn* tends to mean the horn of a unicorn. Informal words for animals blending Pegasus and unicorn traits have included pegacorn, unisus and unipeg. For more on the Longma, see Endnote 80. The blending of Longma, Pegasus and Unicorn into an Almacorn is a Wize creation.

[91] You can learn about seahorses – which really do change color – at **en.wikipedia.org/wiki/seahorse** , and about the part-human/part-horse centaurs at **en.wikipedia.org/wiki/centaur** .

Chapter 23 Deepening

[92] The author is again using Esperanto for UL. Esperanto builds words out of pieces that always mean the same thing. *Spirito* means

"spirit", and changing the end to *a* (*spee-REE-tah*) makes it the adjective "spiritual". *Lerni* means "to learn", *ejo* (*AY-oh*) means "place", and so *lernejo* (*lair-NAY-yo)* is a learning-place, a school. *Besto* means "beast", *montri* means "to show", *ejo* means "place", and so *bestmontrejo* (*baste-moan-TRAY-yo*) is an animal showplace. To learn about tools to teach yourself Esperanto, enter the term **Esperanto teach yourself** into a search engine such as Google.

[93]   Dali is referring to the twelfth Glad Tiding of the Tablet of Bishárát (Glad-Tidings) in *Tablets of Bahá'u'lláh Revealed After the Kitáb-i-Aqdas*. The complete quotation, on page 26, reads:

"It is enjoined upon every one of you to engage in some form of occupation, such as crafts, trades and the like. We have graciously exalted your engagement in such work to the rank of worship unto God, the True One. Ponder ye in your hearts the grace and the blessings of God and render thanks unto Him at eventide and at dawn. Waste not your time in idleness and sloth. Occupy yourselves with that which profiteth yourselves and others. Thus hath it been decreed in this Tablet from whose horizon the day-star of wisdom and utterance shineth resplendent.

"The most despised of men in the sight of God are those who sit idly and beg. Hold ye fast unto the cord of material means, placing your whole trust in God, the Provider of all means. When anyone occupieth himself in a craft or trade, such occupation itself is regarded in the estimation of God as an act of worship; and this is naught but a token of His infinite and all-pervasive bounty."

[94]   In moderation, 'Abdu'l-Bahá enjoyed honey and candy himself, shared it generously with others, and even offered it as a healing balm for both mental and physical stress. In *The Chosen Highway*, page 202, Lady Blomfield describes a meal where: " 'Abdu'l-Bahá tasted only a few spoonfuls of honey, a little broth, and some olives, and after the meal He slept about an hour." In *Arches of the Years*, page 95, Marzieh Gail relates that, during 'Abdu'l-Bahá's travels in America: "He was paying His own bills, accepting nothing of money value, only such gifts as flowers and candy, which He promptly distributed as was His way." In *Dawn Over Mount Hira*, pages 200–201, she also describes a work meeting with him wherein: "He reached over to His table (throughout this interview He remained standing) – on which He had flowers, papers, rock candy, rose water – and with both hands full of candy He told me to hold out my hands. I laid the Tablets on the table edge, stretched out my cupped hands and He filled them with candy; and still smiling, He took my face in His two hands and said: "Go and eat this candy, and by

the grace and power of the Blessed Beauty thou shalt be enabled to translate from Arabic into English." And in *Tablets of 'Abdu'l-Bahá*, volume 1, page 185, the Master assures an ailing woman that her illness is not on account of sin and suggests, "Take some honey, recite 'Ya Baha-ul-ABHA,' and eat a little thereof for several days."

[95]   In Esperanto, *pordo* means "door". *Ŝlosi* means "to lock," using *iĝ* makes it reflexive (the actor acts upon itself), changing the end to *u* makes it a command, and so *ŝlosiĝu* means "lock yourself".

[96]   Muscle testing exists now. See how to muscle test yourself at **www.lind.com/quantum/muscle%20testing%20yourself.htm** .

[97]   Erdeans act on 'Abdu'l-Bahá's statement, included in selection 39 on pages 15–16 of *A Compilation on Bahá'í Education*:

"Observe how many penal institutions, houses of detention and places of torture are made ready to receive the sons of men, the purpose being to prevent them, by punitive measures, from committing terrible crimes – whereas this very torment and punishment only increaseth depravity, and by such means the desired aim cannot be properly achieved.

"Therefore must the individual be trained from his infancy in such a way that he will never undertake to commit a crime, will, rather, direct all his energies to the acquisition of excellence, and will look upon the very commission of an evil deed as in itself the harshest of all punishments, considering the sinful act itself to be far more grievous than any prison sentence. For it is possible so to train the individual that, although crime may not be completely done away with, still it will become very rare.

"The purport is this, that to train the character of humankind is one of the weightiest commandments of God, and the influence of such training is the same as that which the sun exerteth over tree and fruit. Children must be most carefully watched over, protected and trained; in such consisteth true parenthood and parental mercy".

[98]   Many forms of pest-control fields are already in use to repel insects, arachnids, and small mammals through electromagnetic, ionic, or sonic means. Visit **www.ElectronicPestRepeller.com** to see an example that uses all three types.

[99]   Dali is quoting paragraph 62, page 41, of *The Kitáb-i-Aqdas*. There is, of course, a difference between deliberately taking a person's life, say, to rob them, versus to protect a child they are trying to kill. Just as there's a difference between burning an empty warehouse versus burning a family home. For more detail on this subject, read Note 86, pages 203–204, of *The Kitáb-i-Aqdas*.

[100] This has, unfortunately, happened in numerous wars. And is still happening. If you have a strong stomach, take a look at the report from late 2007 at **hnn.us/blogs/entries/45591.html** .

[101] *Bahiyyih Khanum* was the name of Bahá'u'lláh's daughter, who, along with her family, accompanied Him during His exile and imprisonment. She also upheld the leadership of the Faith during tumultuous transitional years following the death of her elder brother, 'Abdu'l-Bahá. Her name is popular among Bahá'í women as she exemplifies faith, steadfastness, courage, dignity, service, and compassion. You can read more about her character at **https://bahai-library.com/morten_tribute_bahiyyih_khanum.**

[102] "My name is 'Abdu'l-Bahá, my identity is 'Abdu'l-Bahá, my qualification is 'Abdu'l-Bahá, my reality is 'Abdu'l-Bahá, my praise is 'Abdu'l-Bahá. Thraldom to the Blessed Perfection is my glorious refulgent diadem; and servitude to all the human race is my perpetual religion." From *Tablets of 'Abdu'l-Bahá*, vol. 2, p. 430. From the same book, p. 466: "Regarding the station of this servant: My station is 'Abdul-Baha, my name is 'Abdu'l-Bahá, my qualification is 'Abdu'l-Bahá, my praise is 'Abdu'l-Bahá, my title is 'Abdu'l-Bahá."

[103] This dramatic presentation is based on Mrs. Brown's book entitled *Memories of 'Abdu'l-Bahá.*

[104] The actress is quoting a sentence on page 14 of *'Abdu'l-Bahá – The Centre of the Covenant of Bahá'u'lláh.*

[105] An anecdote describes how 'Abdu'l-Bahá once gave away all His family's sheep. Bahá'u'lláh laughed and remarked, "We will have to protect 'Abdu'l-Bahá from himself – someday he will give himself away." Honnold, *Vignettes from the Life of 'Abdu'l-Bahá*, p. 58, from *Star of the West*, vol. Xv, No. 3, p. 74. Also in Vol. XIII, pp. 271-2.

[106] At a Summer School years ago, the author heard the recording of 'Abdu'l-Bahá chanting. The translation is found in *The Bahá'í World*, vol. VII, p. 421, as well as starting on page 7 of **https://www.bahai.org/library/authoritative-texts/abdul-baha/additional-tablets-extracts-talks/additional-tablets-extracts-talks-abdul-baha.pdf?cf5a866b** :

Praise be to God that ye are present in this radiant assemblage and have turned your faces toward the Kingdom of Abhá! That which ye behold is from the grace and bounty of the Blessed Perfection. We are as atoms and He is the Sun of Truth. We are as drops and He is the Most Great Ocean. Poor are we, yet the outpouring of the treasury of the Kingdom is boundless. Weak are we, yet the confirmation of the Supreme Concourse is abundant. Helpless are we, yet our refuge and shelter is Bahá'u'lláh.

Praise be to God! His signs are evident.

Praise be to God! His light is shining.

Praise be to God! His ocean is surging.

Praise be to God! His radiance is intense.

Praise be to God! His bestowals are abundant.

Praise be to God! His favours are manifest.

Glad tidings! Glad tidings! The Morn of Guidance hath dawned.

Glad tidings! Glad tidings! The Sun of Truth hath shone forth.

Glad tidings! Glad tidings! The breeze of favour hath wafted.

Glad tidings! Glad tidings! The showers of the clouds of divine bounty have poured down.

Glad tidings! Glad tidings! The Sun of the supreme horizon hath shed its radiance upon all the world with boundless effulgence.

Glad tidings! Glad tidings! The hearts of all are in the utmost purity.

Glad tidings! Glad tidings! His all-encompassing splendour hath been revealed.

Glad tidings! Glad tidings! The celestial concourse is astir.

Glad tidings! Glad tidings! Zion is rapt in ecstasy.

Glad tidings! Glad tidings! The Kingdom of God is filled with exultation and joy.

[107]   The Day of the Covenant is the Holy Day observed on November 26 to commemorate Bahá'u'lláh's appointment of 'Abdu'l-Bahá as the Center of His Covenant. 'Abdu'l-Bahá instructed that his own birthday not be celebrated, because he was born on the very day that the Báb declared His mission (May 23, 1844) and he said *that* Holy Day must be devoted solely to the Báb's anniversary. But when the early believers pleaded with him for a day to observe in his honor, he graciously acceded and gave them the Day of the Covenant.

[108]   The actress is quoting 'Abdu'l-Bahá's statement on page 339 of *The Promulgation of Universal Peace.*

[109]   Kahlil Gibran (*kah-LEEL jih-BRAWN*) is sometimes spelled as Khalil Gibran. To learn about Kahlil Gibran, including his interaction with 'Abdu'l-Bahá, visit **en.wikipedia.org/wiki/Khalil_Gibran** and **www.bahai-library.org/file.php?file=bushrui_gibran_man_poet** . Scroll to the bottom of the latter link to see one of his sketches of 'Abdu'l-Bahá.

Chapter 24 Animals

[110]   Abby is not familiar with either the *culpeo* or the *dhole*. Visit **en.wikipedia.org/wiki/canidae** to learn about the canine family in

general, and **www.youtube.com/watch?v=HqbVbPvlDoM** to see an amazing video of a woman who taught her dog a pattern and/or is cueing it surreptitiously.

[111]   Abby is seeing a *caracal*. Visit **en.wikipedia.org/wiki/felidae** to learn about the feline family in general.

[112]   Xenophon (*ZEHN-uh-fun*) – circa 430–355 BC – is considered the father of natural horsemanship. He was a Greek soldier, friend of Socrates, historian, poet, writer, and horse trainer. Among other books and short works, he wrote a significant treatise entitled *Peri Hippikēs* (variously called *De Re Equestri, On Horsemanship*, and *On the Art of Horsemanship*) that covered selecting, caring for, and training horses in a non-abusive manner for general use, classical dressage. and even the military. Visit **classics.mit.edu/Xenophon/xen.horse.html** to read this treatise in Greek and English. Visit **iep.utm.edu/x/xenophon.htm** and **en.wikipedia.org/wiki/Xenophon** to read more about Xenophon.

[113]   Abby quickly recognizes that the animal show's opening narrative is based on the creation story told at the beginning of the Book of Genesis in the Bible.

[114] Many make fun of the animal videos on the internet but it also contains mind-expanding videos of animal capabilities, which contributed to the author imagining this show. For example, see these rescue animals performing in a talent show: **https://www.reshareworthy.com/rescue-animals-pet-shenanigans/**

[115]   Back in Chapter 13, when Abby asked about roping steers, Dali blinked long and slow. That's the first time Abby noticed anyone mentally communicating with their Yuter, though she didn't yet know that's what was happening. Dali was checking an historical record to make sure she understood what Abby meant, then scheduling a reminder to mention it to Abby again at the show. A good starting point for learning more about training cattle is **https://en.wikipedia.org/wiki/Ox** .

[116]   In Spanish-walking, the horse lifts its diagonal front and back feet together and stretches its front leg up and out. A person Spanish-walking beside their horse can lift and stretch their own legs in unison with the horse's front legs. To see a video of a ridden horse Spanish-walking, visit **www.youtube.com/watch?v=lpCvQBALBX0** .

[117]   This segment of the animal-show narration about unity is based on statements by 'Abdu'l-Bahá in *Paris Talks*.

[118]   The continuing animal-show narration about love is based on statements by 'Abdu'l-Bahá on page 88 in the "Divine Love" section of *Foundations of World Unity*.

[119]   In Roman riding, a rider typically stands atop a pair of side-by-side moving horses, with one foot on each horse's back. To see a video

that includes Roman-riding and related teaming and jumping feats, visit **www.youtube.com/watch?v=YXpxpKTnUr8** .

[120]   To see a picture of the Spanish Riding School's arena, visit **en.wikipedia.org/wiki/File:Spanische_Hofreitschule3,_Vienna.jpg** .

[121]   Much of the author's inspiration for the horse part of the animal show came from the amazing Cavalia touring show. To learn more, visit **www.cavalia.net** .

[122]   The quotation on the STEED OF FAITH sculpture appears on page 5 of *The Seven Valleys and the Four Valleys*.

Chapter 25 School

[123]   In a letter quoted in item 75, page 30, of *A Compilation on Bahá'í Education*, 'Abdu'l-Bahá wrote of children that: "From the age of five their formal education must begin. That is, during the daytime they should be looked after in a place where there are teachers, and should learn good conduct."

[124]   "If possible the children should all wear the same kind of clothing, even if the fabric is varied. It is preferable that the fabric as well should be uniform; if, however, this is not possible, there is no harm done. The more cleanly the pupils are, the better; they should be immaculate." *Selections from the Writings of 'Abdu'l-Bahá*, #110, p. 135. Entire passage: **https://www.bahai.org/library/authoritative-texts/abdul-baha/selections-writings-abdul-baha/6#514751316** .

[125]   This is Morse Code jewelry, with one large bead standing for a dash and one smaller bead representing a dot. Petra has made sayings and verses out of beads in this technique.

[126]   Abby is remembering Christ's first Beatitude, from Luke 6:20: "Blessed are you who are poor, for yours is the kingdom of God."

[127]   Petra is familiar with this saying from Bahá'u'lláh's *Tablet to a Physician*: "A light meal in the morning is as a light to the body." From *Star of the West*, vol. 13, no. 9, December 1922, p. 252.

[128]   Petra is quoting from selection 138 on page 159 of *Selections from the Writings of 'Abdu'l-Bahá*. You can read the whole selection at **https://www.bahai.org/library/authoritative-texts/abdul-baha/selections-writings-abdul-baha/6#809863038** .

[129]   In *The Concept of Spirituality*, page 16, William S. Hatcher says: " 'Abdu'l-Bahá often responded to Bahá'ís who felt overwhelmed by the task of refining their character by stressing the necessity of patience and daily striving. 'Be patient, be as I am,' He would say. Spirituality was to be won 'little by little; day by day.' "

[130]   Yoga for teens is a "thing" and can be very helpful. One resource is the book with DVD, *Breathe: Yoga for Teens* by Mary Kaye

Chryssicas, DK Publishing, 2007. Some schools are even substituting yoga, meditation and mediation for punishments. **https://www.higherperspectives.com/detention-meditation-school-2606986894.html** is one of many reports.

[131] Petra is quoting from a verse on page 21 of *The Hidden Words of Bahá'u'lláh*, specifically Arabic #71: "O Son Of Man! Write all that We have revealed unto thee with the ink of light upon the tablet of thy spirit. Should this not be in thy power, then make thine ink of the essence of thy heart. If this thou canst not do, then write with that crimson ink that hath been shed in My path. Sweeter indeed is this to Me than all else, that its light may endure for ever."

[132] TerraCycle was featured in the National Geographic Channel program "Garbage Moguls" for making useful products from discarded "trash" such as newspapers, cereal boxes, and cookie wrappers. Visit **channel.nationalgeographic.com/episode/garbage-moguls-4314** to view videos. Also, according to a news article – "RICHLITE now green, growing" – at **www.thenewstribune.com/voelpel/story/739980.html** , two RICHLITE products are made from 100% recycled paper, and the company has also developed a way to recycle/reuse production heat. Visit **www.richlite.com** to see paper-based products from cutting boards and countertops to skateboard ramps and industrial panels.

[133] In Esperanto, *instrui* means "to teach"; the students are using the root *instru* as a loving honorific, as in "Good morning, Teach!" *Ĝentilajo* means "courtesy"; and since using *aj* indicates a concrete example of an abstract idea, calling Ms. Reed *Ĝentilajo* in this case indicates that the students consider her the embodiment of courtesy.

[134] The teacher is referring to the Lawh-i-Dunyá (Tablet of the World) in *Tablets of Bahá'u'lláh Revealed After the Kitáb-i-Aqdas* p. 88.
. "O people of God! I admonish you to observe courtesy, for above all else it is the prince of virtues. Well is it with him who is illumined with the light of courtesy and is attired with the vesture of uprightness. Whoso is endued with courtesy hath indeed attained a sublime station." He then expresses the hope that *everyone*: "…may be enabled to acquire it, hold fast unto it, observe it, and fix our gaze upon it."

[135] Maybe a student asks if this incident is about controlling emotions, and recalls sia training in controlling emotions, as passed on to the world from the Inuits (and perhaps other cultures too). **https://www.npr.org/sections/goatsandsoda/2019/03/13/685533353/a-playful-way-to-teach-kids-to-control-their-anger**

Chapter 26 Lunch

[136] For more information on Tranquility Zones, a style of devotional gathering some Bahá'ís in Northern Ireland started and others adapted, visit **https://bahaipedia.org/Tranquillity_Zone** . Perhaps Ms. Reed played "Sapient, A Cantata of Peace" by Steven Chesne, which can be found at **https://www.amazon.com/Sapient-Steven-Chesne/dp/B076MG4TMC** . It contains chants and songs of peace from 17 different religious and spiritual traditions; the 18th and 19th tracks blend the previous vocals into magnificent calls for peace.

[137] A fascinating spiritual concept described by an early American believer after her pilgrimage to 'Abdu'l-Bahá in Haifa, Palestine. On the heart-wrenching day that the group was to leave Palestine, 'Abdu'l-Bahá gave them words to remember during their separation:

"Pray that your hearts may be cut from yourselves and from the world, that you may be confirmed by the Holy Spirit and filled with the fire of the love of God. The nearer you are to the light, the further you are from the darkness; the nearer you are to heaven, the further you are from the earth; the nearer you are to God, the further you are from the world. You have come here among the first and your reward is great. There are two visits; the first is for a blessing; then ye come and are blessed and are sent forth to work in God's vineyard; the second ye come with music and the banners flying, like soldiers, in gladness and triumph to receive your reward. If in times past those who have risen up and gone forth in the Cause of God have been helped and confirmed by His spirit, even to suffering death for Him, how much greater is the flood of life with which ye shall be flooded now! For this is the end and the full revelation, and I say unto you that anyone who will rise up in the Cause of God at this time shall be filled with the spirit of God, and that He will send His hosts from heaven to help you and that nothing shall be impossible to you if you have faith. And now I give you a commandment which shall be for a covenant between you and Me – that ye have faith; that your faith be steadfast as a rock that no storms can move, that nothing can disturb, and that it endure through all things even to the end; even should ye hear that your Lord has been crucified, be not shaken in your faith; for I am with you always, whether living or dead, I am with you to the end. As ye have faith so shall your powers and blessings be. This is the balance – this is the balance." From *An Early Pilgrimage* by May Bolles Maxwell, most accurate rendition by George Ronald Publishing, 1953. Special thanks to Bahá'í David Bowie of British Columbia, Canada for the correct reference.

[138] For a 10-minute video on one tribe's hand games, watch **https://youtu.be/_BBHge8wzR0** (Last character is a zero).

[139] From their earliest years, Erdean children learn about cooperation. We have great resources now, such as:

- **http://www.ultimatecampresource.com/site/camp-activities/cooperative-games.page-1.html**
- *The Cooperative Sports & Games Book* by Terry Orlick, Pantheon Press, 1978, from which the author imagined Petra's "Collective-Score Monsterball Volleyball," on p. 51. Her version would be wheelchair- and differently-abled-friendly, with several nets set up and teams trying to bump their planet-ball over the net as many times as possible.
- Another classic reference, which contains the Group Sit game as "The Lap Game" on p. 171, is *The New Games Book* by the New Games Foundation, 1976.

[140] Pentathlon for the five fields of STEAM (Science, Technology, Engineering, Art and Math). Perhaps it has events such as those listed at **https://scioly.org/wiki/index.php/Pentathlon** .

[141] At Dali's request, the yuter again accesses its ancient archives and discovers references from our present about problems with cow's milk, such as that found in an article about "Cows' Milk Allergy in Infants" at **www.MedicalNewsToday.com/articles/73741.php** .

[142] The yuter also discovers articles from our present about health problems resulting from ingesting chemicals, colorings, preservatives, and so on, such as the one on chemicals found in commonplace things at **alternet.org/story/146938/can_everyday_things_cause_cancer?** and the one on dairy products found at **drweil.com/drw/u/id/QAA400175** . The effects of naturally occurring hormones in milk may be further aggravated if the farmers also feed their cattle growth hormones.

[143] Do a web search on any of those conditions and you'll find that, while the cause is not known, it is known that dietary changes can often help them. Search a little deeper and you'll find that medical science barely recognizes the critical role of nutrition in health. People are finding out for themselves, however; and medicine is slowly allowing for the influence of diet as a preventative factor.

[144] Dali is quoting from selection 134, page 153, in *Selections from the Writings of 'Abdu'l-Bahá*. You can read the complete selection at **https://www.bahai.org/library/authoritative-texts/abdul-baha/selections-writings-abdul-baha/6#729204486** . And for interesting information on food combining, enter the term **food combining** into a search engine such as Google.

[145] In a letter to an individual Bahá'í, 'Abdu'l-Bahá wrote: "The child must, from the day of his birth, be provided with whatever is conducive to his health; and know ye this: so far as possible, the mother's milk is best for, more agreeable and better suited to the child, unless she should fall ill or her milk should run entirely dry." As a former certified childbirth educator, the author can add the option of feeding a baby breastmilk donated by another mother. The excerpt quoted appears on page 461 in Volume 1 of *The Compilation of Compilations*, which is available in *Ocean*.

[146]   Dali adapts a saying by Maya Angelou:
"Do the best you can until you know better. Then when you know better, do better." **http://wisdomquotes.com/maya-angelou-quotes/** .

[147]   Petra is quoting from selection 72, page 110, of *Selections from the Writings of 'Abdu'l-Bahá*.

[148]   One Bahá'í writer has discussed giving and taking offence. Read it as an appendix, and other quotes about speech, in *Wise Utterance* by Lisa Bradley Godward. Find it on Amazon.

[149]   Dali is quoting from the Tablet of Tarazát (Ornaments) in *Tablets of Bahá'u'lláh Revealed After the Kitáb-i-Aqdas*. The complete sentence, on pages 35–36, reads: "The first Taráz and the first effulgence which hath dawned from the horizon of the Mother Book is that man should know his own self and recognize that which leadeth unto loftiness or lowliness, glory or abasement, wealth or poverty." *Taráz* is the singular noun meaning "ornament".

Chapter 27 Return

[150]   The song Melissa is singing – "The Remover of Difficulties" – is a prayer by the Báb; it appears on page 226 of *Bahá'í Prayers*.

[151]   Melissa and Jon are singing a short healing prayer revealed by Bahá'u'lláh. It is well-known among Bahá'ís and appears on page 96 of *Bahá'í Prayers* and on numerous sites on the internet, including **https://www.bahaiprayers.org/healing2.htm** . The full prayer is, "Thy name is my healing, O my God, and remembrance of Thee is my remedy. Nearness to Thee is my hope, and love for Thee is my companion. Thy mercy to me is my healing and my succor in both this world and the world to come. Thou, verily, art the All-Bountiful, the All-Knowing, the All-Wise."

[152]   Versions of this saying by Friedrich Wilhelm Nietzsche include: "What does not kill me, makes me stronger." "What does not destroy me, makes me stronger." "That which does not kill us makes us stronger." "He turns all of his injuries into strengths, that which does not kill him makes him stronger." Coincidentally, Nietzsche was born in the year that the Bahá'í Era began: 1844.

[153]   Visit **www.kidshealth.org/kid/talk/qa/coma.html** to learn about comas.

[154] Visit **en.wikipedia.org/wiki/Near-death_experience** to learn about the experiences of people who have been very close to death or briefly clinically dead.

[155] Visit **https://www.youtube.com/watch?v=cF_dIME8b_Q** to hear this song in Zulu and English. Melissa's rendition of the Zulu is shown in single syllables because various websites group the syllables into words differently. The songwriter is Benjamin Dlamini.

[156] Melissa quotes from Lucki Melander Wilder's *The Three Onenesses and the Foundational Verities,* **www.earthstarworks.com** .

[157] The Bahá'ís of Suriname keep an interesting website at: **https://en.bahai.sr/** .

Chapter 28 Phonecall

[158] Melissa has read *World Order of Bahá'u'lláh,* pages 57-58, and, with certain additional understandings and qualifiers, refers to Shoghi Effendi's sentence, "Its declared, its primary purpose, is to enable every adherent of these Faiths to obtain a fuller understanding of the religion with which he stands identified, and to acquire a clearer apprehension of its purpose."

[159] Melissa is referring to parts of section 15, starting on page 29, of *Selections from the Writings of 'Abdu'l-Bahá,* where he says: "Thou didst begin thy letter with a blessed phrase, saying: 'I am a Christian.' O would that all were truly Christian! It is easy to be a Christian on the tongue, but hard to be a true one. Today some five hundred million souls are Christian, but the real Christian is very rare: he is that soul from whose comely face there shineth the splendour of Christ, and who showeth forth the perfections of the Kingdom; this is a matter of great moment, for to be a Christian is to embody every excellence there is. I hope that thou, too, shalt become a true Christian." And later in the same letter, he says: "O honoured lady! For a single purpose were the Prophets, each and all, sent down to earth; for this was Christ made manifest, for this did Bahá'u'lláh raise up the call of the Lord: that the world of man should become the world of God, this nether realm the Kingdom, this darkness light, this satanic wickedness all the virtues of heaven–and unity, fellowship and love be won for the whole human race, that the organic unity should reappear and the bases of discord be destroyed and life everlasting and grace everlasting become the harvest of mankind." You can read the whole selection at: **https://www.bahai.org/library/authoritative-texts/abdul-baha/selections-writings-abdul-baha/3#870877966** .

[160] *One in All*, a 1952 book compiling quotes from the world's major faith traditions, is the first interfaith book the author read. Out of print and rare, it includes quotes on nine topics related to one's preparation, path, and goal: the search for knowledge and truth, purification and sincerity, non-attachment, love and charity, humility and devotion, renunciation and surrender, enlightenment and new life, the one-in-all concept, and identification. Many other books have since collected and grouped similar concepts from the different faiths. One excellent current book that reads like a loving trip down a gentle river of hope is *Ancient Wisdom, Common Ground* by the author's friend E.G. Acosta. Find it at **https://www.amazon.com/dp/146094934X** .

[161]   In a letter dated March 11, 1936 and included in *The World Order of Bahá'u'lláh*, page 203, Shoghi Effendi states: "A mechanism of world inter-communication will be devised, embracing the whole planet, freed from national hindrances and restrictions, and functioning with marvelous swiftness and perfect regularity."

[162]   "Should a man try to fly with the wing of religion alone he would quickly fall into the quagmire of superstition, whilst on the other hand, with the wing of science alone he would also make no progress, but fall into the despairing slough of materialism." 'Abdu'l-Bahá. Read the entire, excellent talk on "The Acceptance of the Relation Between Religion and Science" at:
https://www.bahai.org/library/authoritative-texts/abdul-baha/paris-talks/5#351420434 or in the book *Paris Talks*, pp 145-150, depending on the edition.

[163]   For an outstanding analysis of the unworkable, outmoded approaches as well as the necessary, logical solutions to world peace, there's hardly a better source than *The Promise of World Peace*, a statement by the Universal House of Justice to the peoples of the world. It is available in paper from Special Ideas, **www.bahairesources.com** and online at **https://www.bahai.org/documents/the-universal-house-of-justice/promise-world-peace** .

[164]   "In Persia there is a wonderful breed of horses which are trained to run long distances at very great speed. They are most carefully trained at first. They are taken out into the fields and made to run a short course. At the commencement of their training they are not able to run far. The distance is gradually increased. They become thinner and thinner, wiry and lean, but their strength increases. Finally, after months of rigid training, their swiftness and endurance become wonderful. They are able to run at full speed across rough country many parasangs of distance. At first this would have been impossible. Not until they become trained, thin and wiry, can they endure this severe test.

"In this way I shall train you. *Kam-kam, kam-kam* (little by little,

little by little), until your powers of endurance become so increased that you will serve the Cause of God continually, without other motive, without other thought or wish. This is my desire.

"You must become impervious to criticism, unconscious of attack and abuse, nay, rather welcoming persecution, hostility and bitterness as the means of testing and increasing your supreme faith in God; even as His Holiness Christ instructed His disciples 'Bless them that curse you; pray for them that despitefully use you.'. Be therefore as spiritual adamant against these darts, arrows and swords of infliction. We will help each other to bear them. First by love and increased zeal in the Heavenly Cause. For by exercise the spirit grows stronger, more capable of withstanding, just as the muscle of the outer body increases its fibre through continual action. You must help me and I will help you to increase our service in the Cause of Bahá'u'lláh Secondly; we will help each other grow more and more accustomed to punishment and persecution. Years ago in Baghdád the usual punishment for offenders and lawbreakers was the bastinado. The governor noticed that a certain band of men came repeatedly before him for trial. They were regularly found guilty of breaking the law, sentenced and whipped upon the feet. While the bastinado was being inflicted they appeared quite comfortable and evidently unconscious of pain. In a few days these same offenders would be back again, going through the same process. The governor made careful inquiry about them. It was learned that they lived together in a house and that every day it was their custom to bastinado each other until the skin upon their feet had become so hardened to the whip that the legal bastinado gave them no inconvenience whatever.

"Now we, as offenders against the opinions of our friends and enemies, must assist each other to become impervious to their criticism, unconscious of attack, welcoming their whips. You must beat me and I will beat you with the whips of love. The more we beat each other the more capable of withstanding we will become. When the enemies find they are increasing our love, enkindlement and service in the pathway of Bahá'u'lláh, they will wonder and say, 'How is this? Our words have no effect upon them except to make them love us more and give thanks to God for our scourging.'

"The Blessed Beauty Bahá'u'lláh won the hearts of his jailers and tormentors. No one could withstand Him. The intense flame of His love melted the hardest stone of hearts. The more chains of iron they put upon His body, the more He imprisoned them in chains of love. They looked upon Him in wonder; they became His followers." 'Abdu'l-Bahá, *Star of the West*, Vol. IV:6, 24 June 1913, pp. 104-5.

[165] Melissa might have been thinking of the advice to think of the acronym HALT: Hungry, Angry, Lonely, Tired: the four powerful conditions we shouldn't let overlay our speech, because it warps our communications. Or perhaps the self-checking reminder, THINK: Is it True? Helpful? Inspiring? Necessary? Kind?

She might also have heard of this one of three similar Buddhist quotes about the five factors to gauge our speech with:

"Monks, a statement endowed with five factors is well-spoken, not ill-spoken. It is blameless & unfaulted by knowledgeable people. Which five?

"It is spoken at the right time. It is spoken in truth. It is spoken affectionately. It is spoken beneficially. It is spoken with a mind of good-will.

"A statement endowed with these five factors is well-spoken, not ill-spoken. It is blameless & unfaulted by knowledgeable people." AN 5.198, PTS: A iii 243, Vaca Sutta: A Statement translated from the Pali by Thanissaro Bhikkhu, © 2000 and quoted on :
https://fakebuddhaquotes.com/if-you-propose-to-speak-always-ask-yourself-is-it-true-is-it-necessary-is-it-kind/

And social media regularly circulates variations on this idea: "Before you speak, let your words pass through three gates: Is it true? Is it necessary? Is it kind?" Variously attributed, sometimes to the much-loved 13th-century Islamic Persian mystic Rumi. Definitely a Victorian England poem, "Is It True? Is It Necessary? Is It Kind?" published in *Miscellaneous Poems* by Mary Ann Pietzker, 1872 by Griffith and Farran of London (at the "corner of St. Paul's Churchyard"), and before that to a Rev. Mr. Stewart's work from before 1848. Might Rumi's words have found their way to Europe and then America?

[166] In the statement Melissa and her mother read, Selection 57 of *Some Answered Questions*, 'Abdu'l-Bahá says:

"In the innate nature of things there is no evil—all is good. This applies even to certain apparently blameworthy attributes and dispositions which seem inherent in some people, but which are not in reality reprehensible. For example, you can see in a nursing child, from the beginning of its life, the signs of greed, of anger, and of ill temper; and so it might be argued that good and evil are innate in the reality of man, and that this is contrary to the pure goodness of the innate nature and of creation. The answer is that greed, which is to demand ever more, is a praiseworthy quality provided that it is displayed under the right circumstances. Thus, should a person show greed in acquiring science and knowledge, or in the exercise of compassion, high-mindedness, and justice, this would be most praiseworthy. And should he direct his anger and wrath against the bloodthirsty tyrants who are like ferocious beasts, this too would be most praiseworthy. But should he display these qualities under other conditions, this would be deserving of blame."

[167]   Melissa is referring to one of Bahá'u'lláh's teachings, quoted on page 6 of *Consultation: A Universal Lamp of Guidance*, exhorting the Bahá'ís to: "Take ye counsel together in all matters, inasmuch as consultation is the lamp of guidance which leadeth the way, and is the bestower of understanding." One option is to take an interpersonal problem to a Local Spiritual Assembly, and try to avoid defaming the other person's character in describing the problematic actions to that council.

The author is a big fan of Bahá'í consultation and has published a very short summary of steps she has found useful when working through solitary, interpersonal or group project problems. Find *Applied Bahá'í Consultation* at **https://www.amazon.com/dp/B077SM43T6** . This work is also included in the author's broader work, *Wise Utterance*, also available on Amazon and covering the topic of speech and utterance in many situations.

[168]   The idea that it only takes one steady-ish, loving person in our lives to keep us sane may have originated in a 1980's or 90's book by noted psychotherapist M. Scott Peck. It has spread into wider culture and some therapists suggest that this idea can now be found by Googling **The Resilient Child** or **Emotionally Resilient Children**.

[169]   *A Selection of Bahá'í Prayers and Holy Writings,* printed in Malaysia; *The Three Onenesses and the Foundational Verities* and the handouts by Lucki Melander Wilder can be found and ordered from **http://www.earthstarworks.com/BooksCatalog.html** . *Paris Talks* was the author's first Bahá'í book.

[170]   In paragraph 149, pages 73–74, of *The Kitáb-i-Aqdas*, Bahá'u'-lláh says:

"Pride not yourselves on much reading of the verses or on a multitude of pious acts by night and day; for were a man to read a single verse with joy and radiance it would be better for him than to read with lassitude all the Holy Books of God, the Help in Peril, the Self-Subsisting. Read ye the sacred verses in such measure that ye be not overcome by languor and despondency. Lay not upon your souls that which will weary them and weigh them down, but rather what will lighten and uplift them, so that they may soar on the wings of the Divine verses toward the Dawning-place of His manifest signs; this will draw you nearer to God, did ye but comprehend."

And in selection 214, pages 268–269, of *Selections from the Writings of 'Abdu'l-Bahá*, the Master says: "Follow thou the way of thy Lord, and say not that which the ears cannot bear to hear, for such speech is like luscious food given to small children. However palatable, rare and rich the food may be, it cannot be assimilated by the digestive organs of a suckling child. Therefore unto every one who hath a right, let his settled measure be given."

[171]   Yes, Erden was real, not a dream or hallucination. She didn't wake up from a dream of Erden; she time-traveled to it and then away from it.

[172]   Abby used this advice commonly attributed to Ponca Chief White Eagle: "When you are in doubt, be still, and wait; when doubt no longer exists for you, then go forward with courage. So long as mists envelop you, be still; be still until the sunlight pours through and dispels the mists – as it surely will. Then act with courage."

[173]   This is part of the Tablet of Ahmad that Ms. Bahiyyih chanted and the yuter translated at the deepening in Lodlan. See **Endnote 101**.

Chapter 29 Reentry

[174]   "The first duty prescribed by God for His servants is the recognition of Him Who is the Dayspring of His Revelation and the Fountain of His laws, Who representeth the Godhead in both the Kingdom of His Cause and the world of creation. *Kitab-i-Aqdas*, p. 19.

"(T)he children have the duty to obey their parents – the parents do not obey the children..." from a longer quote, one of many about Parenting and Families, and here applied to the issue of spiritual autonomy. **http://bahai-library.com/compilation_family_life** .

"Once the child comes of age, however, he should be given full freedom to choose his religion, irrespective of the wishes and desires of his parents...." Shoghi Effendi, *Messages of Shoghi Effendi to the Indian Sub-continent,* p. 192.

[175]   One of the most egregious examples is the 16-year-old Mona Mahmudnizhad, hanged for teaching children's classes. Read more at **https://en.wikipedia.org/wiki/Mona_Mahmudnizhad** . Watch Canadian Doug Cameron's 1984 music video and find other links at **https://www.bahaiblog.net/2014/12/doug-cameron-mona-children/** .

[176]   A 1949 letter on behalf of Shoghi Effendi explains that:
"...there is absolutely nothing keeping those who have broken the Covenant, whether Bahá'u'lláh's or the Master's, out of the Cause of God except their own inner spiritually sick condition...Unfortunately a man who is ill is not made well just by asserting there is nothing wrong with him! Facts, actual states, are what count. Probably no group of

people in the world have softer tongues, or proclaim more loudly their innocence, then those who in their heart of hearts, and by their every act, are enemies of the Center of the Covenant. The Master well knew this, and that is why He said we must shun their company, but pray for them. If you put a leper in a room with healthy people, he cannot catch their health; on the contrary they are very likely to catch his horrible ailment." *Lights of Guidance* #618, p. 188.

[177]   For a glimpse into how the Native Americans helped shape (but then whose role was minimized or even largely forgotten), visit **http://www.californiaindianeducation.org/educational_news/roycoo k/2011/american_politics.html** and **https://www.pbs.org/native-america/blogs/native-voices/how-the-iroquois-great-law-of-peace-shaped-us-democracy?sfns=xmo** .

[178]   The author especially likes the quote on page 209 of *A General Theory of Love*: "Happiness is within range only for adroit people who give the slip to America's values. These rebels will necessarily forgo exalted titles, glamorous friends, exotic vacations, washboard abs, designer everything – all the proud indicators of upward mobility – and in exchange, they may just get a chance at a decent life."

[179]   In paragraphs 122–125, pages 63–64, of *The Kitáb-i-Aqdas*, Bahá'u'lláh says:

"Consider the pettiness of men's minds. They ask for that which injureth them, and cast away the thing that profiteth them. They are, indeed, of those that are far astray. We find some men desiring liberty, and priding themselves therein. Such men are in the depths of ignorance.

"Liberty must, in the end, lead to sedition, whose flames none can quench. Thus warneth you He Who is the Reckoner, the All-Knowing. Know ye that the embodiment of liberty and its symbol is the animal. That which beseemeth man is submission unto such restraints as will protect him from his own ignorance, and guard him against the harm of the mischief-maker. Liberty causeth man to overstep the bounds of propriety, and to infringe on the dignity of his station. It debaseth him to the level of extreme depravity and wickedness.

"Regard men as a flock of sheep that need a shepherd for their protection. This, verily, is the truth, the certain truth. We approve of liberty in certain circumstances, and refuse to sanction it in others. We, verily, are the All-Knowing.

"Say: True liberty consisteth in man's submission unto My commandments, little as ye know it. Were men to observe that which We have sent down unto them from the Heaven of Revelation, they would, of a certainty, attain unto perfect liberty. Happy is the man that hath apprehended the Purpose of God in whatever He hath revealed from the Heaven of His Will that pervadeth all created things. Say: The liberty that profiteth you is to be found nowhere except in complete servitude unto God, the Eternal Truth. Whoso hath tasted of its sweetness will refuse to barter it for all the dominion of earth and heaven.

[180]   Some references on the process Abby is discovering:

"When you wish to reflect upon or consider a matter, you consult something within you. You say, shall I do it, or shall I not do it? Is it better to make this journey or abandon it? Whom do you consult? Who is within you deciding this question? Surely there is a distinct power, an intelligent ego. Were it not distinct from your ego, you would not be consulting it. It is greater than the faculty of thought. It is your spirit which teaches you, which advises and decides upon matters. Who is it that interrogates? Who is it that answers? There is no doubt that it is the spirit and that there is no change or transformation in it, for it is not a composition of elements, and anything that is not composed of elements is eternal." 'Abdu'l-Bahá, *The Promulgation of Universal Peace,* p. 242.

"It is an axiomatic fact that while you meditate you are speaking with your own spirit. In that state of mind you put certain questions to your spirit and the spirit answers: the light breaks forth and the reality is revealed." Find this and other enlightening quotes online at **https://www.bahai.org/library/authoritative-texts/compilations/importance-prayer-meditation-devotional-attitude/importance-prayer-meditation-devotional-attitude.pdf?314624f0** , #30.

Also see the short book on Bahá'í Consultation by Lisa Bradley Godward. We can consult within ourselves, and with others. **https://www.amazon.com/dp/B077SM43T6** .

Chapter 30 Sunday

[181]   To read the April 2002 Letter to the Worlds Religious Leaders, visit **https://www.bahai.org/library/**.

[182]   For all the lyrics of this song based on 'Abdu'l-Bahá's words, visit **https://www.youtube.com/watch?v=jyx-YILIUOM** .

[183]   Visit **https://www.youtube.com/watch?v=IclFQj4l3F0** for the melody and lyrics to this song by Malvina Reynolds.

[184]   The full prayer by 'Abdu'l-Bahá is: O God, guide me, protect me, make of me a shining lamp and a brilliant star. Thou art the Mighty and the Powerful. **https://www.bahaiprayers.org/child7.htm** .

[185]   For the lyrics – as well as the melody – of this prayer turned

into song, visit **https://www.youtube.com/watch?v=nKrt_HKgc98** .

[186]   Hear the melody of Shine Your Light on Me, Bahá'u'lláh at **https://www.youtube.com/watch?v=aluJfMb6cFk** .

[187]   *Arising To Serve*, Book 2 in the Ruhi Institute series.

[188]   LaKeesha uses *Teaching Children's Classes: Grade 1*, Book 3 in the Ruhi Institute series, as her guide in teaching children's classes. The "staying connected to God" drawing activity is not from the book; the author made it up and used it in teaching children.

[189]   One child's drawing refers to a passage on page 34, in the Tablet of Tarazát (Ornaments), of *Tablets of Bahá'u'lláh Revealed After the Kitáb-i-Aqdas*: "O my Lord! Thou beholdest them clinging to the rope of Thy grace and holding fast unto the hem of the mantle of Thy beneficence. Ordain for them that which may draw them nearer unto Thee, and withhold them from all else save Thee."

[190]   Part of a prayer with several other memorable metaphors. **http://www.thebahaiprayers.com/quotepage.php?Prayers%2FClinging+to+the+Cord** .

[191]   "(W)henever We desire to quote the sayings of the learned and of the wise, presently there will appear before the face of thy Lord in the form of a tablet all that which hath appeared in the world and is revealed in the Holy Books and Scriptures. Thus do We set down in writing that which the eye perceiveth."-Bahá'u'lláh, Tablet of Wisdom (Lawh-i-Hikmat), *Tablets of Bahá'u'lláh*, p. 149.

"No, I do not know everything. But when I need to know something, it is pictured before Me." Quoting 'Abdu'l-Bahá, in *Memories of 'Abdu'l-Bahá* by Stanwood Cobb, pp. 20-21. Longer Endnote at #88.

Author's Notes

[192]   *Proper Pronunciation of Arabic* – dated 1995-08-08, prepared by the Research Department of the Universal House of Justice, and posted at **bahai-library.org/file.php?file=uhj_pronunciation_arabic** – ends with the statement: "Bahá'ís who are neither Arabs nor Persians have generally picked up a pronunciation similar to that of the Persians because they have learned it from Persian Bahá'ís, but there is no constraint on them to follow this pattern if they are familiar with Arabic and wish to pronounce Arabic words in the Arabic manner."

Resources

Online

- *Bahá'í Faith:* Visit the Bahá'í World Centre's website – in English, with links to French, Spanish, Portuguese, Chinese, Persian, and Arabic pages – at **www.bahai.org** for links to contact information for your country and for Bahá'í publishers. Every country in the world has Bahá'ís, and most are listed. Also look in your local white pages to see if there's a listing for **Bahá'í** (Faith or Center) near you.
- *Bahá'í Writings:* Many books of Bahá'í Scripture, exposition, and research are freely available online. Some very good resources are the *Bahá'í Reference Library* at **bahai.org/library,** the *Bahá'í Library Online* at **bahai-library.org** and, finally, the downloadable – but not necessarily proofread or with the most up-to-date editions – *Ocean Library of World Religions* at **www.bahai-education.org/ocean**.
- *The Bible:* Visit **www.mechon-mamre.org/p/pt/pt0.htm** for the 1917 Jewish Publication Society version of the Bible of Judaism. Visit **www.drbo.org/** for the 1582/1609 Douay-Rheims version of the Catholic branch of Christianity. Visit **www.kingjamesbibleonline.org/** for the 1611 King James version of the Protestant branch of Christianity.
- *Cavalia:* This homage to the poignant history and fascinating bond between humans and horses blends dramatic visual effects, live music, dance, and acrobatics with the bold presence of magnificent horses. Learn more about it at www.cavalia.net .
- *Cricket Magazine Group:* Starting with *Cricket Magazine*, Carus Publishing (Peterborough, NH; 800-821-0115) expanded to fourteen children's magazines serving children ranging from toddlers to teens. Interestingly, as a child ages, their subscription can be changed from one magazine to another at no extra cost. Learn more about them at **www.CricketMag.com/shop_magzines.asp** .
- *Daisy Kingdom:* There is no website for Daisy Kingdom. The brand name and designs are now owned by the Springs Creative Products Group (Rock Hill, SC), which has a useful Fabric Dictionary posted at **www.SpringsCreative.com/site/fabric-dictionary** . To find websites with examples of patterns, though, enter the term **daisy kingdom patterns** into a search engine such as Google.
- *Earthstar Works:* From its humble beginnings as a bricks-and-mortar purveyor of eco-assemblage art and, later, chapbooks to select audiences, Earthstar Works (Chicago, IL) is expanding to the web. Learn more about their art and craft pieces, chapbooks and plays, greeting-card designs, artist/aficionado links, and various online goodies at **www.EarthstarWorks.com** .

- *Harry Potter:* Visit **en.wikipedia.org/wiki/Harry_Potter** to learn about the series. The official Harry Potter publication site in the U.S. is **www.scholastic.com/harrypotter**; it contains videos, games, discussions, downloads, and more. The official *HP* movie site in the U.S. is **harrypotter.warnerbros.com**; it contains trailers, games, newsletters, downloads, and more.
- *Keepsake Quilting:* Learn more about fabrics, patterns, kits, and quilting aids by Keepsake Quilting (Center Harbor, NH; 800-865-9458) at **www.KeepsakeQuilting.com** .
- *National Geographic Society:* Learn more about the Society's magazines and TV channel at **wwwNationalGeographic.com** .
- *Natural Horsemanship:* Visit **www.parelli.com** to learn more about the Parelli Program of Natural Horsemanship (Pagosa Springs, CO; 800-642-3335). You can find many video clips on **www.youtube.com** using the SEARCH term **Parelli**. To find websites with information regarding other such programs, enter the term **natural horsemanship** into a search engine such as Google.
- *Reader's Digest Association:* Learn more about the Association at **phx.corporate-ir.net/phoenix.zhtml?c=71092&p=sitemap** and its flagship and other magazines at **www.rd.com**, where you can also sign up for free newsletters on topics such as do-it-yourself projects, health, humor, and simple solutions.
- *Ruhi Institute Resources:* Learn more about the Ruhi books and how they are used at **www.ruhi.org** .
- *Special Ideas:* Air fresheners to buttons, calendars to DVDs, flags to greeting cards, jewelry to mugs, postcards to stickers, T-shirts to who-knows-what and, of course, scads of books...inspiration is the name of the game for Special Ideas (Heltonville, IN; 800-326-1197). Learn more about them at **www.BahaiResources.com** .
- *The Trail of Painted Ponies:* Building on the concept of a public art project held in New Mexico, Trail of Painted Ponies (Carefree, AZ; 800-500-5779) produces collectible figurines – and many related items – celebrating the beauty and majesty of horses. Learn more about them at **www.TrailOfPaintedPonies.com** . One very cool thing about this site is that, when you clink on the DETAILS button of a figurine, you have the option to access a picture that you can rotate through a 360° circle to see the horse from all sides.
- *Western Saddle Guide:* Whether you're a novice or an experienced rider, **www.western-saddle-guide.com** has answers to just about every question you might ask about Western saddles.

Magazines

Monthly magazines usually hit the stands the month *before* their issue date. So Abby could read September-dated magazines in August.

- *Cowboys & Indians*: This is published monthly by USFR Media Group (Houston, TX; 800-982-5370). Learn more about this magazine at **www.CowboysIndians.com** .
- *Horse Illustrated*: This is published monthly by BowTie Magazines (Irvine, CA). Learn more about this and other horse magazines at **www.BowtieInc.com/BowtieInc/home.aspx** by clicking on **MAGA-ZINES** > PETS & ANIMALS > Horses .
- *Star of the West*: This was the first Bahá'í magazine published in the Western world; the first issue being March 1910. All 25 volumes are available on a single CD, $65.00, by phone from Special Ideas or by online credit-card system at **https://bahai.works/Star_of_the_West** .

Books

Efforts have been made to use the American editions wherever possible.

- *'Abdu'l-Bahá – The Centre of the Covenant of Bahá'u'lláh* by H.M. Balyuzi. Published 1971 by George Ronald.
- *The Advent of Divine Justice* by Shoghi Effendi. Published 1969 by the Bahá'í Publishing Trust of the U.S.
- *American Heritage Dictionary of the English Language*, fourth edition. Published 2006 by Houghton Mifflin Company.
- *Arches of the Years* by Marzieh Gail. Published 1991 by George Ronald.
- *Bahá'í Prayers*. Published 2002 by the Bahá'í Publishing Trust of the U.S.
- *A Basic Bahá'í Dictionary* by Wendi Momen. Published 1989 by George Ronald.
- *The Book of Certitude*. See *The Kitáb-i-Íqán*.
- *The Chosen Highway* by Lady Blomfield. Published 1975 by the Bahá'í Publishing Trust of the U.S.
- *The Compilation of Compilations, 1963-1990, Volumes 1 and 2*. Prepared by the Universal House of Justice. Published 1991 by Bahá'í Publications Australia.
- *A Compilation on Bahá'í Education*. Published 1976 by the Bahá'í World Centre.
- *The Concept of Spirituality* by William S. Hatcher. Published 1987 by the Association for Bahá'í Studies, and now available online at **bahai-library.org/?file=hatcher_bw18_spirituality** .
- *Consultation: A Universal Lamp of Guidance* by John E. Kolstoe. Published 1985 by George Ronald.

- *Cooperative Sports & Games Book* by Terry Orlick, Pantheon Press, 1978
- *Dawn Over Mount Hira and Other Essays* by Marzieh Gail. Published 1976 by George Ronald.
- *Developing Distinctive Bahá'í Communities: Guidelines for Spiritual Assemblies.* Published 1992 by the National Spiritual Assembly of the Bahá'ís of the United States.
- *The Diary of Juliet Thompson.* Published 1983 by Kalimat Press, and now available online at **bahai-library.org/books/thompson**.
- *Fire & Gold: Benefitting from Life's Tests* compiled by Brian Kurzius. Published 1995 by George Ronald.
- *Foundations of World Unity* by 'Abdu'l-Bahá. Published 1972 by the Bahá'í Publishing Trust of the U.S.
- *A General Theory of Love* by Thomas Lewis, Fari Amini, and Richard Lannon. Published 2001 by Vintage Books.
- *Gleanings from the Writings of Bahá'u'lláh.* Published 1990 by the Bahá'í Publishing Trust of the U.S.
- *God Passes By* by Shoghi Effendi. Published 1979 by the Bahá'í Publishing Trust of the U.S.
- *The Hidden Words of Bahá'u'lláh.* Published 1954 by the Bahá'í Publishing Trust of the U.S.
- *Horses for Dummies* by Audrey Pavia with Janice Posnikoff, DVM. Published 1999 by Hungry Minds, Inc.
- *The Kitáb-i-Aqdas (The Most Holy Book)* by Bahá'u'lláh. Published 1992 by the Bahá'í World Centre.
- *The Kitáb-i-Íqán (The Book of Certitude)* by Bahá'u'lláh. Published 1950 by the Bahá'í Publishing Trust of the U.S.
- *Lights of Guidance* compiled by Helen Hornby. Published 1994 by the Bahá'í Publishing Trust of India.
- *Memories of 'Abdu'l-Bahá: Recollections of the Early Days of the Bahá'í Faith in California* by Ramona Allen Brown. Published 1980 by the Bahá'í Publishing Trust of the U.S.
- *The Most Holy Book.* See *The Kitáb-i-Aqdas.*
- *Native American Wisdom.* Published 1993 by Running Press.
- *One in All: An Anthology of Religion from the Sacred Scriptures of the Living Faiths* compiled by Edith B. Schnapper. Published 1952 by John Murray.
- *Paris Talks* by 'Abdu'l-Bahá. Published 1972 by the Bahá'í Publishing Trust of the UK.
- *The Priceless Pearl* by Rúhíyyih Rabbaní. Published 1969 by the Bahá'í Publishing Trust of the UK.
- *The Proclamation of Bahá'u'lláh.* Published 1967 by the Bahá'í World

Centre.
- *The Promulgation of Universal Peace* compiled by Howard MacNutt. Published 1982 by the Bahá'í Publishing Trust of the U.S.
- *The Revelation of Bahá'u'lláh, Volumes 1, 2, 3, and 4* by Adib Taherzadeh. Published 1976, 1977, 1984, and 1987, respectively, by George Ronald.
- *The Secret of Divine Civilization* by 'Abdu'l-Bahá. Published 1990 by the Bahá'í Publishing Trust of the U.S.
- *A Selection of Bahá'í Prayers and Holy Writings.* Published 1985 by the Bahá'í Publishing Trust Committee of Malaysia.
- *Selections from the Writings of 'Abdu'l-Bahá.* Published 1978 by the Bahá'í World Centre.
- *The Call of the Divine Beloved* by Bahá'u'lláh. Available online at **https://www.bahai.org/library/authoritative-texts/bahaullah/call-divine-beloved/** .
- *Some Answered Questions* by 'Abdu'l-Bahá. Available online at **https://www.bahai.org/library/authoritative-texts/abdul-baha/some-answered-questions/** .
- *Stories of Bahá'u'lláh* compiled by 'Alí-Akbar Furútan. Published 1986 by George Ronald.
- *Tablets of 'Abdu'l-Bahá, Volumes 1, 2, and 3.* Published 1909, 1915, and 1916, respectively, by the Bahá'í Publishing Society.
- *Tablets of Bahá'u'lláh Revealed After the Kitáb-i-Aqdas.* Published 1988 by the Bahá'í Publishing Trust of the U.S.
- *Ten Days in the Light of 'Akká* by Julia M. Grundy. Published 1979 by the Bahá'í Publishing Trust of the U.S.
- *The Three Onenesses and the Foundational Verities* by Lucki Melander Wilder, Published 2008 by Earthstar Works.
- *The World Order of Bahá'u'lláh: Selected Letters* by Shoghi Effendi. Published 1991 by the Bahá'í Publishing Trust of the U.S.
- *Zen Cowboy* by Michael W. Domis; illustrated by Richard A. Goldberg. Published 2005 by Peter Pauper Press.

Counted Cross-Stitch Patterns

Below are the charts and instructions for you to stitch the patterns I designed. I start with the easier "No Hate" chart. Once you learn with that, you should be ready to stitch the "World Peace" chart.

Look at each chart and read its instructions *completely* before beginning. See the photo on the preceding page for models.

Each chart may be easiest to work with if you photocopy or scan/ print it from this book, so you can highlight completed stitching as you go, to mark your place and progress. **You have my permission to copy it *for your own use only*. You do *not* have my permission to copy it for or e-mail it to anyone else, post it online, or sell the needlework you make from it.**

Supplies:
- Charts
- Scissors
- Floss:
- Two 6-inch squares of 14-count Aida fabric
- Tapestry (blunt) needle, size 24 or 26
- Highlighter to mark completed steps/squares
  - No Hate – **Black** such as DMC 310 (adding Kreinik 005HL if a metallic sheen is desired); **Red** such as DMC 666 (adding Kreinik 003HL if a metallic sheen is desired).
  - World Peace – **Gold** such as DMC 972; **Green** such as DMC 910; maybe **Light Blue** such as DMC 809. (For a shaded look, use variegated thread – dyed darker and lighter in one skein – such as "Brandy" gold, "Blue Jay" blue, and "Spring Grass" green. See the photo on the book cover for this variation.)

To begin:
1. **Look at the fabric.** See the regularly spaced holes? They divide the fabric into little squares with holes at the four corners of each square, so the needle can easily go through the fabric.

   There is no space between the squares; for example, the holes at the bottom corners of one square are also the holes at the top corners of the square below it.

   The squares in the fabric correspond to the squares on the chart. You stitch an **X** on the fabric to correspond with each symbol on the chart. Each symbol tells you what color to make that **X**. I use the symbols "**M**" and "**O**" and "**–**" as they are easy to tell apart.

2. **Pick one side of the fabric to be the top side** (the sides are the same, it doesn't matter). With a pencil, mark a backslash (\ ) in the upper left corner. This marks the top side of the fabric AND shows you which way the bottom, or first, arm of the stitch should be made AND tells you which way to orient the fabric (and the design).

3. **Find the center of the fabric.** Fold the fabric in half vertically and pinch it with your fingers to make a small crease. Open the fabric. Fold it in half horizontally and make another crease. Open the fabric again. The two creases cross at the center of the fabric.

   Note: If you have a bigger than 6" x 6" piece of fabric and want to position the design elsewhere than in the center to conserve fabric or for artistic reasons, use a ruler and your basic math skills to ensure your crossed creases allow enough space to complete the design in all directions.

4. **Look at the chart.** The design is 27 x 27 squares. See the five black squares? They mark the horizontal center line, the vertical center line, and the exact center of the pattern. Use these indicators to help keep track of where you are and to center the design on the fabric.

5. **Find the center square of the chart:** the black square with the white symbol in it. The center-square symbol indicates which color thread to start with. In the "No Hate" chart, the first color is Red; in the "World Peace" chart, it is Gold.

6. **Measure and cut a length of floss cord.** Regular cotton embroidery floss comes in 6-strand cords, usually bundled into skeins. Holding the skein in one hand, find a cut end of the cord and unwrap or pull it with the other hand until it reaches your elbow, then cut it. You now have a cord about 12 to 16 inches long.

   Note: Always **leave the paper bands** on skeins to keep them tidy and document their exact brand name, color name, and color code.

7. **Separate the cord into strands.** Don't peel the strands apart; they will snarl and maybe break. Instead, grab the cord in one hand, with about 2 inches sticking out the top of your fist, like a bouquet of flowers. With the other hand, carefully pick out the end of one strand and slowly but firmly pull one strand straight up. The downward-hanging cord will coil up against the bottom of your fist, but should uncoil after you pull the strand completely out. If not, bounce your hand until it uncoils. Repeat this twice more, until you have three strands pulled out. (You also have three unseparated strands left in your fist, which you'll use later. Set it aside for now.)

Note: If you add metallic thread, you'll separate out ONE metallic strand and join it with TWO separated plain strands. The metallic will show through irregularly for attractive sparkle.

8. **Thread the needle.** Take three plain strands (or two plain and one metallic strand), group them into a 3-strand thread, and thread the needle with them. Pull the thread so you have about 2 inches of thread on one side of the needle hole and all the rest on the other side. Don't tie a knot at the end of the thread.

   Note: Whenever the needle runs out of thread, rethread the needle using the strands you have already separated, or by cutting and separating more cord.

9. **Look at the center of the chart.** In the "No Hate" pattern, it is the black square in the middle of the diagonal Red line; in the "World Peace" pattern, it is the black square in the middle of the vertical Gold line. This square shows where to start stitching.

10. **Start stitching the first (center) X.** Hold the fabric so your topside mark is in the upper left corner. Poke the threaded needle up from the underside through the hole closest to where the center-creases cross, and then pull it through on the topside. This is now the upper left corner of the first square.

    Note: **Leave a 1-inch start-tail** of thread on the underside of the fabric, and keep it there while stitching the first several half-stitches by pressing the tail against the fabric with a finger so you don't accidentally pull the thread all the way through the fabric.

11. **To continue the X**, use the needle tip to find the bottom right hole of the square you started, poke the needle down into the hole from the topside, then pull the needle and thread through on the underside. The first topside stitch now looks like a back-slash (\).

    Note: Be sure to **pinch the thread** on both sides of the needle's eye when pulling the needle, so it doesn't unthread.

12. **To finish the X,** poke the needle up through the top right hole from the underside, then push it down through the bottom left hole. Feel for the holes with the needle tip, or turn the fabric over to look (be sure to reorient the fabric when flipping and rotating). The second topside stitch now looks like a forward-slash (/) lying across the back-slash, so that the two stitches form the **X**.

    Note: **Pull the thread** just hard enough so that each stitch on both the topside and the underside lies right against the fabric, but not so hard that the fabric puckers.

13. **Anchor the start-tail on the underside.** As you make the next several stitches, stitch over the 1-inch start-tail on the underside of the fabric, so that it is enclosed and anchored in place by underside stitches. You can clip off any extra start-tail after anchoring it with half a dozen stitches.

Note: Do not try to run the needle *through* the start-tail; just nudge the threads to make the underside stitches lie *across* or *over* the start-tail.

14. **Count the squares on the chart and on the fabric** to see where the next stitches go. In the "No Hate" pattern, the second **X** is one square right and one square down; in the "World Peace" pattern, the second **X** is one square up.

Refer to the individual charts for design-specific instructions.

Note: You will do lots and *lots* of counting, recounting, and counting again to ensure you **follow the pattern**. That's why it's called *counted* cross-stitch. The effort is well repaid, though, when you see your finished result. And people who like counted cross-stitch even find the counting soothing, like chanting or auto-hypnotism.

15. **For every X you make,** do the back-slash stitch (upper left to lower right) first and the forward-slash stitch (upper right to lower left) second. That way, every **X** looks exactly the same, which makes your work look neater and more polished.

Note: If you accidentally start an X in the same hole where you ended the previous X, it will make the previous X come partially undone. However, doing so intentionally is a handy way to **undo a mistake**, undoing stitches as far back as you need to. Another way to undo stitches is to slide the needle off the thread, use the eye-end to carefully lift out incorrect stitches without shredding the floss, then rethread the needle and continue correctly.

16. **When only two needle-lengths of thread remain on the needle,** slide the needle back under the last half-dozen stitches on the underside, then pull the needle off the thread. This anchors the end-tail of thread without tying a knot, which would make a lump on the finished piece. Cut off any extra end-tail after anchoring it.

17. **Plan your stitching route carefully.** Stitch as far as possible with one thread. However, if the thread must travel along the underside across more than four empty squares on the chart, despite careful

planning, then end and anchor it (just as if only two needle-lengths of thread remained on the needle), because any long loose threads can catch on things and even show through to the topside.

Note: To **backtrack past completed stitches** to another part of the pattern, slide the needle under the completed stitches on the underside until you reach the place to start stitching again. When you restart stitching, do not pull so hard that the fabric puckers.

18. **Once you have finished the stitching,** you may cut the fabric to form a long narrow bookmark, a round patch, a square or rectangle suitable for framing, etc. Be sure to leave enough fabric for your choice of finish.

19. **To finish off the fabric** after the design is done, so that the edges of the fabric do not unravel, you have many options, such as:

   a. Invisibly turn under and hem the edges with thread the same color as the fabric.

   b. Decoratively whip-stitch the edges using one of the colors in the pattern (see small World Peace patch in photo preceding this section).

   c. Bind the edges either with narrow binding or, as in photo of the No Hate bookmark, cut a backing fabric about ½" wider than dimensions of item, pin in place wrong side next to the back side of the stitching, fold twice over the raw edge to make a 1/8" binding while also backing the item, and sew edge of binding to top side of item.

   d. Decoratively seal the edges with puffy or fabric paint.

How to get really good:

Like everything in life, getting good takes practice. Don't be hard on yourself if your first pieces don't look quite as smooth as you wish. Congratulate yourself for doing as well as you did.

And if you liked it, do more. You'll get better with more trying.

Beginners should stick to small projects that have only a few colors. Keep your projects manageable. Don't pick a big or complex project, find it too hard, get discouraged, and quit. Build your successes and feelings of accomplishment by setting goals you can meet.

"No Hate" Chart

27x27 design, 29x29 chart, and instructions © 2010 Lisa Bradley

M = Red: Stitch one **X** with red embroidery floss DMC 666 or a similar color. For metallic sheen, add Kreinik 003HL.

O = Black: Stitch one **X** with black embroidery floss DMC 310 or a similar color. For metallic sheen, add Kreinik 005HL.

"No Hate" Instructions

Having done the first Red **X** at the center:

1. Stitch the Red diagonal line downwards into the circle (9 more stitches), anchoring the start-tail.

2. Stitch the Red circle all the way around.

3. Backtrack under your original diagonal stitches to reach the unfinished part of the diagonal line, then continue to stitch downwards until the diagonal line is completed.

4. Anchor the end-tail under several Red stitches, then cut the thread.

Having finished the Red stitching (congratulations!), thread the needle with Black and, being careful to skip *under* each Red **X** that crosses a Black line:

5. Start at the bottom left corner of the Black letter **H** and stitch upwards to the top left corner (13 stitches), anchoring the start-tail.

6. Backtrack under your latest stitches to reach the crossbar, then stitch the crossbar and the top right leg of the **H**.

7. Backtrack under your latest stitches to reach the unfinished leg of the **H**, then stitch downwards until the **H** is completed.

8. On the underside, lay the thread across one empty square to the right and, at the second square, begin stitching upwards to complete the left side of the **A**.

9. Stitch across the top of the **A,** down the top right leg to the crossbar, and across the crossbar.

10. Backtrack under the crossbar to reach the unfinished leg of the **A**, then stitch downwards until the **A** is completed.

11. On the underside, lay the thread across three empty squares and, at the fourth square, begin stitching upwards to complete the upright of the **T.**

12. Stitch the top left arm of the **T**.

13. Backtrack to the upright, and stitch the top right arm of the **T**.

14. On the underside, lay the thread across one empty square and, at the second square, stitch the top arm of the **E**.

15. Backtrack under the top arm to reach the left side of the **E**, stitch down the top left leg to the crossbar, then stitch the crossbar.

16. Backtrack under the crossbar to reach the unfinished leg of the **E**,

then stitch down the leg and across the bottom arm until the **E** is completed.

17. Anchor the end-tail under several Black stitches, then cut the thread.

Congratulations with thunderous applause…especially if this is your first-ever piece of counted cross-stitch!

"Out and Back" Technique:

Now that you've completed one piece, let me describe the "out and back" technique: a way to work from the beginning to the end and then back to the beginning of a row (and, once you get good at it, a column or even a diagonal line) of stitches. It is an alternative to backtracking, uses less thread, and demands greater concentration.

As an example, let's say you're starting the top arm of the **E**. Instead of completing five **X** stitches starting at the left side of the **E** and going all the way across, then backtracking on the underside, try this:

1. Make a rightward running line of five back-slashes (\\\\\), with each back-slash (after the first) starting in the hole directly above the hole where the previous back-slash ended.
2. At the end of the row, go to the hole directly above the hole where the final back-slash ended and start a leftward running line of five forward-slashes (/////) lying across the back-slashes, so that the ten slashes form **XXXXX**.
3. You are now back where you started and ready to continue down the left side of the **E**.

However, trying to start the next **X** in the usual manner would, in this example, simply undo your latest stitch. (This is not always true, but it occasionally is, and you need to watch out for it.) On the next row down, in such a case, make your first back-slash from the bottom right corner of the square to the top left corner. Then continue to make the rest of your slash-stitches as usual.

"World Peace" Chart

```
                        M M M M M ■ M M M M M
                  M M - - - - M - - - - O M M
               M O - - - - - M - - - O O O M
             M O - - - - - - M - - O O O O M
           M O O - - - - - - M - O O O - - O O M
         M O O O - - - - - - M - O O O - - - - - M
       M O O O O O - - - - - - M - - - - - O O O O O M
     M O O O O O O O - - - - - - M - - - - O O O O O O O M
     M O O O - - O - - - - - - - M - - O O O O O O O O O O M
 M - - O O - - - - - - - - - M - O O O O O O O O O O O M
 M - - - O O - - - - - - - - M - O O O O O O O O O O O M
 M - - - O - - - - - - - - - M - O O O O O O O O O O O M
 M - - - - O - - - - - - - - M - - O O O O O O O O O O M
■M - - - - O O O - - - - - ■M - - - - O O O O O O O O M■
 M - - - - O O O O O - - - M M M - - - - - O O O O O O M
 M - - O O O O O O O O O M - M - M - - - - - O O O O O M
 M - O O O O O O O O O M - - M - - - M - - - - O O O O M
 M - O O O O O O O O M O - - M - - - - M - - - O O O O M
   M O O O O O O O M O - - - M - - - - - M - - - O O O M
   M - O O O O O M O - - - - M - - - - - - M - - - O O M
     M - O O M O - - - - - M - - - - - - - M - - O M
       M - M O O - - - - - M - - - - - - - - M - M
         M - O O - - - - - M - - - - - - - - - M
           M - O - - - - - M - - - - - - - - - M
             M - O - - - - - M - - - - - - - M
               M M - - - - M - - - - M M
                 M M M M M ■ M M M M M
```

27x27 design, 29x29 chart, and instructions © 2010 Lisa Bradley

M = Gold: Stitch one **X** with gold embroidery floss DMC 972 or a similar color.

O = Green: Stitch one **X** with black embroidery floss DMC 910 or a similar color.

— = option: You have two options:

- **— = blank**
  Leave the oceans the color of the fabric; do not stitch any square containing this symbol.

- **— = Light Blue**
  Stitch one **X** with Light Blue embroidery floss DMC 809 or a similar color. (Don't use blue and green of the same intensity; they'll blend visually.)

"World Peace" Instructions

Having done the first Gold **X** at the center – and feeling free to (a) use the "out and back" technique wherever you see "backtrack" and (b) start your stitches at the "wrong" end of the slash if necessary to keep from undoing stitches, as long as you do the back-slash first and the forward-slash second:

1. Stitch the Gold vertical line upwards into the circle (13 more stitches), anchoring the start-tail.

2. Stitch the Gold circle all the way around.

3. Anchor the end-tail and cut the thread.

4. Find the first Gold **X** you stitched (at the center), move the needle one square right and one square down, and stitch the next Gold **X** in the right diagonal line.

5. Continue stitching diagonally, anchoring the start-tail, until you meet the circle.

6. Slide the needle under the 8 stitches forming the bottom right arc of the circle and, when you reach the exact center of the circle bottom, stitch upwards to complete the vertical line.

7. Stitch the left diagonal line to exactly mirror the existing right diagonal line.

8. Anchor the end tail under several Gold stitches, then cut the thread.

Having finished the Gold stitching, thread the needle with Green and, being careful to skip *under* each Gold **X** that crosses South America:

9. In the left half of the circle, and using your circle as a guide, stitch the lone Green **X** at the top, or row 1, of North America.

10. Move the needle one square left and one square down, and stitch the Green **X** in row 2 of North America, starting to anchor the start-tail.

11. Move the needle one square down, and stitch row 3 (2 stitches) from right to left, continuing to anchor the start-tail.

12. Move the needle one square left and one square down, and stitch row 4 from left to right, anchoring the remainder of the start-tail.

13. Work downwards one horizontal row at a time through the lone Green **X** in row 24, being sure that you skip the two empty squares separating Florida from Texas and that South America touches the Gold circle in only two places.

14. Anchor the end-tail under several Green stitches, then cut the thread. You have completed the Western Hemisphere continents.

15. In the right half of the circle, and again using your circle as a guide, stitch the lone Green **X** at the top, or row 1, of Europe.

16. Move the needle two squares left and one square down, and stitch row 2 (3 stitches) of Europe from right to left, starting to anchor the start-tail.

17. Stitch row 3 from left to right, anchoring the remainder of the start-tail.

18. Work downwards one horizontal row at a time through the lone Green **X** in row 21, being sure that you skip the two empty squares separating Italy and Spain.

19. Anchor the end-tail under several Green stitches, then cut the thread. You have completed the Eastern Hemisphere continents.

If you've decided to leave the oceans blank, you're done! Congrats!

However, if you want to stitch the oceans, thread the needle with Light Blue and:

20. On the left side of the circle, start stitching at the top of the Pacific Ocean where it meets the west coast of North America, moving down the rows in alternate directions. Do not cross over into the Atlantic Ocean at Central America. Be sure to include the narrow Pacific Ocean coastline of South America.

21. After you complete the last stitch of the Pacific Ocean, next to the southern tip of South America, move the needle two squares right and one square down and start stitching the bottom of the Atlantic Ocean, moving up the rows in alternate directions. Be careful to skip *under* each Gold **X** that crosses the Atlantic Ocean.

22. When you reach the southern tip of Europe, treat the Mediterranean Sea as part of the Atlantic Ocean rows, being careful to skip *under* each Green **X** in Spain.

23. When you complete the top row of the Atlantic Ocean, anchor the end-tail under several Light Blue stitches, then cut the thread.

24. Make sure there are now no empty squares within the circle. (If there are, go back and fill them in, being sure to use the right color and to anchor the start-tail and the end-tail.)

Now you are really and truly finished. Good work!

Additional Responses to
Abby Wize: AWĀ ("away")

I liked the story; Abby and her activities felt authentic. As a horse owner, I would have enjoyed even more horse experiences. Seamlessly interwoven is a clear, unobtrusive explanation of the Bahá'í Faith.

This book caused me to give more thought to what an ideal world would look like. Today, people often complain of too much government, but if people would control themselves, laws to control people would be only minimally necessary. My experience as a classroom teacher bears that out; as we develop away from the I/Me/My priority, the world will become much more like that of Abby's experience.

Abby Wize: Awā presents ideas of the future that hold much hope and are more realistic than so-called advanced visions of a world with superior gadgets and ineffective interpersonal relationships. For example, people in those 'future' scenarios haven't learned to collaborate, respect each other, and build on each other's strengths – all necessary skills to a productive and mutually beneficial society.

I enjoyed reading a version of what a Bahá'í-inspired world might be. Very thought-provoking!
-Mrs. Jill Stepp Johnston, retired teacher, Vader, WA

I loved the book! I liked the future: you showed how we learn to live with nature, learning our lesson and turning the planet away from our current course of self-destruction. Accurately represents the concerns of a 13-year-old without being childish. I think the proportion of horses, spirituality and adolescent issues were really nicely balanced.

I loved learning about the Bahá'í Faith; it seems like a very loving and caring religion. The religious part wasn't pushed down my throat, you could just take it or leave it. I like how she wrestled with coming back to our time period and she learned how to cope with everything better because of her experience in the perfect future.

I like your writing style; it's very captivating, fluid and well-written, and you kept my interest really well.

                    -Mr. Bob Nelson, entrepreneur/artist, naturalist

I love the main character…all the characters. I actually went to HS with a girl whose mother was like Abby's mother. Disturbing but realistic.

I love horses, rode them growing up, so I could really relate to all the horse parts, especially the lesson. It rang really true that the riding instructors are often kids who don't know much more than the students.

I loved the horse fantasy and all the wonderful people she meets in the future. How it's just so…well, it would be so nice if it was really like that.

It made me want to go visit the Bahá'í Temple in Chicago next summer when I go visit my mom. I don't know if you're aware that everyone in the area lovingly calls it God's Orange Juice Squeezer.

I like that you have the notes in the back; you can choose to read them or not.

Some people are going to turn off on the religion parts, some are going to like it. I personally loved it. I think it's going to depend on their spiritual orientation.

I especially like that in the future we all get along and avoid raping the land.

I could definitely slip into her fantasy!

            -Ms. Jean Simon, longtime actress, Jew,
                    mermaid performer, avid reader

About the Author

While earning her college degree in journalism and art in Nebraska, USA, Lisa Paulson Bradley Godward discovered the Bahá'í Faith. Inspired by that unfolding vision of justice and peace, Lisa eventually conceived and wrote *Abby Wize – AWAY*. It is the first in the Abby Wize spiritual, horse-loving time travel series. She lives on a ranch in Arizona, USA, and practices the Parelli method of horse whispering.

About the Book Award

This Revised Edition of *Abby Wize – AWAY* won a Finalist award in the November 2018 Best Book Awards contest's "Fiction: Religious" category in the competition run by American Book Fest. **www.amerbookfest.com** .

Cover Art
Cover art by Sean Michael Robinson
under the direction of Lisa Bradley Godward.
www.livingtheline.com .

Title Font

Many Weatz (Many Weatz) font was designed by Måns Grebäck,

Örebro, Sweden. **www.mansgreback.com** .
The font was modified by American graphic designer
Lindsay Montgomery (linmon8803@gmail.com)
for the breezy, artsy, energetic title of this Revised Edition of

Abby Wize – Away

CPSIA information can be obtained
at www.ICGtesting.com
Printed in the USA
LVHW091931141221
706070LV00028B/153